Praise for PETER ROBINSON and
PAST REASON HATED

"An expert plotter with an eye for telling detail."
The New York Times Book Review

"Robinson proves the equal of legends of the genre such as
P.D. James and Ruth Rendell. He delights in subtly
misleading the reader, weaving a complex plot replete with
blind alleys and base villains disguised as amiable country folk.
Here is an entertaining challenge, trying to discover just
where the evildoer is hidden amidst quaint tea shops,
rustic pubs, and sylvan English lanes."
St. Louis Post-Dispatch

"Finely crafted . . . a terrific crime novel . . .
a gifted writer . . . a superior series. Robinson has
intriguing characters, a solid-gold Yorkshire setting,
and a slam-bang plot that keeps moving
right up to the final chapter . . .
Robinson wastes no time pulling us into the story."
Toronto Globe and Mail

"The finest traditional British detective novel of the year . . .
Robinson tells a good story, with believable red herrings and
a fascinating cast of characters."
Virginian-Pilot and Ledger-Star

"A memorable mystery novel."
Providence Journal

Books by Peter Robinson

STRANGE AFFAIR
THE FIRST CUT
PLAYING WITH FIRE
CLOSE TO HOME
AFTERMATH
GALLOWS VIEW
COLD IS THE GRAVE
IN A DRY SEASON
BLOOD AT THE ROOT
INNOCENT GRAVES
FINAL ACCOUNT
WEDNESDAY'S CHILD
PAST REASON HATED
THE HANGING VALLEY
A NECESSARY END
A DEDICATED MAN

PETER ROBINSON

PAST REASON HATED

An Inspector Banks Mystery

AVON BOOKS
An Imprint of HarperCollinsPublishers

This is a work of fiction. Names, characters, places, and incidents are products of the author's imagination or are used fictitiously and are not to be construed as real. Any resemblance to actual events, locales, organizations, or persons, living or dead, is entirely coincidental.

AVON BOOKS
An Imprint of HarperCollins*Publishers*
10 East 53rd Street
New York, New York 10022-5299

First Avon Books paperback printing: October 2000

Avon Trademark Reg. U.S. Pat. Off. and in Other Countries, Marca Registrada, Hecho en U.S.A.
HarperCollins® is a trademark of HarperCollins Publishers Inc.

Printed in the U.S.A.

10 9 8 7 6 5

This one is for the
Usual Suspects

ONE

I

Snow fell on Swainsdale for the first time that year a few days before Christmas. Out in the dale, among the more remote farms and hamlets, the locals would be cursing. A heavy snowfall could mean lost sheep and blocked roads. In past years, some places had been cut off for as long as five weeks. But in Eastvale, most of those crossing the market square on the evening of December 22 felt a surge of joy as the fat flakes drifted down, glistening in the gaslight as they fell, to form a lumpy white carpet over the cobble-stones.

Detective Constable Susan Gay paused on her way back to the station from Joplin's newsagents. Outside the Norman church stood a tall Christmas tree, a gift from the Norwegian town with which Eastvale was twinned. The lights winked on and off, and its tapered branches bent under the weight of half an inch of snow. In front of the tree, a group of children in red choir-gowns stood singing "Once in Royal David's City." Their alto voices, fragile but clear, seemed especially fitting on such a beautiful winter's evening.

Susan tilted her head back and let the snowflakes melt on her eyelids. Two weeks ago she would not have allowed herself to do something so spontaneous and frivolous. But now that she was *Detective* Constable Gay, she could afford to relax a little. She had finished with courses and exams, at least until she tried for sergeant. Now there would be no more arguing with David Craig over who made the coffee. There would be no more walking the beat, either, and no more traffic duty on market day.

The music followed her as she headed back to the station:

> *And He leads His children on*
> *To the place where He is gone.*

Directly in front of her, the new blue lamp hung like a shop-sign over the doorway of the Tudor-fronted police station. In an attempt to change the public image of the force, tarnished by race riots, sex scandals and accusations of high-level corruption, the government had looked to the past: more specifically, to the fifties. The lamp was straight out of "Dixon of Dock Green." Susan had never actually seen the program, but she understood the basic idea. The image of the kindly old copper on the beat had caused many a laugh around Eastvale Regional Headquarters. Would that life were as simple as that, they all said.

Her second day on the job and all was well. She pushed open the door and headed for the stairs. Upstairs! The inner sanctum of the CID. She had envied them all for so long— Gristhorpe, Banks, Richmond, even Hatchley—when she had brought coffee or messages, or stood by taking notes while they interrogated female suspects. No longer. She was one of them now, and she was about to show them that a woman could do the job every bit as well as a man, if not better.

She didn't have her own office; only Banks and Gristhorpe were allowed such luxuries. The hutch she shared with Richmond would have to do. It looked over the car-park out back, not the market square, but at least she had a desk, rickety though it was, and a filing cabinet of her own. She had inherited them from Sergeant Hatchley, now exiled to the coast, and the first thing she had had to do was rip down the nude pin-ups from the cork bulletin board above his desk. How anybody could work with those bloated mammaries hanging over them was beyond her.

About forty minutes later, after she had poured herself a cup of coffee to keep her awake while she studied the latest regional crime reports, the phone rang. It was Sergeant Rowe calling from the front desk.

"Someone just phoned in to report a murder," he said.

Susan felt the adrenalin flow. She grasped the receiver tighter. "Where?"

"Oakwood Mews. You know, those tarted-up *bijou* terraces back of King Street."

"I know them. Any details?"

"Not much. It was a neighbor that called. Said the woman next door went rushing into the street screaming. She took her in but couldn't get much sense out of her except that her friend had been murdered."

"Did the neighbor take a look for herself?"

"No. She said she thought she'd better call us right away."

"Can you send PC Tolliver down there?" Susan asked. "Tell him to check out the scene without touching anything. And tell him to stay by the door and not let anyone in till we get there."

"Aye," said Rowe, "but shouldn't—"

"What's the number?"

"Eleven."

"Right."

Susan hung up. Her heart beat fast. Nothing had happened in Eastvale for months—and now, only her second day on the new job, a murder. And she was the only member of the CID on duty that evening. Calm down, she told herself, follow procedure, do it right. She reached for her coat, still damp with snow, then hurried out the back way to the car-park. Shivering, she swept the snow off the windscreen of her red Golf and drove off as fast as the bad weather allowed.

II

> *Four and twenty virgins*
> *Came down from Inverness,*
> *And when the ball was over*
> *There were four and twenty less.*

"I think Jim's a bit pissed," Detective Chief Inspector Alan Banks leaned over and said to his wife, Sandra.

Sandra nodded. In a corner of the Eastvale Rugby Club banquet room, by the Christmas tree, Detective Sergeant Jim Hatchley stood with a group of cronies, all as big and brawny as himself. They looked like a parody of a group of carol-singers, Banks thought, each with a foaming pint in his hand. As they sang, they swayed. The other guests stood by the bar or sat at tables chatting over the noise. Carol Hatchley—*née* Ellis—the sergeant's blushing bride, sat beside her mother and fumed. The couple had just changed out of their wedding clothes into less formal attire in readiness for their honeymoon, but Hatchley, true to form, had insisted on just one more pint before they left. That one had quickly turned into two, then three. . . .

> *The village butcher, he was there,*
> *Chopper in his hand.*
> *Every time they played a waltz,*
> *He circumcised the band.*

It didn't make sense, Banks thought. How many times could you circumcise one band? Carol managed a weak smile, then turned and said something to her mother, who shrugged. Banks, leaning against the long bar with Sandra, Superintendent Gristhorpe and Philip Richmond, ordered another round of drinks.

As he waited, he looked around the room. It was done up for the festive season, no doubt about that. Red and green concertina trimmings hung across the ceiling, bedecked with tinsel, holly and the occasional sprig of mistletoe. The club tree, a good seven feet tall, sparkled in all its glory.

It was twenty past eight, and the real party was just beginning. The wedding had taken place at Eastvale Congregationalist Church late in the afternoon, and it had been followed by a slap-up meal at the rugby club at six. Now the speeches had been made, the plates cleared away and the tables moved for a good Yorkshire knees-up. Hatchley had hired a DJ for the music, but the poor lad was still waiting patiently for a signal to begin.

> *Singing "Balls to your father,*
> *Arse against the wall.*
> *If you've never been shagged on a Saturday night,*
> *You've never been shagged at all."*

"Four and Twenty Virgins" was coming to a close, Banks could tell. There would be a verse about the village schoolmistress (who had unusually large breasts) and one about the village cripple (who did unspeakable things with his crutch), then a rousing finale. With a bit of luck, that would be the end of the rugby songs. They had already performed "Dinah, Dinah, Show Us Yer Leg (A Yard Above Your Knees)," "The Engineer's Song" and a lengthy, improvised version of "Mademoiselle from Armentieres." The sulky DJ, who had been pretending to set up his equipment for the past hour, would soon get his chance to shine.

Banks passed the drinks along to the others and reached for a cigarette. Gristhorpe frowned at him, but Banks was used to that. Phil Richmond was also smoking one of his occasional panatellas, so the superintendent was having a particularly hard time of it. Sandra had stopped smoking completely, and Banks had agreed not to smoke in the house. Luckily, although most of the police station had been declared a non-smoking area, he was still permitted to light up in his own office. Things had got so bad, though, that even alleged criminals brought in for interrogation could legally object to any police officer smoking in the interview rooms. It was a sorry state of affairs, Banks mused: you could beat them to your heart's content, as long as the bruises didn't show, but you couldn't smoke in their presence and get away with it.

Sandra raised her dark eyebrows and breathed a sigh of relief when "Four and Twenty Virgins" came to an end. But her joy was short-lived. The choir of rugby forwards refused to leave the stage without giving their rendition of "Good King Wenceslas." Despite groans from the captive audience, a dirty look from the DJ and a positive flash of fury from Carol's eyes, Sergeant Hatchley led them off:

> *Good King Wenceslas looked out*
> *Of his bedroom window.*
> *Silly bugger, he fell out . . .*

Gristhorpe looked at his watch. "I think I'll be off after this one. I just overheard someone say it's snowing pretty heavily out there now."

"Is it?" Sandra said. Banks knew she loved snow. They walked over to the window at the far end of the room and glanced out. Clearly satisfied with what she saw, Sandra pulled the long curtains open. It had been snowing only lightly when they had arrived for pre-dinner drinks at about five, but now the high window framed a thick swirl of white flakes falling on the rugby field. Others turned to look, oohing and aahing, touching their neighbors on the arm to tell them what was happening. As they walked back, Banks took Sandra in his arms and kissed her.

"Got you," he said, then he looked up and Sandra followed his gaze to the mistletoe hanging above them.

Sandra took his arm and walked beside him back to the bar. "I don't mean to be rude or anything," she said, "but when's this racket going to end? Don't you think someone should have a word with Jim? After all, it *is* Carol's wedding day. . . ."

Banks looked at Hatchley. Judging by his flushed face and

the way he swayed, there wouldn't be much of a wedding
night for the bride.

> *Brightly shone his arse that night,*
> *Though the frost was cruel . . .*

Banks was just about to walk across and say something—
only concerned that he might sound too much like the boss
when he was just a wedding guest—when he was saved by
the DJ. A long and loud blast of feedback issued from the
speakers and stopped Hatchley and his mates in their tracks.
Before they could regather their wits for a further onslaught,
several quick-thinking members of the party applauded. At
once, the singers took this as their cue for a bow and the DJ
as his opportunity to begin the real music. He adjusted a couple of dials, skipped the patter, and before Hatchley and his
mob even knew what had hit them the hall was filled with
the sound of Martha and the Vandellas singing "Dancing in
the Street."

Sandra smiled. "That's more like it."

Banks glanced over at Richmond, who looked very pleased
with himself. And well he might. There had just been a big
change-around at Eastvale Regional Police Headquarters. Sergeant Hatchley had been a problem for some time. Not suitable material for promotion, he had stood in Richmond's way,
even though Richmond had passed his sergeant's examination
with flying colors and shown remarkable aptitude on the job.
The trouble was, there just wasn't room for two detective
sergeants in the small station.

Finally, after months of trying to find a way out of the
dilemma, Superintendent Gristhorpe had seized the first opportunity that came his way. Official borders had been re-
drawn and the region had expanded eastwards to take in a
section of the North York Moors and a small stretch of coastline between Scarborough and Whitby. It seemed a good idea
to place a small CID outpost on the coast to deal with the
day-to-day matters that might arise there, and Hatchley came

to mind as the man to head it. He was competent enough, just lazy and inattentive to detail. Surely, Gristhorpe had reasoned to Banks, he couldn't do much damage in a sleepy fishing village like Saltby Bay?

Hatchley had been asked if he fancied living by the seaside and he had said yes. After all, it was still in Yorkshire. As the time of the move coincided with his impending marriage, it had seemed sensible to combine the two celebrations. Though Hatchley remained a sergeant, Gristhorpe had managed to wangle him a small pay increase, and—more important—he would be in charge. He was to take David Craig, now a detective constable, with him. Craig, soaking up the ale at the other end of the bar, didn't look too pleased about it. Hatchley and his wife were off to Saltby Bay that night—or, the way things were going, the next morning—where he was to take two weeks' leave to set up their cottage by the sea. His only complaint was that it wouldn't be summer for a long time. Apart from that, Hatchley seemed happy enough with the state of affairs.

In Eastvale, Richmond had got his promotion to detective sergeant at last, and Susan Gay had been brought upstairs as their new detective constable. It was too early to know whether the arrangement would work, but Banks had every confidence in both Richmond and Gay. Still, he felt sad. He had been in Eastvale almost three years, and during that time he had grown to like and depend on Sergeant Hatchley, despite the man's obvious faults. It had taken Banks until last summer to call the sergeant by his first name, but he felt that Hatchley, with Superintendent Gristhorpe, had been responsible for helping him adapt to Yorkshire ways after his move from London.

The music slowed down. Percy Sledge started singing "When a Man Loves a Woman." Sandra touched Banks's arm. "Dance?"

Banks took her hand and they walked toward the dance-floor. Before they got there, someone tapped him gently on the shoulder. He turned and saw DC Susan Gay, snowflakes still melting on the shoulders of her navy coat and in her short, curly blond hair.

"What is it?" Banks asked.

"Can I have a word, sir? Somewhere quiet."

The only quiet places were the toilets, and they could hardly go charging off into the gents' or ladies'. The alternative was the corner opposite the DJ, which seemed to be deserted. Banks asked Sandra if she minded missing this one. She shrugged, being used to such privations, and went back to the bar. Gristhorpe, Banks noticed, gallantly offered her his arm, and they went onto the dance-floor.

"It's a murder, at least a possible murder," DC Gay said, as soon as they had found a quieter spot. "I didn't see the superintendent when I came in, so I went straight to you."

"Any details?"

"Sketchy."

"How long ago was this?"

"About ten minutes. I sent PC Tolliver to the house and drove straight over here. I'm sorry to spoil the celebrations, but I couldn't see what else—"

"It's all right," Banks said, "you did fine." She hadn't, but that was hardly her fault. She was new to the job and a murder report had cropped up. What should she have done? Well, she could have gone to check out the scene herself, and she might have found, as nine times out of ten one did, that there had been some mistake, or a prank. Or she might have waited for the PC to call in and let her know the situation before running off and dragging her chief inspector away from his ex-sergeant's wedding celebration. But Banks didn't blame her. She was young yet, she would learn, and if they really were dealing with a murder, the time saved by Susan's direct action could prove invaluable.

"I've got the address, sir." She stood there looking at him, keen, expectant. "It's on Oakwood Mews. Number eleven."

Banks sighed. "We'd better go then. Just give me a minute."

He went back to the bar and explained the situation to

Richmond. The music speeded up again, into the Supremes' "Baby Love," and Gristhorpe led Sandra back from the dance-floor. When he heard the news, he insisted on accompanying Banks to the scene, even though it was by no means certain they would find a murder victim there. Richmond wanted to come along, too.

"No, lad," said Gristhorpe, "there's no point. If it's serious, Alan can fill you in later. And don't tell Sergeant Hatchley. I don't want it spoiling his wedding day. Though judging by the look on young Carol's face he might have already done that himself."

"Are you taking the car?" Sandra asked Banks.

"I'd better. Oakwood Mews is a fair distance from here. There's no telling how long we'll be. If there's time, I'll come back and pick you up. If not, don't worry, Phil will take good care of you."

"Oh, I'm not worried." She slipped her arm in Richmond's and the new detective sergeant blushed. "Phil's a lovely mover."

Banks kissed her quickly and set off with Gristhorpe.

Susan Gay stood waiting for them by the door. Before they got to her, one of Hatchley's rugby club cronies lurched over and tried to kiss her. From behind, Banks saw him put his arms around her, then double up and stagger back. Everyone else was too busy dancing or chatting to notice. Susan looked flushed when Banks and Gristhorpe got there. She put her hand to mouth and muttered, "I'm sorry," while the rugby player pointed, with a hurt expression on his face, to the sprig of mistletoe over the door.

III

It was no false alarm; that much, at least, was clear from the expression on PC Tolliver's face when Banks and the others reached number eleven Oakwood Mews. After Gristhorpe had issued instructions to send for Dr. Glendenning and the scene-of-crime team, the three detectives went inside.

The first thing Banks noticed when he entered the hall was the music. Muffled, coming from the front room, it sounded familiar: a Bach cantata, perhaps? Then he opened the living-room door and paused on the threshold. The scene possessed a picturesque quality, he felt, which even extended, at first, to masking the ugliness of the corpse on the sofa.

A log fire crackled in the hearth. Its flames tossed shadows on the sheepskin rug and over the stucco walls. The only other light came from two red candles on the polished oak table in the far corner, and from the Christmas tree lights in the window. Banks stepped into the room. The flames danced and the beautiful music played on. On the wall above the stereo was a print of one of Gauguin's Tahitian scenes: a coffee-skinned native woman, naked to the waist, carrying what looked like a bowl of red berries as she walked beside another woman.

As he approached the sofa, Banks noticed that the sheep-skin rug was dotted with dark blotches, as if the fire had spat sparks, which had seared the wool. Then he became aware of that sickly, metallic smell he had come across so often before.

A log shifted on the fire; flames leapt in all directions and their light played over the naked body. The woman lay stretched out, head propped up on cushions in what would have been a very inviting pose had it not been for the blood that had flowed from the multiple stab wounds in her throat and chest and drenched the whole front of her body. It glistened like dark satin in the firelight. From what Banks could see, the victim was young and pretty, with smooth, olive skin and shoulder-length, jet-black hair. Bending over her, he noticed that her eyes were blue, the intense kind of blue that makes some dark-haired people all that much more attractive. Now their stare was cold and lifeless. In front of her, on the low coffee table, stood a half-empty teacup on a coaster and a chocolate layer-cake with one slice missing. Banks covered one fingertip with his handkerchief and touched the cup. It was cold.

The spell broke. Banks became aware of Gristhorpe's voice in the background questioning PC Tolliver, and of Susan Gay standing silent beside him. It was her first corpse, he realized, and she was handling it well, better than he had. Not only was she not about to vomit or faint, but she, too, was glancing around the room, observing the details.

"Who found the body?" Gristhorpe asked PC Tolliver.

"Woman by the name of Veronica Shildon. She lives here."

"Where is she now?" Banks asked.

Tolliver nodded toward the stairs. "Up there with the neighbor. She didn't want to come back in here."

"I don't blame her," said Banks. "Do you know who the victim is?"

"Her name's Caroline Hartley. Apparently, she lived here too."

Gristhorpe raised his bushy eyebrows. "Come on, Alan, let's go and hear what she has to say. Susan, will you stay down here till the scene-of-crime team arrives?"

Susan Gay nodded and stood aside.

There were only two rooms and a bathroom-toilet upstairs. One had been converted into a sitting room, or a study, with bookcases covering one wall, a small roll-top desk under the window and a couple of wicker armchairs arranged below the track-lighting. The bedroom, Banks noticed from the landing, was done out in coral and sea-green, with Laura Ashley wallpaper. If two women lived in the house and there was only one bedroom, he reasoned, then they must share it. He took a deep breath and went into the study.

Veronica Shildon sat in one of the wicker chairs, head in hands. The neighbor, who introduced herself as Christine Cooper, sat beside her. The only other place to sit was the hard-backed chair in front of the desk. Gristhorpe took it and leaned forward, resting his chin on his fists. Banks stood by the door.

"She's had a terrible shock," Christine Cooper said. "I

don't know if she'll be able to tell you much."

"Don't worry, Mrs. Cooper," Gristhorpe said. "The doctor will be here soon. He'll give her something. Is there anyone she can stay with?"

"She can stay with me if she wants. Next door. We've got a spare room. I'm sure my husband won't mind."

"Fine." Gristhorpe turned toward the crying woman and introduced himself. "Can you tell me what happened?"

Veronica Shildon looked up. She was in her mid-thirties, Banks guessed, with a neat cap of dark brown hair streaked with gray. Handsome rather than pretty, her thin face and lips, and everything in her bearing, spoke of dignity and refinement, perhaps even of severity. She held a crumpled tissue in her left hand and the fist of her right was clenched so tightly it was white. Even as he admired her appearance, Banks looked for any signs of blood on her hands or her clothing. He saw none. Her gray-green eyes, red around the rims, couldn't quite focus on Gristhorpe.

"I just got home," she said. "I thought she was waiting for me."

"What time was this?" Gristhorpe asked.

"Eight. A few minutes after." She didn't look at him when she answered.

"Where had you been?"

"I'd been shopping." She looked up, but her eyes appeared to be staring right through the superintendent. "That's just it, you see. I thought for a moment she was wearing the present I'd bought her, the scarlet camisole. But she couldn't have been, could she? I hadn't even given it to her. And she was dead."

"What did you do when you found her?" Gristhorpe asked.

"I . . . I ran to Christine's. She took me in and called the police. I don't know. . . . Is Caroline really dead?"

Gristhorpe nodded.

"Why? Who?"

Gristhorpe leaned forward and spoke softly. "That's what

we have to find out, love. Are you sure you didn't touch anything in the room?"

"Nothing."

"Is there anything else you can tell us?"

Veronica Shildon shook her head. She was clearly too distraught to speak. They would have to leave their questions until tomorrow.

Christine Cooper accompanied Banks and Gristhorpe to the study door. "I'll stay with her till the doctor comes, if you don't mind," she said.

Gristhorpe nodded and they went downstairs.

"Organize a house-to-house, would you?" Gristhorpe asked PC Tolliver before they returned to the living room. "You know the drill. Anyone seen entering or leaving the house." The constable nodded and dashed off.

Back inside the front room, Banks noticed for the first time how warm it was and took off his raincoat. The music stopped, then the needle came off the record, returned to the edge of the turntable and promptly started on its way again.

"What *is* that music?" Susan Gay asked.

Banks listened. The piece—elegant, stately strings accompanying a soprano soloist singing in Latin—sounded vaguely familiar. It wasn't Bach at all, Italian in style rather than German.

"Sounds like Vivaldi," he said, frowning. "But it's not what it is bothers me so much, it's why it's playing, and especially why it's been set to repeat."

He walked over to the turntable and knelt by the album cover lying face down on the speaker beside it. It was indeed Vivaldi: *Laudate pueri*, sung by Magda Kalmár. Banks had never heard of her, but she had a beautiful voice, more reedy, warm and less brittle than many sopranos he had heard. The cover looked new.

"Should I turn it off?" Susan Gay asked.

"No. Leave it. It could be important. Let the scene-of-crime boys have a look."

At that moment the front door opened and everyone stood

aghast at what walked in. To all intents and purposes, their visitor was Santa Claus himself, complete with beard and red hat. If it hadn't been for the height, the twinkling blue eyes, the brown bag and the cigarette dangling from the corner of his mouth, Banks himself wouldn't have known who it was.

"I apologize for my appearance," said Dr. Glendenning. "Believe me, I have no wish to appear frivolous. But I was just about to set off for the children's ward to give out their Christmas presents when I got the call. I didn't want to waste any time." And he didn't. "Is this the alleged corpse?" He walked over to the sofa and bent over the body. Before he had done much more than look it over, Peter Darby, the photographer, arrived along with Vic Manson and his team.

The three CID officers stood in the background while the specialists went to work collecting hair and fabric samples with tiny vacuum cleaners, dusting for prints and photographing the scene from every conceivable angle. Susan Gay seemed enthralled. She must have read about all this in books, Banks thought, and even taken part in demonstration runs at the police college, but there was nothing like the real thing. He tapped her on the shoulder. It took her a few seconds to pull her eyes away and face him.

"I'm just nipping back upstairs," Banks whispered. "Won't be a minute." Susan nodded and turned to watch Glendenning measure the throat wounds.

Upstairs, Banks knelt in front of the armchair. "Veronica," he said gently, "that music, Vivaldi, was it playing when you got home?"

With difficulty, Veronica focused on him. "Yes," she said, with a puzzled look on her face. "Yes. That was odd. I thought we had company."

"Why?"

"Caroline . . . she doesn't like classical music. She says it makes her feel stupid."

"So she wouldn't have put it on herself?"

Veronica shook her head. "Never."

"Whose record is it? Is it part of your collection?"

"No."

"But you like classical music?"

She nodded.

"Do you know the piece?"

"I don't think so, but I recognize the voice."

Banks stood up and rested his hand on her shoulder. "The doctor will be up soon," he said. "He'll give you something to help you sleep." He took Christine Cooper's arm and drew her onto the landing. "How long have they been living here?"

"Nearly two years now."

Banks nodded toward the bedroom. "Together?"

"Yes. At least I . . ." She folded her arms. "It's not my place to judge."

"Ever any trouble?"

"What do you mean?"

"Rows, threats, feuds, angry visitors, anything?"

Christine Cooper shook her head. "Not a thing. You couldn't wish for quieter, more considerate neighbors. As I said, we didn't know each other very well, but we've passed the time of day together now and then. My husband . . ."

"Yes?"

"Well . . . he was very fond of Caroline. I think she reminded him of our Corinne. She died a few years ago. Leukemia. She was about Caroline's age."

Banks looked at Christine Cooper. She seemed to be somewhere in her mid-fifties, a small, puzzled-looking woman with gray hair and a wrinkled brow. That would make her husband about the same age, or a little older perhaps. A paternal attachment, most likely, but he made a mental note to follow it up.

"Did you notice anything earlier this evening?" he asked.

"Like what?"

"Any noise, or anyone calling at the house?"

"No, I can't really say I did. The houses are quite solid, you know. I had my curtains closed, and I had the television on until eight o'clock, when that silly game show came on."

"You heard nothing at all?"

"I heard doors close once or twice, but I couldn't be sure whose doors."

"Can you remember what time?"

"When I was watching television. Between seven and eight. I'm sorry I'm not more use to you. I just didn't pay attention. I didn't know it would be important."

"Of course not. Just one more small point," Banks said. "What time did Mrs. Shildon arrive at your house?"

"Ten past eight."

"Are you sure?"

"Yes. I was in the kitchen then. I looked at the clock when I heard someone shouting and banging on my door. I hadn't heard any carol-singers, and I wondered who could be calling at that time."

"Did you hear her arrive home?"

"I heard her door open and close."

"What time was that?"

"Just after eight—certainly not more than a minute or two after. I'd just switched the television off and gone to start on Charles's dinner. That's why I heard her. It was quiet then. I thought it was my door at first, so I glanced up at the clock. It's a habit I have when I'm in the kitchen. There's a nice wall-clock, a present . . . but you don't want to know about that. Anyway, I wasn't expecting Charles back so early so I . . . Just a minute! What are you getting at? Surely you can't believe—"

"Thank you very much, Mrs. Cooper, that'll be all for now."

When Mrs. Cooper had gone back into the study, Banks had a quick look through the bedroom for any signs of blood-stained clothing, but found nothing. The wardrobe was clearly divided into two halves: one for Veronica's more conservative clothes and the other for Caroline's, a little more modern in style. At the bottom sat a carrier bag full of what looked like unwrapped Christmas presents.

The whole house would have to be searched thoroughly before the night was over, but the scene-of-crime team could do that later. What bothered Banks for the moment was the gap of almost ten minutes between Veronica Shildon's arriving home and her knocking on her neighbor's door. A lot could be accomplished in ten minutes.

Back downstairs, Banks led Vic Manson over to the turntable.

"Can you get this record off and dust the whole area for prints? I want the cover and the inside sleeve bagged for examination, too."

"No problem." Manson set to it.

Everyone looked up when the music stopped. It had cast such a spell over the scene that Banks felt like a dancer cut off in the middle of a stately pavan. Now everyone seemed to notice for the first time exactly what the situation was. It was harsh and ugly, especially with all the lights on.

"Have they found anything interesting yet?" Banks asked Gristhorpe.

"The knife. It was on the draining-board in the kitchen, all washed, but there are still traces of blood. It looks like one of their own, from a set. Did you notice that cake on the table in front of the sofa?"

Banks nodded.

"It's possible she'd used the knife to cut herself a slice earlier."

"Which would make it the handiest weapon," Banks said, "if it was still on the table."

"Yes. And there's this." The superintendent held out a crumpled sheet of green Christmas wrapping paper with silver bells and red holly-berries on it. "It was over by the music center." He shrugged. "It might mean something."

"It could have come from the record," Banks said, and told Gristhorpe what Veronica had said.

Dr. Glendenning, who had taken off his beard and hat and unbuttoned the top half of his Father Christmas outfit, walked over to them and stuck another cigarette in his mouth.

"Dead three or four hours at the most," he said. "Bruise on the left cheek consistent with a hard punch or kick. It might easily have knocked her out. But cause of death was blood loss due to multiple stab wounds—at least seven, as far as I can count. Unless she was poisoned first."

"Thanks," Gristhorpe said. "Any way of telling how it happened?"

"At this stage, no. Except for the obvious—it was a bloody vicious attack."

"Aye," said Gristhorpe. "Was she interfered with sexually?"

"On a superficial examination, I'd say no. No signs of it at all. But I won't be able to tell you any more until after the postmortem, which I'll conduct first thing tomorrow morning. You can have the lads cart her to the mortuary whenever they're ready. Can I be off now? I hate to keep those poor wee kiddies waiting."

Banks asked him if he would drop in on Veronica Shildon first and give her a sedative. Glendenning sighed but agreed. The ambulance men, who had been waiting outside, came in to take away the body. Glendenning had covered the hands with plastic bags to preserve any skin caught under the fingernails. As the ambulance men lifted her onto the stretcher, the cuts around her throat gaped open like screaming mouths. One of the men had to put his hand under her head so that the flesh didn't rip back as far as the spine. That was the only time Banks saw Susan Gay visibly pale and look away.

With Caroline Hartley's body gone, apart from the blood that had sprayed onto the sheepskin and the sofa cushions, there was very little left to indicate what horror had occurred in the cozy room that night. The forensic team bundled up the rug and cushions to take with them for further examination, and then there was nothing left to show at all.

It was after ten-thirty. PC Tolliver and another two uniformed constables were still conducting house-to-house inquiries in the area, but there was little else the CID could do until morning. They needed to know Caroline Hartley's movements that evening: where she had been, who she had seen and who might have had a reason to want her dead.

Veronica Shildon could probably tell them, but she was in no state to answer questions.

Gristhorpe and Susan Gay left first. Then, after leaving instructions for the scene-of-crime team to search the house thoroughly for any signs of blood-stained clothing, Banks returned to the rugby club to see if Sandra was still there. Snow swirled in front of his headlights and the road was slippery.

When Banks pulled up outside the rugby club in the northern part of Eastvale it was almost eleven o'clock. The lights were still on. In the foyer, he kicked the clinging snow off his shoes, brushed it from his hair and the shoulders of his camel-hair overcoat, which he hung up on the rack provided, and went inside.

He stood in the doorway and looked around the softly lit banquet hall. Hatchley and Carol had finally left, but plenty of others remained, still holding drinks. The DJ had taken a break and someone sat at the piano playing Christmas carols. Banks saw Sandra and Richmond sitting on their stools at the bar. He stood and watched them sing for a few moments. It was a curiously intimate feeling, like watching someone sleep. And like sleepers, their faces wore innocent, tranquil expressions as their lips mouthed the familiar words:

> *Silent night, holy night*
> *All is calm, all is bright*

TWO

I

"What have we got so far?" Gristhorpe asked at eight o'clock
the following morning. As Banks knew from experience, the
superintendent liked to call regular conferences in the early
stages of an investigation. Although he had been at the scene
the previous evening, he would now leave the fieldwork to
his team and concentrate on co-ordinating their tasks and
dealing with the press. Gristhorpe, unlike some supers Banks
had worked with, believed in letting his men get on with the
job while he handled matters of politics and policy.

In the conference room, the four of them—Gristhorpe,
Banks, Richmond and Susan Gay—reviewed the events of
the previous evening. Nothing had come in yet from forensics
or from Dr. Glendenning, who was just about to start the post-
mortem. The only new information they had obtained had
resulted from the house-to-house inquiry. Three people had
been seen visiting number eleven Oakwood Mews separately
that evening. Nobody could describe them clearly—after all,
it had been dark and snowing, and the street was not well
lit—but two independent witnesses seemed to agree that one
man and two women had called there.

The man had called first, around seven o'clock, and Caroline had admitted him to the house. Nobody had seen him
leave. Not very long after, a woman had arrived, talked briefly
to Caroline on the doorstep, then left without entering the

21

house. One witness said she thought it might have been some-one collecting for charity, what with it being Christmas and all, but then a collector wouldn't have missed the opportunity of knocking on everyone else's door as well, would she? And no, there had been no obvious signs of a quarrel.

The final visitor—according to the sightings—called shortly after the other woman left and went inside the house. Nobody had noticed her leave. That, as far as they could pin down, was the last time Caroline Hartley had been seen alive by anyone but her killer. Other visitors may have called be-tween about half past seven and eight, but nobody had seen them. Everybody had been watching "Coronation Street."

"Any ideas about the record?" Gristhorpe asked.

"I think it might be important," Banks said, "but I don't know why. According to Veronica Shildon, it wasn't hers, and the Hartley girl didn't like classical music."

"So where did it come from?" Susan Gay asked.

"Tolliver said that one of the witnesses thought the man who called was carrying a shopping bag of some sort. It could have been in there—a present, say. That would explain the wrapping paper we found."

"But why would anyone bring a woman a present of some-thing she didn't like?" Susan asked.

Banks shrugged. "Could be any number of reasons. Maybe it was someone who didn't know her tastes well. Or it might have been intended for Veronica Shildon. All I'm saying is that it's odd and I think we ought to check it out. It's also strange that someone should put it on the turntable and delib-erately leave it to repeat *ad infinitum*. We can be reasonably certain that Caroline wouldn't have played it, so who did, and why? We might even be dealing with a psycho. The music could be his calling card."

"All right," Gristhorpe said after a short silence. "Susan, why don't you get down to Pristine Records and see if they know anything about it."

Susan made a note in her book and nodded.

"Alan, you and Detective Sergeant Richmond here can see

what you can get out of Veronica Shildon." He paused. "What do you make of their relationship?"

Banks scratched the little scar by the side of his right eye. "They were living together. And sleeping together, as far as I could tell. Nobody's spelled it out yet, but I'd say it's pretty obvious. Christine Cooper implied much the same."

"Could that give us an angle?" Gristhorpe suggested. "I don't know much about lesbian relationships, but anything off the beaten track could be worth looking into."

"A jealous lover, something like that?" Banks said.

Gristhorpe shrugged. "You tell me. I just think it's worth a bit of scrutiny."

The meeting broke up and they went their separate ways, but not before Sergeant Rowe came up to them in the corridor with a form in his hand.

"There's been a break-in at the Community Center," he said, waving the sheet. "Any takers?"

"Not another!" Banks groaned. It was the third in two months. Vandalism was becoming as much of a problem in Eastvale as it seemed to be everywhere else in the country.

"Aye," said Rowe. "Dustbin men noticed the back door broken open when they picked up the rubbish half an hour ago. I've already notified the people involved with that Amateur Dramatic Society. They're the only ones using the place at the moment—except for your wife, sir."

Rowe was referring to Sandra's new part-time job managing Eastvale's new gallery, where she arranged exhibitions of local art, sculpture and photography. The Eastvale Arts Committee had applied as usual for its grant, fully expecting significant cuts, if not an outright refusal. But that year, whether due to some bureaucratic blunder or a generous fiscal whim, they had been given twice what they had asked for and found themselves looking for ways to spend the money before someone asked for it back. The check didn't bounce; months passed and they received no letter beginning, "Due to a clerical oversight, we are afraid. . . ." So the large upstairs room of the Community Center was set aside and redecorated for gallery space.

"Any damage upstairs?" Banks asked.

"We don't know yet, sir."

"Where's the caretaker?"

"On holiday, sir. Gone to the in-laws in Oldham for Christmas."

"All right, we'll take care of it. Susan, drop by there before you go to the record shop and see what's going on. It shouldn't take long."

Susan Gay nodded and set off.

Banks and Richmond turned down by the side of the police station toward King Street. The snow had stopped early in the morning, leaving a covering about six inches thick, but the sky was still overcast, heavy with more. The air was chill and damp. On the main streets cars and pedestrians had already churned the snow into brownish-gray slush, but in those narrow, winding alleys between Market Street and King Street it remained almost untouched except for the odd set of footprints and the patches that shopkeepers had shoveled away from the pavement in front of their doors.

This was the real tourist Eastvale. Here, the antique dealers hung up their signs and antiquarian booksellers advertised their wares alongside numismatists and bespoke tailors. These weren't like the cheap souvenir shops on York Road; they were specialty shops with creaking floors and thick, mullioned windows, where unctuous, immaculately dressed shopkeepers called you "Sir" or "Madam."

Oakwood Mews was a short cul-de-sac, a renovated terrace with only ten houses on each side. Black-leaded iron railings separated each small garden from the pavement. In summer, the street blossomed in a profusion of colors, with many houses sporting bright hanging baskets and window boxes. It had even won a "prettiest street in Yorkshire" prize several years ago, and the plaque to prove it was affixed to the wall of the first house. Now, as Banks and Richmond approached number nine, the street looked positively Victorian. Banks almost expected Tiny Tim to come running up to them and throw his crutches away.

Banks knocked on the Coopers' door. It was made of light, paneled wood, and the shiny knocker was a highly polished brass lion's head. A wealthy little street this, obviously, Banks thought, even if it was only a terrace block of small houses. They were brick built, pre-war, and had recently been restored to perfection.

Christine Cooper answered the door in her dressing-gown and invited them in. Unlike the more cozy, feminine elegance of number eleven, the Cooper place was almost entirely modern in decor: assemble-it-yourself Scandinavian furniture and off-white walls. The kitchen, into which she led them, boasted plenty of shelf- and surface-space and every gadget under the sun, from microwave to electric tin-opener.

"Coffee?"

Banks and Richmond both nodded and sat down at the large pine breakfast table. It had been set close to a corner to save space, and someone had fixed bench-seating to the two adjacent walls. Both Banks and Richmond sat on the bench with their backs to the wall. Banks had no trouble fitting himself in, as he was only a little taller than regulation 172 centimeters; but Richmond had to shift about to accommodate his long legs.

Mrs. Cooper faced them from a matching chair across the table. The electric coffee-maker was already gurgling away, and they had to wait only a few moments for their drinks.

"I'm afraid Veronica isn't up, yet," Mrs. Cooper said. "Your doctor gave her a sleeping pill and she was out like a light as soon as we got her into bed. I explained everything to Charles. He's been very understanding."

"Where is your husband?" Banks asked.

"At work."

"What time did he get home last night?"

"It must have been after eleven. We sat up and talked about . . . you know . . . for a while, then we went to bed about midnight."

"He certainly works long hours."

Mrs. Cooper sighed. "Yes, especially at this time of year. You see, he runs a chain of children's shops in North Yorkshire, and he's constantly being called from one crisis to another. One place runs out of whatever new doll all the kids want this year and another out of jigsaw puzzles. I'm sure you can imagine the problems."

"Where was he yesterday evening?"

Mrs. Cooper seemed surprised at the question, but she answered after only a slight hesitation. "Barnard Castle. Apparently the manager of the shop there reported some stock discrepancies."

There was probably nothing in it, Banks thought, but Charles Cooper's alibi should be easy enough to check.

"Maybe you can give us a bit more background on Caroline Hartley while we're waiting for Mrs. Shildon," he said.

Richmond took out his notebook and settled back in the corner seat.

Mrs. Cooper rubbed her chin. "I don't know if I can tell you much about Caroline, really. I knew her, but I didn't feel I *really* knew her, if you know what I mean. It was all on the surface. She was a real sparkler, I'll say that for her. Always full of beans. Always a smile and a hello for everyone. Talented, too, from what I could gather."

"Talented? How?"

"She was an actress. Oh, just amateur like, but if you ask me, she'd got what it takes. She could take anybody off. You should have seen her impression of Maggie Thatcher. Talk about laugh!"

"Was this theatrical work local?"

"Oh, yes. Only the Eastvale Amateur Dramatic Society."

"Was this her first experience with theater?"

"I wouldn't know that. It was only a small part, but she was excited about it."

"Where does she come from?"

"Do you know, I can't say. I know nothing about her past.

She could be from Timbuktu for all I know. As I said before, we weren't *really* close."

"Do you know if she had any enemies? Did she ever tell you about any quarrels she might have had?"

Mrs. Cooper shook her head, then blushed.

"What is it?" Banks asked.

"Well," Mrs. Cooper began, "it's nothing really, I don't suppose, and I don't want to go getting anybody into trouble, but when two women live together like . . . like they did, then somebody somewhere's got to be unhappy, haven't they?"

"What do you mean?"

"Veronica's ex-husband. She was a married woman before she came here. I shouldn't think he'd be very happy about things, would he? And I'll bet there was someone in Caroline's life, too—a woman or a man. She didn't seem the kind to be on her own for too long, if you know what I mean."

"Do you know anything about Veronica Shildon's ex-husband?"

"Only that they sold the big house they used to have outside town and split the money. She bought this place and he moved off somewhere. The coast, I think. The whole thing seemed very hush-hush to me. She's never even told me his name."

"The Yorkshire coast?"

"Yes, I think so. But Veronica can tell you all about him."

"You didn't see him in the neighborhood yesterday evening, did you?"

Mrs. Cooper pulled her robe together at the front, looking down and making a double chin as she did so. "No. I told you all I saw or heard last night. Besides, I wouldn't recognize him from Adam. I've never seen him."

Banks heard stairs creak and looked around to see Veronica Shildon standing in the doorway. She was dressed as she had been the previous evening—tight jeans, which flattered her slim, curved hips, trim waist and flat stomach, and a high-necked, chunky-knit green sweater, which brought out the color in her eyes. She was tall, about five foot ten, and poised.

Banks thought there was something odd about seeing her in such casual wear; she looked as if she belonged in a pearl silk blouse and a navy business suit. She had taken the time to brush her short hair and put a little make-up on, but her face still looked drawn underneath it all, and her eyes, disarmingly honest and naked, were still red from crying.

Banks tried to stand up, but he was too closely wedged in by the table.

"I'm sorry to bother you so soon," he said, "but the quicker we get moving the more chance we have."

"I understand," she said. "Please don't worry about me. I'll be all right."

She swayed a little as she walked toward the table. Mrs. Cooper took her elbow and guided her to a chair, then brought her some coffee and disappeared, muttering something about things to attend to.

"In cases like this," Banks began, "it helps if we know what the person was doing, where she was, previous to the incident." He knew he sounded trite, but somehow he couldn't bring himself to say "victim" and "murder."

Veronica nodded. "Of course. As far as I know Caroline went to work, but you'll have to check that. She runs the Garden Café on Castle Hill Road."

"I know it," Banks said. It was an elegant little place, very up-market, with a stunning view of the formal gardens and the river.

"She usually finishes at three on a weekday, after the lunchtime crowd. They don't open for tea off-season. On a normal day she'd come home, do some shopping, or perhaps drop by at the shop for a while to help out."

"Shop?"

"I own a flower shop—or rather my partner and I do. It's mostly a matter of his money and my management. It's just around the corner from here, down King Street."

"You said on a 'normal' day. Was yesterday not normal?"

She looked straight at him and her eyes let him know that his choice of words had been inappropriate. Yesterday, indeed, had not been normal. But she simply said, "No. Yesterday after work they had a rehearsal. They're doing *Twelfth Night* at the Community Center. It's quite a heavy rehearsal schedule as the director's set on actually opening on twelfth night."

"What time did rehearsals run?"

"Usually between four and six, so she would have been home at about quarter past six, if she'd come home immediately."

"And was she likely to?"

"They often went for a drink after, but yesterday she came straight home."

"How do you know?"

"I phoned to see if she was there and to tell her I'd be a bit late because I was doing some shopping."

"What time?"

"About seven."

"How did she sound?"

"Fine . . . she sounded fine."

"Was there any special reason for her not going for a drink with the others yesterday?"

"No. She just said she was tired after rehearsal and she . . ."

"Yes?"

"We've both been so busy lately. She wanted to spend some time with me . . . a quiet evening at home."

"Where had you been that evening?"

Veronica didn't show a flicker of resentment at being asked for an alibi. "I closed the shop at five-thirty, then I went for my six o'clock appointment with Dr. Ursula Kelly, my therapist. She's Caroline's too. Her office is on Kilnsey Street, just off Castle Hill. I walked. We do have a car but we don't use it much in town, mostly just for trips away." She blew on her coffee and took a sip. "The session lasted an hour. After that, I went to the shopping center to buy a few things. Christmas presents mostly." She faltered a little. "Then I walked home. I . . . I got here about eight o'clock."

No doubt it would be possible to check her alibi in the

shopping center, Banks thought. Some shopkeepers might remember her. But it was a busy time of year for them, and he doubted that any would be able to recollect what day and what time they had last seen her. He could examine the receipts, too. Sometimes the modern electronic cash registers gave the time of purchase as well as the date.

"Can you tell me exactly what happened, what you did, from the moment you left the shops and walked home last night?"

Veronica took a deep breath and closed her eyes. "I walked home," she began, "in the snow. It was a beautiful evening. I stopped and listened to the carol-singers in the market square for a while. They were singing 'O, Little Town of Bethlehem.' It's always been one of my favorites. When I got home I . . . I called out hello to Caroline, but she didn't answer. I thought nothing of it. She could have been in the kitchen. And then there was the music . . . well, that was odd. So I took the opportunity and crept upstairs to hide the presents in the wardrobe. Some were for her, you see, the . . ." She paused, and Banks noticed her eyes fill with tears. "It seemed so important just to put them out of sight," she went on. "I knew there would be plenty of opportunity to wrap them later. While I was up there, I washed and changed and went back downstairs.

"The music was still playing. I opened the door to the living room and . . . I . . . at first I thought she was wearing the new scarlet camisole. She looked so serene and so beautiful lying there like that. But it couldn't be. I told you last night, I hadn't given it to her then. I'd just bought her the camisole for Christmas and I'd put it in the bottom of the wardrobe with everything else. Then I went closer and . . . the smell . . . her eyes . . ." Veronica put her mug down and held her head in her hands.

Banks let the silence stretch for a good minute or two. All they could hear was the soft ticking of Mrs. Cooper's kitchen wall-clock and a dog barking in the distance.

"I understand you were married," Banks said, when Veronica had wiped her eyes and reached out for her coffee again.

"I still am, officially. We're only separated, not divorced. He didn't want our personal life splashed all over the newspapers. As you may have gathered, Caroline and I lived together."

Banks nodded. "Why should the newspapers have been interested? People get divorced all the time for all kinds of reasons."

Veronica hesitated and turned her mug slowly in a circle on the table. She wouldn't meet his eyes.

"Look," Banks said, "I hardly need remind you what's happened, how serious this is. We'll find out anyway. You can save us a lot of time and trouble."

Veronica looked up at him. "You're right, of course," she said. "Though I don't see how it can have anything to do with all this. My husband was—is, Claude Ivers. He's not exactly a household name, but enough people have heard of him."

Banks certainly had. Ivers had once been a brilliant concert pianist, but several years ago he had given up performance for composition. He had received important commissions from the BBC, and a number of his pieces had been recorded. Banks even had a tape of his two wind quintets; they possessed a kind of eerie, natural beauty—not structured, but wandering, like the breeze in a deep forest at night. Veronica Shildon was right. If the press had got hold of the story she would have had no peace for weeks. *News of the World* reporters would have been climbing the drainpipes and spying in bedroom windows, talking to spiteful neighbors and slighted lovers. He could just see the headlines: "HIGH-BROW MUSICIAN'S WIFE IN LESBIAN LOVE-NEST."

"Where is your husband now?" Banks asked.

"He lives in Redburn, out on the coast. He said the seclusion and the sea would be good for his work. He always did care about his work."

Banks noticed the bitterness in her tone. "Do you ever see one another?"

"Yes," she said. A smile touched her thin lips. "It was an acrimonious parting in many ways, but there *is* some affection left. We don't seem able to stamp that out, whatever we do."

"When did you last see him?"

"About a month ago. We occasionally go for dinner if he's in town. I rarely visit the coast, but he comes here from time to time."

"To the house?"

"He's been here, yes, though he's always worried someone will see him and know who he is. I try to tell him that people don't actually recognize composers in the street any more than they do writers, that it's only television and film stars have to put up with that, but . . ." She shrugged.

"Did he know Caroline?"

"He could hardly *help* knowing her, could he? They'd met a few times."

"How did they get on?"

Veronica shrugged. "They never seemed to have much to say to one another. They were different as chalk and cheese. He thought she was a scheming slut and she thought he was a selfish, pompous ass. They had nothing in common but affection for me."

"Was there any open antagonism?"

"Open? Good lord, no. That isn't Claude's way. He sniped from time to time, made sarcastic comments, cruel remarks, that kind of thing."

"Directed toward Caroline?"

"Directed toward both of us. But I'm sure he blamed Caroline for leading me astray. That's how he saw it."

"Was it that way?"

Veronica shook her head.

"Was Caroline ever married?"

"Not that I know of."

"Was she living with anyone before she met you?"

Veronica paused and gripped her coffee mug in both hands

as if to warm them. Her fingers were long and tapered and she had freckles on the backs of her hands. She wore a silver ring on the middle finger of her right hand. As she spoke, she looked down at the table. "She was living with a woman called Nancy Wood. They'd been together about eight months. The relationship was going very badly."

"Where does Nancy Wood live?"

"In Eastvale. Not too far from here. At least, she did the last I heard."

"Did Caroline ever see her after they split up?"

"Only by accident once or twice in the street."

"So they parted on bad terms?"

"Doesn't everyone? Much as I admire Shakespeare, I've often wondered where the sweetness is in the sorrow."

"And before Nancy Wood?"

"She spent some time in London. I don't know how long or who with. A few years, at least."

"What about her family?"

"Her mother's dead. Her father lives in Harrogate. He's an invalid, been one for years. Her brother Gary looks after him. I told one of your uniformed men last night. Will someone have called?"

Banks nodded. "Don't worry, the Harrogate police will have taken care of it. Is there anything else you can tell me about Caroline's friends or enemies?"

Veronica sighed and shook her head. She looked exhausted. "No," she said. "We didn't have a lot of close friends. I suppose we tried to be too much to one another. At least that's how it feels now she's gone. You could try the people at the theater. They were her acquaintances, at least. But we didn't socialize very much together. I don't think any of them even knew about her living with me."

"We're still puzzled about the record," Banks said. "Are you sure it isn't yours?"

"I've told you, no."

"But you recognized the singer?"

"Magda Kalmár, yes. Claude and I once saw her in *Lucia*

di Lammermoor at the Budapest Opera. I was very impressed."

"Could the record have been intended as a Christmas present from your husband?"

"Well, I suppose it could...but that means...no, I haven't seen him in a month."

"He could have called last night, while you were out."

She shook her head. "No. I don't believe it. Not Claude."

Banks looked over at Richmond and nodded. Richmond closed his notebook. "That's all for now," Banks said.

"Can I go home?" she asked him.

"If you want." Banks hadn't imagined she would want to return to the house so soon, but there was no official objection. Forensics had finished with the place.

"Just one thing, though," he said. "We'll need to have another good look through Caroline's belongings. Perhaps Detective Sergeant Richmond can accompany you back and look over them now?"

She looked apprehensive at first, then nodded. "All right."

They stood up to leave. Christine Cooper was nowhere in sight, so they walked out into the damp, overcast day and shut the door behind them without saying goodbye.

Veronica opened her front door and went in. Banks lingered at the black iron gate with Richmond. "I'm going to the Community Center," he said. "There should be someone from the theater group there since they've been notified of the break-in. How about we meet up at the Queen's Arms, say twelve or twelve-thirty?" And he went on to ask Richmond to check Veronica Shildon's purchases and look closely at the receipts for corroboration of her alibi. "And check on Charles Cooper's movements yesterday," he added. "It might mean a trip to Barnard Castle, but see if you can come up with anything by phone first."

Richmond went into the house and Banks set off up the steep part of King Street with his collar turned up against the cold. The Community Center wasn't very far; the walk would be good exercise. As he trudged through the snow, he thought about Veronica Shildon. She presented an odd mixture of reserve and frankness, stoical acceptance and bitterness. He was sure she was holding something back, but he didn't know what it was. There was something askew about her. Even her clothes didn't seem to go with the rather repressed and inhibited essence that she projected. "Prim and proper" was the term that sprang to mind. Yet she had left her husband, had gone and set up house with a woman.

All in all, she was an enigma. If anything, Banks thought, she seemed like a woman in the process of great change. Her reference to the analyst indicated that she was at least concerned with self-examination.

It seemed to Banks as if her entire personality had been dismantled and the various bits and pieces didn't quite fit together; some were new, or newly discovered, and others were old, rusted, decrepit, and she wasn't sure whether she wanted to discard them or not. Banks had an inkling of what the process felt like from his own readjustment after the move from London. But Veronica's changes, he suspected, went far deeper. He wondered what she had been like as a wife, and what she would become in the future now that Caroline Hartley had been so viciously excised from her life. For the younger woman had had a great influence on Veronica's life; Banks was certain of that. Was Veronica a killer? He didn't think so, but who could say anything so definite about a personality in such turmoil and transition?

II

On her way to the Community Center, DC Susan Gay thought over her behavior of the previous day and found it distinctly lacking. She had felt even more miserable than usual when she went home from Oakwood Mews that night. Her small flat off York Road always depressed her. It was so barren, like a hotel room, so devoid of any real stamp of her presence, and she knew that was because she hardly spent any time there. Mostly she had been working or off on a course somewhere. For years she had paid no attention to her surroundings or to her personal life. The flat was for eating in, sleeping in and, occasionally, for watching half an hour of television.

It seemed like a lifetime since she'd last had a boyfriend, or anyone more than a casual date, anyone who *meant* something to her. She accepted that she wasn't especially attractive, but she was no ugly sister, either. People had asked her out; the problem was that she always had something more important to do, something related to her career. She was beginning to wonder if the normal sexual impulse had somehow drained away over the years of toil. That incident with the rugby player last night, for example. She knew she shouldn't have responded with such obvious revulsion. He was only being friendly, even if he was a bit rough about it. And wasn't that what mistletoe was for? But she had to overreact. Banks and Gristhorpe had both noticed, she was certain. She wondered what they must think of her.

Damn! The front doors of the Community Center, a Victorian sandstone building on North Market Street, were still locked. That meant Susan would have to double back to the narrow street behind the church. Shivering, she hunched up against the cold and turned around.

It seemed now that the whole of yesterday evening had been a nightmare. First she had run off half-cocked out of the station at the first sign of trouble, without even bothering to check if the call was genuine or not. Then she had gone straight to Banks. She had seen Gristhorpe by the bar, of course, but she hadn't approached him because she was terrified of him. She knew he was said to be a softie, really, but she couldn't help herself. He seemed so self-contained, so sure of himself, so *solid*, just like her father.

The only thing she was proud of was her reaction at the scene. She hadn't fainted, even though it was her first corpse, and a messy one at that. She had managed to maintain a detached, clinical view of the whole affair, watching the experts at work, getting the feel of the scene. There had been only one awkward moment, as the body was being carried away, but anyone could be forgiven for paling a bit at that. No, her behavior at the scene had been exemplary. She hoped Banks and Gristhorpe had noticed that, and not only her faults.

And now she was on her way to investigate a case of vandalism while the others got to work on the murder. It wasn't fair. She realized she was the new member of the team, but that didn't mean she always had to be the one to handle the petty crimes. How could she get ahead if she didn't get to work on important cases? She already had sacrificed so much to her career that she couldn't bear to contemplate failure.

Finally, she got to the back entrance, down an alley off the northern part of York Road. The back door had obviously been jimmied open. Its meager lock was bent and the wood around the jamb had cracked. Susan walked down the long corridor, lit only by a couple of bare sixty-watt bulbs, to where she could hear voices. They came from a room off to her right, a high-ceilinged place with exposed pipes, bare brick walls pied with saltpeter, and more dim lighting. The room smelled of dust and mothballs. There she found a man and a woman bent over a large trunk. They stood up as she walked in.

"Police?" the man asked.

Susan nodded and showed her new CID identification card.

"I must admit, I didn't expect a woman," he said.

Susan prepared to say something withering, but he held up a hand. "Don't get me wrong, I'm not complaining. I'm not a sexist pig. It's just a surprise." He peered at her in the poor light. "Wait a minute, aren't you . . . ?"

"Susan Gay," she said, recognizing him now that her eyes had adjusted to the light. "And you're Mr. Conran." She blushed. "I'm surprised you remember me. I was hardly one of your best students."

Mr. Conran hadn't changed much in the ten years since he had taught the sixteen-year-old Susan drama at Eastvale Comprehensive. About ten years older than her, he was still hand-some in an artsy kind of way, in baggy black cords and a dark polo-neck sweater with the stitching coming away at the shoulder seam. He still had that vulnerable, skinny, half-starved look that Susan remembered so well, but despite it he looked healthy enough. His short fair hair was combed for-ward, flat against his skull; beneath it, intelligent and ironic gray eyes looked out from a pale, hollow-cheeked face. Susan had hated drama, but she had had a crush on Mr. Conran. The other girls said he was a queer, but they said that about everyone in the literature and arts departments. Susan hadn't believed them.

"James," he said, stretching his hand out to shake hers. "I think we can dispense with the teacher-pupil formalities by now, don't you? I'm directing the play. And this is Marcia Cunningham. Marcia takes care of props and costumes. It's she you should talk to, really."

As if to emphasize the point, Conran turned away and be-gan examining the rest of the storage room.

Susan took her notebook out. "What's the damage?" she asked Marcia, a plump, round-faced woman in gray stretch slacks and a threadbare alpaca jacket that looked at least one size too large for her.

Marcia Cunningham sniffed and pointed to the wall. "There's that, for a start." Crudely spray-painted across the bricks were the words "FUCKING WANKERS." "But that'll wash off easy enough," she went on. "This is the worst. They've shredded our costumes. I'm not sure if I can salvage any of them or not."

Susan looked into the trunk. She agreed. It looked like someone had been to work on them with a large pair of scis-sors, snipping the different dresses, suits and shirts into pieces and mixing them all together.

"Why would anyone do that?" Marcia asked.

Susan shook her head.

"At least they left the shoes and wigs alone," she said, gesturing toward the other two boxes of costumes.

"Has anyone checked upstairs?" Susan asked.

Marcia looked surprised. "The gallery? No."

Susan made her way down the corridor to the stairs, cold stone with metal railings. There were several rooms upstairs, some of them used for various groups such as the Philately Society or the Chess Club, others for local committee meetings. All of them were locked. The glass doors to the new gallery were locked too; no damage had been done there. She went back down to the props room and watched Marcia picking up strands of slashed material and moaning.

"All that work, all those people who gave us stuff. Why do they do this?" Marcia asked again. "What bloody point is there?"

Susan knew numerous theories of hooliganism, from poor potty-training to the heartlessness of modern England, but all she said was, "I don't know." People don't want to hear theories when something they value has been destroyed. "And short of catching them red-handed, we can't promise much, either."

"But this is the *third* time!" Marcia said. "Surely by now you must have some kind of lead?"

"There are a few people we're keeping our eye on," Susan told her, "but it's not as if they've stolen anything."

"Even that would be more understandable."

"What I mean is, we'd find no evidence even if we suspected someone. There's no stolen property to trace to them. Have you thought of employing a night-watchman?"

Marcia snorted. "A night-watchman? How do you think we can afford that? I know we got a bonanza grant this year, but we didn't get that much. And most of it's gone already on costumes and stuff."

"I'm sorry," Susan said. She realized this was an inadequate response, but what else was there to say? A constable walked the beat, but he couldn't spend his whole night in the alley at the back of the Community Center. There had been other break-ins, too, and other incidents of vandalism. "I'll make out a report," she said, "and let you know if we come up with anything."

"Thanks a lot."

"Don't be so rude, Marcia." James Conran reappeared and put his hand on Marcia's shoulder. "She's only trying to help." He smiled at Susan. "Aren't you?"

Susan nodded. His smile was so infectious she could hardly keep from responding, and the effort to maintain a detached expression made her flush.

Marcia rubbed her face until her plump cheeks shone. "I'm sorry, love," she said. "I know it's not your fault. It's just so bloody frustrating."

"I know." Susan put her notebook back in her handbag. "I'll be in touch," she said.

Before she could turn to leave, they heard footsteps coming along the corridor. Conran looked surprised. "There's nobody else supposed to be coming here, is there?" he asked Marcia, who shook her head. Then the door creaked open and Susan saw a familiar face peep around. It was Chief Inspector Banks. At first she was relieved to see him. Then she thought, why the hell is he here? Checking up on me? Can't he trust me to do a simple job properly?

III

Detective Sergeant Philip Richmond was glad that Veronica Shildon had not wanted to stand over him as he searched the two upper rooms. He never could tolerate the feel of someone looking over his shoulder. Which was one of the reasons he liked working with Banks, who usually left him to get on with the job his own way.

The bedroom smelled of expensive cologne or talcum. As he looked at the large bed with its satiny coral spread, he thought of the two women in there together and the things they did to each other. The images embarrassed him and he got back to work.

Richmond took the bag of presents out of Veronica's half of the wardrobe and spread them on the bed: a Sheaffer fountain-pen and pencil set, a green silk scarf, some Body Shop soaps and shampoos, a scarlet camisole, the latest Booker Prize winner . . . all pretty ordinary stuff. The receipts were dated but none of them gave the time the purchase had been made. Richmond made a list of items and shops so the staff could be questioned.

The dresser drawers contained mostly lingerie. Richmond picked his way through it methodically, but found nothing hidden away, nothing that shouldn't be there. He moved on to the study.

In addition to the books—none of them inscribed—there was also a roll-top desk in the corner under the window. There was nothing surprising in it: letters to Veronica Shildon, some from her husband, about practical and financial matters; a few bills; Veronica's address book, mostly empty; a house insurance policy; receipts and guarantees for the oven, the fridge and items of furniture, and that was about all. None of it any use to Richmond.

Just when he was beginning to wonder whether Caroline Hartley had had any possessions at all, he came across a manila envelope with "Caroline" written on the front. Inside were a pressed flower, her birth certificate (which showed she had been born in Harrogate twenty-six years ago), an expired passport with no stamps or visas, and a black-and-white photograph of a woman he didn't recognize. She had piercing, intelligent eyes, and her head was slightly tilted to one side. Her medium-length hair was swept back, revealing a straight hairline and ears with tiny lobes. Her lips were pressed tight together, and there was something about the arrogant intensity of her presence that Richmond found disturbing. He wouldn't have described her as beautiful, but striking, certainly. Across the bottom were the words "To Carrie, Love Ruth," written with a flourish.

Making sure he hadn't missed anything, Richmond went back downstairs, taking the envelope of Caroline's possessions with him. Veronica Shildon turned on the small electric fire in the front room when he entered.

"I'm sorry," she said, "I can't be bothered to light a real fire now. We use this most of the time anyway. It seems to be warm enough. Some tea?"

"Yes, please, if it's no trouble."

"It's already made."

Richmond sat down, avoiding the cushionless sofa in favor of an armchair. After Veronica had poured, he held out the photograph to her. "Who's this woman?" he asked. "Can you tell me anything about her?"

Veronica glanced at the photograph and shook her head. "It's just someone Caroline used to know in London."

"Surely she must have told you something about her."

"Caroline didn't like to talk about her past very much."

"Why not?"

"I don't know. Perhaps it was painful for her."

"In what way?"

"I told you. I don't know. I've seen the picture before, yes, but I don't know who it is or where you can find her."

"Is it an old girlfriend?" Richmond felt embarrassed as he asked the question.

"I should think so, wouldn't you?" Veronica said evenly.

"Mind if I take it with me?"

"Not at all."

"Caroline didn't seem much of a one for possessions," Richmond mused. "There's hardly anything of hers but clothes. No letters, nothing."

"She liked to travel light, and she had no sentimental regard for the past. Caroline always looked ahead."

It was a simple statement, but Richmond heard the irony in Veronica Shildon's voice.

She shrugged. "A few of the books are hers. Some of the jewelry. All the non-classical records. But she didn't go in much for keepsakes."

Richmond tapped the photograph. "Which makes it all the more odd she should have hung onto this. Thank you, Ms. Shildon. I'd better be off now."

"Aren't you going to finish your tea?"

"Best not," he said. "I'll have to get back to work or my boss'll skin me alive. Thanks very much anyway." Richmond could sense her unease. She looked around the room before glancing at him again and nodding.

"All right, if you must."

"Will you be all right?" he asked. "You could always go back to Mrs. Cooper's, if you feel—"

"I'll be all right," she said. "I'm still in a bit of a daze. I can't believe it's really happened."

"Is there no one you can go to, until you're feeling better?"

"There's my therapist. She says I can call her any time, day or night. I might do that. We'll see. But do you know the oddest thing?"

Richmond shook his head.

She folded her arms and nodded toward the room in general. "I can take all this. The room where it happened. I didn't think I'd be able to bear it after last night, but it doesn't bother me in the slightest to be here. It just feels empty. Isn't that strange? It's the loneliness, Caroline's absence, that hurts. I keep expecting her to walk in at any moment."

Richmond, who could think of no reply, said goodbye and walked out into the snow. He still had about an hour before his lunchtime meeting with Banks in the Queen's Arms. He could use that time to check on Charles Cooper's movements the previous evening and perhaps see if he could find out anything about the mysterious Ruth.

THREE

I

The gears screeched as Susan Gay slowed to turn onto the Harrogate road. Luckily, the snow hadn't been so heavy south of Eastvale. It lay piled up against the hedgerows, but the roads had been cleared and the temperature hadn't dropped low enough to make the surface icy. She was out of the Dales now, in the gently rolling country south of Ripon. Nothing but the occasional stretch of stone wall, or a distant hamlet, showed through the thin white veil of snow.

She still felt angry at herself for being so damn jumpy. Banks had only dropped by the Community Center to break the news of Caroline Hartley's death and to discover what time she had left the rehearsal the previous evening. But Susan hadn't known anything about Caroline's part in the play, so how could she help assuming that Banks was checking up on her? Anyway, she had kept quiet and matters had soon become clear to her.

When Banks had gone, she'd walked to Pristine Records in the shopping center by the bus station. The girl with the white-face make-up and hair like pink champagne pointed out the small classical section and, when pushed, leafed idly through the stock cards. No, they hadn't sold a copy of *Lousy whatsit* lately; they hadn't even had a copy in. Ever. Using her own initiative, Susan also checked Boots and W. H. Smith's, both of which had small record departments, but she had no luck there either. The record was imported from Hungary, and whoever had bought it hadn't done so in Eastvale.

Over lunch at the Queen's Arms, information had been pooled and tasks assigned by Superintendent Gristhorpe. According to Banks, Caroline had left the Garden Café just after three o'clock, as usual, probably done a bit of shopping, then attended rehearsal at four. James Conran said they had finished at ten to six and everyone had left by five to. He himself had been the last to leave. He had gone out the back way, as usual, locked up and strolled over to the Crooked Billet on North York Road for a couple of drinks. In the caretaker's absence, he and Marcia Cunningham were the only ones in the drama group to have keys to the center, although an extra one had been lodged at the police station in case of emergencies. Members of the other societies housed in the center also had keys, including Sandra Banks.

Presumably, Caroline had gone straight home, because a neighbor across the street told one of the constables that she had seen Miss Hartley enter the house. It had happened at the same time the neighbor had gone over to her window to close a chink in the curtains during the commercial break in "Calendar," which would have been about six-fifteen.

Richmond had not been able to find out much about Charles Cooper's movements. The clerk who had been at the Barnard Castle shop on the evening in question had the day off today. He planned to visit Barnard Castle and ask around some more after he had talked to Veronica Shildon's therapist and made a start on tracking down Ruth. Banks was off to visit Claude Ivers, Veronica's estranged husband, and Susan herself had drawn the job of talking to Caroline's family in Harrogate. In addition to keeping tabs on the break-in, she was still on the murder team. Thank God the Harrogate police had at least broken the news of Caroline's death. That was one distasteful task she had been spared.

She drove up Ripon Road by the huge Victorian hotels—the Cairn, the Majestic, the St. George—dark stone mansions set back behind vast walled lawns and croquet greens. As she kept an eye on the road, Susan found herself hoping that the Hartley case wouldn't be solved by Christmas. That way she could legitimately beg off visiting her parents in Sheffield. Home visits were always tense. Susan found herself regaled with stories about her brother the stockbroker and her sister the lawyer. Of course, neither of them could ever make it home for Christmas; her brother lived in London and her sister in Vancouver. But she had to hear all about them, nonetheless. And whatever Susan herself achieved was always belittled by her siblings' success stories, pieced together from occasional letters and the odd newspaper clipping, and by her parents' disapproval of the course she had chosen. She could make chief constable and they would still look down on her. With a bit of luck, Caroline Hartley's murder would keep her busy well into the new year. Susan had a feeling they might be dealing with a nutter—the violence of the wounds and the music left playing seemed to point that way—and nutters, she remembered from her training, were always difficult to catch.

The town of Harrogate soon banished thoughts of psychopaths. All formal gardens and elegant Victorian buildings, it was a spa town, like Bath, a place people retired to or visited to attend business conventions. Ripon Road became Parliament as she drove past the Royal Baths and Betty's Tea Room, then its name changed again to West Park. She turned left onto York Place, the road that ran by the Stray, a broad expanse of parkland in the town center renowned for its vibrant flower displays in spring. Now it looked cool and serene under its layer of snow.

The Hartleys lived in a large house off Wetherby Road on the southern outskirts of the town. From the outside, it looked like something out of Edgar Allan Poe: the House of Usher, Susan thought, the way it appeared in that Roger Corman film that used to scare her when she was a little girl. The black stone was rough and pitted like coke, and the upper oriels seemed to stare out like bulging eyes. When Susan rang the doorbell she half expected an enormous manservant with a green complexion to answer and say "You rang?" in a deep

voice. But the boy who came to the door was far from enormous. He was in his late teens, judging by the pale, spotty
face, the spiky hair and the look of dazed contempt for the
world on his face, and he was as skinny as a rake.

"What is it?" he asked in an edgy, high-pitched voice. "We
don't want anything. There's been a death in the family."

"I know," Susan said. "That's why I'm here." She showed
her card and he stepped back to let her in. She followed him
down the gloomy hallway to a room that must once have been
a study or library. The ceiling was high, with curlicues at the
corners and an ornate fixture at the center from which the
chandelier had once hung. Dark wainscotting came waist-
high.

But the room was a mess. Much of the fine oak paneling
was scratched with graffiti and pitted where darts had been
thrown. The huge windows, framed by heavy, moth-eaten
drapes, were filmed with cobwebs and grime. Magazines and
newspapers lay scattered all over the threadbare carpet. Beer
cans and cigarette ends littered the hearth and the old stone
fireplace, and the stuffing was coming out of the huge green
velvet-upholstered settee. The room was an elegant Victorian
sanctuary reduced to a teenager's private wasteland.

The boy didn't ask Susan to sit down, but she found a chair
that looked in reasonable condition. Before she sat, she began
to undo her coat, but as she did so she realized that it was
freezing in the room, as it had been in the hall. There was no
heat at all. The boy didn't seem to notice or care, even though
he was only wearing jeans and a torn T-shirt. He lit a cigarette
and slumped on the settee. More stuffing oozed out, like foam
from a madman's mouth.

"So?" he said.

"I'd like to see your father."

The boy laughed harshly. "You must be the first person to
say that in five years. People don't usually *like* to see my
father. He's a very depressing man. He makes them think of
death. The grim reaper."

The boy's thin face, only a shade less white than the snow

outside, certainly made Susan think of death. He looked in urgent need of a blood transfusion. Could he really be Caroline Hartley's brother? It was hard to see a resemblance between the boy and his sister. Caroline, when she was alive, must have been a beautiful woman. Even in death she had looked more alive than her brother.

"Can I see him?"

"Be my guest." The boy pointed toward the ceiling and flicked his ash toward the littered fireplace.

Susan walked up the broad staircase. It must have been wonderful once, with thick pile carpeting and guests in evening dress standing around sipping cocktails. But now it was just bare, creaky wood, scuffed and splintered in places, and the banister looked like someone had been cutting notches in it. There were pale squares on the walls showing where paintings had been removed.

Without a guide or directions, it took Susan three tries before she opened the right door. Her first try had led her into a bathroom, which seemed clean and modern enough; the second revealed the boy's room, where the curtains were still closed and faint light outlined messy bedsheets and last week's underwear on the floor; and the third took her into a warm, stuffy room that smelled of cough lozenges, camphor and commodes. A one-element electric fire radiated its heat close to the bed, and there, in a genuine four-poster with the curtains open, a shadow of a man lay propped up on pillows. The bags under his eyes were so dark they looked like bruises, his complexion was like old paper, and the hands that grasped the bedclothes around his chest were more like talons. His skin looked as if it would crack like parchment if you touched it. As she approached, his watery eyes darted toward her.

"Who are you?" His voice was no more than a frightened whisper.

Susan introduced herself and he seemed to relax. "About Caroline?" he said. A faraway look came into his ruined eyes, pale yokes floating in glutinous albumen.

"Yes," Susan said. "Can you tell me anything about her?"

"What do you want to know?"

Susan wasn't sure. She had taken statements as a uniformed constable and studied interview techniques at police college, but it had never seemed as haphazard as this. Superintendent Gristhorpe hadn't been much help either. "Find out what you can," he had told her. "Follow your nose." Clearly it was a matter of sink or swim in the CID. She took a deep breath and wished she hadn't; the warmed-up smell of terminal illness was overpowering.

"Anything that might help us find her killer," she said. "Did Caroline visit you recently?"

"Sometimes," he muttered.

"Were you close?"

He shook his head slowly. "She ran away, you know."

"When did she run away?"

"She was only a child and she ran away."

Susan repeated her question and the old man stared at her. "Pardon? When did she go? When she was sixteen. Only a child."

"Why?"

A look of great sadness came into his eyes. "I don't know. Her mother died, you know. I tried the best I could, but she was so hard to manage."

"Where did she go?"

"London."

"What did she do there?"

He shook his head. "Then she came back. That's when she came to see me."

"And again since?"

"Yes."

"How often?"

"When she could. When she could get away."

"Did she ever tell you anything about her life down in London?"

"I was so happy to see her again."

"Do you know where she lived, who her friends were?"

"She wasn't a bad girl, not really a *bad* girl."

"Did she write from London?"

The old man shook his head slowly on the pillow.

"But you still loved her?"

"Yes." He was crying now, and the tears embarrassed him. "I'm sorry . . . could you please . . . ?" He pointed to a box of tissues on the bedside table and Susan passed it to him.

"She wasn't *bad*," he repeated when he'd settled down again. "Restless, angry. But not *bad*. I always knew she'd come back. I never stopped loving her."

"But she never talked about her life, either in London or in Eastvale?"

"No. Perhaps to Gary. . . . I'm tired. Not a *bad* girl," he repeated softly.

He seemed to be falling asleep. Susan had got nowhere and could think of no more questions to ask. Clearly, the old man had not jumped out of bed, hurried over to Eastvale and murdered his daughter. Maybe she would get more out of the son. At least he seemed angry and bitter enough to give something away if she pushed him hard enough. She said goodbye, though she doubted that the old man heard, and made her way back downstairs. The boy was still sprawled on the sofa, a can of lager open beside him on the floor. Despite the cold, she could still smell, underlying the smoke, a faint hint of decay, as if pieces of meat lay rotting under the floorboards.

"When did you last see your sister?" she asked.

He shrugged. "I don't know. A week, two weeks ago? She came when she felt like it. Time doesn't have much meaning around this place."

"But she had visited you recently?"

Gary nodded.

"What did she talk about?"

He lit a cigarette and spoke out of the corner of his mouth. "Nothing. Just the usual."

"What's the usual?"

"You know . . . job, house . . . relationships. . . . The usual crap."

"What's wrong with your father?"

"Cancer. He's had a couple of operations, chemotherapy, but . . . you know."

"How long has he been like this?"

"Five years."

"And you look after him?"

The boy tensed forward and points of fire appeared in his pale cheeks. "Yes. Me. All the fucking time. It's bring me this, Gary, bring me that. Go get my prescription, Gary. Gary, I need a bath. I even sit him on the fucking toilet. Yes, I take care of him."

"Does he never leave his room?"

He sighed and settled back on the sofa. "I told you, only to go to the bathroom. He can't manage the stairs. Besides, he doesn't want to. He's given up."

That explained the state of the place. Susan wondered if the father knew, suspected, or even cared that his son had taken over the huge cold house to live whatever life of his own he could scrounge from the responsibilities of the sick room. She wanted to ask him how he put up with it, but she already knew the scornful answer she would get: "Who else is there to do it?"

Instead, she asked, "How old were you when your sister ran away?"

He seemed surprised by the change in direction and had to think for a moment. "Eight. There's eight years between us. She'd been a bitch for years, had Caroline. The atmosphere was always tense. People were always rowing or on the verge of rows. It was a relief when she went."

"Why?"

He turned away so she couldn't see his eyes. "Why? I don't know. She was just like that. Full of poison. Especially toward me. Right from the start she tormented me, when I was a baby. They found her trying to drown me in my bath once. Of course they said she didn't realize what she was doing, but she did."

"Why should she want to kill you?"

He shrugged. "She hated me."

"Your father says he loved her."

He cast a scornful glance toward the ceiling and said slowly, "Oh yes, she always was the apple of his eye, even after she took off to London to become a tramp. Caroline could do no wrong. But who was the one left looking after him?"

"Why did you say tramp? How do you know?"

"What else would she do? She didn't have any job skills, but she was sixteen. She had two tits and a cunt like any other bird her age."

If Susan was expected to be shocked by his crudity, she was determined not to show it. "Did you ever see her during that period?"

"Me? You must be joking. It was all right for a while till mum got sick and died. It didn't take her longer than a month or two, not five years like that miserable old bastard upstairs. I was thirteen then, when he started. Took to his bed like a fish to water and it's been the same ever since."

"What about school?"

"I went sometimes. He sleeps most of the time, so I'm okay unless he has one of his awkward phases. I left last year. No jobs anyway."

"But what about the Health Service? Don't they help?"

"They send a nurse to look in every once in a while. And if you're going to mention a home, don't bother. I'd have him in one before you could say Jack Robinson if I could, but there's no room available unless you can pay." He gestured around the crumbling house. "As you can see, we can't. We've got his pension and a bit in the bank and that's it. I've even sold the bloody paintings, not that they were worth much. Thank God the bloody house is paid for. It must be worth a fortune now. I'd sell it and move somewhere cheaper if I could but the old bastard won't hear of it. Wants to die in his own bed. Sooner the better, I say."

Susan realized that Gary was drunk. As he'd been talking he'd finished one can of larger and most of a second, and he had obviously drunk a few before she arrived.

"Did you know anything at all about Caroline's life?" she asked.

His bright eyes narrowed. "I knew she was a fucking dyke, if that's what you mean."

"How did you know that?"

"She told me. One of her visits."

"But your father doesn't know?"

"No. It wouldn't make a scrap of difference if he did, though. It wouldn't change his opinion. As far as he's concerned the sun shone out of her arse and that's all there is to it." He tossed the empty can aside and picked up another from the low, cigarette-scarred table.

"How do you feel about her death?"

Gary was silent for a moment, then he looked directly at Susan. "I can't say I feel much at all. If you'd asked me a few years ago, I'd have said I felt glad. But now, nothing at all. I don't really care. She made my life a misery, then she left and lumbered me with the old man. I never had a chance to get out like her. And before that, she made everyone's life miserable at home. Especially mum's. Drove her to an early grave."

"Did you talk to her much when she visited?"

"Not by choice," he said, reaching for another cigarette. "But sometimes she wanted to talk to me, explain things, like she was taking me into her confidence. As if I cared. It was funny, almost like she was apologizing for everything without ever quite getting around to it. Do you know what I mean? 'I want you to know, Gary,' she says, 'how much I appreciate what you're doing for Dad. The sacrifices you're making. I'd help if I could, you know I would . . . ' and all that fucking rubbish." He imitated her voice again: " 'I want you to know, Gary, that I'm living with a woman in Eastvale and I'm happy for the first time in my life. I've really found myself at last. I know we've had problems in the past . . .' Always that 'I want you to know, Gary . . .' as if I fucking cared what she did, the slut. So she's dead. I can't say I care one way or another."

Susan didn't know whether to believe him. There was more pent-up passion and rage in his tone than she could handle, and she wasn't sure where it was coming from. All she knew was that she had to get out of this oppressive house, with its vast cold and crumbling spaces. She was beginning to feel dizzy and nauseated listening to Gary Hartley's high-pitched vitriol, which, she suspected, had as much to do with self-pity at his own weakness as anything else. Quickly, she muttered her farewell and headed for the door. As she walked down the hallway she heard an empty lager can crash against the wainscotting, followed by the screech of the top being ripped off another.

Outside, she breathed in the cold damp air and leaned against the roof of her car. Her gaze fixed on the melting snow that dripped from the branches of a tall tree. Her hands were shaking, but not from the cold.

Before she had driven far, she realized that she needed a drink. She pulled into the parking lot of the first decent-looking pub she saw outside town. There, in a comfortable bar lit and warmed by a real coal fire, she sipped a small brandy and thought about the Hartleys. She felt that her visit had barely scraped the surface. There was so much bitterness, anger and pain festering underneath, so many conflicting passions, that it would take years of psychoanalysis to sort them out.

One thing was clear, though: whatever the reasons for the family's strife, and whatever Caroline's reasons for running away, Gary Hartley certainly had a very good motive for murder. His sister had ruined his life; he even seemed to blame her for his mother's death. Had he been a different kind of person, he would have handled the burden some other way, but because he was weak and felt put upon, blood had turned to vinegar in his veins. As Susan had just seen, it didn't take more than a few drinks to bring the acid to the surface.

It would be very interesting to know what Gary Hartley had been doing between seven and eight o'clock the previous evening. As he had told her, the old man slept most of the time, so it would have been easy for Gary to nip out for a while without being missed. She hadn't asked him for an alibi, and that was an oversight. But, she thought, taking another sip of brandy and warming her hands by the fire, before we start to get all paranoid again, Susan, let's just say that this was only a preliminary interview. It would be a good idea to approach Gary Hartley again with someone else along. Someone like Banks.

As she tilted her head back and finished the rest of her drink, she noticed the bright Christmas decorations hung across the ceiling and the string of cards on the wall above the stone fireplace. That was another thing she remembered about the Hartley house. In addition to the cold and the overwhelming sense of decay, there had been nothing at all in the entire huge place to mark the season: not a Christmas tree, not a card, not a sprig of holly, not a cut-out Father Christmas. In that, she realized bitterly, the place resembled her own flat all too closely. She shivered and walked out to the car.

II

Banks drove carefully down the hill into Redburn as his tape of Bartok's third string quartet neared its end. The gradient wasn't quite as steep as at Staithes, where you had to leave your car at the top and walk, but it was bad enough. Luckily, the snow had petered out somewhere over the heathered reaches of the North York Moors and spared the coast.

The narrow hill meandered alongside the beck down to the sea, and it wasn't until he turned the final corner that Banks saw the water, a heaving mass of gray sloshing against the seawall and showering the narrow promenade with silver spray. Redburn was a small place: just the one main street leading down to the sea, with a few ginnels and snickets twisting off it where cottages were hidden away, half dug into the hillside itself, all sheltered in the crescent of the bay. In summer the jumble of pastel colors would make a picturesque scene, but in this weather they seemed out of place, as if a piece of the Riviera had been dug up and transported to a harsher climate.

Banks turned left at the front, drove to the end of the road and parked outside the Lobster Inn. Where the road ended, a narrow path led up the hillside, providing the only access to the two or three isolated cottages that faced the sea about halfway up: ideal places for artists.

The cold whipped the breath out of him and the air seemed full of sharp needles of moisture, but Banks finally reached his goal, the white cottage with the red pantile roof. Like the rest of the village, it would look pretty in summer with its garden full of flowers, he thought, but in the dull gray air, with the wind curling smoke from the red chimney, it took on a desolate aspect. Banks knocked at the door. Somewhere the wind was whistling and banging a loose shutter. He thought of Jim Hatchley and wondered how much he was enjoying the seaside not many miles away.

The woman who answered his knock had the kind of puzzled expression on her face that he'd expected. There couldn't be many people dropping in on such a day in such an isolated place.

She raised her dark eyebrows. "Yes?"

Banks introduced himself and showed his card. She stood aside to let him in. The room was a haven from the elements. A wood fire crackled in the hearth and the smell of fresh-baked bread filled the air. The wooden furniture looked primitive and well-used, but homely. The woman herself was in her mid-twenties, and the long skirt and blouse she wore outlined her slender figure. She had a strong jaw and full, red lips. Beneath her fringe of dark hair, two large brown eyes watched him go over and rub his hands in front of the fire.

Banks grinned at her. "No gloves. Silly of me."

She held out her hand. "I'm Patsy Janowski. Pleased to meet you." Her grip was firm and strong. Her accent was American.

"I'm here to see Mr. Ivers," he said. "Is he at home?"

"Yes, but he's working. You can't see him now. He hates to be disturbed."

"And I would hate to disturb him," Banks said. "But it's important."

She gave him a thoughtful look, then smiled. It was a radiant smile, and she knew it. She looked at her watch. "Why don't I make us some tea and you can try some of my bread. It's fresh from the oven. Claude will be down in twenty minutes or so for a short break."

Banks considered the options. Either way he would have surprise on his side, and if he let Ivers finish his session, the man would probably be better disposed toward him. Was that what he wanted? At this stage, he decided, it would be helpful. He also felt a great sense of respect for the music the man created and would have been loath to interrupt the creative process. In addition, he had to admit that the prospect of tea and fresh bread was one that appealed very strongly.

He smiled back at Patsy Janowski. "Sounds good to me. Mind if I smoke?"

"Go ahead. I don't myself, but Claude's a pipe man. I'm used to it. I won't be a minute."

Banks sat in front of the fire and lit up. The chair was hard and creaked whenever he shifted position, but in an odd way it was comfortable. A few minutes later, Patsy came back in with a plate full of warm bread and a steaming teapot covered with a pink quilted cozy. She put them on the low table in front of the fire then fetched butter and strawberry jam. That done, she sat opposite Banks.

"Nice place," he said, buttering the bread.

"Yes. Claude bought it after he split up with his wife. They had this enormous mansion near Eastvale, and you know what prices are like these days. This was comparatively cheap. Needed a bit of work. And he always wanted to live by the sea. He says it inspires his work. You know, the sea's rhythms, its music."

As she spoke, Banks noticed, her lively eyes flitted from

one thing to another: his wedding ring, the scar by his right eye, his left foot, the middle button on his shirt. It wasn't as if she were avoiding eye-contact, more as if she were conducting an inventory.

Banks nodded at what she said. He had noticed musical imitations of the ebb and flow of waves in Ivers's previous work. Perhaps such effects would be even more prevalent in the future. Certainly between the hiss and crackle of the fire he could hear waves pounding the rough sea-wall.

"What about you?" Banks asked.

"What about me?"

"What do you do? It's a bit out of the way here, isn't it?"

She shrugged. "Why should you assume I'd prefer the city? Do you think I like cruising the bars, going to discos, taking my credit cards shopping?" She smiled before he could answer. "I love it here. I can amuse myself. I read, I draw a little. I like to cook and go for long walks. And I'm working on my PhD dissertation. That keeps me busy."

"Consider me suitably chastised," Banks said.

"Thank you." She treated him to the radiant smile again, then frowned. "What is it you want with Claude?"

"It's a personal matter."

"We do live together, you know. It's not as if I was just a neighbor dropping in for gossip."

Banks smiled. She had at least answered a question before he'd had to ask it. "Do you know his ex-wife, Veronica Shildon?"

"I've met her. Why, has anything—?"

Banks held up a hand. "Don't worry, nothing's happened to her," he said.

"And she's not really his ex-wife," Patsy said. "They're still married." She sounded as if she didn't like that state of affairs. "Wanted to avoid the scandal. More bread?"

"Mmm, I think I will." Banks reached forward. "A drop more tea as well, if there is any."

"Sure."

"How did you meet Claude Ivers?"

Patsy looked at the pen in Banks's top pocket. "I was studying at York when he was teaching a music appreciation course. I took it and kind of . . . well, he noticed me. We've been living together here for a year now."

"Happily?"

"Yes."

"How often have you met Veronica?"

"Three or four times. They were very civilized about things. At least they were by the time I came onto the scene."

"What about Caroline Hartley?"

Her jaw set. "You'll have to ask Claude about her. I've met her once or twice, but I can't say I know her. Look, if it's—"

At that moment they heard a creaking on the stairs and both turned in unison to see Claude Ivers duck under the low lintel and walk into the room. He made an imposing figure— tall, gaunt, stooped—and there was no doubt about the power of his presence. He wore a jersey and baggy jeans, and his gray hair stuck up in places as if he had been running his hand through it. His skin was reddish and leathery, like that of a man who has spent a lot of time in the wind and sun, and a deep "V" of concentration furrowed the bridge of his nose. He looked to be in his early fifties. An inquisitive glance passed between Ivers and Patsy before she introduced Banks. Ivers shook hands and sat down. Patsy went to see to his coffee.

"What do you want to see me about?" he asked.

Banks repressed a childish urge to tell him he liked his music. "Bad news, I'm afraid," he said. "Caroline Hartley, your wife's companion. She's dead."

Ivers lurched forward and gripped the sides of his chair. "Good God! What? How?"

"She was murdered."

"But that's absurd. Things like that don't happen in real life."

"I'm sorry. It's true."

He shook his head. "Is Veronica all right?"

"She's very upset, obviously, but apart from that she's okay. I take it you still care?"

"Of course I do."

Banks heard something crash down heavily in the kitchen.

"If you don't mind my saying so, Mr. Ivers," he went on, "I find that very difficult to understand. If my wife—"

He waved Banks's comparison aside. "Listen, I went through everything any normal man would go through. Everything. Not just anger and rage, but disbelief, disgust, loss of self-esteem, loss of self-confidence. I went through hell. Christ, it's bad enough when your wife runs away with another man, but another woman . . ."

"You forgave her?"

"If that's the right word. I could never entirely blame Veronica in the first place. Can you understand that? It was as if she'd been led astray, fallen under someone else's influence."

"Caroline Hartley's?"

He nodded.

"Would you tell me what happened?"

For several moments there was silence but for the fire, the sea and muted sounds from the kitchen. Finally, Ivers stared at Banks, then cracked his fingers and stretched back in the chair.

"All right," he said. "You're a stranger. Somehow that makes it easier. And we don't get many people to talk to around here. Sometimes I get a bit stir-crazy, as Patsy puts it. There's not a lot to it, really. One day everything was fine. She was happy, we were happy. At least I thought so. Maybe she got a bit bored from time to time, got depressed now and then, but we had a good solid marriage, or so I thought. Then she started seeing a therapist, didn't tell me why. I don't think she knew herself, but I suspect it was a bit of a trend among bored, middle-class housewives. It didn't seem to be doing her much harm at first so I didn't object, but then, out of the blue, there's this new friend. It's all 'Caroline says this' and 'Caroline says that.' My wife starts to change in front of my eyes. Can you believe that? She even started using this other girl's language, saying things she would never say herself. She started calling things she liked 'neat.' 'Really neat,' she'd say! That wasn't Veronica. And she started dressing differently. She'd always been a bit on the formal side, but now she'd wear jeans and a sweatshirt. And there was all that interminable talk about Jung and self-actualization. I think she once told me I was too much the thinking type, or some such rot. Said my music was too intellectual and not emotional enough. And she got interested in stuff she'd never cared about when I'd tried to interest her—theater, cinema, literature. She was never in, always around at Caroline's. Then she even started suggesting that *I* should go to therapy too."

"But you didn't?"

He stared into the fire and paused, as if he realized he had already given too much away, then he said quietly, "I have my demons, Mr. Banks, but they also fire me. I'm afraid that if I subjected them to therapy I'd have no more fuel, no more creativity. Whatever Veronica might say, my music's born from conflict and feeling, not just technical skill." He tapped his head. "I really hear those things. And I was afraid if I opened my head to some shrink all the music would escape and I would be condemned to silence. I couldn't live like that. No, I didn't go."

Patsy returned with the coffee. Ivers took it, smiled at her, and she sat on the floor beside him with her legs curled under her and her hand resting on his thigh.

"Did you know at the start of the friendship that Caroline was a lesbian?" Banks asked.

"Yes. Veronica told me Caroline was living with a woman called Nancy Wood. Fair enough, I thought. Live and let live. I'm a musician, not the bohemian type, perhaps, but I've been around enough oddballs in my time not to worry about them too much. And I'm fairly broad-minded. So Caroline was a lesbian. I never for a moment thought that my wife . . ."

"So if you blamed anyone it was Caroline?"

"Yes." He hesitated, realizing what he'd said. "But I didn't kill her, if that's what you're getting at."

"What did you do yesterday evening?"

He sipped his coffee and spoke, half into the mug. "Stayed in. With Patsy. We don't go out all that much."

Patsy looked at Banks and nodded in agreement. He saw shadows behind her eyes. He wasn't sure he believed her. "Do you own a car?" he asked.

"We both do."

"Where do you park?"

"We've got spots reserved in the village, behind the pub. Obviously there's no parking up here."

"When did you last see your wife?"

He thought for a moment. "About a month ago. I was in Eastvale on business and I dropped in to see how Veronica was doing. I called at the shop first. I usually do that to avoid meeting Caroline, but sometimes if it's evening I just have to face it out."

"How did Caroline react to these visits?"

"She'd leave the room."

"So you never spoke to her."

"Not much, no. And Veronica would be tense. I'd never end up staying long if Caroline was around."

"Are you sure that was the last time you visited the house, a month ago?"

"Yes, of course I am."

"You didn't go there yesterday evening?"

"I told you. We stayed in."

"You're a musician," Banks said. "You must know Vivaldi's work."

"I—of course I do."

"Do you know the *Laudate pueri*?"

Ivers turned aside and reached for some bread and butter. "Which one? He wrote four, you know."

"Four what?"

"Four settings for the same liturgical piece. I think it's Psalm 112, but I can't be sure. Why do you ask?"

"Have you heard of a singer called Magda Kalmár?"

"Yes. But I—"

"Did you usually buy your wife a Christmas present?"

"I did last year."

"And this year?"

He buttered his bread as he spoke. "I was going to. Am. I just haven't got around to it yet."

"Better hurry up, then," Banks said with a smile. "Only one more shopping day to Christmas." He put his cup down on the hearth and stood up to leave. "Thank you very much for the tea and bread," he said to Patsy, "and it was an honor to meet you Mr. Ivers. I've enjoyed your music for a long time."

Ivers raised an eyebrow. Banks was thankful he just nodded and didn't say anything about being surprised that policemen listened to music.

Banks walked over to the door and Ivers followed him. "About Veronica," he said. "She must be in a terrible state. Do you think she needs me?"

"I don't know," Banks said. He honestly didn't. Did a wife who lost her female lover turn back to her husband for comfort? "Maybe you should ask her."

Ivers nodded, and the last thing Banks noticed before the door closed was the darkening expression in Patsy Janowski's eyes, fixed on the pipe in Ivers's hand.

He made his way against the wind back to the car and drove up the hill again. The Ivers household had left him with a strange feeling. However rustic and cozy it was, he couldn't help but suspect that all was not well, and that nobody had told him the complete truth. He had little doubt that Ivers had bought the record for Veronica and had more than likely delivered it, too. But he couldn't prove it. As soon as he could, he would go back to visit Claude Ivers again.

III

The Queen's Arms was never very busy at five o'clock on a winter's afternoon. It was too late for the lunch-time drinkers and too early for the after-work crowd. The only other customers, apart from Banks, Richmond and Susan Gay, were three or four people with shopping bags full of Christmas presents.

The three of them sat in the deep armchairs around the fire. Banks and Richmond were drinking pints and Susan had accepted a brandy and soda. They had pooled their notes and still had nothing concrete to go on. Richmond had discovered that Nancy Wood had left Eastvale for an extended trip to Australia. A phone call to immigration had established that she was indeed there. Richmond followed with a call to the Sydney police, who got back to him a couple of hours later with positive confirmation. That was one serious suspect eliminated.

Richmond had so far got nowhere with the photograph of Ruth, the mystery woman. The record, too, remained unexplained. They would have to start canvassing classical record shops all over England, and that would take time. Veronica Shildon's therapist had confirmed that Veronica had left her office at about seven o'clock the previous evening, as usual, and that she had mentioned going shopping.

"You said that Caroline ran off to London when she was sixteen?" Banks said to Susan.

"That's what her brother told me."

"And she was down there for about six years before she came up to Eastvale. A lot can happen in that time. Any idea where she was?"

"Sorry, sir, they didn't seem to know anything. Either that or they weren't saying."

"Was that the feeling you got?"

"There was certainly something weird about them." Susan shuddered as she spoke.

"Never mind. We'll find out when we talk to them again.

Maybe you can get a printout from the PNC, Phil? Caroline Hartley might have a record down there. Runaways often get in trouble with the law."

Richmond nodded.

"Any other leads?" Banks asked.

They shook their heads. He smiled. "Don't look so bloody despondent, Susan. At least it means you'll get Christmas Day at home."

"Sir?"

"If we don't solve a murder in twenty-four hours, the odds are we'll be at it a long time. A day here or there isn't going to make a lot of difference unless we come up with a hot lead tomorrow. And it *is* Christmas. Things slow down. You know as well as I do it's impossible to get anything done for a couple of days. Nobody's around, for a start. All we can do is get the statements sorted out and see if we can build up a clear picture of the victim. You find often enough that the seeds of the death are in the life, so to speak, and given the life Caroline Hartley led that may be even more apt in her case. We'll do what we can with the photo, the record and the London connection, and in a day or two we'll visit her family again and push a bit harder. Maybe you and I could have a bit of a chat with the Amateur Dramatic Society again, too, Susan. There might be some connections there—jealousy, rivalry, something like that."

Susan nodded.

"And I don't think Veronica Shildon's coming clean with us, either," Banks went on. "But then she's not likely to. She'll be protecting Caroline's memory, especially if there's any shady business in the girl's past. Her alibi checks out, but there are ten minutes unaccounted for between her return home and going to Christine Cooper's. She could have nipped back earlier, too, say between seven and half-past, if she'd wanted to, and only pretended to arrive later. Then there's Cooper himself, and his wife for that matter. If there was anything odd going on between those two households, who knows what kind of can of worms it might have opened. All

I'm saying is that we should keep an open mind while we let them all stew for a while. Let them enjoy Christmas. Maybe we'll do the rounds again on Boxing Day when they're all full and comfy. An old sparring partner of mine from the Met, Dirty Dick Burgess, always used to prefer Sundays for surprise raids. Boxing Day's probably even better."

Richmond raised his eyebrows at the mention of Burgess. Banks and Dirty Dick had locked horns over a politically sensitive case in Eastvale last spring, and they had hardly parted on the best of terms. Apart from Banks and Burgess, only Richmond knew the full story.

Banks looked at his watch and finished his pint. "Right. I'd better be off now. I want to see if that post-mortem report's turned up yet." It was already dark outside and the snow had just started falling again.

The report had indeed turned up. Banks skipped the technical details for the layman's synopsis that Dr. Glendenning always courteously provided.

There was nothing new at first. She had been hit, probably punched, on the cheek, and the blow could have rendered her unconscious. After that, she had been viciously and repeatedly stabbed with her own kitchen knife. The only blood found at the scene was hers. Her dressing-gown had no bloodstains on it, so it had been removed—or Caroline herself had removed it—before the stabbing. Glendenning had found no signs at all of sexual interference. He had, however, found crumbs of chocolate cake in several of the wounds, which led him to believe that the knife had been lying by the cake on the table. If so, Banks thought, they were probably dealing with a spur-of-the-moment attack, a weapon at hand, grabbed and used in anger. There were no signs of skin or blood under her fingernails, which meant she hadn't had a chance to fight off her attacker.

And that was it, apart from the general information. Banks read idly through—health basically sound, appendix scar, gave birth to a child. . . . He stopped and read that part over again. According to Glendenning, who had been as thorough as usual, the cervix showed a multiparous os, which meant the deceased had, at some point, had a baby.

That cast an interesting new light on things. Not only did it mean she had had at least one heterosexual relationship, it might also explain why she went to London, or what might have happened to her down there. All the more imperative, therefore, to find out exactly where she'd been and what she'd done. Banks felt that the photograph was a clue. Given that it was the only memento she'd kept, apart from a pressed flower, Ruth was obviously someone important from Caroline's past.

Banks walked over to the window and looked out on the market square. It looked like one of Brueghel's winter scenes. The tree was lit up and shoppers crossed the whitened cobbles to and fro with their packages. Banks was glad he'd done his Christmas shopping a week ago. The only thing that remained was the booze. He'd buy that tomorrow: a bottle of port, a nice dry sherry, perhaps some Ciardhu single-malt, if he could afford it. Then his thoughts drifted back to Caroline Hartley. A baby. What a bloody turn-up! And if there was a baby, somewhere there had to be a father. Maybe a father with a grudge.

Eager to find out if there had been any progress on the record and the scrap of wrapping paper, he phoned the forensic lab and asked for Vic Manson.

Manson was slightly breathless when he came on the line. "What is it? I'd just this minute put my overcoat on. I was on my way out."

Banks smiled to himself and lit a cigarette. Manson was always on his way somewhere. "Sorry, Vic. I won't keep you long. Just wanted to know if you've got anything for us on the Hartley murder."

Manson sighed. "Not a lot. No dabs we can't account for. The knife was washed, but we found traces of blood and crumbs where the blade meets the handle."

"What about the record?"

"Nothing. Besides, people usually hold records by the edge.

No room for prints there. The cover and inside sleeve were clean, too."

"Anything else?"

"It looked new, the record. As far as we can tell it was in mint condition, only been played a few times."

"How many?"

"Can't tell for sure—two or three at the most—but take our word, it was new."

"The paper?"

"Common or garden Christmas wrapping paper. Could have come from anywhere. It does look like it had been wrapped around the record, though. It fits to a tee. But there's no gift tag with the murderer's name on, unfortunately."

"Well, at least we've got something. Thanks, Vic. Look, can you send the record over to me when you're done with it?"

"Of course. Tomorrow okay?"

"Fine. Don't let me keep you any longer. And have a good Christmas."

"You too."

Banks hung up, walked back to the window and lit a cigarette. What the hell was it about the music that bothered him? Why did it have to mean something? He would find out as much as he could about Vivaldi's *Laudate pueri*, all four versions. Claude Ivers admitted he knew them, but that didn't mean anything. He must have known that if he'd feigned ignorance, given his musical reputation, Banks would have immediately become even more suspicious. But Ivers knew more than he let on, that was for certain. And so did Patsy Janowski, she of the wandering eyes. Well, give them time, he thought, as he smoked and looked down on the Brueghel scene, they're not going anywhere. Let them think they're safe, then . . .

FOUR

I

James Conran lived in a small terrace house on the north-west edge of town, where Cardigan Drive met North Market Street and turned into the main Swainsdale road. At the far end of his living room, a manual typewriter sat on a table by the window. The view to the west along snow-shrouded Swainsdale was superb. Bookcases flanked the table on both sides with books on all subjects. Banks took a quick glance: history, theater, music, but hardly any fiction. A small sofa and two matching armchairs formed a semicircle around the hearth, where a peat fire smouldered. On the wall above the mantelpiece hung a poster advertising a performance of *The Duchess of Malfi* at Stratford. There was no television set, but a music center with a compact-disc player stood opposite the fireplace. Banks ran his eyes over the records and discs, most of them the works of classical composers: Beethoven, Zelenka, Bax, Stanford, Mozart, Elgar. There was some Vivaldi, including the *Stabat Mater*, but not the *Laudate pueri*.

Conran, having explained to Banks how Susan had once been one of his pupils, was now fussing over her and offering to make tea. Both she and Banks accepted.

"Nice collection of discs," Banks observed. "Are you a musician?"

"Merely a dabbler," Conran said. "I sang with the church choir when I was a boy, then with an amateur outfit in York.

I also directed the choir at Eastvale Comprehensive for a few years—mostly, I might add, because no one else would take on the job. But that's just about the limit of my musical abilities. I *am* a good listener, however."

As Conran made tea in the kitchen, Banks continued reading book and record titles. It helped get a sense of people, he always thought, to discover their tastes in literature and music. Conran definitely read to learn, not for pleasure, which hinted at a certain amount of intellectual and artistic ambition. His record collection, while fairly eclectic, favored choral works, perhaps an unconscious left-over from his choir days. The fact that he owned a compact-disc player showed he was serious about his listening. Though she said she liked classical music, Veronica Shildon only had an old stereo system, a turntable complete with arm and spindle for stacking records. No one who genuinely loved music would play it on such antiquated equipment, especially if they could afford better. No, Veronica Shildon's priorities lay elsewhere than music— in decor, perhaps, in creating the sense of a cozy and comfortable home. But Conran clearly valued his artistic pleasures over material ones.

Banks warmed his hands by the fire. "I should imagine you got to know Caroline Hartley pretty well during rehearsals for *Twelfth Night*," he said. "Can you tell us anything about her?"

"Such as what?"

"Anything at all. Her habits, moods, your impression of her. Believe me, every little bit helps."

"It's very difficult," Conran said. "I mean, I didn't know her that well. None of us did, really."

"What was your relationship with her?"

Conran frowned. "Relationship? I'd hardly say we had a relationship. What are you implying?"

"You were directing her in a theatrical production, isn't that so?"

"Well, yes . . . but—"

"That's a relationship."

"I see . . . I . . . I thought. Anyway, yes, I directed her on stage. It was a purely working relationship. You don't really find out much about people when you're busy telling them where to stand and how to speak, you know."

"What did you think of her?"

"She was a very talented and attractive girl, a natural. It's a real tragedy. She'd have gone far had she lived."

"Yet you only gave her a small part."

"It was her first performance. She needed more experience. But she was quick. It wouldn't have taken her long to get to the top if she'd put her mind to it. *Mercurial*. I think that's the best word to describe her talent."

"How did she get on with the rest of the cast?"

Conran shrugged. "All right, I suppose."

"Did she form any special relationships? Was she close to anyone in particular?"

"Not that I know of. We're all pretty chummy, really, when it comes down to it. After all, this isn't the West End. It's meant to be fun. That's the reason I'm involved."

"She did join you for drinks after rehearsals sometimes, didn't she?"

"Yes, usually. But you can hardly get to know somebody in a group situation like that."

"Who did she talk to?"

"Everyone, really."

"How did she behave?"

"I don't understand."

"Was she comfortable with the group?"

"As far as I could tell."

"Did you know she was a lesbian?" Banks asked.

"Caroline?" He shook his head. "I don't believe it."

"Do you have evidence to the contrary?"

"Of course not," Conran snapped. "Stop twisting everything I say. What I mean is I'm surprised. She . . ."

"She what?"

"Well, you don't expect things like that, do you? She seemed quite normal to me."

"Heterosexual?"

Conran looked at Susan as if pleading for support. "You're doing it again. I've no knowledge of her sex life at all. All I'm saying is she *seemed* normal to me."

"So she didn't tell you anything about her private life?"

"No. She kept herself to herself. I knew nothing at all about what she did when she left the hall or the pub."

"Oh, come on! Surely some of the men in the cast must have tried it on with her. Maybe you even tried yourself. Who wouldn't? How did she respond?"

"I'm not sure what you mean."

"It's obvious enough. Was she cold, polite, friendly, rude . . . ?"

"Oh, I see. Well, no, she certainly wasn't cold. She'd joke and flirt like the rest, I suppose. It's not something I actually thought about. She was always friendly and cheerful, or so it seemed to me."

"Terrible waste, don't you think? A beautiful woman like that, and no man stood a chance with her."

Conran glanced down into his mug and muttered, "It takes all sorts, Chief Inspector."

"Who did she usually sit next to?"

"It varied."

"Did you notice anything at all that hinted at a more than superficial relationship with anyone in the cast, male or female?"

"No."

Banks sipped some tea and leaned back in his chair. "In a close group like that, you must get all sorts of pressures. I've heard that actors sometimes have very fragile egos. Did you get many tantrums or rows? Any professional jealousies?"

"Only over petty matters," Conran said, "like you'd get in any team situation. As I said, we're in it for pleasure, not ambition or fame."

" 'Petty matters'? Can you be a bit more specific?"

"I honestly can't remember any examples."

"Anything involving Caroline Hartley?"

He shook his head.

"Was there any special reason why Caroline didn't join you all for a drink after rehearsal on December twenty-second?"

"Nobody went to the pub that evening. We didn't always go, you know. It was a very casual thing."

"But you went?"

"Yes. Alone. I wanted to mull over the rehearsal. I seem to be able to think better about things like that when there's a bit of noise and festive activity around me."

"Drink much?"

"A bit. I wasn't drunk, if that's what you mean."

"Had anything odd happened between four and six? Any fights, threats, arguments?"

"There was nothing unusual, no. Everybody was tired, that's all. Or they had shopping to do. Surely you can't think one of the cast—"

"Right now, I'm keeping an open mind." Banks put down his mug. "Why did you give up teaching, Mr. Conran?"

If Conran was surprised by the abrupt change in questioning, he didn't show it. "I'd always wanted to write. As soon as I had a little success I decided to burn my bridges. Much as I enjoyed it, teaching made too many demands on my time and energy."

"How do you make your living now? Surely not from the Eastvale Amateur Dramatic Society?"

"Good Lord, no! That's just a hobby, really. I work as a freelance writer. I've also had a few plays produced on television, some radio work."

Banks looked around the room again. "Don't you even watch your own work?"

Conran laughed. "I *do* have a television, as a matter of fact. I don't watch it very often so I keep it upstairs in the spare room. One of the advantages of being a bachelor. Plenty of space."

"Are you working on anything right now?"

Conran beamed and sat forward, hands clasped in his lap. "As a matter of fact, I am. I've just got this wonderful commission from the BBC to dramatize John Cowper Powys's novel, *Weymouth Sands*. It'll be a hard task, very hard, but it pays well, and it's an honor to be involved. I'm not the only writer in the project, of course, but still . . ."

"You're a long way from Weymouth," Banks remarked. "Come from down there?"

"Litton Cheney, actually. You won't have heard of it. It's a small village in Dorset."

"I thought I could spot a trace of that Hardy country burr. Well, Mr. Conran, sorry to have bothered you on Christmas Eve. Hope we haven't kept you from your family."

"I have no family," Conran said, "and you haven't kept me from anything, no." He stood up and shook hands, then helped Susan on with her coat.

Back outside at the car, Banks turned to Susan and said, "Do you know, I think he fancies you."

Susan blushed. "He probably fancies anything in a skirt."

"You could be right. He seemed a bit edgy, didn't he? I wonder if there's more to this dramatic society than meets the eye? You know the kind of thing, fiery passions lurking beneath the surface of dull suburban life."

Susan laughed. "Could be," she said. "Or perhaps he's just shaken up."

"And did I miss something," Banks said, "or did he tell us nothing at all?"

"He told us nothing," Susan agreed. "But I certainly got the impression he knew much more than he let on."

Banks opened the car door. "Yes," he said. "Yes, I think he did, didn't he. That's the trouble with cases like this. Everybody's got something to hide."

II

On Christmas Eve at four o'clock the Queen's Arms was packed. Businessmen, off work early for the holidays, loosened their ties, smoked cigars and laughed themselves red in

the face at dirty jokes; friends met for a last few drinks before
parting to spend the holidays with their families; groups of
female office workers drank brightly colored concoctions and
laughed about the way the mail room boy's hands had roamed
during the office party. A large proportion of the Eastvale
police force, denied their favorite spot by the fire, had pulled
together two round tables with dimpled copper tops and cast-
iron legs for their own party. It was a movable feast; men
nipped over from the station for a quick one, then returned
to cover for others. Even Fred Rowe managed to drop by for
a couple of pints while young Tolliver took over the front
desk. The only real continuity was provided by the CID—
Gristhorpe, Banks, Richmond and Susan Gay—who had
managed to hang onto their chairs amidst the chaos around
them.

Everyone seemed to be having a good time. The atmosphere was cheery with its blazing fire and green-and-red decorations. The only thing Banks found objectionable,
especially after a couple of pints, was the music that Cyril,
the landlord, had piped in for the occasion. It sounded like
airport-music versions of Christmas carols. Gristhorpe didn't
seem to mind, but he was tone-deaf.

After the visit to Conran's, they had achieved very little
that day, and nothing more would be achieved by working
longer. By mid-afternoon it had been almost impossible to
reach anyone on the phone. If you did happen to be lucky
enough, all you got for your trouble was a drunken babble in
the earpiece. Police work may never stop completely, but it
does slow down at times. The only coppers working harder
than ever now would be the road patrols chasing after drunken
drivers.

Richmond had talked to Caroline's staff at the Garden
Café, but found out nothing more about her. No, they had
never suspected she might be a lesbian; she had kept her
private life to herself, just as Conran had said. She was cheerful and friendly, yes, good with customers, but a closed book
when it came to her personal life. She never talked about

boyfriends or shared her problems, as some of the other women did.

Richmond had also dropped in on Christine Cooper and taken her through her story again. The details matched word for word. He had first taken the initiative of phoning his mother and asking her what had happened on the December 22 broadcasts of "Emmerdale Farm" and "Coronation Street." Passing himself off as a fan who had missed his favorite programs, he asked Christine Cooper to give him a blow-by-blow description of them, which she did. That accounted for her whereabouts between seven and eight o'clock. Caroline Hartley had last been seen alive around seven-twenty, answering the door to a female visitor. Unless Christine Cooper had nipped out during the commercials and stabbed her with the handy kitchen knife, or unless she was such a cunning killer she had videotaped the television programs in case someone asked about them, then it looked as if she was out of the running. So far, Richmond had not been able to satisfy himself about her husband's alibi, but he planned to pay a visit to Barnard Castle after Christmas, when the shop reopened.

The only new fact he had discovered, via the PNC, was that Caroline Hartley had been arrested for soliciting in London five years ago. That seemed to back up what her brother, Gary, had said about her life there, but it still left a lot unsaid. Had Gary actually known what she was doing, or had he made an inspired guess? Both he and Caroline's father said that Caroline had never contacted them during her time in London. Were they lying? If so, why?

For the moment, though, the festive season chased away day-to-day concerns. Even Susan Gay was knocking back the Old Peculier and chatting with the others more easily than she usually did.

"What are you doing over the holidays?" Banks asked her over the racket.

"Going home."

"Because if you're stuck for somewhere," he went on, "you

can always join us for Christmas dinner. I know you don't get enough time off to really go anywhere."

"Thanks," Susan said, "but it's all right. Sheffield's not that far."

Banks nodded. Richmond, he knew, would be spending the day with his family in town. Gristhorpe was coming to the Bankses' this year. For their first two Christmases up north, Banks and his family had gone out to his farmhouse where Mrs. Hawkins, the woman "what did for him," had done them proud. This year, however, Mrs. Hawkins and her husband had been invited to their daughter's in Cambridge. It would be the first Christmas away for them, but as the daughter had recently borne them a grandchild, they could hardly refuse. Gristhorpe had played hard-to-get at first, but succumbed without too much of a fight at Banks's third invitation. Banks suspected that it was actually Sandra's telling Gristhorpe that the house was now a "smoke-free environment" that finally tipped the balance.

At five o'clock, Banks decided it was time to leave. He had had three pints of Theakston's bitter, just about the right amount to work up an appetite. Sandra would be expecting him for dinner. He was due to help with the big meal tomorrow—mostly the dull stuff, he imagined, chopping vegetables and setting the table, as his cooking skills were limited—but tonight was Sandra's treat.

He said his goodbyes and wandered out into the snow, which had been falling on and off all day. Opposite, the blue lamp outside the police station shed its avuncular light. Banks didn't know why he hated it so much, but he did. It was phoney, a kind of cheap nostalgia for a time when things were simpler—or at least we fooled ourselves into believing they were simpler—when the goodies wore white and the baddies wore black. Maybe it really had been like that, but Banks doubted it. Certainly nothing could ever have been simple for the Caroline Hartleys and Veronica Shildons of this world.

Anyway, he told himself, no more gloomy thoughts. He stuck on his headphones and fiddled with the Walkman in his pocket. The music he'd chosen was his own tribute to the season: Benjamin Britten's *A Ceremony of Carols*. It was difficult, though, to put the case out of his mind: not the investigation, the details or the leads, but the sheer fact of Caroline Hartley's brutal murder. Even at the pub he had felt at times like a spectator, watching everyone celebrate, but held back from joining in by what he had seen at number eleven Oakwood Mews. Still, it was Christmas Eve and he had to make an effort to be jolly for his family's sake.

The snow was crisp and squeaky. At last Eastvale had the white Christmas it had been screaming for during the past three or four rainy ones. Colored lights winked on and off in windows, and Banks felt for a moment that fleeting sense of peace and relaxation in the air that seems to arise and flourish briefly when the commercial fervor of the season begins to abate.

He remembered his own childhood Christmases: the sleepless nights before the big day; the early mornings opening presents; the disappointment the year his parents hadn't been able to buy him the bicycle he wanted because his father was out of work; the joy two years later when he got an even better one than he had expected.

At home, the trimmings were up, the lights were on and the children were brimming with excitement and curiosity about their presents. At least Tracy was. Brian, being seventeen, was much more cool about the whole thing.

"No, you can't open them tonight," Banks told his daughter.

"But Laura Collins says they do at her house. Oh, go on, Dad. Please!"

"No!" Banks wasn't about to have a lifetime's tradition changed because of Laura Collins. Tracy pouted for a while, but she wasn't the kind to sulk for long.

Brian kept quiet, as though he didn't even care whether he got a present. All that interested him was pop music, and Banks had bought him a second-hand guitar he'd spotted in a shop window. Of course, it would mean a bit of noise to put up with. Banks didn't have much regard for his son's taste, but far be it for him to stand in the way of the lad's musical ambitions. Euterpe, like God, works in mysterious ways; raucous pop music might inspire someone to learn the guitar, but tastes change, and the talent might well end up in the service of jazz, blues or classical music.

Tracy had been a good deal less specific in her demands, but both Banks and Sandra had thought it a good idea to acknowledge that she was no longer a little girl. She was, after all, fifteen, and though her interest in history remained steady, and had even extended to take in literature, she had a new look in her eyes when the subject of boys came up. Banks had also noticed the odd pop star poster surreptitiously making its way onto her bedroom wall. So rather than books, they had bought her some fashionable new clothes and a make-up kit. When Banks looked at his children now, it was with a tinge of sadness in his heart. Next year he would be forty, and soon he would lose them to their own lives completely.

After a tasty beef stew with dumplings—a frugal dinner to counterbalance tomorrow's blow-out—came that time of evening when Banks could start to relax: the children out or occupied in their rooms, the television turned off, a tumbler of good Scotch, quiet music and Sandra beside him on the sofa. When he went for his refill, he remembered the photograph he had brought home in his briefcase along with the record Vic Manson had sent over that afternoon. He had hardly looked at it, but something about it rang a bell. Sandra, with her knowledge of photography, should be able to help him. He took the photograph out and handed it to her.

"What do you think of that?"

Sandra examined it close up, then held it at arm's length. "Do you mean technically?"

"Any way you like."

"Well, it's obviously good, a professional job. You can tell that by the lighting and the way he's made it seem like a relaxed pose. She looks very studious. A striking woman. Good quality paper, too."

"Why would someone have a photograph like that taken?"

"Well, lots of people have portraits done . . . but I see what you mean."

"There's something about it I can't put my finger on," Banks said. "Somehow, I think it's more than a portrait. I just wondered if you had any ideas."

"Hmm. That look in her eyes. Very intelligent, a bit haughty. I wonder if that was her or the photographer."

"What do you mean?"

"Some photographers really capture a person's essence in their portraits, but some create an image—you know, for pop stars or advertising. I'm just not sure what this is."

"That's it!" Banks slapped the chair arm. "An image. A pose. Why would someone want a photographer to create an image?"

Sandra put the photograph carefully aside on the coffee-table. "For publicity, I suppose."

"Right. That's what was bothering me. It must be a publicity picture of some kind. That gives us a chance of tracking her down."

"You need to find this woman?"

"Yes."

"You'll still have a hell of a job. It could be for anything—modeling, movies, theater."

Banks shook his head. "Caroline had an interest in theater, but I get the impression that's more of a recent passion. Still, she could be an actress. She's attractive, yes, but she's no model. You said it yourself—look at the intelligence, the arrogance in that tilt of the head and the eyes. And Veronica Shildon said the woman wrote poetry."

"A book jacket?"

"Those are the lines I was thinking along. It could be a publicity still for an author's tour or something. That should narrow things down a bit. We can check with publishers and theatrical agents." Banks paused for a moment, then went on.

"Speaking of Caroline Hartley, did you ever meet her?"

"I met her a couple of times with the group, when I went for a drink with Marcia after working late in the gallery. But I didn't know her. I never even spoke to her."

"What was your impression?"

"I can only tell you how she acted as part of a group in a pub. She was very beautiful. You couldn't help but notice her smooth complexion and her eyes. Notice and envy." Sandra put her hand to her own cheek, which Banks had always thought of as soft and unblemished. "In looks, she reminded me a bit of that actress who played Juliet in the old film. What's her name? . . . Olivia Hussey. And mostly she was vivacious, sparkling. Though she did seem to have her quiet periods, as if the energy was a bit of a hard act to keep up sometimes."

"Quiet periods?"

"Yes. I just remember her staring into space sometimes, looking a bit lost. Never for long, because there was always somebody wanting to attract her attention, but it was noticeable."

"Did she seem especially close to anyone else in the group?"

"I don't know. She chatted and laughed with them all, but only in a general, friendly way."

"You never saw her arguing with anyone?"

"No."

"Did you know she was a lesbian?"

"Not until you told me. But why would I?"

"I don't know. I just wondered if it was in any way obvious to you."

"No—to both questions."

"Did you ever notice anyone obviously chatting her up?"

Sandra laughed. "Well, most of the men did, yes."

"How did she react?"

"I'd say she played them along nicely. If anything, I'd have said she was a flirt, a bit of a tease, really. But now I know the truth . . ."

"Self-protection, I suppose. What about the women?"

Sandra shook her head. "I didn't notice anything."

"Did James Conran usually turn up for a drink? He's the only one I've met apart from Marcia, the costume manager."

"Usually, yes. He seems like a pleasant fellow. A bit theatrical, highly strung. Drinks a fair bit. I mean, a lot of actors are really shy, aren't they? They have to get themselves tanked up and play parts to express themselves. And he's a bit of a practical joker. Nothing serious, he just likes arranging for someone's drink to be all tonic and no gin, for example, or having the barman tell someone there's none of their favorite pub grub left. I'd say he's a bit of a ladies' man, too. You know, that vulnerable look, the dedicated, suffering artist. He's pretty sure of himself really, I'll bet. He just finds the act useful. And I know for a fact he's been having it off with Olivia."

"Olivia who?"

"I don't know her real name. The actress who's playing Olivia. They had a bit of a tiff in the pub one night, in the corridor that leads to the toilets, and I happened to overhear them arguing. She seemed to think now he'd got what he wanted he wasn't interested anymore, and she told him that was fine with her, because she hadn't liked it much anyway."

"When was this?"

"Quite early on in rehearsals. I can't remember exactly. Mid-November, maybe?"

"Did he ever make a pass at you?"

"No. He knew I was married to a tough detective who'd beat him to a pulp if he did."

Banks laughed. "What about Caroline?"

"You mean did he come on to her?"

"Yes."

"Well, he contrived to sit next to her often enough and arrange for the occasional bit of accidental body contact. I'd say he was putting the moves on her, yes."

No wonder Conran had been so tetchy when Banks had asked about his relationship with Caroline. People often denied their true relationships with victims, especially with murder victims.

"How did she react?" he asked.

"She pretended she didn't notice, but she was always polite and friendly toward him. After all, he *is* the director."

"I should hardly think directors of local amateur dramatic societies have casting couches."

"No, but they could make a person's life difficult if they wanted."

"I suppose so. What about this Olivia? Might she have had good reason to resent Caroline's presence?"

"Not that I noticed. Look, Alan, do you think you could pack it in for a while? It's Christmas Eve. I'm not used to being interrogated in my own home. You know I'm glad to be of help whenever I can, but I didn't know Caroline Hartley was going to get herself murdered, so I didn't pay a lot of attention to who she did or didn't talk to."

Banks scratched his head. "Sorry love. I can't seem to let it drop, can I? Another drink?"

"Please. I don't mean to be—"

Banks held up his hand. "It's okay. You're right. Not another word."

He brought the drinks and turned out the main lights. All they had left was the light from the Christmas tree, from the fake log in the electric fire and a red candle he lit and placed on the low table. He could hear a monotonous pop song playing upstairs on Brian's portable cassette player.

When he sat down again, he put his arm around Sandra.

"That's more like it," she said.

"Mmm. Tell me something. Do you think you could ever see yourself going to bed with another woman?"

"What do you have in mind? Inviting Jenny Fuller over for a threesome?"

"Unfortunately Jenny's away for Christmas."

Sandra hit him gently on the chest. "Beast."

"No, seriously. Could you?"

Sandra was quiet for a moment. Her dark eyebrows knit

together and tiny candle flames burned in her blue eyes. Banks sipped his drink and wished he could have a cigarette. Maybe later, while Sandra was getting ready for bed, he could nip outside in the cold and have a few quick drags. That should soon cure him of the habit.

"Well, hypothetically, the idea doesn't offend me," Sandra said finally. "I mean, it's nothing I think about much, but it doesn't disgust me. It's hard to explain. I've had crushes, what schoolgirl or schoolboy hasn't, but they never led to anything. I can't say I've thought about it a lot over the years, but there's something about the idea of being with another woman that's sort of comforting in a way. It doesn't feel threatening to me, when I think about it. I'm probably not making much sense, but I've had a few drinks, and you did ask."

"I think I understand," Banks said.

"Men always like the idea of two women together, don't they? It excites them."

Banks had to admit that it did, but he didn't know why. So far, he hadn't allowed himself to picture the sexual side of Veronica's relationship with Caroline, though he guessed they had been a passionate couple. And where there's passion, he mused, snuggling closer to Sandra, there's often likely to be violence, even murder.

III

Susan left the pub shortly after Banks, and as soon as she got home to the bare, empty flat, she felt dizzy. First she drank a large glass of water, then she turned on the television and lay down on the sofa. The picture looked blurred. Suddenly she started to feel horribly depressed and nauseated. She remembered the lies she had told Banks about going home to Sheffield for Christmas. She had no intention of going. She would phone and tell her parents she couldn't make it because she was working on an important case. A murder. And she would spend the day in her flat doing a few domestic chores and reading that new American book on homicide investigation. She had enough food—a tin of spaghetti, a frozen chicken dinner—so she didn't need to go out and risk being seen by someone. Because she only lived half a mile or so from Banks, she would have to be careful.

She had bought and wrapped her presents days ago. She would try to pay a visit home next week or early in the new year. Somehow, it was easier on non-festive occasions. The forced enjoyment of the season only exacerbated her discomfort. For the same reason, she had always hated and avoided New Year's Eve parties.

The TV picture still looked blurred. When she closed her eyes, the world spun around and seemed to pull her into a swirling vortex that made her stomach heave. She opened her eyes again quickly. She felt sick but didn't want to get up. The third time she tried, her thoughts settled down and she fell into an uneasy sleep.

In her dream she moved into a room like the one Gary Hartley lived in, and she called it home. A high-ceilinged, dark, cold place crumbling around her as she stood there. And when she looked at the far wall it wasn't a wall at all but a mesh of cobwebs beyond which more ruined rooms with dusty floorboards and walls of flaking plaster stretched to infinity. When she went over to investigate, a huge fat spider dropped from the ceiling and hung inches from her nose. It seemed to be grinning at her.

Susan's own scream woke her. As soon as she came to consciousness she realized that she had been struggling for some time to get out of the nightmare. Her clothes were mussed up and a film of cold sweat covered her brow. Frantically, she looked around her at the room. It was the same, thank God. Dull, empty, characterless, but the same.

She staggered to the kitchen and splashed her face with cold water. Too much to drink. That Old Peculier was powerful stuff. And Richmond had insisted on buying her a brandy and Babycham. No wonder she felt the way she did. She cursed herself for the fool she was and prayed to God she hadn't made an idiot of herself in front of the others.

She looked at her watch: seven o'clock. Her head felt a little clearer now, despite the dull ache behind her eyes.

She couldn't shake the dream, though, or the sense of panic it had caused in her. She made tea, paced about the room while the kettle boiled, switched TV channels; then, suddenly, she knew she had to do something about her bare, joyless flat. She couldn't go home, but neither could she spend Christmas Day in such a miserable place. The visit to Gary Hartley had shaken her up even more than she'd realized.

Panicking that it might be too late, she looked at her watch again. Twenty to eight. Surely some places in the shopping center would be staying open extra hours tonight? Every year, Christmas seemed to get more and more commercial. They wouldn't miss a business opportunity like Christmas Eve, all those last-minute, desperate shoppers, guilty because they've forgotten someone. Susan hadn't forgotten anyone except herself. She grabbed her coat and dashed for the door. Still time. There had to be.

FIVE

I

Christmas Day in the Banks household passed the way Christmas Days usually pass for small families: plenty of noisy excitement and too much to eat and drink. Downstairs at nine o'clock—a great improvement over the ridiculously early hours they had woken up on Christmas mornings past—Brian and Tracy opened their presents while Sandra and Banks sipped champagne and orange juice and opened theirs. Outside, framed in the bay window, fresh snow hung heavy on the roofs and eaves of the opposite houses and formed a thick, unmarked carpet across street and lawns alike.

Banks and Sandra were happy with their presents—mostly clothes, book or record tokens and the inevitable aftershave, perfume and chocolates. Brian quickly disappeared upstairs with his guitar, and Tracy spent an hour in the bathroom preparing herself for dinner.

Gristhorpe arrived about noon. They ate at one-thirty, got the dishes out of the way as quickly as possible, then watched the Queen's Message, which Banks found as dull and pointless as ever. The rest of the afternoon the adults spent variously chatting, drinking and dozing. Around tea-time, Banks and Sandra made a few phone calls to their parents and distant friends.

In deference to Gristhorpe's tin ear, Banks refrained from playing music most of the time, but later in the evening, when

Brian and Tracy had gone up to their rooms and the three adults sat enjoying the peace, he couldn't restrain himself. Off and on, he had been thinking about Caroline Hartley and was anxious to check out the music. He was sure that it had some connection with the murder. Now he could hold back no longer. He searched through his cassette collection for the Vivaldi he thought he had. There it was: the *Magnificat*, with *Laudate pueri* and *Beatus vir* on the same tape.

First he put on the record that Vic Manson had sent over from forensics. The familiar music, with its stately opening and pure, soaring vocal, disturbed him with the memory of what he had seen in Veronica Shildon's front room three days ago. He could picture again the macabre beauty of the scene: blazing fire, Christmas lights, candles, sheepskin rug, and Caroline Hartley draped on the sofa. The blood had run so thickly down her front that she had looked as if she were wearing a bib, or as if an undergarment had slipped up over her breasts. Carefully, he removed the needle.

"I was enjoying that," Sandra said. "Better than some of the rubbish you play."

"Sorry," Banks said. "Try this."

He put the cassette in the player and waited for the music to start. It was very different. The opening was far more sprightly, reminiscent of "Spring" from *The Four Seasons*.

"What are you after?" Sandra asked.

Banks stopped the tape. "They've got the same title, by the same composer, but they're different."

"Any fool can hear that."

"Even me," Gristhorpe added.

"Claude Ivers was right then," Banks muttered to himself. He could have sworn he had a piece by Vivaldi called *Laudate pueri*, but he hadn't recognized the music he heard at the scene.

The sleeve notes for the record told him very little. He turned to the cassette notes and read through the brief biographical sketch: Vivaldi—affectionately called "*il prete rosso*" because of his flaming red hair—had taken holy orders, but ill health prevented him from working actively as a priest. He had served at the *Pietà*, a kind of orphanage-cum-conservatory for girls in Venice, from 1703 to 1740 and would have been asked to compose sacred music when there was no choirmaster.

The blurb went on, outlining the composer's career and trying to pin down dates of composition. The *Laudate pueri* had probably been written for a funeral at the *Peità*. One of its sections—the antiphon, "*Sit nomen Domini*"—revealed the liturgical context as a burial service for very young children. There was more about Vivaldi's setting being hardly solemn enough for a child's funeral, but Banks was no longer paying attention. He went back to the word sheet enclosed in the record sleeve and read through the translation: so few words, so much music.

According to the translator, "*Sit nomen Domini benedictum ex hoc nunc et usque in saeculum*" meant, "Blessed be the name of the Lord; from henceforth now and forever." What that had to do with funerals or children Banks had no idea. He realized he didn't know enough about the liturgy. He would have to talk to a churchman if he really wanted to discover the true relevance of the music.

The main point, however, was that what Banks now knew about the music tied in with the information he had got from Glendenning's post-mortem. Caroline Hartley had given birth to a child. According to Banks's theories so far, this had either been the reason for her flight to London or it had occurred while she had been there. Another chat with Veronica Shildon might clear that up.

Where was the child? What had happened to it? And who was the father? Perhaps if he could answer some of those questions he would know where to begin.

As far as musical knowledge went, Claude Ivers certainly seemed the most likely candidate to have brought the record. Already Banks was far from satisfied with his account of himself. Naturally, Ivers would deny having called at Veronica's house on the night of the murder; he was known to have a grudge against Caroline Hartley. But he must have realized he had left the record. Why take such a risk? Surely he must understand that the police would have ways of finding out who had bought the record, even if there was no gift tag on the wrapping? Or did he? Like many geniuses, his connection with the practical realities of life was probably tenuous. And Ivers couldn't have had anything to do with Caroline Hartley's baby unless they had known one another some time ago. Very unlikely.

"Put some carols on," Sandra said, "and stop sitting on the floor there staring into space."

"What? Oh, sorry." Banks snapped out of it and got up to freshen the drinks. He searched through the pile of records and tapes for something suitable. Kathleen Battle? Yes, that would do nicely. But even as "O Little Town of Bethlehem" began, his mind was on Vivaldi's requiem for a dead child, Caroline Hartley's baby and the photograph of Ruth, the mystery woman. Christmas or not, Veronica Shildon was going to get another visit very soon. He went into the hall, took his cigarettes and lighter from his jacket pocket and slipped quietly out into the backyard for a peaceful smoke.

II

"Veronica Shildon, this is Detective Constable Susan Gay."

It was an embarrassing introduction, but it had to be made. Banks was well aware of the modern meaning of "gay," but he was no more responsible for the word's diminishment than he was for Susan's surname.

Banks noticed the ironic smile flit across Veronica's lips and saw Susan give a long-suffering smile in return—something she would never have done in other circumstances.

Veronica stretched out her hand. "Good to meet you. Please sit down." She sat opposite them, back straight, legs crossed, hands folded in her lap. The excessive formality of her body language seemed at odds with the casual slacks and gray sweatshirt she was wearing. She offered them some sherry, which they accepted, and when she went to fetch it she walked as if she'd put in a lot of time carrying library books on her head.

Finally, when they all had their glasses to hide behind, Veronica seemed ready for questions. Starting gently, Banks first asked her about the furniture, whether she wanted the sofa cushions and the rug back. She said no, she never wished to see them again. She was going to redecorate the room completely, and as soon as the holidays were over and the shops had reopened, she was going to buy a new suite and carpet.

"How are you managing with the flower shop?" he asked.

"I have a very trustworthy assistant, Patricia. She'll take care of things until I feel ready again."

"Did Caroline ever have anything to do with your business? The shop, your partner . . . ?"

Veronica shook her head. "David, my partner, lives in Newcastle and rarely comes here. He was a friend of Claude's, one of the few that stuck with me when . . . Anyway, he regards the shop more as an investment than anything else."

"And Patricia?"

"She's only eighteen. I assume she has her own circle of friends."

Banks nodded and sipped some sherry, then he slipped the signed photograph from his briefcase.

"Are you sure you can't tell me any more about this woman?"

Veronica looked at the photograph again. "It was something personal to Caroline," she answered. "I never pried. There were parts of her she kept hidden. I could accept that. All I know is that her name was Ruth and she wrote poetry."

"Where does she live?"

"I've no idea, but Caroline lived in London for some years before she came up here."

"And you've never met this Ruth, never seen her?"

"No."

Banks bent to slip the photograph back into his briefcase and said casually, before he had even sat up to face her again, "Did you know that Caroline had a conviction for soliciting?"

"Soliciting? I . . . I . . ." Veronica paled and looked away at the wall so they couldn't see her eyes. "No," she whispered.

"Is there anything at all you can tell us about Caroline's life in London?"

Veronica regained her composure. She sipped some sherry and faced them again. "No."

Banks ran his hand through his cropped black hair. "Come on, Ms. Shildon," he said. "You lived with her for two years. She must have talked about her past. As I understand it, you were undergoing therapy. Caroline too. Do you seriously expect me to believe that two people digging into their psyches like that never spoke to one another about important things?"

Veronica sat up even straighter and gave Banks a look as cold and gray as the North Sea. "Believe what you want, Chief Inspector. I've told you what I know. Caroline lived in London for a number of years. She didn't have a very happy time there. What she was working through in analysis was private."

"How was she when you met her?"

"When I . . . ?"

"When you first met."

"I've told you. She was living with Nancy Wood. She seemed happy enough. It wasn't a . . . it was just a casual relationship. They shared a flat, I believe, but there was no deep commitment. What else can I say?"

"Was she more, or less, disturbed back then than she has been lately?"

"Oh, more. Definitely more. As I said, she seemed happy enough. At least on the surface. But she had some terrible problems to wrestle with."

"What problems?"

"Personal ones. Psychological problems, like the ones we

all have. Haven't you read the poem: 'They fuck you up, your mum and dad. / They don't mean to, but they do.' " She reddened when she'd finished, as if just realizing there had been a four-letter word in the literary quotation. "Philip Larkin."

Banks, who had heard from Susan all about the Hartley home, could certainly believe that. He knew something about Larkin's poetry, too, through Gristhorpe and a recent Channel Four special, and made a mental note to have another look at the poem later.

"But she was making progress?" he asked.

"Yes. Slowly, she was becoming whole. The scars don't go away, but you recognize them and learn to live with them. The better you understand why you are what you are, the more you're able to alter destructive patterns of behavior." She managed a wry smile at herself. "I'm sorry if I sound like a commercial for my therapist, but you did ask."

"Was anything bothering her lately? Was she especially upset about anything?"

Veronica thought for a moment and drank more sherry. Banks was coming to see this as a signal of a forthcoming lie or evasion.

"Quite the opposite," Veronica said finally. "As I told you, she was making great progress with regard to her personal problems. Our life together was very happy. And she was excited about the play. It was only a small part, but the director led her to believe there would be better ones to follow. I don't know if Mr. Conran was leading her to expect too much, but from what she told me, he seemed convinced of her talent."

"Did you ever meet James Conran?"

"No. Caroline told me all this."

"Did she ever tell you that he fancied her?"

Veronica smiled. "She said he chatted her up a lot. I think she knew he found her attractive and felt she could use it."

"That's a bit cold-blooded, isn't it?"

"Depends on your point of view."

"How far was she willing to go?"

Veronica put her glass down. "Look, Chief Inspector, I don't mind answering your questions when they're relevant, but I don't see how speaking or implying ill of the dead is going to help you at all."

Banks leaned forward. "Now you listen to me for a moment, Ms. Shildon. We're looking for the person who killed your companion. At the moment we've no idea who this person might be. If Caroline did *anything* that might have led to her death, we need to know, whether it reflects well or badly on her. Now how far was she willing to go with James Conran?"

Veronica, pale and stiff, remained silent a while. When she spoke, it was in a quiet, tired voice. "It was only an amateur dramatic society," she said. "The way you speak, anyone would think we were talking about a movie role. Caroline could flirt and flatter men's egos easily enough, but that's as far as she'd go. She wasn't mercenary or cold."

"But she did lead men on?"

"It was part of her way of dealing with them. If they were willing to be led . . ."

"She didn't sleep with them?"

"No. And I would have known, believe me."

"So everything seemed to be going well for Caroline. There was nothing to worry or upset her?"

Again, the hesitation, the lady-like sip of sherry. "No."

"It's best not to hold anything back," he said. "I've already told you, you can't have any idea what information might be valuable in an investigation like this. Leave decisions like that to us."

Veronica looked directly at him. He could see courage, pain and stubborn evasion in her eyes. He let the silence stretch, then gave Susan, who had been busy taking notes, a discreet signal to go ahead.

"Veronica," Susan asked softly, "did you know about Caroline's baby?"

This time the reaction was unmistakably honest. She almost

spilled her sherry and her eyes widened. "What?"

Veronica Shildon certainly hadn't known about Caroline's baby, and the fact that she hadn't known surprised her. Which meant, Banks deduced, that she probably *did* know a lot more about Caroline than she was willing to let on.

"Caroline had a baby some years ago," Susan went on. "We can't say exactly when, but we were hoping you might be able to help."

Veronica was able only to shake her head in disbelief.

"We're assuming she had it in London," Banks said. "That's why anything you can tell us about Caroline's life there would be a great help."

"A baby," Veronica echoed. "Caroline? She never said a word . . ."

"It's true," Susan said.

"But what happened to it? Where is it?"

"That's what we'd like to know," Banks said. "Did you know that music, the *Laudate pueri*, was used at burial services for children?"

Veronica looked at him as if she didn't understand. Her thin, straight lips pressed tight together and a frown spread over her brow from a deep V at the top of her nose. "What does that have to do with it?" she asked.

"Maybe nothing. But someone put that record on and made sure it was going to stay on. You say it wasn't yours, so someone must have brought it. Perhaps the killer. You said you like classical music?"

"Of course. I could hardly have lived with Claude for ten years if I didn't, could I?"

Banks shrugged. "I don't know. People make the strangest sacrifices for comfort and security."

"I might have sacrificed my independence and my pride, Chief Inspector, but my love for music wasn't feigned, I assure you. I did then and still do enjoy all kinds of classical music."

"But Caroline didn't."

"What does it matter? I was quite happy to enjoy my records when she was out."

Banks, who had often suffered Sandra's opposition to some of the music he liked, understood that well enough. "Is it," he asked, "the kind of present your husband might have given you?"

"If you're expecting me to implicate Claude in this, I won't do it. We may have separated, but I wish him no harm. Are you trying to suggest that there is some obscure link between this music, the baby and Caroline's death?"

"The link seems obvious enough between the first two," Banks said, "but as for the rest, I don't know. If you'd never seen the record before, someone must have brought it over that evening. It would help a lot if we knew who the father of Caroline's child was."

Veronica shook her head slowly. "I didn't know. I really didn't know. About the baby, I mean."

"Does it surprise you to discover that Caroline wasn't exclusively lesbian?"

"No, it's not that. After all, I've hardly been exclusively so myself, have I? Most people aren't. Most people like us." She tilted her head back and fixed him with a cool, gray look. "It might interest you to know, Chief Inspector, just for the record, that I'm not ashamed of what I am, and neither was Caroline. But we weren't crusaders. We didn't go around holding hands and mauling one another in public. Nor did we proselytize on behalf of groups or causes that seem to think sexual preference is an important issue in everything from ordination as a Church minister to what kind of breakfast cereal one buys. Like most people's sex lives, ours was an intimate and private matter. At least it was until the papers got hold of this story. They soon discovered I was married to Claude, and why we parted, and it hasn't taken them long to guess at the nature of my relationship with Caroline."

"I shouldn't worry too much," Banks offered. "People pay much less attention to the gutter press during the Christmas season. Do you know if Caroline had any affairs while she was living with you? With men or women?"

Veronica fingered the neckline of her sweatshirt. "You're very forthright, aren't you?"

"I sometimes have to be. Can you answer the question?"

Veronica paused, then said, "As far as I know she didn't. And I think I would have known. Of course, she was attractive to men, and she knew it. She dealt with it as best she could."

"What were her feelings about men?"

"Fear, contempt."

"Why?"

Veronica looked down into her glass and almost whispered. "Who can say where something like that starts? I don't know."

"What about you?"

"My feelings toward men?"

"Yes."

"I can't see how that's relevant, Chief Inspector, but I certainly don't hate men. I suppose I fear them somewhat, like Caroline, but perhaps not as much. They threaten me, in a way, but I have no trouble dealing with them in the course of business. Mostly they confuse me. I certainly have no desire ever to live with one again." She had finished her sherry and put the glass down on the low table as though announcing the end of the interview.

"Are you sure she wasn't involved with any members of the cast? Things like that do happen, you know, when people work together."

Veronica shook her head. "All I can say is that she never came home late or stayed out all night."

"Did Caroline's brother ever visit you here?" Susan asked.

"Gary? He hardly left the house as far as I know."

"You never met him?"

"No."

"But did he know where the two of you lived?"

"Of course he did. Caroline told me she gave him the address in case of an emergency. She'd drop by every once in a while to see how things were with her father."

"You never went with her?"

"No. She didn't want me to."

Banks could understand why. "Did anyone know you were going shopping after your therapy session the other evening?" he asked.

"Nobody. At least, I . . . I mean, Caroline knew."

"Apart from Caroline."

"She might have told someone, though I can't think why. I certainly don't announce such domestic trivia to the world at large."

"Of course not. But you might have mentioned it to someone?"

"I might have. In passing."

"But you can't remember to whom?"

"I can't even remember mentioning it to anyone other than Ursula, my therapist. Why is it important?"

"Did your husband know?"

She uncrossed her legs and shifted in her chair. "Claude? Why would he?"

"I don't know. You tell me."

Veronica shook her head. "I told you, I've not seen him for a while. He phoned me yesterday to offer his condolences, but I don't think it would be a good time for us to meet again. Not for a while."

"Tell me, is there any chance that your husband knew Caroline Hartley before you introduced them?"

"What a strange question. No, of course he didn't. How could he, without my knowing?"

Banks shook his head and gestured to Susan that they were about to leave. They stood up.

"Thanks for your time," Banks said at the door. "I hope it wasn't too painful for you."

"Not too much, no. Incomprehensible, perhaps, but the pain was bearable."

Banks smiled. "I told you, it's best to leave the sorting out to us."

She looked away. "Yes."

As he turned, she suddenly touched his arm and he swung around to face her again. "Chief Inspector," she said. "This woman, Ruth. If you do find her, would you tell me? I know it's foolish, but I'd really like to meet her. From what Caroline told me, Ruth had quite an influence on her, on the kind of life she'd begun to make for herself. I'm being honest with you. I know nothing more about her than that."

Banks nodded. "All right, I'll see what I can do. And if you remember anything else, please call me."

She started to say something, but it turned into a quick "Goodbye" and a hastily closed door.

The chill hit them as soon as they walked out into Oakwood Mews. Banks shivered and slipped on his black leather gloves, a Christmas present from Sandra. The sky looked like iron and the pavement was slick with ice.

"Well," Susan said, as they walked carefully down the street, "she didn't have much to tell us, did she?"

"She's holding back. I think she's telling the truth about not knowing the woman in the photograph, but she's holding back about almost everything else. Maybe you could pick up the key from the station and drop in at the Community Center. Caroline may have left some of her things there, in a locker maybe, or a dressing-table drawer."

Susan nodded. "Do you think we should bring her in to the station and press her a bit harder? I'm sure she knows something. Maybe if we kept at her for a while, wore down her resistance . . . ?"

Banks looked at Susan and saw a smart young woman with earnest blue eyes, tight blond curls and a slightly snub nose gazing back at him. Good as she is, he thought, she's got a long way to go yet.

"No," he said. "It won't do any good. She's not holding back for reasons of guilt. It's a matter of pride and privacy with her. You might break her, given time, but you'd have to strip her of her dignity to do so, and she doesn't deserve that."

Whether Susan understood or not, Banks didn't really know. She nodded slowly, a puzzled look clouded her eyes, then she shoved her hands deep in the pockets of her navy-blue coat and marched up King Street beside him. The crusted ice crackled and creaked under their winter boots.

III

There were certainly no dressing rooms at the Community Center, not even for the lead players; nor were there any lockers. Susan wondered how they would manage when the play opened and they had to wear costumes and make-up. As she nosed around idly, she reflected on her Christmas.

On Christmas morning she had weakened and considered going to Sheffield, but in the end she had phoned and said she couldn't make it because of an important murder investigation. "A murder?" her mother had echoed. "How lurid. Well, dear, if you insist." And that was that. She had spent the day studying and watching the old musicals on television. But at least, she remembered with a smile, she had been in time on Christmas Eve to buy a small tree and a few decorations. At least she had made the flat look a bit more like a home, even if there were still a few things missing.

There was not much else they could do about identifying the three visitors Caroline Hartley had received on the evening of her death until they had more information about the record and the woman in the photograph. They wouldn't get that until the shops and businesses were back into the swing of things again in a day or two. Banks had suggested a second visit to Harrogate for the following day, and though Susan was hardly looking forward to that, she was interested in what Banks would make of the set-up there.

Susan wasn't sure about Veronica Shildon at all, especially

now that she had met her. The woman was too stiff and thin-lipped—the kind one could imagine teaching in an exclusive girls' school—and her posh accent and prissy mannerisms stuck in her craw. The idea of the two women in bed together made Susan's flesh crawl.

As she poked around, looking for anything that might have been connected with Caroline, she thought she heard a noise down the hallway. It could have come from anywhere. The backstage area, she had quickly discovered, was a warren of store rooms and cubby-holes. Slowly, she walked toward the stage entrance and peeked through a fire-door. The lights were on in the auditorium, which seemed odd, but it was silent and she saw no one. Puzzled, she went to the props room.

Marcia had scrubbed the graffiti from the walls, Susan noticed, leaving only garish smears in places. The trunk of tattered costumes had gone. It was a shame about the vandals, she thought, but there was nothing, really, she could do. As she had told Conran and Marcia, the police had a good idea who the culprits were, but they didn't have the manpower to put a round-the-clock watch on them and could hardly arrest them with no evidence at all. PCs Tolliver and Bradley had had a word with the suspected ringleaders, but the kids were so cool and arrogant they had given nothing away.

Again, Susan thought she heard a noise like something being dragged across a wood floor. She stood still and listened. It stopped, and all she could hear was her own heart beating. Not even a mouse stirred. She shrugged and went on poking about the room. It was no use. She would pick up nothing about Caroline Hartley here by osmosis.

The door creaked open slowly behind her. She turned, ready to defend herself, and saw a uniformed policeman silhouetted in the doorway. What the hell? As far as she knew, they hadn't put a guard inside the place. She couldn't make out who it was; his helmet was too low over his brow and its strap covered his chin. The light behind her in the store room was too dim to be much help.

He stood with his hands clasped behind his back and bent

his knees. "Hello, hello, hello! What have we here?"

It was an assumed voice, she could tell that. Pretentiously deep and portentous. For a moment she didn't know what to do or say. Then he walked into the room and closed the door.

"I'm afraid," he said, "I shall have to ask you to accompany me to the Crooked Billet for a drink, and if you don't come clean there, we'll proceed to Mario's for dinner."

Susan squinted in the poor light and saw that under the ridiculous helmet stood James Conran himself. Out of angry relief, she said, "What the hell are you doing here?"

"I'm sorry," he said, taking off the helmet. "Couldn't resist playing a little joke. I saw you when you peeked into the auditorium. I'd just dropped by to check out some blocking angles from the floor."

"But the uniform," Susan said. "I thought the costumes had all been destroyed."

"This? I found it under the stage with a lot more old stuff. Been there for years. I suppose our previous incarnation must have left it all behind."

Susan laughed. "Do you always dress the part when you ask someone out to dinner?"

Conran smiled shyly. "I'm not the most direct or confident person in the world," he said, unbuttoning the high-collared police jacket. "Especially when I'm talking to an ex-pupil. You may be grown-up now, but you weren't the last time I saw you. Maybe I need a mask to hide behind. But I did mean what I said. Would you consider at least having a drink with me?"

"I don't know." Susan had nothing to do, nowhere to go but home, but she felt she couldn't just say yes. It was partly because he made her feel like that sixteen-year-old schoolgirl with a crush on the teacher again, and partly because he was connected, albeit peripherally, with a case she was working on.

"I think I should arrest you for impersonating a police officer," she said.

He looked disappointed, and a faint flush touched his

cheeks. "At least grant the condemned man his last wish, then. Surely you can't be so cruel?"

Still Susan deliberated. She wanted to say yes, but she felt as if a great stone had lodged in her chest and wouldn't let out the air to form the words.

"Some other time, perhaps, then?" Conran said. "When you're not so busy."

"Oh, come on," Susan said, laughing. "I've got time for a quick one at the Crooked Billet at least." To hell with it, she thought. Why not? It was about time she had some fun.

He brightened. "Good. Just a minute then. Let me change back into my civvies."

"One thing first," Susan said. "Did Caroline or any of the cast keep any of their private things here? I can't seem to find any lockers or changing areas."

"We just have to make do with what we have," Conran said. "It's all right at the moment, as we're not bothering with make-up and costumes, but at dress rehearsal and after . . . well, we'll see what we can do about some of those little cubby-holes off the main corridor."

"So there's not likely to be anything?"

"Afraid not. If people brought their handbags or briefcases to rehearsal, we just left them in here while we were on stage. The back door was locked, so nobody could sneak in and steal anything. Don't go away," he said, and backed out of the room.

Susan put her hand over her mouth and laughed when he had gone. How shy and clumsy he seemed. But he did have charm and a sense of humor.

"Right," he said, peeping around the door a couple of minutes later. "Ready."

They left the Community Center by the back door, locked up and made their way down the alley to York Road. There, midway between the bus station and the pre-Roman site, stood the Crooked Billet. Luckily it wasn't too busy. They found a table by a whitewashed wall adorned with military emblems, and Conran went to fetch the drinks.

Susan watched him. His shirt hung out of the back of his pants, under his sweater, he had rather round shoulders and his hair could have done with a trim at the back. Apart from that he was presentable enough. Slim, though more from lack of proper diet than exercise, she guessed; tall, and if not straight at least endearingly stooped. Very artistic, really. His eyes, she noticed as he came back, were two slightly different shades of blue-gray, one paler than the other. Funny, she had never noticed that at school.

"Here," he said, putting a half of mild in front of her and holding out his pint. "Cheers." They clinked glasses.

"How's the investigation going?" he asked.

Susan told him there was nothing to report on the vandalism. "I'm sorry about Caroline Hartley," she went on. "I noticed how upset you were when the Chief Inspector mentioned her death."

Conran looked down and swirled the beer in his glass. "Yes. As I told you on Christmas Eve, I can't say we were great friends. This was her first role with the company. I hadn't known her very long. Obviously, I didn't know her at all, really. But she was a joy to have around. Such childlike enthusiasm. And what talent! Untrained, but very talented. We've lost an important member of the cast. Not that that's why I was upset. A Maria can easily be replaced."

"But not a Caroline Hartley?"

He shook his head. "No."

"Are you sure you weren't in love with her?"

Conran started as if he'd been stung. "What? What on earth makes you ask that?"

"I don't know," Susan said. And she didn't. The question had just risen, unbidden, to her lips. "Just that everyone says she was so attractive. After all, you are a bachelor, aren't you?"

He smiled. "Yes. I'm sorry. It's just that, well, here we are, having a drink together for the first time—our first date, so to speak—and you ask me if I was in love with another woman. Don't you think that's a bit odd?"

"Maybe. But were you?"

Conran smiled from the corner of his mouth and looked at her. "You're very persistent. I'd guess that's something to do with your job. One day you must tell me all about it, all about your last ten years, why you joined the police."

"And the answer to my question?"

He held his hands out, as if for handcuffs, and said in a Cockney voice, "All right, all right, guv! Enough's enough! I'll come clean."

The people at the next table looked over. Susan felt embarrassed, but she couldn't help smiling. She leaned forward and put her elbows on the table. "Well?" she whispered.

"I suppose every man's a little bit in love with every beautiful woman," Conran said quietly.

Susan blushed and reached for her drink. She didn't consider herself beautiful, but did he mean to imply that she was? "That's a very evasive answer," she said. "And besides, it sounds like a quote."

Conran grinned. "But it's true, isn't it? Depending on one's sexual preference, I suppose."

"I think it's disgusting, the way she lived," Susan said. "It's abnormal. Not that I mean to speak ill of the dead," she blustered on, reddening, "but the thought of it gives me the creeps."

"Well, that was her business," Conran said.

"But don't you think it's perverted?"

"I can think of worse things to be."

"I suppose so," Susan said, feeling she'd let too much out. What was wrong with her? She had been so hesitant about going out with him in the first place, and now here she was, exposing her fears. And to him, of all people. Surely, being in the arts, he must have come across all kinds of perverts. But she hadn't been able to help herself. The image of the two women in bed together still tormented her. And it was especially vivid as she had just come from talking to the cool, elegant Veronica Shildon. Slow down, Susan, she warned herself.

"Do you have any idea who the killer is?" Conran asked. Susan shook her head.

"And what about your boss?"

"I'm never sure I know what he thinks," Susan said. She laughed. "He's an odd one is Chief Inspector Banks. I sometimes wonder how he gets the job done at all. He likes to take his time, and he seems so sensitive to other people and their feelings. Even criminals, I'll bet." She finished her drink.

"You make him sound like a wimp," Conran said, "but I doubt very much that he is."

"Oh no, he's not a wimp. He's . . ."

"Sympathetic?"

"More like empathetic, compassionate. It's hard to explain. It doesn't stop him from wanting to see criminals punished. He can be tough, even cruel, if he has to be. I just get the impression he'd rather do things in the gentlest way."

"You're more of a pragmatist, are you?"

Susan wasn't sure if he was making fun of her or not. It was the same feeling she often had with Philip Richmond. Her eyes narrowed. "I believe in getting the job done, yes. Emotions can get in the way if you let them."

"And you wouldn't?"

"I'd try not to."

"Another drink?" Conran asked.

"Go on, then," she said. "On two conditions."

"What are they?"

"One, I'm buying. Two, no more shop talk. From either of us."

Conran laughed. "It's a deal."

Susan picked up her handbag and went to the bar.

IV

"I've told you," Detective Sergeant Jim Hatchley said to his new wife. "It's not exactly *work*. You ought to know me better than that, lass. Look at it as a night out."

"But what if I didn't want a night out?" Carol argued.

"I'm buying," Hatchley announced, as if that was the end of it.

Carol sighed and opened the door. They were in the carpark at the back of the Lobster Inn, Redburn, about fifteen miles up the coast from their new home in Saltby Bay. The wind from the sea felt as icy as if it had come straight from the Arctic. The night was clear, the stars like bright chips of ice, and beyond the welcoming lights of the pub they could hear the wild crashing and rumbling of the sea. Carol shivered and pulled her scarf tight around her throat as they ran toward the back door.

Inside, the place was as cozy as could be. Christmas decorations hung from beams that looked like pieces of driftwood, smoothed and worn by years of exposure to the sea. The murmur of conversations and the hissing of pumps as pints were pulled were music to Hatchley's ears. Even Carol, he noticed, seemed to mellow a bit once they'd got a drink and a nice corner table.

She unfastened her coat and he couldn't help but look once again at the fine curve of her bosom, which stood out as she took off the coat. Her shoulder-length blond hair was wavy now, after a perm, and Hatchley relished the memory of seeing it spread out on the pillow beside him that very morning. He couldn't get enough of the voluptuous woman he now called his wife, and she seemed to feel the same way. His misbehavior at the reception had soon been forgiven.

Carol spotted the way he was looking at her. She blushed, smiled and slapped him on the thigh. "Stop it, Jim."

"I weren't doing anything." His eyes twinkled.

"It's what you were thinking. Anyway, tell me, what did Chief Inspector Banks say?"

Hatchley reached for a cigarette. "There's this bloke called Claude Ivers lives just up the road from here, some sort of highbrow musician, and he parks his car at the back of the pub. Banks wants to know if he took it out at all on the evening of December twenty-second."

"Why can't he find out for himself?"

Hatchley drank some more beer before answering. "He's got other things to do. And it'd be a long way for him to come, especially in nasty weather like this. Besides, he's the boss, he delegates."

"But still, he needn't have asked *you*. He knows we're supposed to be on our honeymoon."

"It's more in the way of a favor, love. I suppose I could've said no."

"But you didn't. You never do say no to a night out in a pub. He knows that."

Hatchley put a hand as big as a ham on her knee. "I thought you'd be used to going with a copper by now, love."

Carol pouted. "I am. It's just . . . oh, drink your pint, you great lummox." She slapped him on the thigh.

Hatchley obliged and they forgot work for the next hour, chatting instead about their plans for the cottage and its small garden. Finally, at about five to eleven, their glasses only half full, Carol said, "There's not a lot of time left, Jim, if you've got that little job to do."

Hatchley looked at his watch. "Plenty of time. Relax, love."

"But it's nearly eleven. You've not even gone up for a refill. That's not like you."

"Trust me."

"Well, you might not want another, though that's a new one on me, but *I* do."

"Fine." Hatchley muttered something about nagging wives and went to the bar. He came back with a pint for himself and a gin and tonic for Carol.

"I hope it's not all going to be like this," she said when he sat down again.

"Like what?"

"Work. Our honeymoon."

"It's a one-off job, I've told you," Hatchley replied. He drained about half his pint in one go. "Hard work, but some-

one has to do it." He belched and reached for another cigarette.

At about twenty past eleven Carol suggested that if he
wasn't going to do anything they should go home. Hatchley
told her to look around.

"What do you see?" he asked when she'd looked.

"A pub. What else?"

"Nay, lass, tha'll never make a detective. Look again."

Carol looked again. There were still about a dozen people
in the pub, most of them drinking and nobody showing any
signs of hurrying.

"What time is it?" Hatchley asked her.

"Nearly half past eleven."

"Any towels over the pumps?"

"What? Oh . . ." She looked. "No. I see what you mean."

"I had a word with young Barraclough, the local lad at
Saltby Bay. He's heard about this place and he's told me all
about the landlord. Trust me." Hatchley put a sausage finger
to the side of his nose and ambled over to the bar.

"Pint of bitter and a gin and tonic, please," he said to the
landlord, who refilled the glass without looking up and took
Carol's tumbler over to the optic.

"Open late, I see," Hatchley said.

"Aye."

"I do so enjoy a pub with flexible opening hours. Village
bobby here?"

The landlord scowled and twitched his head toward the
table by the fire.

"That's him?" said Hatchley. "Just the fellow I want to
see." He paid the landlord, then went and put the drinks down
at their table. "Won't be a minute, love," he said to Carol,
and walked over to the table by the fire.

Three men sat there playing cards, all of them in their late
forties in varying stages of obesity, baldness or graying hair.

"Police?" Hatchley asked.

One of the men, sturdy, with a broad, flat nose and glassy,
fish-like eyes, looked up. "Aye," he said. "What if I am?"

"A minute of your time?" Hatchley gestured to the table where Carol sat nursing her gin and tonic.

The man sighed and shook his head at his mates. "A policeman's lot . . ." he said. They laughed.

"What is it?" he grunted when they'd sat down at Hatchley's table.

"I didn't want to talk in front of your mates," Hatchley began. "Might be a bit embarrassing. Anyways, I take it you're the local bobby?"

"That I am. Constable Kendal, at your service. If you get to the bloody point, that is."

"Aye," said Hatchley, tapping a cigarette on the side of his package. "Well, that's just it. Ciggie?"

"Hmph. Don't mind if I do."

Hatchley gave him a cigarette and lit it for him. "Yon landlord seems a bit of a miserable bugger. I've heard he's a tight-lipped one, too."

"Ollie?" Kendal laughed. "Tight as a Scotsman's sphincter. Why? What's it to you?"

"I'd like to make a little bet with you."

"A bet? I don't get it."

"Let me explain. I'd like to bet you a round of drinks that you can get some information out of him."

Kendal's brow furrowed and his watery eyes seemed to turn into mirrors. He chewed his rubbery lower lip. "Information? What information? What the bloody hell are you talking about?"

Hatchley told him about Ivers and the car. Kendal listened, his expression becoming more and more puzzled. When Hatchley had finished, the constable simply stared at him open-mouthed.

"And by the way," Hatchley added, reaching into his inside pocket for his card. "My name's Hatchley, Detective Sergeant James Hatchley, CID. I've just been posted to your neck of the woods so we'll probably be seeing quite a bit of one another. You might mention to yon Ollie about his license.

Not that I have to remind you, I don't suppose, when it's an offense you've been abetting."

Pale and resigned, Constable Kendal stood up and walked over to the bar. Hatchley sat back, sipped some more beer and grinned.

"What was all that about?" Carol asked.

"Just trying to find out how good the help is around here. Why do a job yourself if you can get someone else to do it for you? There's some blokes, and I've a good idea that land-lord is one of them, who'll tell you it's pissing down when the sun's out, just to be contrary."

"And you think he'll talk now?"

"Aye, he'll talk all right. No percentage in not doing, is there?" He ran a hand through his fine, straw-colored hair. "I've lived in Yorkshire all my life," he said, "and I've still never been able to figure it out. There's some places, some communities, as wide open as a nympho's legs. Friendly. Helpful. And there's others zipped up as tight as a virgin's— sorry, love—and I reckon this is one of them. God help us if anything nasty happens in Redburn."

"Couldn't you just have asked the landlord yourself?"

Hatchley shook his head. "It'll come better from the local bobby, believe me, love. He's got very powerful motivation for doing this. His job. And the landlord's got his license to think about. Much easier this way. The more highly motivated the seeker, the better the outcome of the search. I read that in a textbook somewhere."

About five minutes later, Kendal plodded back to the table and sat down.

"Well?" said Hatchley.

"He came in to open up at six—they don't go in for that all-day opening here except in season—and he says Ivers's car was gone."

"At six?"

"Thereabouts, aye."

"But he didn't see him go?"

"No. He did see that bird of his drive off, though."

"Oh, aye?"

"Aye. American, she is. Young enough to be his daughter. Has her own car too. Flashy red sportscar. Well, you know these rich folk . . ."

"Tell me about her."

"Ollie says she was getting in her car and driving off just as he came in."

"Which way did she go?"

Kendal looked scornfully at Hatchley and pointed with a callused thumb. "There's only one way out of here, up the bloody hill."

Hatchley scratched his cheek. "Aye, well . . . they haven't issued me my regulation ordnance survey map yet. So let's get this straight. At six o'clock, Ivers's car was already gone and his girlfriend was just getting into hers and driving off. Am I right?"

Kendal nodded.

"Owt else?"

"No." Kendal stood up to leave.

"Just a minute, Constable," Hatchley said. "I won the bet. While you're on your feet I'll have a pint of bitter for myself and a gin and tonic for the missis, if it's no trouble."

SIX

I

"What's Susan up to?" Richmond asked Banks on the way to Harrogate on the afternoon of December 27.

Driving conditions had improved considerably. Most of the main roads had been salted, and for the first time in weeks the sky glowed clear blue and the sun glinted on distant swaths and rolls of snow.

"I've got her chasing down the record," Banks answered. "Some shops might not even bother to reply unless we push them."

"Do you think it'll lead anywhere?"

"It could, but I don't know where. It can't just have been on by accident. It was like some kind of macabre soundtrack. Call it a strong hunch if you like, but there was something bloody odd about it."

"Claude Ivers?"

"Could be. At least we know now he lied to us about being out. We'll talk to him again later. What I want today is a fresh perspective on Caroline Hartley's family background. We've already got Susan's perceptions, now it's time for yours and mine. The old man couldn't have done it, so we'll concentrate on the brother. It sounds like he had plenty of motive, and nobody keeps tabs on his movements. It wouldn't have been hard for him to leave his father to sleep for a couple of hours and slip out. From what Susan said, the old man probably wouldn't have noticed."

"What about transport?"

"Bus. Or train. The services are frequent enough."

They pulled up outside the huge, dark house.

"Bloody hell, it does look spooky, doesn't it?" Richmond said. "He's even got the curtains closed."

They walked up the path through the overgrown garden and knocked at the door. Nobody answered. Banks hammered again, harder. A few seconds later, the door opened slowly and a thin, pale-faced teenager with spiky black hair squinted out at the sharp, cold day. Banks showed his card.

"You can't see Father today," Gary said. "He's ill. The doctor was here."

"It's you we want to talk to," Banks said. "If you don't mind."

Gary Hartley turned his back on them and walked down the hall. He hadn't shut the door, so they exchanged puzzled glances and followed him, closing the door behind them. Not that it made much difference; the place was still freezing.

In the front room, Banks recognized the high ceiling, curlicued corners and old chandelier fixture that Susan had described. He could also see the evidence of what Gary Hartley had done to the place, its ruined grandeur: wainscotting pitted with dart-holes, scratched with obscene graffiti.

Richmond looked stunned. He stood by the door with one hand in his overcoat pocket and the other touching the right side of his mustache, just staring around him. The room was dim, lit only by a standard lamp near the battered green-velvet sofa on which Gary Hartley lay smoking and studiously not looking at his visitors. A small color television on a table in front of the curtained window was showing the news with the sound turned down. Empty lager cans and wine bottles stood along the front of the stone hearth like rows of soldiers. In places, the carpet had worn through so much that only the crossed threads remained to cover the bare floorboards. The room smelled of stale smoke, beer and unwashed socks.

It must have been beautiful once, Banks thought, but a beauty few could afford. Back in the last century, for every family enjoying the easy life in an elegant Yorkshire mansion like this, there were thousands paying for it, condemned to the misery of starving in cramped hovels packed close to the mills that accounted for their every waking hour.

Banks picked a scuffed, hard-backed chair to sit on and swept a pair of torn jeans to the floor. He managed to light a cigarette with his gloves on. "What did your father do for a living?" he asked Gary.

"He owned a printing business."

"So you're not short of a bob or two?"

Gary laughed and waved his arm in an all-encompassing arc. "As you can see, the fortune dwindles, riches decay."

Where did he get such language? Banks wondered. He had already taken in the remains of an old library in ceiling-high bookcases beside the empty fireplace: beautiful, tooled-leather bindings. Cervantes, Shakespeare, Tolstoy, Dickens. Now he saw a book lying open, face down, beside Gary's sofa. The gold embossed letters on the spine told him it was *Vanity Fair*, something he had always meant to read himself. What looked like a red-wine stain in the shape of South America had ruined the cover. So Gary Hartley drank, smoked, watched television and read the classics. Not much else for him to do, was there? Was he knowledgeable about music, too? Banks saw no signs of a stereo. It was eerie talking to this teenager. He couldn't have been more than a year or so older than Brian, but any other similarity between them ended with the spiky haircut.

"Surely there must be *some* money left?" Banks said.

"Oh, yes. It'll see him to his grave."

"And you?"

He looked surprised. "Me?"

"Yes. When he's gone. Will you have some money left to help you leave here, find a place of your own?"

Gary dropped his cigarette in a lager can. It sizzled. "Never thought about it," he said.

"Is there a will?"

"Not that he's shown me."

"What'll happen to the house?"

"It was for Caroline."

"What do you mean?"

"Dad was going to leave it to Caroline."

Banks leaned forward. "But she deserted him, she left you all. You've been taking care of him by yourself for all these years." At least that was what Susan Gay had told him.

"So what?" Gary got up with curiously jerky movements and took a fresh pack of cigarettes from the mantelpiece. "She was always his favorite, no matter what."

"What now?"

"With her gone, I suppose I'll get it." He looked around the cavernous room, as though the thought horrified him more than anything else, and flopped back down on the sofa.

"Where were you on the evening of December twenty-second?" Richmond asked. He had recovered enough to find himself a chair and take out his notebook.

Gary glanced over at him, a look of scorn on his face. "Just like telly, eh? The old alibi."

"Well?"

"I was here. I'm always here. Or almost always. Sometimes I used to go to school so they didn't get too ratty with me, but it was a waste of time. Since I left, I've got a better education reading those old books. I go to the shops sometimes, just for food and clothes. Then there's haircuts and the bank. That's about it. You'd be surprised how little you have to go out if you don't want to. I can do the whole lot in one morning a week if I'm organized right. Booze is the most important. Get that right and the rest just seems to fall into place."

"What about your friends?" Banks asked. "Don't you ever go out with them?"

"Friends? Those wallies from school? They used to come over sometimes." He pointed to the wainscotting. "As you can see. But they thought I was mad. They just wanted to drink and do damage and when they got bored they didn't come back. Nothing changes much here."

"December twenty-second?" Richmond repeated.

"I told you," Gary said, "I was here."

"Can you prove that?"

"How? You mean witnesses?"

"That would help."

"I probably emptied out the old man's potty. Maybe even changed his sheets if he messed the bed. But he won't remember. He doesn't know one day from the next. I might even have dropped in at the off-license for a few cans of lager and some fags, but I can't prove that either."

Every time Gary talked about his father his tone hardened to hatred. Banks could understand that. The kid must be torn in half by his conflicts between duty and desire, responsibility and the need for freedom. He had given in and accepted the yoke, and he must hate both himself for his weakness and his father for making such a demand in the first place. And Caroline, of course. How he must have hated Caroline, though he didn't sound bitter when he spoke of her. Perhaps his hatred had been assuaged by her death and he had allowed himself to feel some simple pity.

"Did you go to Eastvale that evening?" Richmond went on. "Did you call on your sister and lose your temper with her?"

Gary coughed. "You really think I killed her, don't you? That's a laugh. If I was going to I'd have done it a few years ago, when I really found out what she'd lumbered me with, not now."

Five or six years ago, Banks calculated, Gary would have been only twelve or thirteen, perhaps too young for a relatively normal child to commit sororicide—and surely he must have been living a more normal life back then. Also, as Banks had learned over the years, bitterness and resentment could take a long time to reach breaking-point. People nursed grudges and deep-seated animosities for years sometimes before exploding into action. All they needed was the right trigger.

"Did you ever visit Caroline in Eastvale?" Banks asked.

"No. I told you, I hardly go out. Certainly not that far."

"Have you ever met Veronica Shildon?"

"That the lezzie she was shacking up with?"

"Yes."

"No, I haven't."

"But Caroline visited you here?"

He paused. "Sometimes. When she'd come back from London."

"You told the detective constable who visited you a few days ago that you knew nothing of Caroline's life in London. Is that true?"

"Yes."

"So for over five years, when she was between the ages of sixteen and twenty-one, you had no contact."

"Right. Six years, really."

"Did you know she had a baby?"

Gary sniffed. "I knew she was a slut, but I didn't know she had a kid, no."

"She did. Do you know what happened to it? Who the father was?"

"I told you, I didn't even know she'd had one."

He seemed confused by the issue. Banks decided to take his word for the moment.

"Did she ever mention a woman called Ruth to you?"

Gary thought for a moment. "Yeah, some woman who wrote poetry she knew in London."

"Can you remember what she said about her?"

"No. Just that they were friends like, and this Ruth woman had helped her."

"Is that all? Helped her with what?"

"I don't know. Just that she'd helped her."

"What did you think she meant?"

He shrugged. "Maybe took her in off the street or something, helped her with the baby. How should I know?"

"What was her last name?"

"She never mentioned it. Just Ruth."

"Whereabouts in London did she live?"

"I've no idea."

"You're sure there's nothing more you can tell us about her?"

Gary shook his head.

"Do you know anything about music?" Banks asked.

"Can't stand it."

"I mean classical music."

"Any music sounds awful to me."

Another one with a tin ear, Banks thought, just like Superintendent Gristhorpe. But it didn't mean Gary knew nothing about the subject. He read a lot, and could easily have come across the necessary details concerning the Vivaldi piece, perhaps in a biography.

"The last time you saw Caroline," he asked, "did she tell you anything that gave you cause to worry about her, to think she might be in danger, frightened of something?"

Gary appeared to give the question some thought, then he shook his head. "No."

Again, Banks thought he was telling the truth. Just. But there was something on Gary's mind, below the surface, that made his answer seem evasive.

"Is there anything else you want to tell us?"

"Nope."

"Right." Banks nodded to Richmond and they headed for the door. "Don't bother to see us out," Banks said. "We know the way."

Gary didn't reply.

"Jesus Christ," said Richmond when they'd got in the car and turned on the heater. "What a bloody nutcase." He rubbed his hands together.

"You wouldn't think, would you," Banks said, looking at the tall, elegant stone houses, "that behind such a genteel façade you'd find something so twisted."

"Not unless you were a copper," Richmond answered.

Banks laughed. "Time for a pub lunch on the way back,"

he said, "then you can take a trip to Barnard Castle and I'll see about having a chat with the therapist."

"Rather you than me," Richmond said. "If she's anything like she was when I saw her the other day she'll probably end up convincing you you need therapy yourself—after she's chewed your balls off."

"Who knows, maybe I do need therapy," Banks mused, then turned by the Stray, passed the Royal Baths and headed back toward Eastvale.

II

Ursula Kelly's office was on the second floor of an old building on Castle Hill Road. A back room, it was graced with a superb view over the formal gardens and the river to the eyesore of the East End Estate and the vale beyond. Not that you could see much today but a uniform shroud of white through which the occasional clump of trees, redbrick street or telegraph pole poked its head.

The waiting room was cramped and chilly, and none of the magazines were to Banks's taste. It wasn't an interview he was looking forward to. He had a great professional resistance to questioning doctors and psychiatrists during a case; much as they were obliged and bound by law, they had never, in his experience, proved useful sources of information. The only one he really trusted was Jenny Fuller, who had helped him out once or twice. As he looked out the window at the snow, he wondered what Jenny would make of Gary Hartley and the whole situation. Pity she was away.

After about ten minutes, Dr. Ursula Kelly admitted him to her inner sanctum. She was a severe-looking woman in her early fifties, with gray hair swept back tight and held firm in a bun. The lines of what might once have been a beautiful if harsh face were softened only by the plumpness of middle age. Her eyes, though guarded, couldn't help but twinkle with curiosity and irony. Apart from a few bookcases housing texts and journals, and the desk and couch in the corner, the consulting room was surprisingly bare. Ursula Kelly sat behind the desk with her back to the picture window, and Banks placed himself in front of her. She was wearing a fawn cardigan over her cream blouse, no white coat in evidence.

"What can I do for you, Chief Inspector?" she asked, tapping the eraser of a yellow HB pencil on a sheaf of papers in front of her. She spoke with a faint foreign accent. Austrian, German, Swiss? Banks couldn't quite place it.

"I'm sure you know why I'm here," he said. "My detective sergeant dropped by to see you the other day. Caroline Hartley."

"What about her?"

Banks sighed. It was going to be just as hard as he had expected. Question—answer, question—answer.

"I just wondered if you might be able to tell me a little more than you told him. How long had she been a patient of yours?"

"I had been seeing Caroline for just over three years."

"Is that a long time?"

Ursula Kelly pursed her lips before answering. "It depends. Some people have been coming for ten years or more. I wouldn't call it long, no."

"What was wrong with her?"

The doctor dropped the pencil and leaned back in her chair. She eyed Banks for a long time before answering. "Let's get this clear," she said finally. "I'm not a medical doctor, I'm an analyst, primarily using Jungian methods, if that means anything to you."

"I've heard of Jung."

She raised her eyebrows. "Good. Well, without going into all the ins and outs of it, people don't have to be ill to start seeing me. In the sense that you mean, there was nothing wrong with Caroline Hartley."

"So why did she come? And pay? I'm assuming your services aren't free."

Dr. Kelly smiled. "Are yours? She came because she was unhappy and she felt her unhappiness was preventing her from living fully. That is why people come to me."

"And you make them happy?"

She laughed. "Would that it were as easy as that. I do very little, actually, but listen. If the patient makes the connections, they cut so much deeper. The people who consult me generally feel that they are living empty lives, living illusions, if you like. They are aware of what potential they have; they know that life should mean more than it does to them; they know that they are capable of achieving, of feeling more. But they are emotionally numb. So they come for analysis. I'm not a psychiatrist. I don't prescribe drugs. I don't treat schizophrenics or psychotics. I treat people you would perceive as perfectly normal, on the outside."

"And inside?"

"Ah! Aren't we all a mass of contradictions inside? Our parents, whether they mean to or not, bequeath us a lot we'd be better off without."

Banks thought of Gary Hartley and the terrible struggles he had to live with. He also thought of the Philip Larkin poem that Veronica Shildon had quoted.

"Can you tell me anything at all about Caroline Hartley's problems?" he asked. "Anything that might help solve her murder?"

"I understand your concern," Ursula Kelly said, "and believe me, I sympathize with your task, but there is nothing I can tell you."

"Can't or won't?"

"Take it whichever way you wish. But don't think I'm trying to impede your investigation. The things Caroline and I worked on were childhood traumas, often nebulous in the extreme. They could have nothing to do with her death, I assure you. How could the way a child felt about . . . say . . . a lost doll result in her murder twenty years later?"

"Don't you think I'd be the best judge of that, as one professional to another?"

"There is nothing I can tell you. It was her feelings I dealt with. We tried to uncover why she felt the way she did about certain things, what the roots of her fears and insecurities were."

"And what were they?"

She smiled. "Even in ten years, Chief Inspector, we might not have uncovered them all. I can see by the way you're fidgeting you need a cigarette. Please smoke, if you wish. I don't, but it doesn't bother me. Many of my patients feel the need for infantile oral gratification."

Banks ignored the barb and lit up. "I don't suppose I need to remind you," he said, "that the rule of privilege doesn't apply to doctor-patient relationships as it does to those between lawyer and client?"

"It is not a matter of reminding me. I never even thought about it."

"Well, it doesn't. You are, by law, obliged to disclose any information you acquired while practicing your profession. If necessary, I could get a court order to make you hand over your files."

"Pah! Do it, then. There is nothing in my files that would interest you very much." She tapped her head. "It is all in here. Look, the women had problems. They came to me. Neither of them hurt anyone. They are not criminals, and they do not have any dangerous psychological disorders. Isn't that what you want to know?"

Banks sighed. "Okay. Can you at least tell me what kind of progress Caroline was making? Was she happy lately? Was anything bothering her?"

"As far as I could tell, she seemed fine. Certainly she wasn't worried about anything. In fact, we'd come to . . ."

"Yes?"

"Let's just say that she'd recently worked through a particularly difficult trauma. They occur from time to time in analysis and they can be painful."

"I don't suppose you'd care to tell me about it?"

"She had confronted one of her demons and won. And

people are usually happy when they overcome a major stumbling-block, at least for a while."

"Did she ever talk about her brother, Gary?"

"It's not unusual for patients to talk about their families."

"What did she have to say about him?"

"Nothing of interest to you."

"She treated him very badly. Did she feel no guilt?"

"We all feel guilt, Chief Inspector. Do you not think so?"

"Perhaps *he* should have been your patient. He certainly seems to have his problems, thanks to his sister."

"I don't choose my patients. They choose me."

"Veronica Shildon was a patient of yours, too, wasn't she?"

"Yes. But I can say even less about her. She's still alive."

Judging by how little Ursula Kelly had said about Caroline, Banks knew not to expect very much.

"Was Veronica particularly upset about anything that last session?"

She shook her head. "Your sergeant asked me that, and the answer is the same. No. It was a perfectly normal session as far as I was concerned."

"No sudden traumas?"

"None." She leaned forward and rested her hands on the desk. "Look, Chief Inspector, you might not think I've been very forthcoming. That is your prerogative. In my business you soon become privy to the innermost fears and secrets of the people you deal with, and you get into the habit of keeping them to yourself. You're looking for facts. I don't have any. Even if I did tell you what happened during my sessions with Caroline and Veronica, it wouldn't help you. I deal with a world of shadows, of dreams and nightmares, signs and symbols. What my patients *feel* is the only reality we have to work with. And I have already told you, in all honesty, that as far as I know neither Caroline nor Veronica was in any way especially disturbed of late. If you need to know more, try talking to Veronica herself."

"I already have."

"And?"

"I think she's holding back."

"Well, that is your problem."

Banks pushed his chair back and stood up. "I think you're holding back, too," he said. "Believe me, if I find out that you are and that it's relevant to Caroline's murder, I'll make sure you know about it. You'll need twenty years in analysis to rid yourself of the guilt."

Her jaw muscles clenched and her eyes hardened. "Should that occur, it will be my burden."

Banks walked out and slammed the door behind him. He didn't feel good about his anger and his pathetic threat, but people like Ursula Kelly, with her smug generalizations and pompous, self-righteous air, brought out the worst in him. He took a couple of deep breaths and looked at his watch. Five-thirty. Time to catch the end of rehearsal.

III

Richmond parked his car outside a pub on the main street, got out and sniffed the air. There was no reason, he thought, why it should smell so different up here, but it did have a damper, more acrid quality. Barnard Castle was only twenty or so miles from Eastvale, but it was over the Durham border in Teesdale.

According to his map, the shop should be on his right about half-way down the hill just in front of him. It seemed to be the main tourist street, with an Indian restaurant, coffee-house, bookshop and antique shop all rubbing shoulders with places that sold souvenirs along with walking and camping gear.

The toy shop itself was about half-way down the hill. First, Richmond looked in the window at the array of goods. Hardly any of them seemed familiar, nothing at all like the toys he had played with as a child. In fact, mostly he had had to use his imagination and pretend that a stick was a sword. It wasn't that his parents had been exceptionally poor, but they had strict priorities, and toys had come very low on the list.

The bell pinged as he entered and a young woman behind the counter looked up from behind a ledger. He guessed her to be in her mid-twenties, and she had a fine head of tangled auburn hair that cascaded over her shoulders and framed an attractive, freckled, oval face. She wore a long, loose cardigan, gray with a maroon pattern, and from what Richmond could see of her above the counter, she seemed to have a slim, shapely figure. A pair of glasses dangled on a chain around her neck, but she didn't put them on as he walked toward her.

"What can I do for you, sir?" she said with a lilting, Geordie accent in a slightly husky voice. "Would it be something for your boy, or your little girl, perhaps?"

Richmond noticed the glint of humor in her eyes. "I'm not married," he said, mentally kicking himself even before he had got the words out. "I mean, I'm not here to buy anything."

She looked at him steadily, fingering the spectacles chain as she did so.

"CID," he said, fumbling for his identification. "I spoke with the manager a couple of days ago, when you were on holiday."

She raised her eyebrows. "Ah, yes. Mr. Holbrook told me about you. Tell me, do all policemen dress as well as you do?"

Richmond wondered if she were being sarcastic. He took pride in his dress, certainly. He had the kind of tall, trim, athletic body that clothes looked good on, and he always favored a suit, white shirt and tie, unlike Banks, who went in for the more casual, rumpled look.

"I'll take that as a compliment," he said finally. "Look, I'm at a bit of a disadvantage. I'm afraid he didn't tell me your name."

She smiled. "It's Rachel, Rachel Pierce. Pleased to meet you." She held out her hand. Richmond shook it. He noticed there was no sign of either a wedding ring or an engagement ring.

She seemed to be laughing at him with her eyes, and it made him feel foolish and disconcerted. How could he question her seriously when she looked at him like that? He remembered his training and aimed for the correct tone.

"Well, Miss Pierce," he opened, "as you may be aware, we are investigating—"

She burst out laughing. Richmond felt himself flush to the tips of his mustache. "What the—?"

She put her hand to her mouth and quietened down. "I'm sorry," she said, seeming more than a little embarrassed herself. "I don't usually giggle. It's just that you seem so stuffy and formal."

"Well, I'm sorry if—"

She waved her hand. "No, no. Don't apologize. It's my fault. I know you have a job to do. It's just that it gets a bit lonely in here after Christmas and I'm afraid that seems to affect my manners. Look," she went on, "it would make this a lot easier for me if you'd let me lock up and make you a cup of tea before we talk. It's near enough closing time already and the only customer I've had all day was a young lad wanting to exchange his Christmas present."

Richmond, encouraged by her friendliness, smiled. "If you're closing anyway," he said, "maybe we could go for a drink and a bite to eat?"

She chewed on her lower lip and looked at him. "All right," she said. "Just give me a minute to make sure everything's secure."

In ten minutes, they were sitting in a cozy pub, Richmond nursing a pint and Rachel sipping rum and coke.

"I'm ready," she said, sitting back and folding her arms. "Grill away, Mr. CID."

Richmond smiled. "There's not much to ask, really. You know Charles Cooper?"

"Yes. He's the general manager."

"I understand he's been very busy lately making sure everything was in order for Christmas."

Rachel nodded.

"Do you remember December twenty-second?"

She wrinkled her brow and thought, then said, "Yes. He was here that day sorting out some stock problems. You see, Mr. Curtis, the manager, had forgotten to reorder some. . . . But you don't want to hear about that, do you?"

Richmond wasn't too sure. He felt like pinching himself to see if he could escape the way just listening to her voice and watching her animated face made him feel. He tried it—just a little nip at the back of his thigh—but it did no good. He took a deep breath. "How long was he at the shop?" he asked.

"Oh, a couple of hours, perhaps."

"Between what times?"

"He got here about four, or thereabouts, and left at six."

"He left at six o'clock?"

"Yes. You sound surprised. Why?"

"It's nothing." It was, though. Unless he had gone to another branch—and neither Cooper nor his wife had mentioned anything about that—then he had left the shop at six and not got home until eleven. Where the hell had he been, and why had he lied?

"Are you sure he left at six o'clock?" he asked.

"Well, it can't have been much after," Rachel answered. "We closed at seven—extra hours for the holiday period— and he was gone a while before then. He said he'd try to shift some stock over from the Skipton shop before Christmas Eve."

"Did you get the impression he was going to go to Skipton right then?"

"No. They'd be closed, too. Wouldn't be any point, would there?"

"Presumably, if he's general manager, he's got a key?"

"Yes, but he doesn't go carrying boxes of toys around, does he, if he's general manager. He gets some dogsbody to do that."

Richmond fingered his mustache. "Maybe you're right. What was your impression of him? Did you know him well?"

She shook her head. "Not well, no. He'd drop in once in a while. We might have a cup of tea and a chat about how things were going."

"That's all?"

She raised her left eyebrow and squinted her right eye almost shut. "And just what might you mean by that?"

"I'm not sure, really. He didn't make a pass at you or anything?"

"Mr. Cooper? Make a pass?" She laughed. "You obviously don't know him."

"So he never did?"

"Never. The thought of it . . ." She laughed again.

"Did he ever talk about things other than business? Personal things."

"No. He kept himself to himself."

"Did you ever hear him mention a woman called Caroline Hartley?"

She shook her head.

"Veronica Shildon?"

"No. He hardly ever even mentioned his own wife, only when I asked after her. I'd met her once or twice at company do's, you see, so it's only polite to ask after her, isn't it?"

"Was there anything odd about him at all?" Richmond asked. "Think. Surely you must have felt or noticed something at some time?"

Rachel frowned. "Look, there *is* something . . . but I don't like to speak out of turn."

"It's not out of turn," Richmond said, leaning forward. "Remember, this is a murder investigation. What is it?"

"Well, I could be wrong. It was just a couple of times, you know."

"What?"

"I think he's a drinker."

"In what way? We're drinking right now."

"I don't know, but not like this. A secret drinker, a problem drinker, whatever you call it."

"What makes you say that?"

"I could smell it on his breath sometimes, early in the day, when he hadn't bothered to take one of those awful breath mints he usually smelled of. And once I saw him take a little flask out of his pocket in the stockroom when he thought I wasn't looking. I can't be sure what it was, of course, but . . ."

Could there be anything in it? Richmond wondered. Rachel Pierce had certainly given him a new perspective on the Coopers, but whether it would lead him to a murderer, he couldn't tell. So the man drank, so he had lied about his alibi—a silly lie, at that, an easy one to check—but it might not mean anything. One thing was certain, though, Banks would want to visit the Coopers again very soon, and he wouldn't be as gentle as he had been on previous occasions.

Richmond looked over at Rachel. Her glass was nearly empty.

"Another?" he asked.

"I shouldn't."

He glanced at his watch. "I think I can say I'm officially off duty now," he said. "Come on, it won't do any harm."

She looked at him a long time. He couldn't fathom the expression on her face. Then she said, "All right, then. Another one."

"Wonderful. There's just one thing I have to do first."

She raised an eyebrow.

"Call my boss," Richmond said. "Don't go away. I won't be a minute."

He glanced back and saw her smiling into her glass as he made for the telephone.

IV

Disguise, I see thou art a wickedness
Wherein the pregnant enemy does much.

How easy it is for the proper false
In women's waxen hearts to set their forms!
Alas, our frailty is the cause, not we,
For such as we are made of, such we be.
How will this fadge? My master loves her dearly;
And I (poor monster) fond as much on him;
And she (mistaken) seems to dote on me.
What will become of this? As I am man,
My state is desperate for my master's love.
As I am woman (now alas the day!),
What thriftless sighs shall poor Olivia breathe?
O Time, thou must untangle this, not I;
It is too hard a knot for me t'untie.

"Better, Faith darling, much better! Perhaps just a bit more introspection—remember, it *is* a soliloquy—but not too serious." James Conran turned to Banks. "What did you think?"

"I thought she was very good."

"Do you know the play?"

"Yes. Not well. But I know it."

"So you know how it 'fadges' then?"

"They all marry the ones they want and live happily ever after."

Conran stuck a finger in the air. "Ah, not quite, Chief Inspector. Malvolio, remember, ends by vowing revenge on the lot of them for making a fool of him."

All that Banks remembered about the end of *Twelfth Night* was the beautiful song the Clown sang alone when everyone else had walked off to their fates. It was on his Deller Consort tape. "For the rain it raineth every day," the refrain went. It had always seemed a curiously somber song to end a comedy with. But nothing was black-and-white, especially in Shakespeare's world.

"Perhaps you'd care to see us on opening night," Conran said. "Complimentary tickets, of course."

"Yes, I would. Very much." Accepting free tickets to an amateur production could hardly be called being on the take,

Banks thought. "Will you be much longer here?" he asked. "I'd like to talk to some of the cast members. Maybe it would be more comfortable over in the Crooked Billet."

Conran frowned. "What on earth would you want to talk to them about?"

"Police business."

Definitely not pleased, Conran looked at his watch and clapped his hands. The actors walked off stage and went for their coats.

After they had dashed down the alley in the chilly evening, the warmth of the Crooked Billet greeted them like a long lost friend. They unbuttoned their coats and hung them by the door, then pulled two tables together near the fire to accommodate the thirsty thespians. Banks tried to keep track of the introductions and the links between actors and roles. Olivia, played by Teresa Pedmore, and Viola, Faith Green, interested him the most. Marcia Cunningham, the costumes and props manager, was there too. It was a casual and unorthodox method of questioning possible suspects, Banks was aware, but he wanted to get as much of a feel of the troupe as he could before he decided where to go from there.

"I still can't imagine why you want to talk to the cast," Conran complained. "Surely you can't think one of us had anything to do with poor Caroline's death?"

"Don't be so bloody naïve, Mr. Conran. There's a chance that anyone who knew her might have done it. Certainly she seemed to know her killer, as there was no sign of forced entry. How long did you stay at the pub the night she died?"

"I don't know. About an hour, I suppose. Maybe a bit longer."

"Until just after seven?"

"About that, yes."

"Then you went home?"

"Yes. I told you."

"There you are, then. You could be lying. You've got no alibi at all."

Conran reddened and his hand tightened on his glass. "Now just wait—"

But Banks ignored Conran completely and went to the bar for another drink. The director certainly seemed jumpy. Banks wondered why. Maybe it was just his artistic temperament.

When he got back to the table, his seat had been taken by a distraught Sir Toby Belch, who seemed to think his part could do with some expansion (perhaps to match his stomach) despite the limitations Shakespeare had imposed.

Banks managed to squeeze himself in between Teresa Pedmore and Faith Green, not a bad place to be at all. Teresa was deep in conversation with the man on her right, so Banks turned to Faith and complimented her on her rendering of Viola's soliloquy. She blushed and replied quickly, her breathy voice pitched quite low.

"Thank you. It's very difficult. I have no formal training. I'm a schoolteacher and I do like to get involved with the plays the department puts on, but . . . It's so difficult doing *Twelfth Night*. I have to remember that I'm really a woman dressed as a man talking about a woman who seems to have fallen in love with me. It's all very strange, a bit perverted really." She put her hand to her mouth and touched Banks's arm. "Oh God, I shouldn't have said that, should I? Not after poor Caroline . . ."

"I'm sure she'd forgive you," Banks said. "Did you have any idea of her sexual inclinations before her death?"

"None at all. None of us did. Not until I read about it in the papers. If you'd asked me, I'd have said she was man-mad."

"Why?"

Faith waved her hand in the air. "Oh, just the way she behaved. She knew how to string a man along. A woman knows about these things. At least, I thought I did."

"But you never actually saw her with a man?"

"Not in the way you mean, no. I'm talking about her general effect, the way she could turn heads."

"Did you notice any personality conflicts among the cast? Especially involving Caroline."

Faith rubbed one of her long blue tear-drop earrings between her finger and thumb. She was probably in her early twenties, Banks thought, with especially beautiful silvery hair hanging in a fringe and straight down to her shoulders. It looked so vibrant and satiny he wanted to reach out and touch it. He was sure sparks would fly out if he did. Her eyes were a little too close together and her lower lip pouted a bit, but the total effect had an interesting kind of unity. Also, as he had noticed on the stage, she was tall and well-formed. It would be difficult, without very good costumes, to conceal the fact that Faith Green was all woman.

She leaned closer to speak to Banks and he smelled her perfume. It was subtle, and probably not cheap. He also smelled the Martini Rossi on her breath.

"I didn't notice anything in particular," she said, flicking her eyes toward the rubicund Sir Toby and Malvolio, who looked like an undertaker's assistant, "but some of the men aren't too keen on Mr. Conran."

"Oh? Why's that?"

"I think they're jealous."

"But the women like him?"

"Most of them, yes. And that's partly why the others are jealous. You'd be surprised what shady motives people have for joining in amateur events like this." She widened her eyes and Banks noticed that they were smiling. "S-e-x," she said. "But he's not my type. I like my men dark and handsome." She looked Banks up and down. "Not necessarily tall, mind you. I don't mind being bigger than my boyfriends."

Banks noticed the plural. Surely there had never been schoolteachers like this in his time?

"I hear there was something between Mr. Conran and Olivia—Teresa, that is."

"You'll have to ask her about that," Faith said. "I'll not tell tales on my friends out of school." She wrinkled her nose.

"Can you tell me anything more about Caroline?"

Faith shrugged. "Not really. I mean, I hardly knew her. She was beautiful in a petite, girlish sort of way, but I can't say she made much of an impression on me. As I said before, I thought she was a bit of a flirt, myself, but I don't suppose she could help the way the men flocked to her."

"Anyone in particular?"

"No, just in general, really. Most of the men seemed to like being with her, including our director."

"Did he make a pass at her?"

"No, he's too subtle for that. He plays the shy and vulnerable one until women approach him, then he reels them in. At least he did with Teresa." She clapped a hand to her mouth. "Look, I *am* telling tales out of school. How do you do it?"

Banks smiled. "Professional secret. So in your opinion, Caroline Hartley was a flirt, but nothing ever came of it?"

"Yes. I suppose that's how she kept them at bay." Faith shook her head and her hair sparked like electricity. "Maybe I was blind, but I'm damned if I could see what she really was."

"What did you think of her as an actress?"

Faith traced a ring around the top of her glass. "She was young, inexperienced. She had a long way to go. And it was only a small part, after all. Young Maggie over there's taken it on now." She nodded toward a serious-looking young woman sitting next to Conran.

"But she was talented?"

"Who am I to say? Perhaps. In time. Look—"

"Did anything odd happen at rehearsal the day Caroline was killed? Does any incident stand out in your mind, however petty it might have seemed at the time?"

"No, not that I remember. Look, will you excuse me for a min? Have to pee."

"Of course."

Banks waited a moment or two, then attracted Teresa Pedmore's attention. Her hair was as dark as Faith's was silver. She had the healthy complexion of a young countrywoman, and it didn't surprise Banks to discover that she was a milk-man's daughter from Mortsett, now working in the main East-vale Post Office and living in town. But that was where her rusticity ended. The haughty tilt of her head when she spoke and her fierce, dark eyes had nothing to do with simple coun-try life. There was an aura of mystery about her; Banks found its source hard to pin down. Something to do with the econ-omy of her body language, perhaps, or the faintly sardonic tone of her voice. And she was ambitious; he could sense that from the start.

"It's about Caroline Hartley, isn't it?" she said before Banks could open his mouth. As she spoke, Banks noticed, she was looking over at James Conran, who was watching her with a frown on his face.

"Yes," Banks answered. "Can you tell me anything about her?"

Teresa shook her head. Coal-black hair danced about her shoulders. "I hardly knew her. Even less so than I thought at the time, according to the papers."

"I understand you were involved with Mr. Conran?"

"Who told you that? Faith?"

Banks shook his head. "Faith was subtly evasive. Were you?"

"What if I was? We're both single. James is fun once you get to know him. At least he was."

"And did Caroline Hartley spoil that fun for you?"

"Of course not. How could she?"

"Didn't he switch his attentions from you to her?"

"Look, I don't know who's been telling you all this, but it's rubbish. Or are you just making it up? James and I ended our little fling ages ago."

"So you weren't jealous of Caroline?"

"Not at all."

"How did Caroline behave among the other women in the cast?"

Teresa laughed, showing a set of straight white teeth rarely seen outside America. "I don't know what you're getting at."

"Was she close to anyone?"

"No. I thought she always seemed aloof. You know, friendly but distant. Casual."

"So you didn't like her very much."

"I can't say I cared one way or the other. Not that I'm glad she's . . . you know. This is only the second play the company's done since James took over, but it was Caroline's first. None of us knew her that well."

"How did she get the part?"

Teresa raised her dark, arched eyebrows. "Auditioned, I should think. Like everybody else."

"You didn't notice her form any close attachments to other women in the play?"

"There are only three of us. What are you trying to say, that I'm a lesbian too?"

Banks shifted in his seat. "No. No, I'd say that was very unlikely, wouldn't you?"

Slowly, she relaxed. "Well . . ."

"What about Faith?"

Teresa gave her cigarette a short, sharp flick with her thumbnail. "What did she tell you? I saw you talking to her."

"She told me nothing. That's why I'm asking you."

"There was nothing between them, I can assure you of that. Faith's as straight as I am." She took a breath, sipped some milky Pernod and water, then smiled. "As far as the others go, I don't think you've got much chance of finding a murderer among them, quite frankly. Malvolio's such a puritan prig he probably even whips himself for taking part in such a sinful hobby as acting. Sir Andrew's thick as pigshit—excuse my French—and Orsino's so wrapped up in himself he wouldn't notice if Samantha Fox waggled her boobs in front of his face."

Banks looked over at Orsino. He had muscular shoulders—clearly the fruits of regular weight-training—dark, wavy hair, hollow cheeks, bright eyes and an expression set in a permanent sneer, as if all he saw outside a mirror was unworthy of his regard.

"None of them three had much to do with Caroline anyway, as far as I noticed. They had some scenes together, but I never saw them communicate much off-stage. And you can forget the others, too. I know for a fact that Antonio's queer as a three-pound note, Sebastian's very happily married with a mortgage, a dog and two-point-five kids, and the Clown, well . . . he's very quiet actually, and he never seems to socialize with us."

"Have you ever noticed him talking to Caroline off-stage or between scenes?"

"I've never noticed him talking to anyone. Period. One of the strangest transformations you can imagine. A wonderful Clown, but such a dull, depressing-looking man."

Banks asked her a few more general questions but found out nothing else. Before long, Teresa was asking him about his most exciting cases and it was time to move on. He chatted briefly with some of the others but got no further. Finally, he went back to James Conran, excused himself from the company and walked out into the cold evening, but not before Faith Green managed to catch him at the door and slip him her telephone number.

Outside, Banks caught his breath at the cold. Bright stars stabbed pinpoints of light in the clear sky. Who, Banks wondered, had believed that the sky was just a kind of black-velvet curtain and the light of heaven beyond showed through the holes in it? The Greeks? Anyway, on nights like this it felt exactly that way.

There had been something wrong about his conversations in the Crooked Billet. He couldn't put his finger on it, but everything had seemed too easy, too chummy. Everyone he spoke to had been nervous, worried about something. He hadn't missed the way Faith excused herself before answering one of his questions, nor the way Teresa played with her cigarette when he asked her questions she didn't like. Those two would merit further talking to, definitely. Surely there must have been minor tiffs or conflicts among the cast of a play? According to the people he had talked to, it had all been happy families—much too squeaky clean for his liking. What were they covering up, and when had they decided to do so?

He put his headphones on. In winter they acted as earmuffs, too. The tape he had in was a collection of jazz pieces by the likes of Milhaud, Gershwin and Stravinsky performed by Simon Rattle and the London Sinfonietta. Tracy had bought him it for Christmas, clearly under instructions from Sandra. When Banks switched on the Walkman the erotic clarinet glissando at the opening of Gershwin's *Rhapsody in Blue* almost bowled him over. He turned down the volume and walked on.

The tree was still lit up outside the church in the market square, but there were no carol-singers in evidence this evening. The cobble-stones were icy and he had to step carefully. The blue lamp glowed coldly outside the police station. It was seven o'clock. Just time to drop in and see if any new information had turned up before going home for dinner.

He walked into the bustle of the police station and went straight upstairs to his office. Before he could even shut the door, Susan Gay called after him and entered.

Banks sat down and took his headphones off. "Anything new?"

"I followed up on the record shops," she said breathlessly. "Most of them are open now because they're having Boxing Week sales. Anyway, I've tracked down two copies of that *Luddite poori* thing sold in the past three weeks."

"Good work. Where from?"

"One from a small specialty shop in Skipton and another from the Classical Record Shop in Leeds. But there's more, sir," she went on. "It seemed a long shot, but I asked for a description of the purchaser in both instances?"

"And?"

"The Leeds shop, sir. Before I'd even started he told me who'd bought it. The salesman recognized him."

"Claude Ivers?"

"Yes, sir."

"Well, well, well," Banks said. "So he was lying after all. Why aren't I surprised? You've done a great job, Susan. In fact I think you deserve a day at the seaside tomorrow."

Susan smiled. "Yes, sir. Oh, and DS Richmond phoned from Barnard Castle with a message about Charles Cooper's alibi. It seems things are getting a bit complicated, doesn't it?"

SEVEN

I

A sea-mist clung to the coastline when Banks and Susan arrived in Redburn at eleven o'clock the next morning. Icy roads over the vale and freezing rain on the moors had made driving difficult all the way, and now, as they came down from the land to the sea, the clash of the two elements had produced a fog that reduced visibility to no more than a few yards.

Susan, Banks could tell, was surprised at being chauffeured by a senior officer. But she would soon learn. He preferred his own car because of the stereo and the generous mileage allowance, and he actually enjoyed driving in Yorkshire, even in poor conditions such as these. On the way, he had been listening to *Metamorphosen*, Richard Strauss's haunting string elegy for the bombing of the Munich Hoftheater, and he hadn't spoken much. He didn't know whether Susan liked the music. She had been as silent as he and had spent most of the journey looking out the window, lost in thought.

He parked the car outside the Lobster Inn again, and they made their way up the path to Ivers's cottage. The mist seemed to permeate everything, and by the time they got to the cottage they were glad of the fire blazing in the hearth.

Again it was Patsy Janowski who answered the door. This time, when Banks introduced Detective Constable Gay, her big brown eyes clouded with worry and fixed on the door handle. She was wearing tight jeans and a dark-green turtle-neck sweater. Her dark hair, which still fell almost to her eyes in a ragged fringe, was tied back in a pony-tail. Her smooth complexion was tinged with the kind of flush that a brisk walk in fresh weather brings.

"He'll be down in a few minutes," she said. "Sit down and warm yourselves. I'll make some tea."

"Shouldn't we go up, sir?" Susan asked when Patsy had left the room. "It'll give us an edge."

Banks shook his head. "He'll be no trouble. Besides, I want to talk to her alone first." They sat in the creaky wooden chairs near the fire, and Banks rubbed his hands in front of the flames. Although he had been wearing gloves on this trip, the chill seemed to have penetrated right through both leather and flesh. When he felt warm enough, he took off his over-coat and lit a cigarette. Warm air from the fire hooked the smoke and sucked it up the chimney.

Patsy returned with the tea-tray and set it down beside them. There was no fresh-made bread this time.

"What is it?" she asked, joining them by the fire. "Have you found the killer?"

Banks ignored her question and picked up his mug of tea. "Tell me," he asked, "where did you drive to when you left your parking spot behind the Lobster Inn the evening Caroline Hartley was killed?"

Patsy stared at his breast pocket, her eyes wide open and afraid, like a hunted doe's. "I . . . I. . . . You can't expect me to remember a particular night just like that. Days are much the same out here."

"I can imagine that, but it was the evening before my last visit. I asked you then, very specifically, where you'd been the night before, and you both told me you'd stayed in. Now I'm asking you again."

Patsy shrugged. "If I said I stayed in, I guess that's what I did."

"But you were seen leaving the car-park."

"It must have been someone else."

"I don't think so. Unless you're in the habit of lending out your car. Where did you go?"

She stirred a spoonful of sugar into her tea and gazed into the steaming mug as she spoke. "I don't remember going anywhere, but I might have gone for a drive early on. I sometimes do that. But I wouldn't have been gone long. There are some beautiful vantage points along the coast, but you have to drive out there, then walk a fair distance to find them."

"Even in this weather?"

"Sure. I'd hardly live here if I minded a bit of rough weather, would I? I like it when the sea gets all churned up."

She seemed to be regaining her composure, but Banks still didn't believe her story. "Why didn't you mention this little drive?" he asked.

She smiled at the fireplace. "It didn't seem important, I guess. I mean, it was nothing to do with what you were asking about."

"Did you go alone?"

She hesitated, then said, "Yes."

"Where was Mr. Ivers?"

"Back here, working."

"Then who was using *his* car?"

Her hand went to her mouth. "I . . . I don't understand . . ."

"It's simple, really, Ms. Janowski. His car was missing from its usual spot. If he was here working, who was using it?"

Patsy was saved from having to answer by the creak of the stairs as Ivers came down. He was dressed in much the same kind of baggy jeans and loose jersey as he had been on Banks's first visit, but this time he had combed back his longish gray hair. He ducked the low lintel beam and walked into the room, where his height and gaunt features commanded attention. The room had seemed crowded enough with three people in it, but with four it felt cluttered and claustrophobic.

"What's going on?" he asked, looking over at Patsy, who was squeezing her plump lower lip between her fingers and staring out the window.

Banks stood up. "Ah, Mr. Ivers. Please join us. Sit down."

"I hardly need to be invited to sit down in my own house," Ivers said, but he sat.

Banks lit another cigarette and leaned against the stone mantelpiece. Not a tall man himself, he wanted the advantage of height. Susan remained where she was, notebook in her lap. Ivers glanced nervously at her, but Banks didn't introduce them.

"We were just talking about memory," he said. "How deceptive it can be."

Ivers frowned. "I don't understand."

"Seems to be a lot of that about," Banks said.

"Mr. Ivers," Susan asked, "where did you drive to on the evening of December twenty-second?"

He stared at her but didn't appear to see her, then he turned toward Banks and gripped the arms of his chair. He thrust himself forward in as menacing a manner as possible. "What is this? What are you insinuating?"

Banks flicked a column of ash into the fire. "I'm just asking you a simple question," he said. "Where did you go?"

"I told you I didn't go anywhere."

"I know. But you were lying."

Ivers half rose. "Now look—"

Banks stepped forward and gently pushed him back. "No. You look. Let me save us all a lot of time and effort and tell you what happened."

Ivers settled back and fumbled for his pipe and tobacco in his pants pocket. Patsy poured him some tea and passed it over. Her hand was shaking. The corner of his thin mouth twitched for her in what was meant to be a reassuring smile.

"That evening," Banks began, "you decided to take Veronica her Christmas present. It was a record you bought for her at the Classical Record Shop in the Merrion Center in Leeds, Vivaldi's *Laudate pueri*, sung by Magda Kalmár, a singer you knew had impressed her. But when you got to the house, just after seven, say, she was out. Caroline Hartley answered the door and let you in. You were simply going to drop off the present, but something happened, something made you angry. Perhaps she said something about your virility, I don't know, or maybe the rage you felt about her stealing Veronica from you finally boiled over. You fought, hit her, then stabbed her with the kitchen knife you found on the table."

"Ingenious," Ivers said. "But not a word of it is true."

Banks knew full well that this theory was full of holes—the two female visitors Caroline Hartley had received *after* Ivers had apparently left, for example—but he went on regardless. He wanted to shake Ivers up a bit, at the very least.

"I don't know why you put the record on, but you did. Perhaps you wanted to make it look like the work of a psychopath. That could also have been why you removed her robe after you hit her. Anyway, when it was done, you washed the knife in the sink. I imagine you must have got blood on your gloves and sleeves, but it would have been easy enough to destroy that evidence when you got home." Banks flicked his cigarette end into the fire. "Right there."

Ivers shook his head and clamped his teeth down on his pipe.

"Well?" Banks said.

"No," he whispered between clenched teeth. "It didn't happen like that at all. I didn't kill her."

"Did you know that Caroline Hartley once had a baby?" Banks asked.

Ivers took his pipe out of his mouth in surprise. "What? No. All I know is that she was the bitch who corrupted my wife and induced her to leave me."

"Which gives you a very good motive for wanting rid of her," Susan said, looking up from her notebook.

Again Ivers looked at her but hardly appeared to see her.

"Perhaps so," he said. "But I'm not a killer. I create, I don't destroy."

Patsy leaned forward and took his hand in hers. With his other hand, he held onto his pipe.

"What happened?" Banks asked.

Ivers sighed and stood up. He stroked Patsy's cheek and

went to the fireplace, where he knocked out his pipe. He seemed more stooped and frail now, somehow, and his cultured voice no longer held its authoritative tone.

"You're right," he said, "I did go over to Eastvale that evening. I shouldn't have lied. I should have told you the truth. But when you told me what had happened, I was certain I'd be a suspect, and I was right, wasn't I? I couldn't bear the thought of any serious interruption of my work. But I swear, Chief Inspector, that when I left Caroline Hartley the little slut was as alive as you and I. Yes, I went to the house. Yes, Veronica was out shopping. Caroline let me in grudgingly, but she let me in because it was cold and snowing and she didn't want to leave the door open. I wasn't in there more than a few minutes. Out of politeness, I asked how she was and asked about Veronica, then I just handed over the present and left. And that's the truth, whether you believe it or not."

"I'd find it easier to believe if you'd told me the first time I called," Banks said. "You've wasted a lot of our time."

"I've already explained why I couldn't tell you. Good Lord, man, what would you have done in my position?"

Banks always hated it when people asked him that. In ninety-nine percent of cases he would have done exactly as they had: the wrong thing.

"How could you even imagine that we wouldn't trace the buyer of the record?"

Ivers shrugged. "I've no idea what you can or can't do. I don't read mystery novels or watch police shows on television. We don't even have a television. Never have had. I knew I hadn't put a gift tag on the record—I remembered I'd forgotten to do that shortly after I left Veronica's—so when you mentioned Vivaldi last time you called I had a good idea you were only guessing it was me. You never asked me outright whether I took her the record or not."

"When you left," Banks said, "was the record still wrapped or had it been opened?"

"Still wrapped, of course. Why should it have been opened?"

"I don't know. But it was. Could Caroline have opened it?"

"She may have done, just to have a laugh at me and my tastes, I suppose. She always said I was an old bore. She once told Veronica she thought my music sounded like the kind of sounds you'd get from a constipated camel."

If Ivers was telling the truth, Banks wondered, then how had the record come to be unwrapped? Unless either Caroline had opened it out of malicious curiosity—"Hello darling, look what the boring old fart's bought you for Christmas!"—or Veronica Shildon herself had returned to the house and opened it? But why would she do that with a Christmas present? Surely she would have put it under the tree with the rest and waited until the morning of the twenty-fifth? And she certainly wouldn't have done anything so mundane if she had walked into the room and found Caroline's body.

"Did you tell her what it was?" Banks asked.

"Not in so many words."

"What did you say?"

"Just that it was something very special for Veronica."

"How did Caroline react?"

"She didn't. She just glanced at it, and I put it down."

"Did you argue with her?"

Ivers shook his head. "Not this time, no. It was cool between us, but civilized. I've told you, I was out again within five minutes."

"What did you do then?"

"I drove over to the shopping center—I wanted to buy a few last minute things I couldn't get here in the village—then I came home."

"What things?"

Ivers frowned. "Oh, I can't remember. Books, a sweater Patsy wanted, a case of decent claret . . . that kind of thing."

"You didn't by any chance see your wife in the shopping center, did you?"

"No. I'd have mentioned it if I did. It's a fairly large place, you know, and it was very busy."

"Why did you go to Eastvale that night in particular?"

"Because it was so close to Christmas and Patsy and I . . . well, I always leave things till the last minute, and we just didn't want to have to go anywhere over the next few days. I'm very involved in a complex piece of music right now. It's all to do with the rhythms of the winter sea, so I don't want to spend more time than necessary away from here. I have no other commitments until after the new year, so I thought I'd get the shopping and Veronica's present out of the way, then my time would be my own." He returned to the chair and started to refill his pipe. "Believe me, it's nothing more sinister than that. I haven't killed anyone. I couldn't. Not even someone I hated the way I hated Caroline Hartley. If I'd been stupid enough to believe that killing Caroline would bring back Veronica, I'd have done it two years ago. But I've got a new life now, with Patsy. It's been tough getting here, but I've put Veronica behind me now."

"Yet you still took her a *special* Christmas present. Rather a sentimental gesture, wouldn't you say?"

"I never claimed to have no feelings for her. After so long, you can't help that. She put me through hell, but that's over." He took Patsy's hand. "I'm happier now than I've ever been."

It was the second time Banks had heard someone refer to having a motive for killing Caroline some years ago but not in the present. Ivers's story rang truer than Gary Hartley's, though. In the first place, Ivers obviously did have a comfortable life with an attractive younger woman, a cozy cottage by the sea and his music. Gary Hartley had nothing. On the other hand, Ivers could easily have lost his temper and lashed out at something Caroline said. Sometimes, after all the big things have been endured and overcome, some apparently inconsequential matter sets off an explosion. There was no real evidence pointing either way, though the use of a knife so close to hand indicated a spontaneous act. If he charged Claude Ivers with murder now, he wouldn't have much of a case.

"I'd like you to drop by the Eastvale police station tomorrow morning and sign a statement," Banks said, gesturing for Susan to close her notebook.

"Must I . . . ? My work . . ."

"Much as I love your music, Mr. Ivers," Banks said, "I'm afraid you must." He smiled. "Look at it this way, it's a hell of a lot better than being charged with murder and sitting in a cell with the drunks on New Year's Eve."

"You're not charging me?"

"Not yet. But I want you to stay where I can find you. Any unexpected moves on your part will be considered as very suspicious behavior indeed."

Ivers nodded. "I wasn't going anywhere."

"Good. See you tomorrow then."

Banks and Susan made their way back down the winding path to the car. On their left, only partially obscured by wraiths of mist, the sea lay quiet and the small waves lapped and hissed on the sands. Banks wondered what Ivers's winter sea music would sound like. Something along the lines of Peter Maxwell Davies's Third Symphony perhaps, or the "Sea Interludes" from Britten's *Peter Grimes*? There was certainly a lot of potential in the idea.

They had just reached the road when Banks became aware of a figure running after them. It was Patsy Janowski, and she hadn't even bothered to put an overcoat on. They turned, and she stood facing them, shivering, with her arms wrapped around her chest. "I need to talk to you." she said. "Please. It's really important."

Banks nodded. "Go on."

She looked around. "Is there somewhere we can go? I'm freezing."

They were outside the Lobster Inn, and Banks could think of no better place to talk. They went inside and found the lounge almost deserted except for the landlord and a couple of gnarled old men chatting at the bar. The large room was cold and drafty, even by the hearth where they sat. The fire clearly hadn't been lit long and the pub had not yet warmed up.

Banks walked to the bar. The two old men flicked their hooded eyes in his direction and continued talking in low voices, thick with local dialect. The landlord shuffled over and stood in front of Banks drying a glass. He neither spoke nor looked up. Banks found himself marveling at Jim Hatchley for getting information out of such a taciturn old bugger. One day he'd have to ask Jim how he'd managed it.

He asked for three whiskies and the landlord ambled off without a word. The entire transaction took place in silence. When he got back to the table, Banks found Patsy and Susan Gay huddled around the meager fire trying to get warm.

"It's not the cold I mind," Patsy was saying, "but the goddamn *chill*. It's so damp it gets right in your bones."

"Where are you from?" Banks asked.

"Huntington Beach, California."

"Warm there?"

Patsy managed a smile. "All year round. They even play beach volley-ball in winter. Don't get me wrong, though. I love England, even the weather. I'm just not dressed right for outdoors today."

Banks passed her the whiskey. "Here. This should warm the cockles of your heart, as we say up here."

"Thank you." She took a sip and smacked her lips. Her eyes ranged around the pub and settled briefly, like a butterfly, on various objects: a dented ashtray, the range of wine glasses above the bar, an optic, the old fishing print on the far wall.

Banks lit a cigarette and leaned back in his chair. "What was it you wanted to tell us?"

Patsy frowned. "I know it must seem too late to you, that we've told so many lies, but Claude was telling the truth just now, honest he was. We only lied because we knew he'd be the main suspect."

"You must have known we'd find out the truth sooner or later."

She shook her head. "Claude said it's only on television that things like that happen. Not in real life. Despite what he says, he *has* seen television in his life. He said policemen in real life are just thick." She put her hand to her mouth. "Oh shit, I'm sorry."

Banks smiled. "Where *did* you drive to that night?"

"Well, that's just what I came out to tell you. I know Claude can't have killed Caroline Hartley because I went to see her after he'd left, and I can assure you she was still alive then."

"What do you mean?"

Patsy rubbed her temple and frowned. "What I say. Look, I know it's not very nice, but I was . . . well, checking up on him."

"You suspected he was still involved with Veronica Shildon?"

"Yes. He still loves her, there's no doubt about that. You heard what he said. But I did hope he really had put her behind him . . . and I know he loves me, too. I suppose I'm just jealous, possessive. I've been burned before by people hung up on past relationships."

"Did you know him when he split up with her?"

"No. We met afterwards. He was in real bad shape."

"In what way?"

"In every way. Claude is a naturally confident man, used to getting what he wants and having his own way, but after he split with Veronica his self-esteem was at rock-bottom. He felt betrayed and . . . well . . . sexually, too, he felt worthless and unwanted. He told me he never thought another woman would want him as long as he lived." She smiled and looked into the fire. "I know it sounds like a come-on, but it wasn't. You have to know him. When we got together I helped him build up his confidence again. There was nothing wrong with him, not really. It was all just the psychological mess caused by what that woman did to him."

"Caroline?"

"No, Veronica. He always blamed Caroline, and I never contradicted him. But if anyone's the bitch, Veronica is, the way she treated him. All of a sudden, she comes along and tells him, 'I'm not really the woman you think I am. In fact,

I never have been. It's all been an illusion, an act, just to please you. But I can't do it anymore. I've seen the light. I've found someone else—a woman, in fact—and I'm leaving you to go and live with her.' I'm sure you can imagine the impact of something like that on a man better than I can. Especially a man as sensitive and vulnerable as Claude. The bitch! Anyway, he never saw it that way. He always saw Caroline as the enemy, the wife-stealer, and Veronica as the victim. He thought she'd end up getting hurt, discarded, when Caroline had finished with her. After all, there was ten years between them." She held up her hand before anyone could say a word. "All right, I know. I know. I'm nobody to talk. There are nearly thirty years between Claude and me. But that's different."

Nobody challenged her. Banks had almost finished his whiskey. He felt like another one. A single shouldn't put him over the limit for driving. This time Susan offered to go buy the drinks.

"What are you trying to say, Ms. Janowski?" Banks asked, swirling the amber gold in the bottom of the glass. "That you were jealous of Claude Ivers's relationship with his wife and that you followed him that night to find out if he was still seeing her secretly?"

"I didn't exactly follow him," she said. "You've got to understand how difficult all this has been, Claude and me. We've had one or two rows about his seeing Veronica, usually after he's been for dinner with her and got back late. I don't know . . . as I said, I must be a terribly jealous person, but I couldn't just sit back and accept it. Oh, it's not even as if I thought they were having an affair or anything. Sometimes an emotional attachment to another person can seem like just as much of a threat or betrayal as a sexual one— maybe even more so. Can you understand that?" Banks nodded. Susan came back with the drinks. "Anyway," Patsy went on, "he didn't tell me where he was going that evening, and I figured because of the rows we'd had, he was keeping it from me, you know, that he was going to see *her*. That got me all worried. I just couldn't stay in the house alone, so I decided to call at Veronica's to see if I was right."

"And what happened?"

"I couldn't see his car anywhere. You can't park in the street, of course, but it wasn't even anywhere in sight on King Street. Then I finally plucked up my courage and went to the house. I knocked on the door and Caroline Hartley answered. I didn't think she'd recognize me because we'd hardly met, but she did. She must be very good with faces. She asked me in, but I didn't want to go. I asked her if Claude was in the house and she laughed. She told me he had called but Veronica was out and he clearly hadn't wanted to spend a minute longer than he had to with her. He'd left his present and gone. I thanked her and went back to the car. Then I drove home. That's all."

"What time did you arrive at the house?"

"About a quarter after seven, twenty after, maybe. It took about an hour and a quarter to drive from Redburn, then five minutes or so to walk from where I parked the car."

"Did you see anyone else approaching the house as you left?"

Patsy shook her head. "No, I don't think so. The street was quiet. I . . . I can't really remember. There were a few people in King Street, shoppers. I'm so confused about it."

"Think," Banks said. "Try to rerun the scene in your mind. Let us know if you remember anything at all. It could be important. Will you try?"

Patsy nodded. "All right."

"Was Mr. Ivers in when you got home?"

"No. He got back later with the shopping."

"Didn't you ask where he'd been?"

"Yes. We had a row. A bad one. But we made up." She blushed and looked into the fireplace.

Banks lit a cigarette and let a few moments pass, then he asked, "How did Caroline Hartley seem when you saw her?"

Patsy shrugged. "Fine, I guess. I never really thought about it. She was obviously being sarcastic about Claude, but that's only to be expected."

"She didn't seem worried or frightened when she answered the door?"

"Not at all."

"What was she wearing?"

"Some sort of kimono-style bathrobe, as if she'd just come out of the shower or something."

"Could you hear music playing?"

"No."

"Can you remember exactly what she said to you?"

Patsy sipped some whiskey and frowned. "Just that he'd been and gone and left some boring classical record for Veronica. That's all."

"She knew what the present was?"

"Seemed to, yes. She didn't mention the title, the one you talked about the other day, but she did use the words 'boring classical record.' I remember that because I took it as an insult to Claude."

"She could have been just guessing," Susan said. "After all, Mr. Ivers *is* a classical musician, and he knows Veronica's tastes. He'd hardly be likely to bring her the Rolling Stones or something, would he?"

"Possibly not," Banks said. "Either that, or she'd opened it to see what was so special that she didn't know about. Anyway, it doesn't matter for now." He turned back to Patsy. "What happened next?"

"Nothing. I told you. I left and drove home."

Banks stubbed out his cigarette and looked closely at her. She stared back defiantly, lips close together, eyes serious. "Look," she said, "I know what you're thinking. I didn't kill her. Think about it. I'd hardly do that, would I? With her out of the way there was more chance of my losing Claude back to Veronica, wasn't there?"

It made a kind of sense, but Banks knew that murders are rarely so logically committed. Still, he felt inclined to believe her for the moment. For one thing, her story tallied with what the neighbors had seen: one man—Ivers, obviously—and two women. The one who had simply knocked at the door like a salesperson had been Patsy, then, asking after Ivers. And unless she had returned later, she was in the clear.

So if Patsy was the first woman visitor, and she was telling the truth, then who was the next: Faith Green? Teresa Pedmore? Veronica herself? Ruth, the mystery woman from London? Or had someone called even later than the last woman, someone none of the neighbors had seen? A man? It was possible. Gary Hartley? James Conran? Someone else from the Dramatic Society? The father of Caroline's child? A psychopath? Even Ivers himself could have returned. He hadn't been home when Patsy got back to Redburn. Banks made a note to question the neighbors again and see if he could get a better description. It was unlikely, especially after so much time had elapsed, but still worth a try. At least someone might be able to tell them whether the woman who had knocked at the door and gone away was dressed the same as the one who did go in later.

Banks finished his drink. "Thank you, Ms. Janowski," he said. "I think you'd better come along tomorrow with Mr. Ivers and make a statement, all right?"

She nodded. "Yes, yes, of course." Then she knocked back the rest of her drink and left.

"What do you think?" Banks asked Susan.

"I don't know. I'd want to keep an eye on them."

"Maybe I'll ask Jim Hatchley to drop by once or twice over the next few days and make sure they're not up to anything. Any ideas about what did happen that night?"

Susan paused, took a delicate sip of whiskey, then said, "I've been wondering about Veronica Shildon. I know she doesn't seem to have a motive, but I can't help but keep coming back to her. Maybe everything wasn't as wonderful as she made out between her and Caroline Hartley. I mean, what if she was jealous? What if she saw Patsy Janowski leaving the house and thought there was something to it? Maybe there even *was* something to it. Caroline Hartley could have taken her own robe off, and if Veronica had found her naked. . . . She could have charged in, had a row with Caroline and killed her. Then she could have changed her clothes, sneaked out and come back later."

They walked out into the cold and sat in the car while it warmed up. "It's possible," Banks said. "But we checked the entire house for blood-stained clothing and found nothing. There were no pieces of charred cloth in the fire either. I'm not saying she couldn't have found a way, just that I haven't figured it out yet. We seem to have too many suspects. Too many motives, opportunities." He slammed the wheel with the flat of his hand. "I still keep coming back to that damn record, though. Why? Why would somebody put a record on and leave it to repeat?"

"Perhaps Caroline herself put it on."

"She hated classical music. She may have opened it, but I doubt she'd have played it."

"But if Veronica had come back . . . ?"

"If it happened the way you suggest, and she'd seen Patsy leaving, she'd have been on the warpath. She'd hardly have stopped to listen to her Christmas present first, especially on December twenty-second. No. It doesn't make sense." He spoke quietly, almost to himself. "But the music is for the burial of a very small child. Caroline's child could be anything up to nine or ten by now. Maybe if I can track the kid down . . ."

"That's if whoever put the record on knew what it was, knew what it meant."

"Oh, the killer knew all right, I'm sure of that."

"Are you sure you're not making too much of it, sir?"

"I might be. But you've got to admit it's a puzzle."

"Talking about records, sir . . ."

"Yes?"

"Do you think you could play something different on the way back? I don't mean to be rude, sir, but that music you were playing on the way over was so boring it nearly put me to sleep."

Banks laughed and drove off. "Your wish is my command."

II

"Well, well, well, if it isn't Mr. Banks. It's a rare treat seeing you in here."

"Sorry, vicar. There's something about my job that disinclines me to believe in a benevolent deity."

"You catch your criminals sometimes, don't you?"

"Yes."

"Well, there you are. The Lord works in mysterious ways."

The Reverend Piers Catcott's eyes twinkled. He was a slight man in his late forties, who looked more like an accountant than a minister: thick spectacles, thinning silver hair, slight stoop and an anemic, well-scrubbed complexion. He was also, Banks had discovered from their discussions and arguments over pints in the Queen's Arms, an extraordinarily erudite and intelligent man. Pity, Banks thought, about the superstition he deemed fit to embrace.

"Still," Catcott said, "I don't think you made the supreme sacrifice of entering this hallowed place just to argue theology, did you?"

Banks smiled. "That's right, vicar. We can do that much better in the pub. No, it's just some background information I want. Knowledge, rather. I want to pick your brains."

"Oh dear, I should think that'll be much more comfortable sitting down. That is if you've no objection to taking a pew. Or we could go into the vestry?"

"A pew'll do fine," Banks said, "as long as you don't expect me to kneel."

The small church was dim and cool. Weak evening sunlight filtered through the stained-glass windows. Banks had seen more of it from the outside than in, though he had been in once or twice to look at the Celtic cross and stone font. The pews creaked as they sat down.

"What's the liturgy?" Banks asked.

"Oh, come on, Mr. Banks," Catcott said with a thin-lipped smile. "Surely even a heathen like yourself knows that?"

"Humor me."

Catcott put a pale, slender forefinger to his lips. "Very well. The liturgy. The word is often used to refer to the Book of Common Prayer, of course, but the meaning goes back a long time beyond that, a long time. Essentially, it's simply the order of services in the church. As even you probably know, we have different services at different times of the year—Christmas, Easter, Harvest Festival and the like. And, you might remember from your misspent youth, we sing different hymns and have different lessons according to the nature of the service. Do you follow so far?"

Banks nodded.

"There is a liturgical calendar to cover the year's worship. Advent, the fourth Sunday before Christmas, came first, then Christmas itself, ending with Epiphany, the sixth of January, or twelfth night, to you. Then we have the Pre-Lenten season, followed by Lent, when you're supposed to give up bad habits—" Here he paused and cast a narrow-eyed look at Banks, "—and the last three are Eastertide, Pentecost and Trinity. But what on earth do you want to know all this for? Surely you're not thinking of—"

"No, I'm not. And believe me, vicar, you'd be better off not knowing. I'm particularly interested in the music that goes along with these services."

"Liturgical music? Well, that's a slightly different matter. It's very complicated. Goes back to Gregorian chant. But basically, each part of the year has its own biblical texts, and early composers set these to music. People still do it, of course—Vaughan Williams, Finzi and Britten did quite a bit—but it's rarely part of a normal church service these days. What you're probably talking about are biblical texts, or parts of texts, set to music. Actually, most of them were abolished in 1563."

"What kind of music are you talking about?"

"All kinds, right from early polyphonic motets. A composer would take a text, perhaps a psalm, and set it to music. In Latin, of course."

"Like a *Gloria* or a *Magnificat*?"

"Actually, the *Gloria* is part of the Mass, which has its own liturgy. I told you, it can get quite complicated."

Banks remembered the section titles from his tapes of masses and requiems: *Kyrie Eleison, Agnus Dei, Credo.* "I think I'm getting the idea," he said. "What about *Laudate pueri*?"

"Ah, yes, '*Laudate pueri, Dominum . . .*' It means 'Praise the Lord, ye children.' That was a popular liturgical work. Based on Psalm 112, if my memory serves me right."

"Do you know Vivaldi's settings?"

"Indeed I do. Magnificent."

"It says in the notes to my tape that the piece may have been used as part of the burial service for a small child. Is that right?"

Catcott rubbed his smooth chin. "That would make sense, yes."

"Would that be fairly common knowledge?"

"Well, *you* knew it, didn't you? I'd say any reasonably well-educated person might have a chance of knowing."

"Would someone like Claude Ivers know?"

"Ivers? Of course. I remember reading an article about him in *Gramophone* and he's extremely knowledgeable about sacred music. Pity he doesn't see fit to write any himself instead of that monotonous stuff he churns out."

Banks smiled. Catcott had sown the seeds of another Queen's Arms argument, but there was no time to pursue the point now.

"Thank you, vicar." Banks stood up and shook hands with Catcott, then headed out. His footsteps echoed on the cold stone. Just before he got to the door he heard the vicar call out from behind him, "The collection box for the restoration fund is to your right."

Banks felt in his pocket for a pound, dropped it in the box and left.

III

Fortunately, Charles Cooper was at home when Banks and Richmond called just after tea-time that day. Mrs. Cooper flitted about the kitchen offering coffee, but Banks suggested he and Richmond retire with her husband somewhere private. Mrs. Cooper seemed worried by that, but she raised no real objection. They settled for the living room, dominated by a huge television screen, and Richmond took out his notebook.

Cooper, Banks noticed, looked a few years older than his wife. He had a weak chin and a veined nose; his sparse gray hair was combed straight back. He was an odd shape, mostly skin and bone with rounded shoulders, but he had a substantial pot-belly bulging through his gray pullover.

"It's a pleasure to meet you at last," said Cooper. "Of course, I've heard all about the business from my wife. Dreadful."

He seemed nervous and fidgety, Banks thought, though his tone seemed calm and genuine enough.

"What did you do on the evening of December twenty-second?" Banks asked.

"I worked," Cooper said with a sigh. "I seemed to do nothing else around that time."

"I understand you're general manager of a chain of toy shops?"

"That's right."

"And on the twenty-second you were dealing with some stock shortages in the Barnard Castle branch?"

Cooper nodded.

"What time did you leave?"

He paused. "Well, let me see . . . I got home about eleven."

"Yes, but what time did you leave the shop?"

"It's about a half-hour drive, a little slower in the snow. I suppose it'd be about ten-fifteen."

"You left the shop at ten-fifteen and came straight home?"

"Why, yes. Look, is—"

"Are you sure, Mr. Cooper?"

Cooper looked toward the sideboard and nervously licked his lips. "I ought to know," he said.

Richmond glanced up from his notes. "It's just that the lady who works there told me you left about six, Mr. Cooper. Would she have any reason to lie?"

Cooper looked from Richmond to Banks and back. "I . . . I don't understand."

Banks leaned forward. "It's perfectly simple," he said. "You left the shop at six o'clock, not at ten-fifteen, as you led us to believe. What were you doing all that time?"

Cooper pursed his lips and looked down at the liver-spots on the backs of his hands.

"What was your relationship with Caroline Hartley?" Banks asked.

"What do you mean?" he said. "I didn't have a relationship with her."

"Were you fond of her?"

"I suppose so. We were just acquaintances."

"She didn't remind you of your late daughter, Corinne?"

Cooper turned red. "I don't know who told you that, but it's not true. And you've no right to bring my daughter into it. It's exactly as I said. We were neighbors. Yes, I liked the girl, but that's all."

"You didn't attempt to start an affair with her?"

"Don't be ridiculous! She was young enough to be my. . . . Besides, you know as well as I do she wasn't interested in men."

"But you did try?"

"I did no such thing." He grasped the chair arms and started to get up. "I think you ought to leave now."

"We'll leave when we're satisfied, Mr. Cooper," Banks said. "Please sit down."

Cooper slumped back in his chair and started twisting his hands in his lap.

"Do have a drink if you want," Banks said. "That *is* what's on your mind, isn't it?"

"Damn you!" Cooper jumped up with surprising agility, took a bottle of Scotch from the sideboard and poured himself three fingers. He didn't offer any to Banks or Richmond. He sat down again and drank off half of it in one gulp.

"We're not satisfied yet, Mr. Copper," Banks said. "We're not satisfied at all. You've been lying to us. Now, that's nothing new. In our business we expect it." He jerked his thumb toward the wall. "But a young woman was brutally murdered next door on December twenty-second, a woman you liked, who reminded you of your daughter. Now I'd think that unless you killed her yourself you'd want to help, you'd want to tell us the truth."

"I didn't kill her, for God's sake. Why on earth would I do that?"

"You tell me."

"I told you, I didn't kill her. And whatever I did that night has no bearing whatsoever on what happened next door."

"Let me be the judge of that."

Cooper swirled his drink and took another long sip.

"We'll stay until you tell us," Banks said. "Unless you'd prefer to get your coat and—"

"All right, all right." Cooper waved his free hand. "I did leave the shop at six, but I wasn't anywhere near Eastvale until eleven, I swear it."

"Where were you?"

"Does it really matter?"

"We have to check."

Cooper got up and poured himself another drink. He cocked his ear toward the living room door, then, satisfied by the sound of washing-up water running in the kitchen, spoke quietly.

"I drink, Mr. Banks," he said. "Simple as that. Ever since Corinne . . . well, you don't need to know about that. But Christine doesn't approve." He looked at his glass. "Oh, she's not a teetotaller or anything. She'll allow the occasional glass of Scotch after dinner, but more than one and I can even smell the disapproval. So I drink elsewhere."

"Where were you drinking that night?" Banks asked.

"Tan Hill," said Cooper. "It's an isolated spot. I like it up there."

"Were you alone?"

"No. There's a group of regulars."

"Names?"

Cooper gave the names and Richmond wrote them down.

"What time did you leave?"

"About ten-thirty. I daren't be *too* late. And I keep some breath mints in the car so she can't smell anything."

"Anything else to tell us?"

Cooper shook his head. "No, nothing. That's it. Look, I'm sorry, I . . . I didn't mean to cause any problems. It's really nothing to do with poor Caroline's death at all."

"We'll see," said Banks, and got up to leave with Richmond.

"There is one small thing," Cooper said before they got to the door.

Banks turned. "Yes?"

"The driving. I mean, I'd had a few drinks. I wasn't drunk, honestly. You won't do anything to my license, will you?"

"I shouldn't worry about that," Banks said. "I think the statute of limitations has just about run out." He made a mental note to find out the license number of Cooper's car and alert the local police patrols.

"Fancy a trip to Tan Hill?" Banks asked Richmond outside.

"Tonight?"

"Sooner the better, don't you think?"

Richmond looked at his watch and frowned. "Well, I did have a . . . er—"

"Take her with you," Banks said. "It's a routine inquiry. Won't take long."

Richmond touched his mustache. "Not a bad idea," he said. "Not bad at all."

"Off you go then. I'll see if I can get anything more out of the people over the street."

IV

It was a cold night—spiky, needle-sharp cold rather than the damp, numbing chill of the sea-mist—and the crusts of ice over puddles on the pavements cracked as Banks walked over them, hands deep in his fur-lined car-coat pockets. He decided to call first on Patrick Farlowe, who had originally said he was sure he had noticed two women and a man call at the house on separate occasions between about six- and seven-thirty on December 22.

Farlowe was finishing off his meal when Banks arrived, and there was still a little wine left in the bottle. Banks accepted a glass and the invitation to join Farlowe in the den while his wife cleared the table. They certainly lived well in Oakwood Mews, Banks noted: remains of sirloin steaks on the plates, fine cutlery, a cut-glass vase holding two long-stemmed roses. The wine was a decent Crozes-Hermitage.

The den was an upstairs study with two walls of dark bookcases, a deep, leather armchair by a standard lamp and a small teak table beside it for resting cups of coffee, pencils and notepads. The light gleamed on the dark, varnished surfaces of the wood. The Hartley place in Harrogate would have been a larger version of this, Banks thought, before Gary let it fall to ruin.

Farlowe relaxed in his armchair and Banks took the swivel chair in front of the writing-desk. One sniff of the clean, leather-scented air tipped him off that this was a non-smoking room.

"We're very grateful for the information you gave us," Banks began, "but I was just wondering if you remembered anything else about that evening."

Farlowe, a small, roly-poly man with tufts of gray hair over his ears, still wearing a three-piece suit, pressed his damp lips together and scratched the side of his nose. Finally he shook his head. The roll of pink fat around his neck wobbled. "Can't say as I do, no."

"Do you mind if we go over a couple of points?"

"Not at all. Be pleased to."

Banks sipped some wine and asked about the timing.

Farlowe strained to remember for a moment, then answered. "I know the first one, the man, called at about seven o'clock because we'd just had supper and I was in the front room turning the Christmas-tree lights on. Then I caught a glimpse of the woman standing on the doorstep when I went to replace a burned-out bulb a bit later. The door was open and she was talking to the Hartley woman."

"Did you get a clear look at her?"

"No. She had her back to me. Nicely shaped, though."

"So there's no doubt it was a woman?"

"None at all."

"What was she wearing?"

He put a pudgy finger to his lips and whistled while trying to recall the scene. "Let me see. . . . It was a winter jacket of some kind, padded or thickly lined. Waist-length, no longer, because I could see the outline of her hips. That's how I knew it was a woman. A youngish one, I'd say. And she wore tight jeans. Lovely long legs she had." He winked.

"What about her hair?"

"It was wrapped in a scarf. I really couldn't see it at all. And she was silhouetted by the hall light of the house, of course, so I couldn't make out any detail. It was only a quick glimpse I got. I already told all this to your constable the other night."

"I know, and I'm sorry to put you through it again, sir. Sometimes, believe it or not, people do remember more when they're given a few days to think about it. What was Caroline Hartley wearing?"

"As far as I could tell, it was some kind of bathrobe. She held it wrapped tight around her while she stood at the door, as if she was feeling the cold. I'm sorry I can't be of any more help. I'd like to see the blighter caught, of course. Don't like the idea of a murderer stalking the neighborhood."

"The third visitor," Banks asked. "Can you be clearer about the time?"

"I have given the matter some thought," Farlowe said, reaching for a decanter on the table beside him. "Port?"

Banks tossed back the rest of his wine and held his glass out. "Please. And . . . ?"

"I'm trying to recollect why I was at the front window again, but it's slipped my mind. Perhaps I'd heard a noise or something . . ." He tapped the side of his head. "That's it! I remember. I heard some music and I went out to see if we had carol-singers in the street. Plagued by them we are." He made them sound like an infestation of rodents. "I consider I've handed out my fair share this year. Should be restricted to Christmas Eve, if you ask me. Anyway, it was only the wife, putting the radio on."

"Do you remember the time?"

"No. All I remember, now I come to think about it, is hearing 'Away in a Manger' and heading for the window. But there was no one at our door. I noticed a woman going into the house over the street, the house where the woman was murdered."

"Can you add anything to your earlier description?"

"I'm sorry. It all happened so fast. I have to admit, I was rather angry at the thought of more singers and I just caught the figure out of the corner of my eye."

"But you're sure it was a woman?"

"Well, this one was wearing a light coat, belted, I think, because it came in at the waist, right down to mid-calves, and she definitely didn't have any trousers on. I thought I could see the bottom of a dress or skirt, too, as if the coat was just a bit too short to cover the dress. And you could see her legs below that."

"What about height? Any idea?"

"A little taller than the woman who answered the door, Caroline Hartley."

"Hair?"

He shook his head. "Again, her head was covered by a scarf of some kind."

"And this woman definitely entered the house?"

"Oh, yes. She was walking in when I saw her."

"So you didn't notice Caroline Hartley's reaction to seeing her?"

"No, not at all. I didn't even see Caroline that time, just this other woman silhouetted as she walked in the door."

"So Caroline might not have let her in?"

"I suppose that's possible. But there didn't seem anything suspicious about it. She didn't seem to be pushing, and I didn't hear any noise of forced entry or anything like that. It all seemed perfectly normal to me. I try to be a responsible neighbor. If I'd thought there was any trouble I would have called the police."

"Did you see her leave?"

"No. But then I didn't look out the window again. Anybody could have arrived or left between seven-thirty and the time when . . . well, you know . . . and I wouldn't have seen them."

Banks finished his port and stood up. "Thank you for being so co-operative, Mr. Farlowe. Also for the port. It was very good."

Farlowe smiled. "Yes, it is, rather, isn't it. Sixty-three vintage, you know." He struggled to get out of his armchair, floundering like a seal on a beach.

"Please don't bother showing me out," Banks said. "I'll find my own way."

"Oh, very well. Fine, then. Bye." And Banks saw Mr. Farlowe reach for the decanter again as he left the room. A suitable case for gout, that one. A lot of tipplers, it seemed, on Oakwood Mews.

On the way out, he met Mrs. Farlowe in the hall. She had seen nothing that night, but she was able to tell him that the radio had been tuned to Radio Three, as always, when she turned it on. No, she couldn't remember what time, but her husband was right. It was a carol service from King's College. "Away in a Manger" had been playing. Lovely tune, that one, isn't it? Banks agreed and left.

From Mrs. Eldridge at number eight Banks got no further information. She had seen the man go in first, then the woman knocking on the door at about seven-fifteen. No, she hadn't seen the man leave in the meantime, but the woman in the short coat and tight jeans definitely didn't enter the house. And it wasn't the same woman as the one who called later. This one was a bit taller and dressed differently. Some kind of long dress under her coat instead of jeans. The way it looked, unless Patsy Janowski had dashed off, changed clothes and added a few inches to her height in the interim, the third visitor couldn't possibly have been her.

He needed to know who this third woman was. Unless someone else had come after her, someone nobody had seen arrive, or unless Claude Ivers had been in the house all the time and nobody had seen him leave, then she was the one, almost certainly, who had killed Caroline Hartley. Was it Veronica Shildon, as Susan had suggested? Banks didn't think so—her love and grief seemed genuine—but he needed to talk to her again. There was a lot of ground yet to cover before he could hope to understand the people, and therefore the motives, involved in this case.

There was, however, one small, practical piece of information he carried away with him. Both Mr. and Mrs. Farlowe had said that the third woman entered the house—bidden or otherwise—when "Away in a Manger" was being played on Radio Three. It should be possible to find out from the local BBC station what time the program started, the order of carols in the concert and the length of each one. Given that information, it would be simple to work out at exactly what time the mysterious third woman had entered Caroline Hartley's house and, in all likelihood, stabbed her to death with a kitchen knife.

EIGHT

I

Banks walked slowly by the river. He wore his fur-lined suede car-coat, collar up, hands thrust deep in his pockets. As he walked, he breathed out plumes of air. The river wasn't entirely frozen over; ducks paddled as usual, apparently oblivious to the cold, in channels between the lumps of gray ice.

As he walked, he thought about the success he had had that morning with the BBC. A keen young researcher in the local studio took the trouble to dig out and listen to the December 22 taped carol broadcast, using a stop-watch. The program had started at seven sharp. "Away in a Manger" began just over midway through the broadcast—7:21, to be exact—and finished two minutes, fourteen seconds later. Banks marveled at the precision. With such a sense of exact measurement, the young woman perhaps had a future working for the Guinness Book of Records or the Olympic Records Committee. Anyway, they now knew that Caroline's likely killer had been let in between 7:21 and 7:24.

They also knew that it wasn't Charles Cooper. Richmond had talked to the regulars at Tan Hill and confirmed his alibi: Cooper had been drinking there between about six-thirty and ten-thirty on December 22, and on most other evenings leading up to the Christmas period. It would be more difficult for him to explain long absences to his wife at any other time, Banks thought.

Banks started thinking about the victim, Caroline Hartley, again and realized he still didn't know much about her. She had run away from home at sixteen, gone to London, got herself pregnant, picked up a conviction for soliciting, come back up north and shacked up first with Nancy Wood, who was out of the picture now, and then with Veronica Shildon. Attractive to both men and women—but now interested only in the latter—vivacious and enthusiastic, but given to thoughtful, secretive moods, a budding actress, a good mimic. That was about all. It covered ten years of the woman's life, and it didn't add up to a hell of a lot. There had to be more, and the only place to find out—as Caroline's friends and family either wouldn't talk or didn't know—was in London. But where to start?

Banks picked up a flat stone and skimmed it across the water toward The Green. Briefly, he thought of Jenny Fuller, who lived in one of the Georgian semis there. A lecturer in psychology at York, she had helped Banks before. She would be damn useful in this case, too, he thought. But she'd gone away somewhere warm for Christmas. Tough luck.

Up ahead, near the bridge, Banks saw a boy, no older than twelve or thirteen. He had a catapult and was aiming pebbles at the ducks out on the river. Banks approached him. Before saying a word, he took out his identity card and let the boy have a good long look.

The boy read it, then glanced up at Banks and said, "Are you really a copper or just one of those perverts? My dad's warned me about blokes like you."

"Lucky for you, sonny, I'm really a copper," Banks said, and snatched the metal catapult from the boy's hand.

"Hey! What you doing? That's mine."

"That's a dangerous weapon is what that is," Banks said, slipping it in his coat pocket. "Think yourself lucky I don't take you in. What do you want to go aiming at those ducks for anyway? What harm have they ever done you?"

"Dunno," the kid said. "I wasn't meaning to kill them or

anything. I just wanted to see if I could hit one. Can I have my catapult back, mister?"

"No."

"Go on. It cost me a quid, that did. I saved up out of my pocket money."

"Well don't bother saving up for another," Banks said, walking away.

"It's bloody daylight robbery," the kid called after him. "You're no better than a thief!"

But Banks ignored him, and soon the shouting died down. There was something in what the boy had said that interested him: "I wasn't meaning to kill them or anything. I just wanted to see if I could hit one."

Could he really divorce the action from its result as cleanly and innocently as that? And if he could, could a murderer, too? There was no doubt that whoever plunged the knife into Caroline Hartley's body had meant her to be dead, but had that been the killer's original intention? The bruise on the cheek indicated that she had been hit, perhaps stunned, first. How had that come about? Was it the kind of thing a woman would do, punch another woman?

Could it have been some kind of sexual encounter gone out of control, with the original object not so much murder but just a desire to see how far things could go? A sado-masochistic fantasy turned reality, perhaps? After all, Caroline Hartley had been naked. But that was absurd. Veronica and Caroline were respectable, middle-class, conservative lesbians; they didn't cruise the gay bars or try to lure innocent schoolgirls back to the house for orgies, like the lesbians one read about in lurid tabloids. Still, when lovers fight, no matter what sex, they can easily become violent toward one another. What happened between the punch and the stabbing? What warped sequence of emotions did the killer feel? Caroline must have been unconscious, or at least momentarily stunned, and the killer must have picked up the knife, which lay so conveniently on the table by the cake.

What made her do it? Would she have done it if the knife

hadn't been so close to hand? Would she have gone into the kitchen and taken a knife from the drawer and still had the resolve when she got back to the living room? Impossible questions to answer—the kind that Jenny might have been able to help with—but they had to be answered or he would never find the key to this problem. Banks needed to know what happened in the dark area, what it was that pushed someone beyond argument, past reason, past sex, beyond even simple physical assault, to murder.

He turned his back on the river and started walking up the hill by the formal gardens back around the castle to the market square. Back at the station, as soon as he turned from the stairwell to the corridor that led to his upstairs office, he saw Susan Gay come rushing toward him with a sheet of paper flapping in her hand. She looked like the cat that had got the cream. Her eyes gleamed with success.

"Found her," she announced. "Ruth. It's a small London publishing company, Sappho Press. I faxed them the photo and they said they had it taken for a dust jacket and for general publicity."

"Good work," Banks said. "Tell me, what made you call that particular press out of the dozens we had listed?"

Susan looked puzzled. "I got as far as 'S' in the alphabet. It took me all morning."

"Do you know who Sappho was?"

Susan shook her head.

Gristhorpe would have known, Banks thought, but you could hardly demand a degree in classics of everyone who wanted to join the police. On the other hand, perhaps it wouldn't be a bad idea: an elite squad of literary coppers.

"She was an ancient Greek poet from the isle of Lesbos," he said.

"Is that . . . ?" Susan began.

Banks nodded.

She blushed. "Well I'd like to say I got the literary clue, like in Agatha Christie," she said, "but it was down to pure hard slog."

Banks laughed. "Well done anyway. Tell me the details."

"Her name's Ruth Dunne and apparently she's published a couple of books. Doing very well for herself in the poetry scene. The woman I spoke to said one of the bigger publishers might be after her soon. Faber and Faber perhaps."

"What kind of stuff does she write?"

"Well, that's another thing. They told me she started by writing the kind of thing the Sappho Press people support. I assumed it was feminist stuff, but now you mention it. . . . Anyway, she's moved away from that, they said, and it looks like she's shifting into a broader market, whatever that means."

"Did you mention Caroline Hartley?"

"Yes. It's a funny thing. The editor recognized the name. She went to check and then told me Ruth Dunne's second book was dedicated to someone called Caroline. I thought it was odd we didn't find a copy among the victim's things, don't you?"

"She liked to travel light," Banks said. "Still, it would have made it a lot easier for us if we had. Maybe they just lost touch with one another."

Susan passed the paper over. "Anyway, she lives in Kennington. Here's the address. What now?"

"I'm going down there tomorrow. There's a few things I want to talk to Ruth Dunne about. She's the only link we have so far with Caroline Hartley's child and her life down there. I think she might be able to tell us quite a lot."

II

Perhaps I'm pushing too hard, Susan told herself later that evening. She was trying to decide what to wear for her first real date with James Conran, but she couldn't help going over the past two days' events in her mind. Banks had seemed so calm, so sure of himself, with Claude Ivers. Susan, left to her own devices, would have charged into his studio.

She also doubted that she would have left Redburn without bringing both Ivers and the Janowski woman in for a lengthy interrogation at the station. After all, they had both been at the Oakwood Mews house around the time of Caroline Hartley's murder, and both had lied about it. She couldn't understand Banks's obsession with the record and the meaning of the music. In her experience, criminals weren't intelligent enough to leave erudite musical clues behind them. Things like that only happened in the detective stories she had read as a teenager. But the music *had* been playing, she had to admit, and that was very odd indeed.

She decided on the blue cotton blouse and navy mid-length skirt. Neither were so close fitting that they would reveal what she thought of as an unacceptably thick waist. And she mustn't overdress. Mario's was a little up-market, but it wasn't really posh.

The more she thought of the case, the more she thought of Veronica Shildon. Susan had felt intimidated by the woman's reserve and poise; and the mysterious transition from happily married woman to lesbian disturbed her. It just didn't seem possible.

Ivers could be right in blaming Caroline Hartley. Perhaps Veronica knew this too, deep down, and hated herself for allowing herself to fall so low. Then she found Caroline naked after seeing Patsy Janowski leave the house, and she hit out. That seemed as good an explanation as any to her. All they had to do was discover how Veronica had disposed of her bloody clothing. Surely if Banks put his mind to it, instead of dwelling on that damn music, he could come up with something. Gary Hartley, Susan thought, wasn't capable of the crime. He might be bitter, but he was also weak, a captive in his father's cold, decaying mansion.

Banks seemed to suspect everyone except Veronica Shildon—or at least he didn't see her as a serious contender. Perhaps it was to do with his being a man, Susan thought. Men perceived things differently; they were unsuited to spotting subtle nuances. They were basically selfish and saw things only in relation to their own egos, whereas women spun a more general net of consciousness. She knew Banks was astute enough not to get side-tracked by his feelings, at least most of the time, but maybe he was attracted to Veronica Shildon. There was something in that tension between her strait-laced exterior and inner passions that a man might find sexy. And the fact that he couldn't have her would only add to the excitement, make her seem more of a challenge. Didn't men always want unattainable women?

Rubbish, Susan told herself sharply. She was letting her imagination run away with her. Time to apply a bit of lipstick.

When she was ready, she looked again at her small tree and the few trimmings she had hastily put up on Christmas Eve. They made the place look a bit more like a home. As she looked around the room, she couldn't really see what was missing. The wallpaper, red roses on a cream background, was nice enough; the three-piece suite arranged around the gas fireplace looked a little shabby, but nonetheless cozy; and the bookcase added a learned look. There was a beautiful pine table, too, in the corner by the window, where she ate. So what was it?

Looking again at the Christmas trimmings, she realized with a shock what was missing. So simple, really. If she had been on a case looking objectively at a suspect's apartment and had seen one just like this, she would have known immediately. But because it was her own, she hadn't paid it the same attention. The one personal touch, the Christmas decorations, pointed out that there was nothing of *her* there; the room had no personality. The furniture, wallpaper, carpet could all belong to anyone. Where were the knick-knacks that people accumulate over the years? Where were the favorite prints on the walls, the framed photographs of loved ones on the mantelpiece, the ornaments on the windowsill? There were no books, only her textbooks, which she kept in the guest room she used as a study. And where was the music? She had a music center her parents had bought for her twenty-first birthday, but all she ever listened to was the radio. She had no records or tapes at all.

The doorbell rang. Well, she thought, slipping on her coat, perhaps it's time I started. A nice landscape on the wall, over there, a Constable print or something, a couple of china figurines on the mantelpiece, a few books, and a record of that music Banks played in the car on the way back from Redburn yesterday. She had felt embarrassed and stupid when he had asked what she wanted to listen to, because she had no idea. She heard music on the radio, pop and classical, and enjoyed some of it, but could never remember the names of performers or titles of the pieces.

For some reason, she had asked for some vocal music, and he had played a tape of Kiri Te Kanawa singing highlights from *Madama Butterfly*. Even Susan had heard of Kiri Te Kanawa, the soprano from New Zealand who had sung at Prince Charles's wedding to Lady Di. One song in particular sent shivers all the way up her spine and made the hackles at the back of her neck stand on end. Banks had told her the heroine was imagining the return of her lover in the aria, which translated as "One Fine Day." Susan had taken note of the title, and she would buy it for herself tomorrow, as a start to her collection. Perhaps she would also try to find out what happened in the story: did the lover return, as Butterfly dreamed?

The doorbell rang again. Smiling, Susan went downstairs to the front door to meet James. He told her she looked beautiful. She didn't believe him, but she felt wonderful as they got into his car and drove off into the icy night.

III

"Sorry for the mess," Veronica Shildon said as she let Banks in. He looked around. There was no mess, really. He sat down. Veronica stood by the kitchen door with her arms folded.

"The reason I came," he said, "is to tell you that we've tracked down the woman in the picture."

Veronica shifted her weight from one foot to the other. "Yes?"

"Her name is Ruth Dunne. She's a poet, as you said, published by a small feminist press, and she lives in London."

"You have an address?"

"Yes."

"Thank you for telling me, Chief Inspector. I realize it might have been unethical."

"Ms. Shildon, I never do anything unethical." His eyes twinkled when he smiled.

"I—I didn't mean—"

"It's all right."

"Would you like some tea? I was just about to make some."

"Yes, please. It's a bit nippy out there."

"If you'd like something stronger . . . ?"

"No, tea will do fine."

While Veronica made the tea, Banks looked around the room. It was in a state of flux. In the first place, there was hardly anywhere to sit. The suite was gone, leaving only a couple of hard-backed chairs at the table by the window. Also, the sideboard had been moved, and the Christmas tree, along with all the trimmings, was gone, even though it was only December 29. Banks wondered if Veronica could have done it all herself.

"Have you talked to her?" Veronica asked, placing the tray on the table and sitting opposite him.

"No, not yet. I'm going down there tomorrow morning. It wouldn't be wise to phone ahead."

"You don't mean she's a suspect?"

"Until I find out otherwise, she is, and I don't want to give her any reason to run off if she thinks she's sitting pretty."

"It must be an awful job you do," Veronica said.

"Sometimes. But not as awful as what the people we try to catch do."

"Touché."

"Anyway, I just thought I'd let you know."

"And I'm grateful." Veronica put her cup and saucer down. "I'd like to see her," she said. "Ruth Dunne. If it's not too much of an imposition, may I travel down with you?"

Banks scratched the scar by his right eye, then crossed his legs. He knew he should say no. Officially, Veronica Shildon was a major suspect in her lover's murder. He had told her about Ruth Dunne only partly out of goodwill; mainly he had been interested in her reaction to the news. On the other hand, if he got her out of her normal environment, out of this house and out of Eastvale, he might be able to get her to open up a bit more about Caroline's background. Was that worth the risk of her making a break for it? It would be easy for her to disappear in a city as large as London. But why should she? They had no real evidence against her; they couldn't put her under arrest.

"I'm going by train," he said. "I won't be driving down. I never could stand driving in London."

"Are you trying to put me off? I know it's an unusual request to make, Chief Inspector, but I've heard about Ruth often enough from Caroline, though never more than her first name and what a good friend she was. Somehow, now that Caroline's gone, I just feel I'd like to meet her. There's very little else left."

Banks sipped at his tea and let a minute pass. "On two conditions," he said finally. "First of all, I can't allow you to be present at the interview, and second, you'll have to wait until I've talked to her before you see her."

Veronica nodded. "That sounds fair."

"I haven't finished yet."

"But that was two."

"I'll make it three, then. I reserve the right to stop you seeing her at all if for any reason I feel it necessary."

"But why on earth . . . ?"

"It should be obvious. If Ruth Dunne turns out to be even more of a suspect than she is now, I can't allow the two of you to discuss the case together. Do you agree to the terms?"

Veronica nodded slowly. "I suppose I'll have to do."

"And you'll also have to return with me."

"I was thinking of looking up an old friend," Veronica said. "Perhaps staying down for New Year's . . ."

Banks shook his head. "I'm already going out on a limb."

Veronica stood up. "Very well. I understand."

"Right," he said at the door. "Eight-twenty from Eastvale, change at Leeds."

"I'll be there," she said, and closed the door behind him.

IV

Mario's was a cozy restaurant in a narrow cul-de-sac of gift shops off North Market Street. It had a small bar at one end of the long room, stucco walls and small tables with red-and-white-checked cloths and candles in orange pressed-glass jars. A man with a guitar sat on a stool at the far end quietly crooning Italian love songs.

The place was full when James and Susan got there and they had to sit for ten minutes at the bar. James ordered a half-liter of Barolo, which they sipped as they waited.

He looked good, Susan thought. Clearly he had made some sartorial effort, replacing cords and polo-neck with gray slacks, a white shirt and a well-tailored, dark-blue sports jacket. His fair hair, thinning and combed forward flat against his skull, looked newly washed, and he had also shaved, as a couple of nicks under his chin testified. His gray eyes seemed bluer tonight, and they sparkled with life and mischief.

"You'll just love the cannelloni," he said, putting his fingers to his lips and making a kissing gesture.

Susan laughed. How long was it since an attractive man

had made her laugh? She had no idea. But very quickly she seemed to be getting over the idea of James Conran as drama teacher and moving toward. . . . Well, she didn't quite know and didn't really want to contemplate just yet. At least not tonight. James chatted easily with the barman in fluent Italian and Susan sipped her wine, reading the labels of the liqueur bottles behind the bar. Soon, a white-jacketed waiter ushered them with a flourish to a table for two. Luckily, Susan thought, it wasn't too close to the singer, now lost in the throes of *O Sole Mio*.

They examined their menus in silence, and Susan finally decided to take James's advice on the cannelloni. He ordered linguine in a white wine and clam sauce for himself. He had recommended that, too, but she was allergic to shellfish.

"I must say again," he said, raising his glass in a toast, "that you look gorgeous tonight."

"Oh, don't be stupid." Susan felt herself blush. She had done the best she could with her appearance, accenting her rather too thin lips and playing down the extra fat on her cheekbones with powder. She knew she wasn't bad looking; her large eyes were a beautiful ultramarine color and her short, blond hair, naturally thick and curly, gave her no trouble at all. If she could just lose a couple of inches from her waist and three or four from her hips, she thought, she'd be more inclined to believe compliments and wolf-whistles. Still, it was a long time since she'd gone to such lengths for a date. She smiled and clinked glasses with James.

"All you lack is confidence," he said, as if reading her thoughts. "You have to believe in yourself more."

"I do," Susan answered. "How do you think I've got where I am?"

"I mean your personality, the image you project. Believe you're lovely and people will see you that way."

"Is that what you do?"

James winced in mock agony. "Oh, now you're being cruel."

"I'm sorry."

"It's all right. I'll survive." He leaned forward. "Tell me, I've always wondered, what did you think of me when you were at school? I mean, what did the girls think of me?"

Susan laughed and put her hand to her mouth. "They thought you were gay."

James's face showed no expression, but a sudden chill seemed to emanate from him.

"I'm sorry," Susan said, feeling flustered. "I didn't mean anything by it. *I* didn't think so, if that's any consolation. And it was just because you were in the arts."

"In the arts?"

"Yes, you know how people in the performance arts always seem to be thought gay. If it'll make you feel any better, they thought Mr. Curlew was that way, too."

James stared at her, then burst into laughter. "Peter Curlew? The music teacher?"

Susan nodded.

"Well, that's a good one. I do feel better now. Curly was a happily married man with four kids. Devoted family man."

Susan laughed with him. "That just shows you how wrong we were, I suppose. I liked the way he used to conduct to himself whenever he played a record for us. He really got quite worked up, in a world of his own."

"Of course, you lot were all snickering at him behind your hands, weren't you?"

"Yes. Yes, I'm afraid we were." Susan felt strangely ashamed to admit it now, though she hadn't thought of Mr. Curlew for years.

"He was a very talented pianist, you know. He could have gone a long way, but those years of dreary teaching broke his spirit."

Susan felt embarrassed. "How are you getting on without Caroline?" she asked, to change the subject.

James paused for a few seconds, as if deep in thought, before answering. "Fine, I suppose. It wasn't a difficult part, it was just that, well, Caroline was special, that's all. Are you any closer?"

Susan shook her head. Not that she would have said even if they were closer to finding Caroline's killer. She frowned. "Do you think anyone in the production could have been involved in her death?"

He cupped his chin in his hand and thought for a moment.

"No," he said finally. "No, I can't see it. Nobody knew her that well."

"Her killer didn't need to know her well. She let him or her in, but he or she could have been merely an acquaintance, someone come to talk to her about something."

"I still can't see it."

"There must have been friction with the other women, the leads."

"Why?"

"Competition."

"Over what?"

"Anything. Men. Lines. Parts."

"There wasn't. I'm not saying we were a totally happy family, we had our ups and downs, our off days, but you're grasping at straws. Remember, it's the *Amateur* Dramatic Society. People join for pleasure, not profit. I'd like to think, though, that we're far from amateur in quality."

Susan smiled. "I'm sure you are. Tell me, what was Caroline Hartley really like?"

"I'm sorry, Susan, it's still very upsetting for me, such a loss. I just don't want to—ah, look, here's our food." He rubbed his hands together. "Delightful. And another half-liter of your best Barolo, please, Enzo."

"Do you think we should?" Susan asked. "I've still got half a glass left. I'm not certain I can drink any more."

"Well if you can't, I can. I know I should be drinking white with the linguine, but what the hell, I prefer Barolo. Worry not, not a drop will be wasted. What did you do for Christmas?"

"I—I—"

"Well, what? Did you visit your parents?" He gathered a

forkful of food and lifted it to his mouth, his eyes probing her face for an answer all the time.

Susan looked down at her plate. "I . . . not really, no, I didn't. I was busy with the case."

"You don't get on with them, do you?" he said, still looking directly at her, with just a glint of satisfaction in his eyes. She found his gaze disconcerting and looked down at her plate again to cut off a bite of cannelloni.

"I don't suppose I do," she admitted when she'd finished chewing. She shrugged. "It's nothing serious. Just that holidays at home can be awfully depressing."

"I suppose so," James said. "I'm an orphan myself and I always find Christmas terribly gloomy. It brings back memories of those awful orphanage dinners and enforced festivities. But you have a family. You shouldn't neglect them, you know. One day, it'll be too late."

"Look," Susan said, reaching for her glass, "when I want a lecture on a daughter's responsibility, I'll ask for one."

James stood up. "I'm sorry, really I am." He patted her arm. "Excuse me for a moment. Men's room."

Susan held her anger in check and tossed back the last of her wine. The second half-liter arrived. She refilled her glass and took a long swig. To hell with caution; she could get as pissed as the next person if she wanted to. Why couldn't she talk about her parents without getting so damned emotional? she asked herself. She picked away at her cannelloni, which was very good, until James came back. Then she took a deep breath and put down her knife and fork.

"I'm the one that should apologize," she said. "I didn't mean to blow up like that. It's just that it's *my* problem, all right?"

"Fine," James said. "Fine. So what *did* you do?"

She sighed. "I stayed at home. I had quite a nice day actually. I'd dashed out and bought a small tree and a few trimmings the night before, so the place looked quite seasonal. I watched the Queen's Message, a variety show, read a book on homicide investigation."

James laughed, a forkful of pasta halfway to his mouth. "You read a textbook on homicide on Christmas Day?"

Susan blushed. At that moment the manager walked by. He nodded at James as he passed.

"I don't believe it," James said. "You sitting there by the Christmas tree listening to carols, reading about dead bodies and poisons and ballistics."

"Well it's true," Susan said, managing a smile. "Anyway, if my job dis—"

But she had no time to finish. Before she could even get the word out, a man appeared beside her and began singing into her ear. She didn't know the song, but she could make out words like *bella* and *amore*. She wished she could shrink to nothing and disappear down a crack in the floor. James sat opposite, hands folded on his lap, watching with cool amusement in his eyes. When the singer had gone and Susan had grudgingly thanked him, she turned to James with fury in her eyes.

"You set that up, didn't you, when you went to the gents?' You talked to the manager. Go on, admit it."

"Very well." James turned his hands palms up. "*Mea culpa.* I just thought you might enjoy it, that's all."

"I've never been so embarrassed in my life. I've a good mind—" Susan dropped her napkin on the table and pushed back her chair, but James leaned forward and put his hand gently on her arm. She could see the mild amusement in his eyes turn to concern.

"Don't go, Susan. I just meant I thought it might cheer you up, after a Christmas spent alone. Honest, I didn't mean to embarrass you. I never thought you wouldn't like it. How could I know?"

Looking at his eyes again, she could see he was sincere. Not so much that, but it hadn't even occurred to him that the singer might embarrass her. She eased the chair toward the table again and relaxed.

"All right," she said, forcing a smile. "I'll let you off just this once. But don't you ever—"

"I won't," James said. "I promise. Scout's honor. Cross my heart and hope to die. Come on, eat your cannelloni and drink your wine. Enjoy." And he let his hand rest on hers on the checked table-cloth for a long moment before taking it away.

V

Banks switched off Milhaud's "Creation" as he pulled up outside Faith Green's block of flats. It was a small unit, only three stories high, with six flats on each floor. He looked at his watch: 8:50. Plenty of time for Faith to have come home from the Crooked Billet, if she hadn't gone out on a date.

Luckily, she was in. When he knocked, he heard someone cross the room and saw the tiny peep-hole in the door darken.

"Inspector Banks!" Faith said as she pulled the door open with a dramatic flourish. "What a surprise. Do come in. Let me take your coat." She hung up his car-coat, then took his arm and led him into the spacious living room. A number of framed posters from old movies hung on the pastel-green walls: Bogart in *Casablanca*, Garbo in *Camille*, John Garfield and Lana Turner in *The Postman Always Rings Twice*. Faith gestured toward the modular sofa that covered almost two walls, and Banks sat down.

"Drink?"

"Maybe just a small Scotch, if you have it."

"Of course." Faith opened up a glass-fronted cocktail cabinet and poured them both drinks. Banks's was about two fingers taller than he would have liked.

"To what do I owe this pleasure?" Faith asked in her husky voice. "If only you'd told me you were coming, I could have at least put my face on. I must look terrible."

She didn't. With her beautiful eyes and silvery, page-boy hair, it would have been difficult for Faith Green to look terrible. She wore no make-up, but that didn't matter. Her high cheekbones needed no highlights, her full, pink lips no coloring. In skin-tight black slacks and a dark-green silk blouse, her figure, slim at the waist, nicely curved at the hips and well-rounded at the bust, looked terrific. The perfume she wore was the same one Banks remembered from their brief chat at the Crooked Billet—very subtle, with a hint of jasmine.

She settled close to Banks on the sofa and cradled a glass of white wine in her hands. "You should have phoned first," she said. "I gave you my number."

"Maybe you didn't know I was married."

She laughed. "I've never known that to make very much difference to men." Given the way she was sitting and looking at him, he could well believe her. He fiddled for his cigarettes.

"Oh, you're not going to smoke, are you?" She pouted. "Please don't. It's not that I'm so anti, but I just can't bear my flat smelling of smoke. Please?"

Banks removed his hand from his jacket pocket and took a long swig of Scotch. He waited until the pleasant burning sensation had subsided, then said, "Remember the last time we talked? About how things were going between the people in the play?"

"Of course I do." Her eyes twinkled. "I told you I liked my men dark and handsome, and not necessarily tall."

If Banks had been wearing a tie, he would have loosened it at this point. "Miss Green—"

"Faith, please. It's not such a bad name, is it? There are three of us, sisters, but my parents never were that well up on the Bible. The youngest's called Chastity."

Banks laughed. "Faith it is, then. You told me you had no idea that Caroline Hartley was a lesbian. Are you sure you didn't?"

Faith frowned. "Of course not. What an odd question. She didn't walk around with it written on her forehead. Besides, it's not as obvious in a woman as it sometimes is in a man, is it? I mean, I've known a few homosexuals, and most of them don't mince around and lisp, but you have to admit that some conform to the stereotype. How could you possibly tell with a woman unless she went about dressed like a man or something?"

"Perhaps you would just sense it?"

"Well, I didn't. Not with Caroline. And *she* certainly didn't walk around dressed like a man."

"So she told no one?"

"Not as far as I know, she didn't. She certainly didn't tell me. I can't vouch for the others. Another drink?"

Banks looked at his glass, amazed to find it empty so soon. "No thanks."

"Oh, come on," Faith said, and took it from him. She brought it back only slightly fuller than the last time and sat about six inches closer. Banks held his ground.

"There's something missing," he said. "Some factor, maybe just a little thing, and I'm trying to find out what it is. I get the feeling that people—you especially—are holding something back, hiding something."

"Little me? Hiding something? Like what?" She spread her hands and looked down as if to indicate that all she had was on display. She wasn't far from the truth.

"I don't know. Do you think there might be a chance that Caroline Hartley was having an affair with someone other than the woman she was living with, perhaps someone in the theater company?"

Faith stared at him, then backed away a few inches, burst out laughing and pointed at her chest. "Me? You think I'm a lesbian?"

Given the situation, her physical closeness and the heady aura of sex that seemed to emanate from her, it did seem rather a silly thing to think.

"Not you specifically," Banks said. "Anyone."

When Faith had stopped laughing, she moved closer again and said, "Well, I can assure you *I'm* not." She shifted her legs. The material swished as her thighs brushed together. "In fact, if you let me, I can even prove to you I'm not."

Banks held her gaze. "It's quite possible for a person to be bisexual," he said. "Especially if he or she is over-sexed to start with."

Faith seemed to recede several feet into the distance, though she hadn't moved at all. "I ought to be insulted," she said with a pout, "but I'm not. Disappointed in you, yes, but not insulted. Do you really think I'm over-sexed?"

Banks put his thumb and forefinger close together and smiled. "Maybe just a little bit."

All the seductiveness, the heat and smell of sexuality, had gone from her manner, and what sat next to him was a very attractive young woman, perhaps a little shy, a little vulnerable. Perhaps it had all been an act. Could she turn her sexual power on and off at will? Why did he keep forgetting that there were so many actors on the fringes of Caroline Hartley's death?

"I didn't mean it as an insult," Banks went on. "It just seemed the best way to cut the games and get down to business. I really do need information. That's why I'm here."

Faith nodded, then smiled. "All right, I'll play fair. But I'm not just all talk, you know." Just for a moment she upped the voltage again and Banks felt the current.

"Could Caroline have been seeing someone?" he asked quickly.

"She could have been, yes. But I can't help you there. Caroline kept herself to herself. Nobody knew anything about her private life, I'm certain. After a couple of drinks, she'd go off home—"

"By herself?"

"Usually. If it was an especially nasty night James would give her a lift. And before you make too much out of that, he would take Teresa too, and drop her off last." She paused for effect, then added huskily, "At his place, sometimes."

"Teresa told me she didn't care about James's attraction to Caroline. What would you say about that?"

Faith put a slender finger to her lips, then said, "Well, I wouldn't quite put it that way. I don't like to tell tales out of school, but . . ."

"But what? It could be important."

"Teresa's very emotional."

"You mean she fought with Caroline?"

"Not exactly."

"With James Conran?"

Faith swirled her drink and nodded slowly. "I heard them talking once or twice," she said. "Caroline's name came up."

"In what way?"

Faith lowered her voice and leaned closer to Banks.."Usually as that 'prick-teasing little bitch.' Teresa's a good friend," she added, settling back, "but you *did* say it was important."

So Teresa Pedmore had more of a grudge against Caroline Hartley than she had cared to admit. She could have been the woman who visited Caroline's house after Patsy Janowski. On the other hand, so could Faith Green, who was being much more circumspect about her own involvement in the thespian intrigues, if she had any. Both were a little taller than Caroline Hartley. Banks would have to have a word with Teresa later and see what she, in turn, had to say about her friend.

"You say James seemed attracted enough to Caroline to upset Teresa," he said. "How strong would you say his interest was?"

"He flirted with her in the pub. That was all I ever saw."

"How did she react?"

"She gave as good as she got."

"Did they sleep together?"

"Not as far as I know."

"Teresa never referred to them doing that?"

"No, just to the way James fussed about her. It wasn't Caroline who maneuverd the seating in the pub. If anyone, Teresa should have blamed James, not Caroline."

"People aren't very logical when it comes to blame," Banks said, thinking of what Claude Ivers and Patsy Janowski had said about Caroline and Veronica.

"Where did you all go after the rehearsal on the day of Caroline's death?"

"I came home. Honestly. I was tired. I didn't even have a date."

"Why didn't you all go for a drink as usual?"

Faith shrugged. "No special reason. Sometimes we just didn't, that's all. People just wandered off home. There's nothing more to it than that. It was close to Christmas. There was shopping to do, family to visit."

Banks didn't believe her. She fiddled with her pearl necklace as she spoke and looked away from him. She also spoke as if there was nobody listening to her.

"Did something happen at that rehearsal, Faith?" he asked. "Was there a row between Caroline and Teresa?"

Faith shifted in her seat. She turned her eyes on him again. They gave away nothing. A waft of perfume drifted over.

"Another drink?"

"No. Tell me what happened."

"Leave me alone. Nothing happened."

Banks put his glass down on the St. Ives coaster and stood up.

Faith scratched the inside of her elbow. "Are you going now?" she asked. All of a sudden she seemed like a frightened girl whose parents were about to turn the lights out.

"Yes. Thanks very much for the drinks. You've been a great help."

She touched his arm. "Nothing happened. Really. Believe me. We just finished our rehearsal and we all went home. Don't you believe me?"

Banks moved toward the door. Faith walked beside him, still holding on. "You must catch him soon, you know," she said.

"Him?"

"Whoever killed Caroline. Was it a woman? I suppose it could have been. But you must."

"Don't worry. We will. With or without your help. Why are you so concerned?"

Faith let go of his arm. "The rest of us are in danger, aren't we? It stands to reason."

"What do you mean?"

"Whoever killed Caroline. He might be stalking the cast. A serial killer."

"A psychopathic killer? It's possible, but I don't think so. You've been reading too many books, Faith."

"So you really don't think the rest of us are in danger?"

"No. But you might as well keep your door locked anyway. And always look and see who's there." He paused, half out the door.

"What is it?" Faith asked.

"Some of you *could* be in danger," he added slowly, "if you know more about the crime than you're telling, and if the killer knows you know, or suspects that you do."

Faith shook her head. "I know nothing more than I told you."

"Then you've nothing to worry about, have you?"

Banks smiled and left. He wanted to get Teresa's version of that final night, but she would have to wait. It was going on for ten o'clock, he was tired, and he was going to London early in the morning. If he still needed to talk to her when he got back, he could do it then.

As he walked over the brittle ice listening to the rest of the Milhaud piece, he recalled Faith Green's expression at the door. She had told him that she knew nothing, but had looked distinctly worried when he had hinted she might be in danger. Of course, knowing her, it could have been just another act, but perhaps, he thought, it wouldn't be a bad idea to have Richmond and Susan Gay keep an eye on the thespians while he was in London.

NINE

I

It wasn't until the Intercity train pulled out of Leeds City Station that Veronica Shildon seemed to relax.

Banks had met her at Eastvale Station early that morning and they had paced the platform, shivering and breathing plumes of mist, until the overheated old diesel rattled in and carried them off. Silent but for small talk, they'd watched the shrouded landscape roll by. South of Ripon, the dales and moors to the west gave way to rolling farmland, where patches of frozen brown earth and clumps of bare trees showed through the gauze of snow, and, finally, to the suburbs and industrial estates of the city itself. They had endured a half-hour wait on the cold, grimy platform at Leeds, breathing in the diesel smell of warm engines and listening to the crackly voice over the loudspeaker.

Now, well past the sign at the station's entrance in honor of the local beer magnate—"Joshua Tetley Welcomes You to Leeds"—Banks looked over his shoulder and watched the city recede into the distance. First it filled the horizon, an urban sprawl under a heavy sky. Tall chimneys and church spires poked through the gray-brown snow; the Town Hall dome and the white university library tower dominated the distance. Then the city was gone and only bare fields stretched east and west.

Veronica took off her heavy blue winter coat and, folding

it carefully, placed it in the luggage rack. Then she smoothed her tweed skirt and sat back down opposite Banks, resting her hands on the table between them.

"I'm sorry," she said with an embarrassed smile. "I know I must be a burden, but I didn't like the idea of traveling down by myself. It's a while since I've been anywhere alone."

"That's all right," said Banks, who had been uncharitably wishing he could spend the journey with the *Guardian* crossword and some Poulenc chamber music on his Walkman. "Coffee?"

"Yes, please."

The buffet car hadn't opened yet, but a British Rail steward was making his way slowly along the corridor with an urn and a selection of biscuits. Banks headed him off, bought two coffees and pushed one over the smooth table to Veronica. Automatically, he reached for his cigarettes, then remembered he was in a non-smoking carriage.

It wasn't Veronica's fault; she would have been happy to sit anywhere with him since he had allowed her to come along. The problem was that there was only one smokers' car on the entire train and, as usual, it was almost full and completely unventilated. Even Banks refused to sit in it. He could do without a cigarette for a couple of hours, easily. It might even do him good. As an alternative, he caught up with the steward and bought a Penguin biscuit.

After Wakefield, they sped along past dreary fields and embankments trying to sip the hot, weak coffee without spilling any. Their carriage was unusually quiet and empty. Perhaps, Banks guessed, this was because they were in that limbo between Christmas and New Year's. Everyone was both broke and in need of a brief hibernation or period of recovery between the two festive occasions.

Deep into South Yorkshire, Banks noticed Veronica looking out at the desolate landscape of pit-wheels and slag-heaps and asked her what she was thinking about.

"It's funny," she said, "but I was thinking how I still feel only half here. Do you know what I mean? I can accept that

Caroline is gone, that she's dead and I'll never see her again, but I can't believe that my life is whole, or even real, without her." She nodded toward the window. "Even the world out there doesn't seem real, somehow. Not anymore."

"That's understandable," Banks said. "It takes time. How did you meet her?"

Veronica gave him a long, appraising look and then leaned forward and rested her arms on the table, clasping her slim, freckled hands.

"It must seem very odd to you. Perverted, even. But it's not. There was nothing sordid about it."

Banks said nothing.

Veronica sighed and went on. "I first met Caroline at the café where she worked. I used to go for long walks by the river . . . oh, just thinking about my life and how empty it felt . . . somehow, the moving water seemed to help soothe me. We got on speaking terms, then once I saw her in the market square and we went for a coffee. We discovered we were both in therapy. After that . . . well, it didn't happen quickly."

"What attracted you to her?"

"I didn't even know I *was* attracted to her at first. Could you imagine someone like me admitting I'd fallen in love with a woman? But Caroline was so alive, so childlike in her enthusiasm for life. It was infectious. I'd felt half dead for years. I'd been shutting the world out. It's possible to do that, you know. So many people accept what life dishes out to them. Apart from the occasional day-dream, they never imagine it could be any different, any better. Even the half-life I have now is preferable to what my life was like before Caroline. There's no going back. I was living like a zombie, denying everything that counts, until Caroline came along. She showed me how good it was to *feel* again. She made me feel alive for the first time. She got me interested in things because she was so passionate about them herself."

"Like what?"

"Oh, theater, books, film. So many neat things. And music. Claude was always trying to get me interested in music, and it really frustrated him that I didn't seem to care as much as he did, or notice as much about it as he did. I suppose I loved opera most of all, but he never had much time for it. Most seasons I went to Leeds to see Opera North by myself. I liked to listen—I still do like classical music—but I never actually bought records for myself. There always seemed something stuffy about the music we listened to, perhaps because Claude hated anything popular, anything outside the classical field. But with Caroline it was jazz and blues and folk music. Somehow it just seemed more alive. We even went to clubs to see folk groups perform. I'd never done that before. Ever."

"But your husband's a musician himself. He loves music. Didn't he mean anything to you? Why couldn't you respond to his enthusiasm?"

Veronica lowered her head and scratched the table surface with her thumb-nail. The train hit a bumpy stretch of track and rocked.

"I don't know. Somehow I just felt completely stifled by his existence. That's the only way I can put it. Like it didn't matter what I thought or felt or did because he was the one our lives revolved around. I depended on him for everything, even for my tastes in music and books. I was suffocated by his presence. Anything I did would have been insignificant beside what he did. He was the great Claude Ivers, after all, always the teacher, the master. One dismissive comment from him on anything that mattered to me and I was reduced to silence, or tears, so I learned not to let things matter. I was the great man's wife, not a person in my own right."

She sat up straight, her brow furrowed. "How can I explain it to you? Claude wasn't cruel, he didn't do any of it on purpose. It's just the way he is, and the way I am, or was. I still have my problems, more than ever now Caroline's gone, I suppose, but when I look back I can't believe I'm the same person I was then. She worked an act of magic—she breathed life into dust. And I know I can carry on somehow, no matter how hard, just because of her, just because I had her in my life, even for such a short time." She paused and glanced out the window. Banks could read the intense feeling in the set of her jaw, the way the small muscles below her cheekbones seemed drawn tight.

"Do you see?" she went on, turning her clear, gray-green eyes on Banks. "It wasn't black-and-white. He wasn't a bad husband. Neglectful, maybe. Certainly the last few years he was far too wrapped up in his work to notice me. And I was dying, drying up inside. If Caroline hadn't come along I don't know what would have become of me."

"But you started seeing the therapist before you met Caroline," Banks said. "What made you do that?"

"Desperation, despair. I'd read an article about Jungian therapy in a women's magazine. It sounded interesting, but not for me. Time passed and I became so miserable I had to do something or I was frightened I would try to kill myself. I suppose I told myself therapy was a sort of intellectual fun, not anything deep and personal. More like going to an evening class—you know, pottery, basket-weaving or creative writing. It wasn't like going to the real doctor or to a psychiatrist, and somehow I could handle that. It still took a lot of nerve, more than I believed I ever had. But I was so unhappy. And it helped. It can be a painful process, you know. You keep circling things without ever really zooming in on them, and sometimes you feel it's a waste of time, it's going nowhere. Then you do focus on things and you find you were circling them for good reason. Occasionally you get some kind of insight, and that sustains you for a while. Then I met Caroline."

"Had you ever experienced feelings like that before?" Banks asked.

"Towards another woman?"

"Yes."

Veronica shook her head. "I hadn't experienced feelings like that for *anyone* before, male or female. Somehow or other, her being a woman just wasn't an issue. Not after a while, anyway. Everything began to feel so natural I didn't even have to think."

"What about your past, your upbringing?"

Veronica smiled. "Yes, isn't it tempting to try and put everything down to that? I don't mean to be dismissive, but I don't think it's so. I had no horrible experiences with men in my past. I'd never been abused, raped or beaten." She paused. "At least not physically."

"What was your family background like?"

"Solid, suburban, upper middle class. Very repressed. Utterly cold. We never spoke about feelings and nobody told me about the facts of life. My mother was well-bred, very Victorian, and my father was kind and gentle but rather distant, aloof. And he was away a lot. I never had much contact with boys while I was growing up. I went to convent school, and even at university I didn't mix very much. I was in an all-girls residence and I tended to stay home and study a lot. I was shy. Men frightened me with their deep voices and their aggressive mannerisms. I don't know why. When I met Claude he was a guest lecturer for a music appreciation course. It was the kind of thing genteel young ladies did, appreciate music, so I took the course. I was fascinated by his knowledge and his obvious passion for his subject—the very things I came to hate later. For some reason he noticed me. He was an older man, much safer than the randy boys in the campus pub. I was twenty-one when I married him."

"So you never had any other boyfriends?"

"Never. I was reclusive, frightened as a mouse. Believe it or not, when Claude seemed to lose interest in sex, that suited me fine. Now, when I look back, I can't remember what I did from day to day. How I got through. I was a housewife. I had no outside job. I suppose I cleaned and cooked and watched daytime television in a kind of trance. Then there was the Valium, of course."

"How long were you married?"

"We were together for fifteen years. I never complained. I never took an interest in life outside his circle of friends and acquaintances. I had no passions of my own. I don't blame Claude for that. He had his own life, and music was more important to him even than marriage. I think it has to be like that with a great artist, don't you? And I believe Claude *is* a great artist. But great artists make lousy husbands."

"Did you ever think of having children?"

"I did. But Claude thought they would interfere with his peace and quiet. He never really liked children. And I suppose I was, am, afraid of childbirth. Terrified, to be honest. Anyway, he just went ahead and had a vasectomy. He never even told me until it was done. What do you think of childless marriages, Mr. Banks?"

Banks shrugged. "I wouldn't know. Never had one."

"Some people say there's no love in them, but I don't agree. Sometimes I think it would be best if we were all childless. Childless and parentless." She caught the paradox and smiled. "Impossible, I realize. There'd be no one here to feel anything. I know I feel alone and it hurts because Caroline isn't here. But at the same time I seem to be saying we'd all be better off without any feelings or any attachments. I want it both ways, don't I?"

"Don't we all? Look, this philosophy's made me thirsty. I know it's early, but how about a drink?"

Veronica laughed. "Have I driven you to drink already? All right, I'll have a gin and tonic."

Banks made his way down to the buffet car, holding on to the tops of seats to keep his balance in the rocking train. Most of the other passengers seemed to be business people with their heads buried deep in the *Financial Times* or briefcases full of papers open in front of them. One man even tapped away at the keys of a laptop computer. After a short queue, Banks got Veronica's drink and a miniature Bell's for himself. Going back one-handed was a little more difficult, but he made it without falling or dropping anything.

Back in his seat, he poured the drinks. They passed a small town: smoking chimneys; grimy factory yards stacked with pallets; a new redbrick school with hardly any windows; a roundabout; snow-covered playing fields as white as the rugby posts. The train's rhythm was soothing, even if it wasn't the same as the steam-train journeys Banks remembered taking with his father when he was young. The sound was different, and he missed the tangy smell of the smoke, the sight of it curling over trees by a wooded embankment where the track curved and he could see the engine through the window.

Veronica seemed content to sip her drink in silence. There was so much more he wanted to ask her, to understand about her relationship with Caroline Hartley, but he didn't feel he could justify his questions. He thought of what she had said about a childless and parentless life and remembered the Philip Larkin poem, which he had recently reread. It was certainly depressing—the ending as much as the beginning—but he found something in the wit and gusto of Larkin's colloquial style that brought a smile to the lips, too. Perhaps that was the secret of great art, it could engender more than one feeling in the spectator at the same time: tragedy and comedy, laughter and tears, irony and passion, hope and despair.

"What's your wife like?"

The suddenness of the question surprised Banks, and he guessed he must have shown it.

"I'm sorry," Veronica went on quickly, blushing, "I hope I'm not being presumptuous."

"No. I was just thinking about something else, that's all. My wife? Well, she's just an inch or so shorter than I am. She's slim, with an oval face, blond hair and dark eyebrows, what I'd call a no-nonsense personality and . . . let me think . . ."

Veronica laughed and held up her hand. "No, no. That'll do. I didn't want a *policeman's* description. I suppose I hadn't thought how difficult it is to answer off the cuff like that. If anyone had asked me to describe Caroline I wouldn't have known where to start."

"You did well enough earlier."

"But that was just scratching the surface."

She drank some more gin and tonic and looked at her reflection in the window, as if she couldn't believe what she was seeing.

"I suppose my wife and I are still together," Banks said, "because she has always been determined and independent. She'd hate to be a housewife worrying about meals and three-pence-off coupons in the papers. Some people might see that as a fault, but I don't. It's what she is and I wouldn't want to turn her into some sort of chattel or slave. And she wouldn't want to depend on me to entertain her or keep her happy. Oh, we've had some dull patches and a few close shaves on both sides, but I think we do pretty well."

"And you put it down to her independence?"

"Mostly, yes. More an independent spirit, really. And intelligence. It's very hard being a policeman's wife. We're a high-divorce profession. It's not so much the worry, though that's there, but the long absences and the unpredictability. I've seen plenty of marriages go down the tubes because the wife hasn't been able to take it anymore. But Sandra has always had a mind of her own. And a life of her own—photography, the gallery, friends, books. She doesn't let herself get bored—she loves life too much—so I don't feel I have to be around to entertain her or pay attention to her all the time."

"That sounds like Caroline and me. Though I suppose I depended on her quite a lot, especially at first. But she helped me become more independent, she and Ursula."

Banks wondered why on earth he had opened up that way to Veronica. There was something about the woman he couldn't quite put his finger on. A terrible honesty, a visible effort she made to communicate, to be open. She was working at living, not simply coasting through life like so many. She didn't shirk experience, and Banks found it was impossible not to be as frank in return with someone like that. Was he letting his feelings overrun his judgment? After all, this woman *could* be a murderess.

"How long had you known Caroline before you left your husband?" Banks asked.

"Known her? A few months, but mostly just casually."

"But how did you know how you felt, what you wanted to do?"

"I just knew. Do you mean sexually?"

"Well . . ."

"I don't know," she went on, cutting through his embarrassment. "Certainly it wasn't anything I'd experienced or even thought about before. I suppose I must have, but I don't remember. Of course, there were crushes and a little petting at school, but I imagine everyone indulges in that. I don't know. It was awkward. We were at her flat and she just . . . took me. After that, I knew. I knew what had been missing in my life, what I had been repressing, if you like. And I knew I had to change things. I was buoyant with love and I suppose I expected Claude to understand when I told him."

"But he didn't?"

"It was the closest he ever came to hitting me."

Banks remembered the ex-husband's anger, his humiliation. "What happened?"

"Oh, I know what I did wrong now. At least I think I do." She laughed at herself. "I was crazy with joy then. I expected him to feel happy for me. Can you believe that? Anyway, I moved out the next day and went to live with Caroline in her flat. Then he sold the house and left Eastvale. Later we got the little place on Oakwood Mews. The rest you know."

"And you never looked back."

"Never. I'd found what I was looking for."

"And now?"

Veronica's face darkened. "Now I don't know."

"But you wouldn't go back to him?"

"To Claude? I couldn't do that. Even if he wanted to." She shook her head slowly. "No, whatever the future holds for me, it's certainly not more of my miserable mistake of a past."

In the silence that followed, Banks glanced out the window and was surprised to find the train was passing Peterborough. The landmarks were so familiar: the tall kiln chimneys of the brick factory growing straight from the ground; the white sign of the Great Northern Hotel against its charcoal-gray stone; the truncated cathedral tower.

"What is it?" Veronica asked. "You look so engrossed. Have you seen something?"

"My home town," Banks explained. "Not much of a place, but mine own."

Veronica laughed.

"Where do you come from?" Banks asked.

"Crosby. Near Liverpool, but light-years away, really. It's a horribly stuck-up suburb, at least it was then."

"I'd hardly say Peterborough was stuck-up," Banks said. "Doesn't your poet, Larkin, have something to say about childhood places?"

"You've been doing your research, I see. Yes, he does. And he set it on a train journey like this. It's very funny and very sad. It ends, 'Nothing, like something, can happen anywhere.' "

"Do you read a lot of poetry?"

"Yes. Quite a bit."

"Do you read any journals?"

"Some. The *Poetry Review* occasionally. Mostly I read old stuff. I prefer rhyme and meter, so I tend to stay away from contemporary work, except Larkin, Seamus Heaney and a couple of others, of course. That's one area Caroline and I disagreed on. She liked free verse and I never could see the point of it. What was it Robert Frost said: Like playing tennis without a net?"

"But you've never noticed Ruth Dunne's name in print, never come across her work?"

Veronica tightened her lips and looked out the window. She seemed irritated that Banks had broken the spell and plunged into what must have felt like an interrogation.

"I don't remember it, no. Why?"

"I just wondered what kind of stuff she writes, and why Caroline didn't tell you about her."

"Because she tended to be secretive about her past.

Sketchy, anyway. I also suspect that maybe she didn't want to make me jealous."

"Were they still seeing one another?"

"As far as I know, Caroline made no trips to London while we were together. I haven't even been myself for at least three years. No, I mean jealous of a past lover. It can happen, you know—people have even been jealous over *dead* lovers—and I was especially vulnerable, being in such a new and frightening relationship."

"Frightening?"

"Well, yes. Of course. Especially at first. Do you imagine it was easy for me, with my background and my sheltered existence, to go to bed with a woman, to give up my marriage and live with one?"

"Was there anyone else who might have been jealous enough of Caroline's relationship with you?"

Veronica raised her eyebrows. "You're never very far away from your job, are you? It makes it hard to trust you, to open up to you. I can never tell what you're thinking from your expression."

Banks laughed. "That's because I'm a good poker player. But seriously, despite all evidence to the contrary, I *am* a human being. And I'd be a liar if I didn't admit that the foremost thing on my mind is catching Caroline's killer right now. The work is never far away. That's because somebody took something they had no right to."

"And do you think catching and punishing the criminal will do any good?"

"I don't know. It becomes too abstract for me at that point. I told you, I like concrete things. Put it this way, I wouldn't like to think that the person who stabbed Caroline is going to be walking around Eastvale, or anywhere else for that matter, whistling 'Oh, What a Beautiful Morning' for the rest of his or her life. Do you know what I mean?"

"Revenge?"

"Perhaps. But I don't think so. Something more subtle, more *right* than mere revenge."

"But why do you take it so personally?"

"Somebody has to. Caroline isn't around to take it so personally herself."

Veronica stared at Banks. Her eyes narrowed, then she shook her head.

"What?" Banks asked.

"Nothing. Just trying to understand, thinking what a strange job you do, what a strange man you are. Do all policemen get as involved in their cases?"

Banks shrugged. "I don't know. For some it's just a day's work. Like anyone else, they'll skive off as much as they can. Some get very cynical, some are lazy, some are cruel, vicious bastards with brains the size of a pea. Just people."

"You probably think I don't care about revenge or justice or whatever it is."

"No. I think you're confused and you're too shaken by Caroline's death to think about whoever did it. You're also probably too civilized to feel the blood-lust of revenge."

"Repressed?"

"Maybe."

"Then perhaps a little repression is a good thing. I'll have to tell Ursula that before she releases the raging beast inside me."

Banks smiled. "I hope we've got the killer safely behind bars long before that."

The train passed a patch of waste ground scattered with bright yellow oil drums and old tires, then a factory yard, a housing estate and a graffiti-scarred embankment. Soon, Banks could see Alexander Palace through the window.

"Better get ready," he said, standing up and reaching for his camel-hair overcoat. "We'll be at King's Cross in a few minutes."

II

Half an hour later, Banks looked across the street at the Gothic extravaganza of St. Pancras, complete with its chimneys, crocketed towers and crenellated gables. So, here he was, back in London for the first time in almost three years. Black taxis and red double-decker buses clogged the roads and poisoned the streets with exhaust fumes. Horns honked, drivers yelled at one another and pedestrians took their lives into their hands crossing the street.

Veronica had taken a taxi to her friend's house. For Banks, the first priority was lunch, which meant a pint and a sandwich. He walked down Euston Road for a while, taking in the atmosphere, loving it almost as much as he hated it. There didn't appear to have been much snow down here. Apart from occasional lumps of gray slush in the gutters, the streets were mostly clear. The sky was leaden, though, and seemed to promise at least a cold drizzle before the end of the day.

He turned down Tottenham Court Road, found a cozy pub and managed to elbow himself a place at the bar. It was lunchtime, so the place was crowded with hungry and thirsty clerks come to slag the boss and gird up their loins for another session at the grindstone. Banks had forgotten how much he liked London pubs. The Yorkshire people were so proud of their beer and their pubs, it had been easy to forget that a London boozer could be as much fun as any up north. Banks drank a pint of draft Guinness and ate a thick ham-and-cheese sandwich. As always in London, such gourmet treats cost an arm and a leg; even the pint cost a good deal more than it would in Eastvale. Luckily, he was on expenses.

The raised voices all around him, with their London accents, brought it all back, the good and the bad. For years he had loved the city's streets, their energy. Even some of the villains he'd nicked had a bit of class, and those that lacked class at least had a sense of humor.

He pushed his plate aside and lit a cigarette. The bottles ranged at the back of the bar were reflected in the gilt-edged mirror. The barmaid had broken into a sweat trying to keep up with the customers—her upper lip and brow were moist with it—but she managed to maintain her smile. Banks ordered another pint.

He couldn't put his finger on when it had all started to go wrong for him in London. It had been a series of events, most likely, over a long period. But somehow it all merged into one big mess when he looked back: Brian getting into fights at school; his own marriage on the rocks; anxiety attacks that had convinced him he was dying.

But the worst thing of all had been the job. Slowly, subtly, it had changed. And Banks had found himself changing with it. He was becoming more like the vicious criminals he dealt with day in, day out, less able to see good in people and hope for the world. He ran on pure anger and cynicism, occasionally thumped suspects in interrogation and trampled over everyone's rights. And the damnedest thing was, it was all getting him good results, gaining him a reputation as a good copper. He sacrificed his humanity for his job, and he grew to hate himself, what he had become. He had been no better than Dirty Dick Burgess, a superintendent from the Met with whom he had recently done battle in Eastvale.

Life had dragged on without joy, without love. He was losing Sandra and he couldn't even talk to her about it. He was living in a sewer crowded with rats fighting for food and space: no air, no light, no escape. The move up north, if he admitted it, had been his way of escape. Put simply, he had run away before it got too late.

And just in time. While everything in Eastvale hadn't been roses, it had been a damn sight better than those last months in London, during which he seemed to do nothing but stand over corpses in stinking, run-down slums: a woman ripped open from pubes to breast bone, intestines spilling on the carpet; the decaying body of a man with his head hacked off and placed between his legs. He had seen those things, dreamed about them, and knew he could never forget. Even in Eastvale, he sometimes awoke in a cold sweat as the head tried to speak to him.

He finished his pint quickly and walked outside, pulling up his overcoat collar against the chill. So, he was back, but not to stay. Never to stay. So enjoy it. The city seemed noisier, busier and dirtier than ever, but a fresh breeze brought the smell of roast chestnuts from a street vendor on Oxford Street. Banks thought of the good days, the good years: searching for old, leather-bound editions of Dickens on autumn afternoons along Charing Cross Road: Portobello Road market on a crisp, windy spring morning; playing darts with Barney Merritt and his other mates in the Magpie and Stump after a hard day in the witness box; family outings to Epping Forest on Sunday afternoons; drinks in the street on warm summer nights at the back of Leicester Square after going to the pictures with Sandra, the kids safe with a sitter. No, it hadn't all been bad. Not even Soho. Even that had its comic moments, its heart. At least it had seemed so before everything went wrong. Still, he felt human again. He was out of the sewer, and a brief visit like this one wasn't going to suck him back into it.

First he made a phone call to Barney Merritt, an old friend from the Yard, to confirm his bed for the night. That done, he caught the Tube to the Oval. As he sat in the small compartment and read the ads above the windows, he remembered the countless other Underground journeys he had made because he always tried to avoid driving in London. He remembered standing in the smoking car, crushed together with a hundred or more other commuters, all hanging on their straps, trying to read the paper and puffing away. It had been awful, but part of the ritual. How he'd managed to breathe, he had no idea. Now you couldn't even smoke on the platforms and escalators, let alone on the trains.

He walked down Kennington Road and found the turn-off, a narrow street of three-story terrace houses divided into flats, each floor with its own bay window. At number twenty-three, a huge cactus stood in the window of the middle flat, and in the top oriel he could see what looked like a stuffed toy animal of some kind. Her name was printed above the top bell: R. Dunne. No first name, to discourage weirdos, but all the weirdos knew that only women left out their first names. There was no intercom. Banks pushed the bell and waited. Would she be in? What did poets do all day? Stare at the sky with their eyes in a "fine frenzy rolling?"

Just when he was beginning to think she wasn't home, he heard footsteps inside the hall and the door opened on a chain. A face—*the* face—peered around at him.

"Yes?"

Banks showed his identification card and told her the purpose of his visit. She shut the door, slid off the chain and let him in.

Banks followed the slender, boyish figure in turquoise slacks and baggy orange sweatshirt all the way up the carpeted stairs to the top. The place was clean and brightly decorated, with none of the smells and graffiti he had encountered in such places so often in the past. In fact, he told himself, flats like this must cost a fortune these days. How much did poets make? Surely not that much. It would be rude to ask.

The flat itself was small. The door opened on a narrow corridor, and Banks followed Ruth Dunne to the right into the living room. He hadn't known what to expect, had no preconceived idea of what a poet's dwelling should look like, but whatever he might have imagined, it wasn't this. There was a divan in front of the gas fire covered with a gaudy, crocheted quilt and flanked on both sides by sagging armchairs, similarly draped. He was surprised to find no bookshelves in evidence and assumed her study was elsewhere in the flat, but what was there surprised him as much as what wasn't: several stuffed toys—a green elephant, a pink frog, a magenta giraffe—lay around in alcoves and on the ledge by the bay window, and on three of the four walls elaborate cuckoo clocks ticked, all set at different times.

"It must be noisy," Banks said, nodding at the clocks.

Ruth Dunne smiled. "You get used to it."

"Why the different times?"

"I'm not interested in time, just clocks. In fact my friends tell me I'm a chronically late person."

On the low table between the divan and the fire lay a coffeetable book on watch-making, a couple of bills, an ashtray and a pack of unfiltered Gauloises.

"Make yourself comfortable," Ruth said. "I've never been interrogated by the police before. At least not by a detective chief inspector. Would you like some coffee?"

"Please."

"It's instant, I'm afraid."

"That'll do fine. Black."

Ruth nodded and left the room. If Banks had expected a hostile welcome, for whatever reason, he was certainly disarmed by Ruth Dunne's charm and hospitality. And by her appearance. Her shiny brown hair, medium length, was combed casually back, parted at one side, and the forelock almost covered her left eye. Her face was unlined and without make-up. Strong-featured, handsome rather than pretty, but with a great deal of character in the eyes. They'd seen a lot, Banks reckoned, those hazel eyes. Felt a lot, too. In life, she looked far more natural and approachable than the arrogant, knowing woman in the photograph, yet there was certainly something regal in her bearing.

"How did you find me?" she asked, bringing back two mugs of steaming black coffee and sitting with her legs curled under her on the divan. She held her mug with both hands and sniffed the aroma. The gas fire hissed quietly in the background. Banks sat in one of the armchairs, the kind that seem to embrace you like an old friend, and lit a cigarette. Then he showed her the photograph, which she laughed at, and told her.

"So easy," she said when he'd finished.

"A lot of police work is. Easy and boring. Time-consuming, too."

"I hope that's not a subtle way of hinting I should have come forward earlier?"

"No reason to, had you? Did you know about Caroline's death?"

Ruth reached for the blue paper packet of Gauloises, tapped one out and nodded. "Read about it in the paper. Not much of a report, really. Can you tell me what happened?"

Banks wished he could, but knew he couldn't. If he told her, then he'd have no way of checking what she already knew.

She noticed his hesitation and waved her hand. "All right. I suppose I should think myself lucky to be spared the gory details. Look, I imagine I'm a suspect, if you've come all this way. Can we get that out of the way first? I might have an alibi, you never know, and it'll make for a hell of a more pleasant afternoon if you don't keep thinking of me as a crazed, butch dyke killer." She finally lit the cigarette she'd been toying with, and the acrid tang of French tobacco infused the air.

Banks asked her where she had been and what she had been doing on December 22. Ruth sucked on her Gauloise, thought for a moment, then got up and disappeared down the corridor. When she reappeared, she held an open appointment calendar and carried it over to him.

"I was giving a poetry reading in Leamington Spa, of all places," she said. "Very supportive of the arts they are up there."

"What time did it start?"

"About eight."

"How did you get there?"

"I drove. I've got a Fiesta. It's life in the fast lane all the way for us poets, you know. I was a bit early, too, for a change, so the organizers should remember me."

"Good audience?"

"Pretty good. Adrian Henri and Wendy Cope were reading there, too, if you want to check with them."

Banks noted down the details. If Ruth Dunne had indeed

been in Leamington Spa at eight o'clock that evening, there was no conceivable way she could have been in Eastvale at seven-twenty or later. If she was telling the truth about the reading, which could be easily checked, then she was in the clear.

"One thing puzzles me," Banks said. "Caroline had your picture but we couldn't find a copy of your book among her things. Can you think why that might be?"

"Plenty of reasons. She wasn't much of a one for material possessions, wasn't Caroline. She never did seem to hang onto things like the rest of us, acquire possessions. I always envied her that. I did give her a copy of the first book, but I've no idea what happened to it. I sent the second one, too, the one I dedicated to her, but I wasn't sure what her address was then. The odds are it went to an old address and got lost in the system."

Either that or Nancy Wood had run off with both of them, Banks thought, nodding.

"But she hung onto the photograph."

"Maybe she liked my looks better than my poetry."

"What kind of poetry do you write, if you don't mind me asking?"

"I don't mind, but it's a hard one to answer." She tapped the fingers holding the cigarette against her cheek. The short blond hairs on the back of her hand caught the light. "Let me see, I don't write confessional lesbian poetry, nor do I go in for feminist diatribes. A little wit, I like to think, a good sense of structure, landscape, emotion, myth. . . . Will that do to be going on with?"

"Do you like Larkin?"

Ruth laughed. "I shouldn't, but I do. It's hard not to. I never much admired his conservative, middle class 'little Englandism,' but the bugger certainly had a way with a stanza." She cocked her head. "Do we have a literary copper here? Another Adam Dalgliesh?"

Banks smiled. He didn't know who Adam Dalgliesh was.

Some television detective, no doubt, who went around quoting Shakespeare.

"Just curious, that's all," he answered. "Who's your favorite?"

"H. D. A woman called Hilda Dolittle, friend of Ezra Pound's."

Banks shook his head. "Never heard of her."

"Ah. Clearly *not* a literary copper then. Give her a try."

"Maybe I will." Banks took another sip of his coffee and fiddled for a cigarette. "Back to Caroline. When did you last see her?"

"Let me see. . . . It was years ago, five or six at least. I think she was about twenty or twenty-one at the time. Twenty going on sixty."

"Why do you say that?" Banks remembered Caroline as beautiful and youthful even in death.

"The kind of life she was leading ages a woman fast— especially on the inside."

"What life?"

"You mean you don't know?"

"Tell me."

Ruth shifted into the cross-legged position. "Oh, I get it. You ask the questions, I answer them. Right?"

Banks allowed himself a smile. "I'm not meaning to be rude," he said, "but that's basically how it goes. I need all the information I can get on Caroline. So far I don't have a hell of a lot, especially about the time she spent in London. If it'll make talking easier for you, I can tell you that we already know she had a conviction for soliciting and gave birth to a child. That's all."

Ruth looked down into her coffee and Banks was surprised to see tears rolling over her cheeks.

"I'm sorry," she said, putting the mug down and wiping her face with the back of her hand. "It just sounds so sad, so pathetic. You mustn't think I'm being flippant, the way I talk. I don't get many visitors so I try to enjoy everyone I meet. I was very upset when I read about Caroline, but I hadn't seen her for a long time. I'll tell you anything I can." A marmalade cat slipped into the room, looked once at Banks, then jumped on the divan next to Ruth and purred. "Meet T. S. Eliot," Ruth said. "He named so many cats, so I thought at least one should be named after him. I call him T. S. for short."

Banks said hello to T. S., who seemed more interested in nestling into the hollow formed by Ruth's crossed legs. She picked up her coffee again with both hands and blew gently on the surface before drinking.

"Caroline started as a dancer," she said. "An exotic dancer, I believe they're called. Well, it's not too much of a leap from that to pleasing the odd, and I do mean *odd*, punter or two for extra pocket-money. I'm sure you know much more about vice here than I do, but before long she was doing the lot: dancing, peep-shows, turning tricks. She was a beautiful child, and she looked even younger than she was. A lot of men around that scene have a taste for fourteen- or fifteen-year-olds, or even younger, and Caroline could fulfill that fantasy when she was eighteen."

"Was she on drugs?"

Ruth frowned and shook her head. "Not as far as I know. Not like some of them. She might have had the odd joint, maybe an upper or a downer now and then—who doesn't?— but nothing really heavy or habitual. She wasn't hooked on anything."

"What about her pimp?"

"Bloke called Reggie. Charming character. One of his women did for him with a Woolworth's sheath-knife shortly before Caroline broke away. You can check your records, I'm sure they'll have all the details. Caroline wasn't involved, but it was a godsend for her in a way."

"How?"

"Surely it's obvious. She was scared stiff of Reggie. He used to bash her about regularly. With him out of the way, she had a chance to slip between the cracks before the next snake came along."

"When did she break away?"

Ruth leaned forward and stubbed out her cigarette. "About a year before she went back up north."

"And you knew her during that period?"

"We lived together. Here. I got this place before the prices rocketed. You wouldn't believe how cheap it was. I knew her before for a little while, too. I'd like to think I played a small part in getting her out of the life."

"Who played the largest part?"

"She did that herself. She was a bright kid and she saw where she was heading. Not many you can say that about. She'd been wanting out for a while, but Reggie wouldn't let go and she didn't know where to run."

"How did you come to meet her?"

"After a poetry reading. Funny, I can remember it like it was yesterday. Out in Camden Town. All we had in the audience was a prostitute and a drunk who wanted to grab the mike and sing 'Your Cheating Heart.' He did, too, right in the middle of my best poem. Afterwards we drove down to Soho—not the drunk, just me and my fellow readers—to the Pillars of Hercules. Know it?"

Banks nodded. He'd enjoyed many a pint of draft Beck's there.

"We just happened to be jammed in a corner next to Caroline and another girl. We got talking, and one thing led to another. Right from the start Caroline struck me as intelligent and wise, wasted on that scummy life. She knew it too, but she didn't know what else she could do. We soon became close friends. We went to the theater a lot and she loved it. Cinema, art exhibitions." She gave a small laugh. "Anything but classical music or opera. She didn't mind ballet, though. It was all a world she'd never known."

"Was that all there was to your relationship?"

Ruth paused to light another Gauloise before answering. "Of course not. We were lovers. But don't look at me as if I was some kind of corrupter of youth. Caroline knew exactly what she was doing."

"Were you the first woman she'd had such a relationship with?"

"Yes. That was obvious right from the start. She was shy about things at first, but she soon learned." Ruth inhaled the smoke deeply and blew it out. "God, did she learn."

One of the cuckoo clocks went through its motions. They waited until it stopped.

"What do you think turned her into a lesbian?" Banks asked.

Ruth shifted on the sofa and T. S. scampered off. "It doesn't happen like that. Women don't suddenly, quote, turn into lesbians, unquote. They discover that's what they are, what they always were afraid to admit because there was too much working against them—social morality, male domination, you name it."

"Do you think there are a lot of women in that situation?"

"More than you imagine."

"What about the men in her life?"

"Work it out for yourself. What do you think it does to a woman to have gross old men sticking their willies in her and meek suburban husbands asking if they can pee in her mouth? You've got the pimp at one end and the perverts at the other. No quarter."

"So Caroline discovered her lesbianism under your guidance?"

Ruth flicked a column of ash into the tray. "You could put it like that, yes. I seduced her. It didn't take her long to figure out that she loathed and feared sex with men. The only difficult thing was overcoming the taboos and learning how to respond to a woman's body, a woman's way of making love. And I'm not talking about dildos and vibrators."

"Why did you split up?"

"Why does anybody split up? I think we'd done what we could for each other. Caroline was restless. She wanted to go back up north. There were no great rows or anything, just a mutual agreement, and off she went."

"Did you know she had a baby?"

"Yes. Colm's. But that was before I met her. She told me she'd just arrived in London and was lucky enough to meet Colm in a pub. Apparently he was a decent enough bloke, just broke all the time. Some of his mates weren't so decent and that's partly what got Caroline involved in the game to start with. You know, just a temporary dancing job at this club, no harm in it, is there? Bit of extra cash, no questions asked. Creeps. In all fairness, I don't think Colm knew. At least not for a while. Then she had his baby and they put it up for adoption."

"Do you remember the name of the club?"

"Yes. It was the Hole-in-the-Wall, just off Greek Street. Dingy looking place."

"This Colm," Banks asked. "Do you know his second name?"

"No. It's funny, but come to think of it, Caroline never used last names when she spoke about people."

"Seen him lately?"

"Me? I've never seen him."

"How come you know so much about him?"

"Because Caroline told me about him when we were first getting to know each other."

"Where did he live?"

"Notting Hill somewhere. Or it could have been Muswell Hill. I'm not sure. Honestly, I can't help you on that one. She never was much of a one for details, just the broad gesture."

"Are you sure Caroline wasn't already pregnant when she arrived in London?"

Ruth frowned and paused, as if she had suddenly remembered something. She turned her eyes away, and when she spoke there was an odd, distant tone to her voice. "What do you mean?"

"I'm just asking."

"As far as I know she wasn't. Unless she was lying to me. I suppose Colm will be able to confirm it if you can find him."

"Why did that question upset you so much?"

She put her hand to her chest. "I don't know what you're talking about."

"You're more defensive than you were earlier."

Ruth shrugged. "It just reminded me of something, that's all."

"Reminded you of what?"

Ruth reached for her coffee cup, but it was empty. Banks waited. He noticed her hand was shaking a little.

"Something that was bothering Caroline. It's not important," Ruth said. "Probably not even true."

"Let me decide."

"Well, it was those dreams she'd been having, and the things she'd been remembering. At least she thought she had. She didn't really know if they were memories or fantasies."

"What about?"

Ruth looked him in the eye, her cheeks flushed. "Oh hell," she said. "Caroline was beginning to think she'd been molested as a child. She felt she'd repressed the incident, but it was making its way back up from her subconscious, perhaps because of all the weird johns she was servicing."

"Molested? When? Where? Who by?"

"I've told you, she wasn't sure she believed it herself."

"Do you know?"

"Shit, yes. When she was a kid. At home. By her father."

TEN

I

"You knew, didn't you?" Banks challenged Veronica Shildon later that evening. They were eating in an Indonesian restaurant in Soho. The view out the window was hardly romantic—a peep show offering "NAKED GIRLS IN BED" for 50 p—but the food was excellent and the bar served Tiger beer.

Veronica played with her *nasi goreng*, mixing the shrimp in with the rice. "Knew what?"

"About Caroline's past."

"No. Not the way you think."

"You could have saved me a lot of time and effort."

Veronica shook her head. Her eyes looked watery, on the verge of tears. Banks couldn't be sure whether it was emotion or the hot chili peppers. His own scalp was prickling with the heat and his nose was starting to run. He took another swig of cold Tiger.

"Some things I knew," she said finally. "I knew Caroline had been on the streets, but I didn't know any of the names or places involved. When she talked about Ruth she always spoke with affection, but she never mentioned her second name or where they'd lived."

"You knew they were lovers, though?"

"Yes."

"But weren't you jealous? Didn't you question Caroline about it?"

Veronica snorted. "I had little right to be jealous, did I? Remember where I was coming from. Caroline told me there'd been others. She was even living with Nancy Wood when I first met her. And I was with Claude. You must be very naïve, Mr. Banks, if you think we walked into our relationship like a couple of virgins with no emotional baggage. And, somehow, I don't honestly believe you are naïve."

"No matter what the rules are," Banks said, "no matter what people try to convince themselves about what they accept and understand, about how open-minded they are, they still can't stop feeling things like jealousy, hatred and fear. Those are powerful, primitive emotions—instincts, if you like—and you can't convince me that you were both so bloody civilized you calmly decided not to feel anything about one another's pasts."

Veronica put down her fork and poured some more beer into her half empty glass. "Quite a speech. And not so long ago you were telling me I was too civilized to feel the need to revenge Caroline's murder."

"Perhaps you are. But that's another matter. Can you answer my question?"

"Yes. I didn't feel jealous about Ruth Dunne. For one thing, it was years ago, and for another, from what I could gather she'd done Caroline a big favor, perhaps the same kind of favor Caroline later did for me. As I said, I didn't know all the details, but I know the gist. And when I talked to Ruth this afternoon after you'd been to see her, I liked her. I was *glad* to think Caroline had met and loved someone like her. That's my answer. Believe it or not, as you choose. Or do you think people like us are just so perverted that all we do is rip each other's clothes off and jump into bed together?"

Banks said nothing. He ate a mouthful of pork *satay* and washed it down with beer. Attracting the waiter's attention, he then ordered two more Tigers. He did believe Veronica. After all, she had felt secure in her relationship with Caroline, and Ruth Dunne had certainly posed no threat.

"So why didn't you tell me what you did know about Caroline's past?" he asked after the beers had arrived.

"I've already told you. I hardly knew anything."

"Maybe not, but if you'd told us what you *did* know, it would have made it easier for us to find out the rest."

Veronica slammed her knife and fork down. Her cheeks flushed and her eyes narrowed to glaring slits. "All right, damn you! So I'm sorry. What more do you want me to say?"

Some of the other diners looked around and frowned, whispering comments to one another. Veronica held Banks's gaze for a few seconds, then picked up her fork again and speared a spicy shrimp far too violently. A few grains of rice skipped off the edge of her plate onto the napkin on her knee.

"What I want to know," Banks said, "is why you didn't tell me what you knew, and whether there's anything else you've been keeping to yourself. See, it's simple really."

Veronica sighed. "You're an exasperating man," she said. "Do you know that?"

Banks smiled.

"All right. I didn't tell you because I didn't want to . . . to soil Caroline's memory. She wasn't that kind of person anymore. I couldn't see how it would do any good to drag all that up and let the newspapers get hold of it. Is that good enough?"

"It's a start. But I'll bet there's more to it than that."

Veronica said nothing. Her mouth was pressed shut so tight the edges of her lips turned white.

Banks went on. "You didn't want me or anyone else to think you were the kind of woman to be living with someone with such a lurid past. Am I right?"

"You're a bastard, is what you are," said Veronica through gritted teeth. "What you don't understand is that it takes more than a couple of years of therapy to undo a lifetime's damage. Christ, all the time I keep hearing my mother's voice in my mind, calling me dirty, calling me perverted. Maybe you're right and I didn't want that guilt by association. But I still don't see what good knowing that does you."

"The reason for Caroline's murder could lie in her past.

She was running with a pretty rough crowd. I know some of them. I worked the vice squad in Soho for eighteen months, and it's not as glamorous as "Miami Vice," you can be sure of that. Drugs. Prostitution. Gambling. Big criminal business. Very profitable and very dangerous. If Caroline maintained any kind of involvement with these people it could explain a lot."

"But she didn't," Veronica insisted, pressing her hands together and leaning across the table. "She didn't. I lived with her for two years. In all that time we never went to London and she never mentioned much about her life there. Don't you see? It was the future we wanted, not the past. Both of us had had enough of the past."

Banks pushed his empty plate aside, asked Veronica's permission to smoke and reached for his cigarettes. When he'd lit one and inhaled, he took a sip of beer. Veronica folded her napkin in a perfect square and laid it on the coral table-cloth beside her plate. A small mound of rice dotted with chunks of garlic, onion and diced pork remained, but the shrimp were all gone.

Banks glanced out the window and watched a punter in a cloth cap and donkey jacket hesitate outside the peep-show. He was probably having a hard time making up his mind with so much to choose from: "NUDE NAUGHTY AND NASTY" down the street, "LIVE EROTIC NUDE BED SHOW" next door, and now "NAKED GIRLS IN BED" opposite. Shoving his hands in his pockets, he hunched his shoulders and carried on toward Leicester Square. Either lost his bottle or come to his senses, Banks thought.

Veronica had been watching him, and when Banks turned back to face her she gave him a small smile. "What were you looking at?"

"Nothing."

"But you were watching so intently."

Banks shrugged. "Coffee? Liqueur?"

"I'd love a Cointreau, if they've got any."

"They'll have it." Banks called the waiter. He ordered a Drambuie for himself.

"What did you see out there?" Veronica asked again.

"I told you, it was nothing. Just a man, likely down from the provinces for a soccer match or something. He was checking out Soho. Probably surprised it was so cheap."

"What do you get for 50 p?"

"Brief glance at a naked tart, if you're lucky. It's a loss leader, really," Banks said. "Supposed to give you a taste for the real action. You sit in a booth, put your coin in the slot and a shutter slides aside so you can see the girl. As soon as your meter's up, so to speak, the shutter closes. Of course, Soho's been cleaned up a lot lately, but you can't really keep its spirit down." Already, Banks noticed, his accent and his patterns of speech had reverted to those of his London days. He had never lost them in almost three years up north, but they had been modified quite a bit. Now here he was, to all intents and purposes a London copper again.

"Do you approve?" Veronica asked.

"It's not a matter of approval. I don't visit the booths or the clubs myself, if that's what you mean."

"But would you like to see it all stamped out of existence?"

"It'd just spring up somewhere else, wouldn't it? That's what I mean about the spirit. Every big city has its vice area: the Red Light district in Amsterdam, the Reeperbahn, Times Square, the Tenderloin, the Yonge Street strip in Toronto. . . . They're all much the same except for what local laws do and don't allow. Prostitution is legal in Amsterdam, for example, and they even have licensed brothels in parts of Nevada. Then there's Las Vegas and Atlantic City for gambling. You can't really stamp it out. For better or for worse, it seems to be part of the human condition. I admire its energy, its vitality, but I despise what it does to people. I recognize its humor, too. In my job, you get to see the funny side from time to time. Maybe it actually makes policing easier, so much vice concentrated in one small area. We can keep closer tabs on it. But we'll never stamp it out."

"I feel so sheltered," Veronica said, looking out the window again. "I never knew any of this existed when I was growing up. Even later, it never seemed to have anything to do with my life. I couldn't even imagine what people did together except for . . . you know." She shook her head.

"And now you're worldly wise?"

"I don't think so, no. But after Caroline, after she brought me to life, at least I was able to see what all the fuss was about. If that's what it felt like, then no wonder everyone went crazy over it. Do you know that Shakespeare sonnet, the one that starts 'The expense of spirit in a waste of shame?' I never understood it until a couple of years ago."

"It's about lust, isn't it?" Banks said. " 'Had, having, and in quest to have, extreme.' " Christ, he thought, I'm getting just like that Dalgliesh fellow Ruth Dunne mentioned. Better watch it. He nodded toward the window. "Suits that lot out there more than it suits you."

Veronica smiled. "No, you don't know what I mean. At last I could understand. Even *lust* I could finally understand. Do you see?"

"Yes." Banks lit another cigarette and Veronica held the glass of Cointreau in her hand. "About Caroline's child," he said.

"She never told me."

"Okay. But did she ever make any references to a person called Colm?"

"No. And I'm sure I'd remember a name like that."

"She had no contact with anyone you didn't know, no mysterious letters or phone calls?"

"Not that I ever found out about. I'm not saying she couldn't have had. She could be very secretive when she wanted. What are you getting at?"

Banks sighed and swirled his Drambuie in its glass. "I don't know. I thought she might have kept in touch with the foster parents, adopters, whatever."

"Surely that would have been just too painful for her?"

"Maybe so. Forgive me, I'm grasping at straws." And he

was. The child must be about nine or ten now. Far too young to hunt out his mother and stab her with a kitchen knife for abandoning him, or her. Far too young to see the irony in leaving a requiem for himself on the stereo. "There is one thing you might be able to help me with, though," he said.

"Yes?"

"Ruth mentioned that Caroline had begun to suspect she'd been sexually abused as a child. Do you know anything about that?"

Veronica blushed and turned her face to the window. Her profile looked stern against the gaudy neon outside, and the muscle at the corner of her jaw twitched.

"Well?"

"I . . . I can't see what it's got to do with—"

"We've already been through that. Let me be the judge."

"Poor Caroline." Veronica looked directly at Banks again and her expression seemed to relax into sadness. "Melancholy" was a better word, Banks decided, a good Romantic word. Veronica looked melancholy as she fingered her glass and tilted her head before she spoke. "I suppose I didn't tell you for the same reason I didn't tell you anything else about her past. I didn't think it mattered and it would only look bad. Now I feel foolish, but I'm not afraid."

"Did she talk to you about it?"

"Yes. At first it was like Ruth said. She had dreams, terrible dreams. Do you know what sexual abuse does to a child, Mr. Banks?"

Banks nodded. Jenny Fuller, the psychologist who occasionally helped with cases, had explained it to him once.

"Then you know they begin to hate themselves. They lose all self-respect, they get depressed, they feel suicidal, and they often seek reckless, self-destructive ways of life. All those things happened to Caroline. And more."

"Is that why she left home?"

"Yes. But she'd had to wait a long time to get out. Till she was sixteen."

"What do you mean? When did this start happening?"

"When she was eight."

"Eight? Jesus Christ! Go on. I take it this is fact, not fantasy?"

"I can't offer you irrefutable proof, especially now Caroline's dead, but you can take my word for it if you're willing. As I said, at first it was just dreams, fears, suspicions, then when she started working on it with Ursula, more memories began to surface. She'd buried the events, of course, which is perfectly natural under the circumstances. Just imagine a child's confusion when the father she loves starts to do strange and frightening things with her body and tells her she must never tell anybody or terrible things will happen to her. It ties her in knots emotionally. It must be good, because Daddy is doing it. Perhaps she even enjoys the attention. But it doesn't *feel* good, it hurts. And why will she go to hell if she ever tells anyone?"

"What happened?"

"As far as she could piece it together, it occurred first when she was eight. Her mother was having a difficult pregnancy and spent the last two weeks of her term in hospital under close observation. Something to do with her blood pressure and the possibility of toxaemia. Caroline was left alone in the big house with her father, and he started coming to her bedroom at nights, asking her to be a good girl and play with him. Before long he was having intercrural sex with her. It's not very clear how far he went. She remembered pain, but not extreme agony or bleeding. Obviously, he was careful. He didn't want anyone to find out."

"What does 'intercrural' mean?" Banks asked. "I've never heard the word before."

Veronica blushed. "I suppose it is a bit technical. It was Ursula who used it first. It means between the thighs, rather than true penetration."

Banks nodded. "What happened when the mother came home?"

"It continued, but with even more caution. It didn't stop until she was twelve and had her first period."

"He wasn't interested after that?"

"No. She'd become a woman. That terrified him, or so Ursula reckoned."

Banks drew on his cigarette and looked out at the peep show. Two swaying teenagers in studded leather jackets stood in the foyer now, arguing with the cashier. A girl slipped out past them. She couldn't have been more than seventeen or eighteen from what Banks could see of her pale drawn face in the street light. She clutched a short, black, shiny plastic coat tightly around her skinny frame and held her handbag close to her side. She looked hungry, cold and tired. As far as he could make out, she wasn't wearing stockings or tights—in fact she looked naked but for the coat—which probably meant she was on her way to do the same job in another club nearby, after she'd stopped off somewhere for her fix.

"Gary Hartley told DC Gay that his sister had always hated him," Banks said, almost to himself. "He said she even tried to drown him in his bath once when he was a baby. Apparently, she made his life a misery. Her mother's, too. Gary blamed her for sending his mother to an early grave. I've met him myself, and he's a very disturbed young man."

Veronica said nothing. She had finished her drink and had only the dregs of her coffee left to distract her. The waiter sidled up with the bill.

"What I'd like to know is," Banks said, picking it up, "did Gary know why she'd treated him that way right from the start? Just imagine the psychological effect. There he was, someone new and strange, the root and cause of all her suffering at her father's hands. Her mother had deserted her, and now when she came back she was more interested in this whining, crying little brat than in Caroline herself. My sister was born when I was six and I clearly remember feeling jealous. It must have been countless times worse for Caroline, after what had happened with her father. Of course, Gary couldn't have known at the time, not for years perhaps, but did she ever tell him that her father had abused her sexually?"

Veronica started to speak, then stopped herself. She glanced at Banks's cigarette as if she wanted one. Finally, when she could find nowhere to hide, she breathed, "Yes."

"When?"

"As soon as she felt certain it was true."

"Which was?"

"A couple of weeks before she died."

II

Banks walked Veronica to Charing Cross Road and got her a taxi to Holland Park, where she was staying with her friend. After she'd gone, he paused to breathe the night air and feel the cool needles of rain on his face, then went back down Old Compton Street to club-land. It was Friday night, about ten-thirty, and the punters were already deserting the Leicester Square boozers for the lure of more drink and a whiff of sex.

In a seedy alley off Greek Street, notable mostly for the rubbish on its pavements, Banks found the Hole-in-the-Wall. Remarkable. It had been there in his days on the vice squad, and it was still there, looking just the same. Not many places had such staying power—except the old landmarks, almost traditions by now, like the Raymond Revue Bar.

He kicked off a sheet of wet newspaper that had stuck to his sole and walked down the steps. The narrow entrance on the street was ringed with low-watt bulbs, and photos in a glass display case showed healthy, smiling, busty young women, some in leather, some in lacy underwear. The sign promised a topless bar and "LIVE GIRLS TOTALLY NUDE."

The place was dim and smoky inside, noisy with customers trying to talk above the blaring music. It took Banks a minute or so to get his bearings. During that time, a greasy-haired lad with a sloth-like manner had relieved him of his admittance fee and indicated in slow-motion that there were any number of seats available. Banks chose to sit at the bar.

He ordered a half of lager and tried not to have a heart attack when he heard the price. The woman who served him had a nice smile and tired blue eyes. Her curly blond hair framed a pale, moon-shaped face with too much red lipstick and blue eye-shadow. Her breasts stood firmly and proudly to attention, evidence, Banks was sure, of a recent silicone job.

Other waitresses out on the dim floor weaving among the smoky spotlights didn't boast the barmaid's dimensions. Still, they came, like fruit, in all shapes and sizes—melons, apples, pears, mangoes—and, as is the way of all flesh, some were slack and some were firm. The girls themselves looked blank and only seemed to react if some over-eager punter tweaked a nipple, strictly against house rules. Then they would either scold him and walk off in a huff, call one of the bouncers or make arrangements for tweaking the other nipple in private later.

On the stage, gyrating and chewing gum at the same time to a song that seemed to be called "I Want Your Sex," was a young black woman dressed only in a white G-string. She looked in good shape: strong thighs, flat, taut stomach and firm breasts. Perhaps she really wanted to be a dancer. Some girls on the circuit did. When she wasn't dancing like this to earn a living, Banks thought, she was probably working out on a Nautilus machine or doing ballet exercises in a pink tutu in a studio in Bloomsbury.

Watching the action and thinking his thoughts in the hot and smoky club, Banks felt a surge of the old excitement, the adrenaline. It was good to be back, to be here, where anything could happen. Most of the time his job was routine, but he had to admit to himself that part of its appeal lay in those rare moments out on the edge, never far from trouble or danger, where you could smell evil getting closer and closer.

The lager tasted like piss. Cat's piss, at that. Banks shoved it aside and lit a cigarette. That helped.

"Can I get you anything more, sir?" the barmaid asked. He

was sitting and she was standing, which somehow put her exquisitely manufactured breasts at Banks's eye-level. He shifted his gaze from the goose-bumps around her chocolate-colored nipples to her eyes. He felt his cheek burn and, if he cared to admit it, more than just that.

"No," he said, his mouth dry. "I haven't finished this one yet."

She smiled. Her teeth were good. "I know. But people often don't. They tell me it tastes like cat's piss and ask for a real drink."

"How much does a real drink cost?"

She told him.

"Forget it. I'm here on business. Tuffy in?"

Her eyes narrowed. "Who are you? You ain't law, are you?"

Banks shook his head. "Not down here, no. Just tell him Mr. Banks wants to see him, will you, love?"

Banks watched her pick up a phone at the back of the bar. It took no more than a few seconds.

"He said to go through." She seemed surprised by the instruction and looked at Banks in a new light. Clearly, anyone who got in to see the boss that easily had to be a somebody. "It's down past the—"

"I know where it is, love." Banks slid off the bar stool and threaded his way past tables of drooling punters to the fire-door at the back of the club. Beyond the door was a brightly lit corridor, and at the end was an office door. In front stood two giants. Banks didn't recognize either of them. Turnover in hired muscle was about as fast as that in young female flesh. Both looked in their late twenties, and both had clearly boxed. Judging by the state of their noses, neither had won many bouts; still, they could make mincemeat of Banks with their hands tied behind their backs, unless his speed and slipperiness gave him an edge. He felt a tremor of fear as he neared them, but nothing happened. They stood back like hotel doormen and opened the door for him. One smiled and showed the empty spaces of his failed vocation.

In the office, with its scratched desk, threadbare carpet, telephone, pin-ups on the wall and institutional green filing cabinets, sat Tuffy Telfer himself. About sixty now, he was fat, bald and rubicund, with a birthmark the shape of a teardrop at one side of his fleshy red nose. His eyes were hooded and wary, lizard-like, and they were the one feature that didn't seem to fit the rest of him. They looked more as if they belonged to some sexy Hollywood star of the forties or fifties—Victor Mature, perhaps, or Leslie Howard—rather than an ugly, aging gangster.

Tuffy was one of the few remaining old-fashioned British gangsters. He had worked his way up from vandalism and burglary as a juvenile, through fencing, refitting stolen cars and pimping to get to the dizzy heights he occupied today. The only good things Banks knew about him were that he loved his wife, a peroxide ex-stripper called Mirabelle, and that he never had anything to do with drugs. As a pimp, he had been one of the few *not* to get his girls hooked. Still, it was no reason to get sentimental over the bastard. He'd had one of his girls splashed with acid for trying to turn him in, though nobody could prove it, and there were plenty of women old before their time thanks to Tuffy Telfer. Banks had been the bane of his existence for about three months many years ago. The evil old sod hadn't been able to make a move without Banks getting there first. The police had never got enough evidence to arrest Tuffy himself, though Banks had managed to put one or two of his minions away for long stretches.

"Well, well, well," said Tuffy in the East-end accent he usually put on for the punters. He had actually been raised by a meek middle class family in Wood Green, but few people other than the police knew that. "If it ain't Inspector Banks."

"*Chief* Inspector now, Tuffy."

"I always thought you'd go far, son. Sit down, sit down. A drink?" The only classy piece of furniture in the entire room was a well-stocked cocktail cabinet.

"A real drink?"

"Wha'? Oh, I get it." Telfer laughed. "Been sampling the lager downstairs, eh? Yeah, a real drink."

"I'll have a Scotch then. Mind if I smoke?"

Telfer laughed again. "Go ahead. Can't indulge no more myself." He tapped his chest. "Quack says it's bad for the ticker. But I'll get enough second-hand smoke running this place to see me to my grave. A bit more won't do any harm."

Tuffy was hamming it up, as usual. He didn't have to be here to run the Hole-in-the-Wall; he had underlings who could do that for him. Nor was he so poor he had to sit in such a poky office night after night. The club was just a minor outpost of Tuffy's empire, and nobody, not even vice, knew where all its colonies were. He had a house in Belgravia and owned property all over the city. He also mixed with the rich and famous. But every Friday and Saturday night he chose to come and sit here, just like in the old days, to run his club. It was part of his image, part of the sentimentality of organized crime.

"Making ends meet?" Banks asked.

"Just. Times is hard, very hard." One of the musclemen put Banks's drink—a generous helping—on the desk in front of him. "But what can I say?" Tuffy went on. "I get by. What you been up to?"

"Moved up north. Yorkshire."

Tuffy raised his eyebrows. "Bit drastic, in'it?"

"I like it fine."

"Whatever suits."

"Not having a glass yourself?"

Tuffy sniffed. "Doctor's orders. I'm a sick man, Mr. Banks. Old Tuffy's not long for this world, and there'll not be many to mourn his passing, I can tell you that. Except for the nearest and dearest, bless her heart."

"How is Mirabelle?"

"She's hale and hearty. Thank you for asking, Mr. Banks. Remembers you fondly, does my Mirabelle. Wish I could say the same myself." There was humor in his voice, but hardness in his hooded eyes. Banks heard one of the bruisers shift from foot to foot behind him and a shiver went up his spine. "What can I do you for?" Tuffy asked.

"Information."

Tuffy said nothing, just sat staring. Banks sipped some Scotch and cast around for an ashtray. Suddenly, one appeared from behind his shoulder, as if by magic. He set it in front of him.

"A few years ago you had a dancer working the club, name of Caroline Hartley. Remember her?"

"What if I do?" Telfer's expression betrayed no emotion.

"She's dead. Murdered."

"What's it got to do with me?"

"You tell me, Tuffy."

Telfer stared at Banks for a moment, then laughed. "Know how many girls we get passing through here?" he said.

"A fair number, I'll bet."

"A fair number indeed. The punters are constantly demanding fresh meat. See the same dancer twice they think they've been had. And you're talking how many years ago?"

"Six or seven."

Telfer rested his pale, pudgy hands on the blotter. "Well, you can see my point then, can't you?"

"What about your records?"

"Records? What you talking about?"

Banks nodded toward the filing cabinets. "You must keep clear and accurate records, Tuffy—cash flow, wages, rent, bar take. For the taxman, remember?"

Telfer cleared his throat. "Yeah, well, what if I do?"

"You could look her up. Come on, Tuffy, we've been through all this before, years ago. I know you keep a few notes on every girl who passes through here in case you might want to use her again, maybe for a video, a stag party, some special—"

Telfer held up a hand. "All right, all right, I get your drift. It's all above-board. You know that. Cedric, see if you can find the file, will you?"

One of the bruisers opened a filing cabinet. "Cedric?" Banks whispered, eyebrows raised.

Telfer shrugged. His chins wobbled. They sat silently, Telfer tapping his short fat fingers on the desk while Cedric rummaged through the files, muttering the alphabet to himself as he did so.

"Ain't here," Cedric announced finally.

"You sure?" Telfer asked. "It begins with a 'aitch—Hartley. That comes after 'gee' and before 'eye.' "

Cedric grunted. "Ain't here. Got a Carrie 'Eart, but no Caroline 'Artley."

"Let's have a look," Banks said. "She might have used a stage name."

Telfer nodded and Cedric handed over the file. Pinned to the top-left corner was a four-by-five black-and-white picture of a younger Caroline Hartley, topless and smiling, her small breasts pushed together by her arms. She could easily have passed for a fourteen-year-old, even a mature twelve-year-old. Below the photo, in Telfer's surprisingly neat and elegant hand, were the meager details that had interested him about Caroline Hartley: "Vital statistics: 34-22-34. Color of hair: jet-black. Eyes: blue. Skin: olive and satiny" (Banks hadn't suspected Tuffy had such a poetic streak). And so it went on. Telfer obviously gave his applicants quite an interview.

The one piece of information that Banks hoped he might find was at the end, an address under her real name: "Caroline Hartley, % Colm Grey." It was old now, of course, and might no longer be of any use. But if it was Colm Grey's address, and he was poor, he might well have hung onto his flat, unless he'd left the city altogether. Also, now Banks had his last name, Colm Grey would be easier to track down. He recognized the street name. It was somewhere between Notting Hill and Westbourne Park. He had lived not far from there himself twenty years ago.

"Got what you want?" asked Telfer.

"Maybe." Banks handed the file back to Cedric, who replaced it, then finished his Scotch.

"Well, then," said Tuffy with a smile. "Nice of you to drop in. But you mustn't let me keep you." He stood up and shook hands. His grip was firm but his palm was sweaty. "Not staying long, are you? Around here, I mean."

Banks smiled. "No."

"Not thinking of coming back to stay?"

"No."

"Good. Good. Just wanted to be sure. Well, do pop in again the next time you're down, won't you, and we'll have another good old natter."

"Sure, Tuffy. And give my love to Mirabelle."

"I will. I will, Mr. Banks."

The bruisers stood aside and Banks walked out of the office and down the corridor unscathed. When he got back to the noisy smoky club, he breathed a sigh of relief. Tuffy obviously remembered what a pain in the arse he'd been, but working on the edge of the law, as he did, he had to play it careful. True, plenty of his operations *were* above-board. It was a game—give and take, live and let live—and both sides knew it. Banks had come close to breaking the rules once or twice, and Tuffy wanted to be sure he wouldn't be around to do that again. Questions that sounded like friendly curiosity were often, in fact, thinly veiled threats.

"Another drink, dear?" the mammarially magnificent barmaid said as Banks passed by.

"No, love. Sorry, have to be off now. Maybe another time."

"Story of my life," she said, and her breasts swung as she turned away.

Outside, Banks fastened his overcoat, shoved his hands deep in his pockets and walked along Greek Street toward the Tottenham Court Road Tube station. He had thought of taking a taxi, but it was only midnight, and Barney lived a stone's throw from the Central line. At Soho Square he saw a drunk in a tweed overcoat and trilby vomiting in the gutter. A tart, inadequately dressed for the cold, stood behind him and leaned against the wall, arms folded across her chest, looking disgusted.

How did that poem end? Banks wondered. The one Veronica had quoted earlier that evening. Then he remembered. After its haunting summary of the horrors of lust, it finished, "All this the world well knows; yet none knows well/To shun the heaven that leads men to this hell." Certainly knew his stuff, did old Willie. They didn't call him "the Bard" for nothing, Banks reflected, as he turned up Sutton Row toward the bright lights of Charing Cross Road.

III

The next morning, after a chat with Barney over bacon and eggs, Banks set out to find Colm Grey. He had arranged to have lunch with Veronica and had asked Barney to check Ruth Dunne's alibi and to see what he could find on the stabbing of Caroline's pimp, Reggie, just to cover all the angles.

The rush-hour crowd had dwindled by the time he got a train, and he was even able to grab a seat and read the *Guardian*, the way he used to do.

He got off at Westbourne Park and walked toward Notting Hill until he found the address on St. Luke's Road. Five names matched the bells beside the front door, and he was in luck: C. Grey was one of them, flat four.

Banks pushed the bell and stood by the intercom. No response. He tried again and waited a couple of minutes. It looked like Grey was out. The way things stood at the moment, Grey was hardly a prime suspect, but he was a loose end that had to be tied up. He was the only one who knew the full story about Caroline Hartley's child. Just as Banks started to walk away, he thought he heard a movement behind the door. Sure enough, it opened and a young man stood there, hair standing on end, eyes bleary, stuffing a white shirt in the waist of his jeans.

He frowned when he saw Banks. "Wharrisit? What time is it?"

"Half past nine. Sorry to disturb you." Banks introduced himself and showed his identification. "It's about Caroline Hartley."

The name didn't register at first, then Grey suddenly gaped and said, "Bloody hell! You'd better come in."

Banks followed him upstairs to a two-room flat best described as cozy. The furniture needed reupholstering and the place needed dusting and a damn good tidying up.

"I was sleeping," Grey said as he bent to turn on the gas fire. "Excuse me a minute." When he came back he had washed his face and combed his hair and he carried a cup of instant coffee. "Want some?" he asked Banks.

"No. This shouldn't take long. Mind if I smoke?"

"Be my guest."

Grey sat opposite him, leaning forward as if hunched over his steaming coffee cup. He was lanky with a long pale face, pitted from ancient acne or chicken-pox. He needed a shave and a trim, and his slightly protruding eyes were watery blue.

"Is it bad news?" he asked, as if he were used to life being one long round of bad news.

"You mean you don't know?"

"Obviously, or I wouldn't be asking. Well?"

Banks took a deep breath. He had assumed Grey would have read about the murder in the papers. "Caroline Hartley was murdered in Eastvale on December twenty-second," he said finally.

At first, Grey didn't seem to react. He couldn't have been much paler, so losing color would have been no indication, and his eyes were already watery enough to look like they were on the verge on tears. All he did was sit silent and still for about a minute, completely still, and so silent Banks wondered if he were even breathing. Banks tried to imagine Grey and Caroline Hartley as a couple, but he couldn't.

"Are you all right?" he asked.

"Can I have one?" Grey indicated the cigarettes. "Supposed to have chucked it in, but . . ."

Banks gave him a cigarette, which he lit and puffed on like a dying man on oxygen. "I don't suppose this is a social call, either?" he said.

Banks shook his head.

Grey sighed. "I haven't seen Caroline for about eight years. Ever since she started running with the wrong crowd."

"Tuffy Telfer?"

"That's the bastard. Just like a father to her, he was, to hear her speak."

Banks hoped not. "Did you ever meet him?"

"No. I wouldn't have trusted myself with him for ten seconds. I'd have swung for the bastard."

Not a chance, Banks thought. Colm Grey couldn't have got within a hundred yards of Tuffy Telfer without getting at least both arms and legs broken. "What caused you and Caroline to split up?" he asked.

"Just about everything." Grey flicked some ash onto the hearth by the gas fire and reached for his coffee again. "I suppose it really started going downhill when she got pregnant."

"What happened? Did you try to give her the push?"

Grey stared at Banks. "Couldn't be further from it. We were in love. I was, anyway. When she got pregnant she just turned crazy. I wanted to have it, the kid, even though we were poor, and she didn't want rid of it at first. At least I don't think she did. Maybe I pushed her too hard, I don't know. Maybe she was just doing it to please me. Anyway, she was miserable all the time she was carrying, but she wouldn't have an abortion either. There was time, if she'd wanted, but she kept putting it off until it was too late. Then she was up and down like a yoyo, one day wishing she could have a miscarriage, taking risks walking out in icy weather, maybe hoping she'd just slip and fall, the next day feeling guilty and hating herself for being so cruel. Then, as soon as the child was born, she couldn't wait to get shut of the blighter."

"Where is the child now?"

"No idea. Caroline never even wanted to see it. As soon as it was born it was whisked off to its new parents. She didn't even want to know whether it was a girl or a boy. Then things started getting worse for us, fast. Caroline worked at getting her figure back, like nothing had ever happened. As soon as she got introduced to Telfer's crowd, that was it. She seemed hell-bent on self-destruction, don't ask me why."

"Who introduced her to Telfer?"

Colm bit his lower lip, then said, "I blamed myself, after I found out. You know what it's like, a man doesn't always choose his friends well. The crowd we went about with, Caroline and me, it was a pretty mixed bunch. Some of them liked to go up west on a weekend and do the clubs. We went along too a few times. Caroline seemed fascinated by it all. Or horrified, I never could make out which. She was well into the scene before I even found out, and there was nothing I could do to stop her. She was a good-looking kid, a real beauty, and she must have caught someone's eye. I should think they're always on the look-out for new talent at those places.

"One night she came home really late. I was beside myself with worry and it came out as anger—you know, like when your mother always yelled at you if you were late. We had a blazing row and I called her all the names under the sun. It was then she told me. In detail. And she rubbed my face in it, laughed at me for not catching on sooner. Where did I think her new clothes were coming from? How did I think we could afford to go out so often? I was humiliated. I should have walked out there and then, but I was a fool. Maybe it was just a wild phase, maybe it would go away. That's what I tried to convince myself. But it didn't go away. The trouble was, I still loved her." Colm rested his chin in his hand and stared at the floor. "A couple of months later we split up. She left. Just walked out one evening and never came back. Didn't even take her belongings with her, what little she had." He smiled sadly. "Never much of a one for possessions, wasn't Caroline. Said they only tied her down."

"Had you been fighting all that time?"

"No. There was only the one big row, then everything was sort of cold. I was trying to accept what she was up to, but I couldn't. It just wasn't working with her coming in at all hours—or not at all—and me knowing what she'd been up to, imagining her in bed with fat, greasy punters and dancing naked in front of slobbering businessmen."

"Where did she go?"

"Dunno. Never saw or heard from her again. She was a great kid and I loved her, but I couldn't stand it. I was heading for a breakdown. She was living life in the fast lane, heading for self-destruct. I tried to stop her but she just laughed at me and told me not to be such a bore."

"Did she ever tell you anything about her past?"

"Not a lot, no. Didn't get on with her mum and dad so she ran off to the big city. Usual story."

"Ever mention her brother?"

"No. Didn't know she had one."

"Did she ever tell you about her dreams?"

"Dreams?" he frowned. "No, why?"

"It doesn't matter. What about you? What did you do after she'd gone?"

"Me? Well, I didn't exactly join the Foreign Legion, but I did run away and try to forget. I sublet the flat for a year and drifted around Europe. France mostly, grape-picking and all that. Came back, got a job as a bicycle courier, and now I'm doing 'the Knowledge.' Nearly there, too. With a bit of luck I'll 'Get Out' and have my 'Bill and Badge' inside a year."

"Good luck." Banks had heard how difficult it was riding around on a moped day after day in the traffic fumes, memorizing over eighteen thousand street names and the numerous permutations of routes between them. But that was what one had to do to qualify as a London taxi driver. "Did you forget her?" he asked.

"You never do, do you, really? What did she do after she left me? Do you know?"

Banks gave him a potted history of Caroline's life up to her death, and again Grey sat still after he'd finished.

"She always was funny about sex," he said. "Not that I'd have guessed, like, that she was a lezzie. I've nothing against them—live and let live, I say—but sex always seemed like some kind of trial or test with her, you know, as if she was trying to find out whether she really liked it or not. I suppose not liking it made it easier for her to live on the game, in a way. It was just a job. She didn't have to like it."

Banks nodded. It was common knowledge that a lot of prostitutes were lesbians.

There was nothing more to say. He stood up and held out his hand. Grey leaned forward and shook it.

"Were you working on the twenty-second?" Banks asked.

Grey smiled. "My alibi? Yes, yes I was. You can check. And I've got to get started today, too. When you're doing 'the Knowledge' you eat, breathe and sleep it."

"I know."

"Besides, I don't even know where Eastvale is."

On his way out, Banks offered Grey another cigarette, but he declined. "It didn't taste all that good, and I couldn't justify starting again. Thanks for telling me . . . you know . . . about her life. At least someone seemed to make her happy. She deserved that." He shook his head. "She was just one fucked-up kid when I knew her. We never had a chance."

Outside, Banks turned up his collar and walked through the squares and side-streets toward Notting Hill Gate. This area had been his first home in London when he had come as a student. Back then, the tall houses with their white facades had been in poor repair, and small flats were just about affordable. Banks had paid seven pounds a week for an L-shaped room, with free mice, in a house that included one out-of-work jazz trumpeter, an earnest social worker, a morose and anorexic-looking woman on the second floor who wore beads and a kaftan and never spoke to anyone, and

Jimmy, the cheerful and charming bus driver who Banks suspected of selling marijuana on the side.

He passed the house, on Powis Terrace, and felt a twinge of nostalgia. That small room, now with lace curtains in the window, was where he and Sandra had first made love in those carefree days when he had been unhappy with his business studies courses but still hadn't quite known what to do with his life.

Back then the area had been very much a swinging sixties enclave with its requisite mixture of musicians, poets, artists, dopers, revolutionaries and general drop-outs. It had suited Banks at the time. He enjoyed the music, the animated discussions and the aura of spontaneity, but he could never wholeheartedly turn on, tune in and drop out. He had wanted to get away from home, from the dull routine of Peterborough, and the Notting Hill flat had been both a cheap and exciting way of finding out what life was all about. Ah, to be eighteen again. . . .

He walked up to the main intersection and took the Underground at Notting Hill Gate. He was on the Central line, and he still had some time to kill, so he got off at Tottenham Court Road, in the same general area he'd been in the previous evening. He was feeling vaguely depressed after his talk with Colm Grey, which had reduced a couple of his favorite theories to shreds, and thought a city walk in the bracing air might help blow away the blues.

Soho was another world in the daytime. The clubs and love shops and peep-shows were still there, but somehow the glitz and sleaze only managed to look anemic in daylight. The gaudy lights held no allure; they were washed out, paled by even the gray winter light. In the daytime, the siren-song of sex for hire was muted to a distant, nagging whine; there was no hiding the cheap, shabby reality of the product.

But another kind of vital street life took the ascendant—the world of markets, of business. Banks wandered among the stalls on Berwick Street, which seemed to sell everything from pineapples and melons to cotton panties, cups and saucers, watches, mixed nuts and egg-cutters. Under one stall, a big brown dog lay sheltered watching the passers-by with mournful eyes.

Feeling better, he found a phone booth on Great Marlborough Street and called Barney Merritt at Scotland Yard. As Banks had expected, and hoped, Ruth Dunne's alibi checked out.

The stabbing of Reggie Becker was also as clear-cut as could be. The killer, a seventeen-year-old prostitute called Brenda Meers, had stabbed Becker five times in broad daylight on Greek Street. At least two of the wounds had nicked major arteries and he had bled to death before the ambulance got there. Eyewitnesses abounded, though fewer came forward later than were present at the time. When asked why she had done it, Brenda Meers said it was because Reggie was trying to make her go with a man who wanted her to drink his urine and eat his feces. She had been with him before and didn't think she could stand it again. She had begged Reggie all morning not to make her go, but he wouldn't relent, so she walked into Woolworth's, bought a cheap sheath-knife and stabbed him. As far as the police were concerned, Reggie Becker was no great loss, and Brenda would at least get the benefit of psychiatric counseling.

So that was that: the London connection ruled out. But maybe he hadn't wasted his time entirely. He now had a much fuller picture of Caroline Hartley, even if he did have to throw out that neat theory of a connection between the Vivaldi *Laudate pueri* and the child she had given birth to. He still believed the music was important, but he could no longer tell how or where it fit.

He looked at his watch. Just time to buy Sandra and Tracy presents in Liberty's, and maybe something for Brian from Virgin Records on Oxford Street. Then it would be time to meet Veronica for lunch and set off. He wondered what, if any, developments would be waiting for him back in Eastvale.

ELEVEN

I

"You don't think he did it, do you?" Susan Gay asked Banks over coffee and toasted teacakes in the Golden Grill. It was two, largely frustrating days after his return from London.

"Gary Hartley?" Banks shrugged. "I don't know. I don't suppose it makes much sense. Gary finds out Caroline was abused as a child so he kills her? All I know is that she told him about it a couple of weeks before she was killed. But you're right, we've no real motive at all. On the other hand, she *did* make his life a misery. Then she ran off and left him stuck with the old man. A thing like that can fester into hatred. The timing is interesting, too."

"Does he know anything about classical music?"

"We'll have to find out. He's certainly well-read. Look at all those books around the place, and the way he speaks, his vocabulary. He's way beyond the range of most teenagers. He could easily have come across the information about *Laudate pueri* somewhere, then seen the record at Caroline's."

"So you're going to see him?"

"Yes. And I'd like you to come along if you can spare the time. Anything happening with the break-ins?"

"Nothing that can't wait."

"Good. Remember, Gary's lied to us before. I want to see the old man, too. Who knows, we might be able to get something out of him."

"He was pretty useless last time," Susan said. "I'm not convinced he's all there." She shivered.

"Cold?"

She shook her head. "Just the thought of that house."

"I know what you mean. Let Phil know, will you? I want the three of us in on this. I'll be with the super, filling him in." Banks looked at his watch. "Say half an hour?"

Susan nodded and left.

Thirty minutes later they sat in an unmarked police Rover with Susan at the wheel and Banks hunched rather glumly in the back, missing his music. Sandra was using the Cortina to buy photographic supplies in York, so they had had to sign a car out of the pool. Susan's driving was assured, though not as good as Richmond's, Banks noted. Sergeant Hatchley had been the worst, he remembered, a bloody maniac on the road.

Despite more snow, road conditions were clear enough. It was, in fact, much brighter in the north, for once, than it had been in London, and a weak winter sun shone on the distant snow-covered fells, spreading a pastel coral glow.

In under an hour they pulled into the familiar Harrogate street and rang Hartley's doorbell. As expected, Gary answered. Giving nothing but a "you again" look, he wandered back into the front room, leaving them to follow.

The room hadn't been cleaned or tidied since their last visit, and a few more beer cans and tab ends had joined the wreckage on the hearth. The air smelled stale, like a pub after closing-time. Banks longed to open the window to let in some air. Before he could get there, Richmond beat him to it, yanking back the heavy curtains and raising the window. Gary squinted at the burst of sunlight but said nothing.

"We've got a few more questions to ask you," Banks said, "but first I'd like a word with your father."

"You can't. He's sick, he's resting." Gary gripped the chair arm and sat up. He reached for a cigarette and lit it. "Doctor's orders."

"I'm sorry, Gary. I already know most of it. I just need him to fill me in on a few details."

"What do you know? What are you talking about?"

"Caroline . . . your father."

Gary sagged back into his chair. "Oh God," he whispered. "You know?"

"Yes."

"Then you can hardly imagine he's going to tell you anything, can you? He's asleep, anyway. Practically in a bloody coma."

Banks stood up. "Stay with him, will you, Phil? Susan, come with me."

Susan followed Banks upstairs. They both heard Gary cry "No!" as they went.

"This way, sir." Susan pointed to Mr. Hartley's door and Banks pushed it open.

If only Gary had turned off the electric fire, Banks thought later, the smell wouldn't have been so bad. As it was, Susan put her hand over nose and mouth and staggered back, while Banks reached for a handkerchief. Neither advanced any further into the room. The old man lay back on his pillows, emaciated almost beyond recognition. Judging by the reddish discoloration of the veins in his scrawny neck, Banks guessed he had been dead at least two days. It would take an expert to fix the time more exactly than that, though, as there were many factors to take into consideration, not least among them his age, the state of his health and the warm temperature of the room.

"Call the local CID," Banks told Susan, "and tell them to arrange for a police surgeon and a scene-of-crime team. You know the drill."

Susan hurried downstairs and went to phone while Banks gently closed the door and returned to the front room. Gary looked at him as he entered. The boy seemed drained of all emotion, tired beyond belief. Banks motioned for Richmond to stand by the window, where Gary couldn't see him, then sat down close to Gary and leaned forward.

"Want to tell me about it, son?" he asked.

"What's to tell?" Gary lit a new cigarette from the stub of his old one. His long fingers were stained yellow with nicotine around the nails.

"You know." Banks pointed at the ceiling. "What happened?"

Gary shrugged. "Is he dead?"

"Yes."

"I told you he was sick."

"How did he die, Gary?"

"He had cancer."

"How long has he been dead?"

"How should I know?"

"Why didn't you call a doctor?"

"No point, was there?"

"When did you last look in on him, take him some food?"

Gary sucked on his cigarette and looked away into the cold hearth, littered with butts and empty beer cans. Sweat formed on his pale brow.

"When did you last go up and see him, Gary?" Banks asked again.

"I don't know."

"Yesterday? The day before?"

"I don't know."

"I'm no expert, Gary, but I'd say you haven't been up there for at least three days, have you?"

"If you say so."

"Did you kill him?"

"He was sick, getting worse."

"But did you kill him?"

"I never touched him, if that's what you mean. Never laid a finger on the old bastard. I couldn't bear . . ."

Banks noticed the boy was crying. He had turned his head aside but it was shaking, and strange snuffling sounds came from between the fingers he had placed over his mouth and nose.

"You deserted him. You left him up there to die. Is that what you did?"

Banks couldn't be sure, but he thought Gary was nodding.

"Why? For God's sake why?"

"You know," he said, wiping his nose with the back of his hand and turning to face Banks angrily. "You told me. You know all about it. What he did . . ."

"For what he did to Caroline?"

"You know it is."

"What about Caroline? Did you kill her too?"

"Why should I do that?"

"I'm asking. She tried to kill *you* once. Did you?"

Gary sighed and tossed his half-smoked cigarette into the grate. "I suppose so," he said wearily. "I don't know. I think *he* did, but maybe we all did. Maybe this miserable bloody family killed her."

II

By mid-afternoon the sun had disappeared behind smoke-colored clouds and Banks had turned his desk lamp on. They sat in his office—Banks, Gary Hartley and Susan Gay—taking notes and waiting for a pot of coffee before getting started on the interrogation.

Gary, sitting in a hard-backed chair opposite Banks, looked frightened now. He wasn't fidgeting or squirming, but his eyes were filled with a kind of resigned, mournful fear. Banks, still not completely sure what had gone on in that large, cold house, wanted him to relax and talk. Fresh, hot coffee might help.

While he waited, Banks glanced over the brief notes the forensic pathologist had made after his preliminary investigation of the scene. He'd estimated time of death at not less than two days and not more than three. For three days then, perhaps—since shortly after Banks's and Richmond's visit—

the poor, frightened kid in front of them had sat in the cold ruin of a room, smoking and drinking, knowing the corpse of his father lay rotting upstairs in the heat of an electric fire. The doctor hadn't called; he had no reason to as long as Mr. Hartley had a full prescription of pain-killers and someone to take care of his basic needs.

"Rigor mortis disappeared . . . greenish discoloration of the abdomen," the report read, "reddish veins in neck, shoulders and thighs . . . no marbling as yet." The temperature would have speeded the process of decomposition considerably, Banks realized. Also, the air was dry, and some degree of mummification might have occurred if the old man had lain there much longer. Banks suspected that cause of death was starvation—Gary had simply left him to die—but it would be a while before more exact information about cause and time could be known. Older persons decompose more slowly than younger ones, and thin ones more slowly than fat ones. Bodies of diseased persons break down quickly. Stomach contents would have to be examined and inner organs checked for the degree of putrefaction.

All very interesting, Banks thought, but none of it really mattered if Gary Hartley confessed.

Finally, PC Tolliver arrived with the coffee and styrofoam cups. Susan poured Gary a cup and pushed the milk and sugar toward him. He didn't acknowledge her. Banks walked over to the window and glanced out at the gray market square, then sat down to begin. He spoke quietly, intimately almost, to put the boy at ease.

"Earlier, Gary, you seemed confused. You said you supposed that you had killed Caroline, then you told me you think your father killed her. Can you be a bit clearer about that?"

"I'm not sure. I . . . I . . ."

"Why not tell me about it, the night you killed her? Start at the beginning."

"I don't remember."

"Try. It's important."

Gary screwed up his eyes in concentration, but when he opened them, he shook his head. "It's all dark. All dark inside. And it hurts."

"Where does it hurt, Gary?"

"My head. My eyes. Everywhere." He covered his face with his hands and shuddered.

Banks let a few seconds pass, then asked, "How did you get to Eastvale?"

"What?"

"To Eastvale? Did you go by bus or train? Did you borrow a car?"

Gary shook his head. "I didn't go to Eastvale. I wasn't in Eastvale."

"Then how did you kill Caroline?"

"I've told you, I don't know." He hung his head in his hands. "I just don't know."

"What happened to your father, Gary?"

"He's dead."

"How did he die? Did you kill him?"

"No. I didn't go near him."

"Did you stop going up to his room? Did you stop feeding him?"

"I couldn't go. Not after Caroline, not after I knew. I thought about it and I carried on for a while, but I couldn't." He looked at Banks, his eyes pleading. "You must understand. I couldn't. Not after she was dead."

"So you stopped tending to him?"

"He killed her."

"But he couldn't have, Gary. He was an invalid, bedridden. He couldn't have gone to Eastvale and killed her."

Suddenly, Gary banged the metal desk with his fist. Susan moved forward but Banks motioned her back.

"I've told you it wasn't in Eastvale!" Gary yelled. "How many times do I have to tell you? Caroline didn't die in Eastvale."

"But she did, Gary. Come on, you know that."

He shook his head. "He killed her. And I killed her too."

Susan looked up from her notes and frowned. "Tell me how he killed her," Banks asked.

"I don't know. I wasn't there. But he did it like . . . like. . . . Oh Christ, she was just a child . . . just a little child!" And he put his head in his hands and sobbed, shaking all over.

Banks stood up and put a comforting arm over his shoulder. At first, Gary didn't react, but then he yielded and buried his head in Banks's chest. Banks held on to him tightly and stroked his hair, then when Gary's grasp loosened, he extricated himself and returned to his chair. Now he thought he understood why Gary was talking the way he was. Now he knew what had happened. Now he understood the Hartley family. But he still had no idea who had killed Caroline Hartley, and why.

III

When Susan Gay got to the Crooked Billet at six o'clock, James Conran wasn't there. Casting around for a suitable place to sit, she caught the eye of Marcia Cunningham, the costumes manager, who beckoned her over. Marcia seemed to be sitting with someone, but a group of drinkers blocked Susan's view.

Susan elbowed her way through the after-work crowd, loosening her overcoat as she went. It was cold outside, and enough snow had fallen to speckle her shoulders, but in the pub it was warm. She took off her green woolly gloves and slipped them in her pocket, then, when she reached Marcia, removed her coat and hung it on a peg by the bar. She noted that the buttons of the pink cardigan Marcia was wearing were incorrectly fastened, making the thing look askew.

"They've not finished yet," Marcia said. "What with it being so close to first night, or should I say *twelfth* night, James thought an extra half hour might be in order. Especially with the new Maria. They didn't need me, so he asked me to pass on his apologies if I saw you. He'll be in a little later."

"Thank you." Susan smoothed her skirt and sat down.

"How rude of me," Marcia said, indicating the woman beside her. "Susan Gay, this is Sandra Banks." Then she put her hand to her mouth. "Silly me, I'm forgetting you probably know each other already."

Susan certainly recognized Sandra. With her looks, she would be hard to miss—that determined mouth, lively blue eyes, long blond hair and dark eyebrows. She possessed a natural elegance. Susan had always envied her and felt awkward and dowdy when she was around.

"Yes," Susan said, "we've met once or twice. Good evening, Mrs. Banks."

"Please, call me Sandra."

"Sandra was just finishing up some work in the gallery so I popped in and asked if she'd like a drink."

Susan noticed that their glasses were empty and offered to get a round. When she came back, there was still no sign of James or the others. She didn't know how she was going to maintain small talk with Sandra Banks for the next twenty minutes or so, especially after the emotional scene she had just witnessed between Banks and Gary Hartley. She felt embarrassed. Strong emotion always made her feel that way, and when Banks had hugged the boy close she had had to avert her gaze. But she had seen her boss's expression over the back of the boy's head. It hadn't given much away, but she had noticed compassion in his eyes and she knew from the set of his lips that he shared the boy's pain.

Luckily, Marcia saved her. In appearance rather like one of those plump, ruddy-cheeked characters one sees in illustrations of Dickens novels, she had an ebullient manner to match.

"Any closer to catching those vandals?" she asked.

Conscious of Sandra watching her, Susan said, "Not yet, I'm afraid. A couple of kids did some damage to a youth club in the north end and we think it's the same ones. We've got our eye on them."

"Do you think you'll ever catch them?"

Susan caught Sandra smiling at the question and could hardly keep herself from doing the same. Her discomfort waned slightly. Instead of feeling resentful, under scrutiny, she was beginning to feel more as if she had an ally. Sandra had been through it all, knew what it was like to be police in the public eye. But Susan knew she would still have to be cautious. Sandra was, after all, the detective chief inspector's wife, and if Susan made any blunders they would certainly be passed on to Banks.

"Hard to say," she replied. "We've got a couple of leads and several likely candidates. That's about all."

What she hadn't said was that they had at least found a pattern to the kind of places the kids liked to wreck. Most of them were community centers of some kind, never private establishments like cinemas or pubs. As there was a limited number of such social clubs in Eastvale, extra men had been posted on guard. Their instructions were to lie low, blend in and catch the kids in the act, rather than stand as sentries and scare them off. Soon they might put a stop to the trail of vandalism that had cost the town a fortune over the past few months.

"It was such a mess," Marcia said, shaking her head. "All those costumes, ruined. I almost sat down and cried. Anyway, I took them home and now I've a bit of time I'm sorting through the remnants to see if I can't resurrect some. I've put a couple together already. I hate waste."

"That sounds a hell of a job," said Sandra. "I don't think I could face it."

"Oh, I love sewing, fixing things, making things. It makes me feel useful. And I see what I've done at the end. Job satisfaction, I suppose, though it's a pity there's no pay to match."

Sandra laughed. "I'd offer to help but I've got two left thumbs when it comes to sewing. I can't even get the bloody thread through the needle. Poor Alan has to sew his own buttons on."

Susan tried to imagine Detective Chief Inspector Alan Banks sewing buttons on a shirt, but she couldn't.

"It's all right," Marcia said. "Keeps me out of mischief these cold winter evenings. Since Frank's been gone I find I need to do more and more to occupy myself."

"Marcia's husband died six months ago," Sandra explained to Susan.

"Aye," said Marcia. "Just like that, he went. Good as new one moment, then, bang, curtains. And never had a day's illness in his life. Didn't drink and gave up his pipe years ago. Only sixty, he was."

Susan shook her head. "It does seem unfair."

"Whoever told us life would be fair, love? Nobody did, that's who. Anyway, enough of that. Walking out with Mr. Conran are you?"

Susan felt herself blushing. "Well I . . . I . . ."

"I know," Marcia went on. "It's none of my business. Tell me to shut up if you want. I'm just an old busybody, that's all."

Now Susan couldn't help laughing. "We've been out to dinner a couple of time, and to the pictures. That's all."

Marcia nodded. "I wasn't probing into your sex life, lass, just curious, that's all. What's he like when he's out of his director's hat?"

"He makes me laugh."

"There's a few in that theater over there could do with a laugh or two."

Susan leaned forward. "Marcia, you know that girl who was killed, Caroline Hartley? Was there really anything between her and James?"

"Not that I know of, love," Marcia answered. "Just larked around, that's all. Besides, she was one of *them*, wasn't she? Not that I . . . well, you know what I mean."

"Yes, but James didn't know that. None of you did."

"Still," Marcia insisted, "nothing to it as far as I could see. Oh, he had his eye on her all right. What man wouldn't?

Maybe not your *Playboy* material, but dangerous as dynamite nonetheless."

"What makes you say that?" Sandra chipped in.

"I don't really know. Maybe it's hindsight. I just get feelings about people sometimes, and I knew from the start that one was trouble. Still, it looks as if she meant trouble for herself mostly, doesn't it?"

"Is James Conran a suspect?" Sandra asked.

"Your husband seems to think so," Susan said. "But everyone who had anything to do with Caroline Hartley is a suspect."

"Aren't you worried about getting involved with him?" Sandra asked.

"A bit, I suppose. I mean, not that I think James is guilty of anything, just that being involved might blur my objectivity. It's an awkward position to be in, that's all. Besides," she laughed, "he's my old teacher. It feels strange to be having dinner with him. I like him, but I'm keeping him at arm's length. At least until this business is over."

"Good for you," Sandra said.

"Anyway, I don't see as it should matter. The chief inspector went off to London with Veronica Shildon, and I'd say she's a prime suspect." Susan realized too late what she had implied, and wondered if an attempt to backtrack and make her meaning clear would only make things worse.

All Sandra said was, "I'm sure Alan knows what he's doing." And Susan could have sworn she noticed a ghost of a smile on her face. "I know. I'm sorry. I didn't mean to imply . . . just . . ."

"It's all right," Sandra said. "I just wanted to point out that what he's doing isn't the same. I'm not criticizing you."

"I don't suppose I understand his methods yet."

"I'm not sure I do, either." Sandra laughed.

Suddenly, Susan's world turned pitch-black. She felt a light pressure on her brow and cheeks and she could no longer see Sandra and Marcia. The bustling pub seemed to fall silent, then a voice whispered in her ear, "Guess who?"

"James," she said, and her vision was restored.

IV

Banks felt unusually tired when he got home about eight o'clock that evening. The paperwork was done, and Gary Hartley had been sent back to Harrogate to face whatever charges could be made.

Sandra had just got home herself, and both children were out. Over a dinner of left-over chicken casserole, Sandra told him about her evening with Susan and Marcia. In turn, Banks tried to explain Gary Hartley to her.

"He'd always hated Caroline, all his life. She was the bane of his existence. She used to tease him, torment him, torture him, and he never had any idea why. She even tried to drown him once. To cap it all, she left home and he got lumbered with looking after his invalid father, who made it perfectly clear that he still preferred Caroline. When you look at it like that, it's not a bad motive for murder, wouldn't you say?"

"Did he do it?" Sandra asked.

Banks shook his head. "No. Not literally. When she told him what had happened when her mother had been in hospital having him, he suddenly realized why she hated him. She wanted to apologize, make up even, if she could. But Gary's sensitive. It's not something you can really work out in your mind. Christ, most people don't even talk about it. And Caroline had blanked out the memory for years. It was always there, though, under the surface, shoving and cracking the crust. Gary just reacted emotionally. He was overwhelmed by what she said, and suddenly his whole world was turned upside-down. All his anger had been pointed in the wrong direction—at her—for so long."

"He killed his father?"

"He sat in his room downstairs and let the old man starve to death."

Sandra shivered. "Good God!"

She was right to be so appalled, Banks thought. It was an act of utmost cruelty, the kind for which a public ignorant of the facts might demand a return of the noose. But still, he couldn't forget Gary's pain and confusion; he couldn't help but feel pity for the boy, no matter what atrocity he had committed. He gave Sandra the gist of their discussion.

"I can see what he meant when he said her father had killed her," she said, "but why implicate himself too? You said he didn't do it."

"But he blamed himself—for being born, if you like. After all, that's when it started. That's when Caroline was left alone with her father. He couldn't give us any concrete details of the crime because he hadn't done it. But in his mind he was responsible. All he could say was that it was all dark to him. Dark and painful."

"I don't understand," Sandra said, frowning.

"I think he was describing being born," Banks said. "Dark. Dark and painful."

"My God. And you said Caroline tried to drown him, too?"

"Yes. He was about four and she was twelve. He can't remember the details clearly, of course, and there's no one else alive to tell what happened, but he thinks his mother left him for a moment to fetch some clean towels. She left the bathroom door open and Caroline walked in. He said he remembers how she pulled his feet and his head went under the water. The next thing he knew, he was up again in his mother's arms gasping for air and Caroline was gone. Nobody ever spoke about it afterwards."

"He must have been terrified of her."

"He was. And he didn't know why she was treating him that way. She didn't know, either. He turned in on himself to shut it all out."

"Is he insane?" Sandra asked.

"Not for me to say. He's in need of help, certainly. Just

imagine the hatred of all those years boiling over, finding its true object at last. All the humiliation. His own life ruined, knowing he was only second-best to his sister. The only wonder is he didn't do it sooner. It took Caroline's murder and the truth about her childhood to set him free."

Banks remembered the slouching figure that had shuffled out of his office after telling everything. He would be under care in Harrogate now, perhaps going through the whole story again at the hands of less sympathetic interrogators. After all, look at what he'd done. But Gary Hartley wouldn't be hanged. He wouldn't even be sent to jail. He would first be bound over for psychiatric evaluation, then he might well spend a good part of his life in mental institutions. Which was better? It was impossible for Banks to decide. Gary's life was blighted, just as his sister's had been, though, unlike Caroline, Gary hadn't even managed to snatch his few moments of happiness.

"Then who *did* kill Caroline Hartley?" Sandra asked.

Banks scratched his head. "I'm buggered if I know. I'm pretty sure we can rule out Gary now, and her friends in London. When Caroline moved on, she always seemed to burn her bridges."

"Which leaves?"

"Well, unless we're dealing with a psycho, we're back to the locals. Ivers and his girlfriend aren't home-free yet, whatever they told us. They lied to us at the start, and Patsy Janowski has a good motive for corroborating everything Ivers might claim. She loves the man and wants to hang onto him. And then there's the amateur theater crowd. I've been intending to have another talk with Teresa Pedmore."

"And Veronica Shildon?" Sandra asked. "Susan Gay seems to think you've been overlooking her."

"Susan's prejudiced."

"Are you sure you're not?"

Banks stared at her. "Don't you know me better than that?"

"Just asking."

He shook his head. "Officially she's a suspect, of course,

but Veronica Shildon didn't do it. I must be overlooking something."

"Any idea what?"

Banks brought his fist up slowly to his temple. "Damned if I know." Then he stood up. "Hell, it's been a rough day. I'm having a stiff Scotch then I'm off to bed." He poured the drink and went into the hall to his jacket. When he came back he said, "And I'm having a bloody cigarette as well, house rule or no house rule."

TWELVE

I

The wind numbed Banks to the marrow when he got out of his car near the Lobster Inn the following afternoon. It was January 3—only three days to twelfth night. The sky was a pale eggshell blue with a few wispy gray clouds twisting over the horizon-like strips of gauze. But the sun had no warmth in it. The wind kicked up little whitecaps as it danced over the ruffled water and slid up the rough sea-wall right onto the front. Banks dashed into the pub.

There already, ensconced in front of the meager fire, sat Detective Sergeant Jim Hatchley, pint in one ham-like hand and a huge, foul-smelling cigar smouldering between two sausage-shaped fingers of the other. Banks thought he had put on weight; his bulk seemed to loom larger than ever. The sergeant shifted in his seat when Banks came over and sat opposite him.

"Miserable old bugger saves all his coal till evening," he said, by way of greeting, gesturing over at the landlord who sat on a high stool behind the bar reading a tabloid. "Bigger crowd then, you see."

Banks nodded. "How's married life treating you?"

"Can't complain. She's a good lass. I could do without being at the bloody seaside in winter, though. Plays havoc with my rheumatism."

"Didn't know you had it."

"Nor did I."

"Never mind. Just wait till spring. You'll be the envy of us all then. Everyone will want to come out and visit you on their weekends off."

"Aye, maybe. We'll have to see about renting out the spare room for bed and breakfast. Carol's got some fancy ideas about starting a garden, too. Sounds like a lot of back-breaking work to me."

And Banks knew what Hatchley felt about work, the dreaded four-letter word, back-breaking or not. "I'm sorry to lumber you with this, Jim," he said. "Especially on your honeymoon."

"That's all right. Gets me out of the house. We're not spring chickens, you know. Can't expect to be at it all the time." He winked. "Besides, a man needs time alone with his pint and his paper."

Banks noticed a copy of the *Sun* folded in Hatchley's pocket. From the little he could see, it looked to be open at page three. An attractive new wife, and he still ogled the naked page-three girl. Old habits die hard.

The landlord stirred; his newspaper began to rustle with impatience. Clearly it was all very well for him to be rude to customers, but customers were not expected to be rude to him by warming themselves in front of the sparse flames for too long without buying a drink. Banks walked over and the paper rose up again, covering the man's beady eyes.

"Two pints of bitter, please," Banks said, and slowly the paper came to rest on the bar. With a why-can't-everyone-leave-me-alone sigh, the man pulled the pints and plonked them down in front of Banks, holding his other hand out for the money as soon as he had done so. Banks paid and walked back to Sergeant Hatchley.

"Anything come up?" Banks asked, reaching for a cigarette.

Hatchley pulled a cigar tube from his inside pocket. "Have one of these. Christmas present from the in-laws. Havana. Nice and mild."

Banks remembered the last cigar he had smoked, one of Dirty Dick Burgess's Tom Thumbs, and declined. "Best stick with the devil you know," he said, lighting the cigarette.

"As you like. Well," Hatchley said, "there's nowt been happening around here. I've been up with Carol a couple of evenings, for a drink, like, and noticed that Ivers and his fancy woman in here once or twice. Tall chap in need of a haircut. Looks a bit like that Irish bloke from *Camelot*, Richard Harris, after a bad night. And that lass of his, young enough to be his granddaughter I'd say. Still, it takes all sorts. Lovely pair of thighs under them tight jeans, and a bum like two peaches in a wet paper bag. Anyroad, they'd come in about nine-ish, nod hello to a few locals, knock back a couple of drinks and leave about ten."

"Ever talk to them?"

"No. They don't know who I am. They keep themselves to themselves, too. The local constable's a very obliging chap. I've had him keeping an eye open and he says they've done nothing out of the ordinary. Hardly been out of the house. Are they still in the running?"

Banks nodded. "There's a couple of problems with the timing, but nothing they couldn't have worked out between them."

"Between them?"

"Yes. If they killed Caroline Hartley, they must have been in it together. It's the only way they could have done it."

"But you're not sure they did?"

"No. I'm just not satisfied with their stories."

"What about motive?"

"That I don't know. The husband had one, clearly enough, but the girl didn't share it. It'd have to be something we don't know about."

"Money?"

"I don't think so. Caroline Hartley didn't have much. It would have to be something more obscure than that."

"Perhaps she's the kind who'd do anything for him, just to hang onto him?"

"Maybe."

"Or they didn't do it?"

"Could be that, too."

"Or maybe you're over-complicating things as usual?"

Banks grinned. "Maybe I am."

"So what now?" Hatchley asked.

"A quick visit, just to let them know we haven't forgotten them."

"Me too?"

"Yes."

"But they'll recognize me. They'll know me in future."

"It won't do them any harm to know we're keeping an eye on them. Come on, sup up."

Grudgingly, Sergeant Hatchley drained his pint and stubbed out his cigar. "Still another ten minutes left in that," he complained.

"Take it with you."

"Never mind."

Hatchley followed Banks out into the sharp wind. Thin ice splintered as they made their way up the footpath to Ivers's cottage, from which a welcoming plume of smoke curled and drifted west. Hatchley groaned and panted as they walked. Banks knocked. This time, Ivers himself answered the door.

"Come in. Sit down. Sit down," he said. Hatchley took the bulky armchair by the mullioned window and Banks lowered himself into a wooden rocker by the fire. "Have you caught him?" Ivers asked. "The man who killed Caroline?"

Banks shook his head. "Afraid not."

Ivers frowned. "Oh . . . well. Patsy! Patsy! Some tea, if you've got a minute."

Patsy Janowski came in from her study, glared at Banks's right shoe-lace and went into the kitchen.

"How do you think I can help you again?" Ivers asked.

"I'm not sure," Banks said. "First, I'd just like to go over one or two details."

"Shall we wait for Patsy with the tea?"

They waited. Banks passed the time talking music with

Ivers, who was excited about the harmonic breakthroughs he had made over the past two days. Hatchley, hands folded in his lap, looked bored.

Finally, Patsy emerged with a tray and put it down on the table in front of the fire. She wore jeans with a plain white shirt, the top two buttons undone. Banks noticed Hatchley take a discreet look down the front as she bent to put the tray down. She didn't seem pleased to see Banks, and if either of them recognized Sergeant Hatchley, they didn't show it. This time, Patsy was surly and evasive and Ivers seemed open and helpful. Luckily, Banks had learned never to take anything at face value. When tea was poured, he began with the questions.

"It's the timing that's important, you see," he opened. "Can you be any clearer about what time you delivered the Christmas present, Mr. Ivers?"

"I'm sorry, I can't. Sometime around seven, I'm sure of that."

"And you stayed how long?"

"No more than five minutes."

"That's rather a long time, isn't it?"

"What do you mean?"

"People have funny ideas about time, about how short or long various periods are. I'd say five minutes was a bit long to spend with someone you didn't like on an errand like that. Why not just hand over the present and leave?"

"Maybe it wasn't that long," Ivers said. "I just went in, handed it over, exchanged a few insincere pleasantries and left. Maybe two minutes, I don't know."

Banks sipped some tea, then lit a cigarette. Patsy, legs curled under her on the rug in front of the fire, passed him an ashtray from the hearth.

"What pleasantries?" he asked. "What did you say to each other?"

"As I said before, I asked how she was, how Veronica was, made a remark about the weather. And she answered me politely. I handed over the record, told her it was something special for Veronica for Christmas, then I left. We'd at least reached a stage where we could behave in a civilized manner toward one another."

"You said it was something special?"

"Something like that."

"How did she react?"

Ivers closed his eyes for a moment and frowned. "She didn't, really. I mean, she didn't say anything. She looked interested, though. Curious."

"That may be why she opened it, if she did," Banks said, almost to himself. "Did she seem at all strange to you? Did she say anything odd?"

Ivers shook his head. "No."

"Did she seem to be expecting someone?"

"How would I know? She certainly didn't say anything if she was."

"Was she on edge? Did she keep glancing toward the door? Did she give the impression she wanted you out of the way as soon as possible?"

"I'd say yes to the latter," Ivers answered, "but no to the others. She seemed perfectly all right to me."

"What was she doing?"

"Doing?"

"Yes. When you called. You went into the front room, didn't you? Was she listening to music, polishing the silver, watching television, reading?"

"I don't know. Nothing . . . I . . . eating, perhaps. There was some cake on the table. I remember that."

"What was she wearing?"

"I can't remember."

"Claude's hopeless about things like that," Patsy cut in. "Half the time he doesn't even notice what *I'm* wearing."

Taking in the stooped, lanky figure of the composer in his usual baggy clothes, Banks was inclined to believe her. Here was the genius so wrapped up in his music that he didn't notice such mundane things as what other people said, did or wore.

On the other hand, Ivers obviously had a taste for attractive women. In different ways, both Veronica and Patsy were evidence enough of that. And what red-blooded male would forget a woman as beautiful as Caroline Hartley answering the door in her bathrobe? Surely a man with a taste for so seductive a woman as Patsy Janowski couldn't fail to remember, or to react? But then Ivers knew Caroline; he knew she was a lesbian. Perhaps it was all a matter of perspective. Banks pressed on.

"What about you, Ms. Janowski? Can you remember what she was wearing?"

"I didn't even go into the house. I only saw her standing in the doorway."

"Can you remember?"

"It looked like some kind of bathrobe to me, a kimono-style thing. Dark green I think the color was. She was hugging it tight around her because of the cold."

"What time did you arrive?"

"After seven. I left here about twenty minutes after Claude."

"How long after seven?"

"I'm not sure. I told you before. Maybe about a quarter after, twenty past."

"What were you wearing?"

"Wearing?" Patsy frowned. "I don't see what that's—"

"Just answer, please."

She shot his right lapel a baleful glance. "Jeans, boots and my fur-lined jacket."

"How long is the jacket?"

"It comes down to my waist," Patsy said, looking puzzled. "Look, I don't—"

"Would you say that Caroline was expecting someone else? Someone other than you?"

"I couldn't say, really."

"Did she react as if she had been expecting someone else when she saw you standing there at the door? Did she show any disappointment?"

"No, not especially." Patsy thought for a moment. "She was real nice, given who I am. I'm sorry, but it all happened so quickly and I was too concerned about Claude to pay much attention."

"Did she seem nervous or surprised to see you, anxious for you to leave quickly?"

"No, not at all. She was surprised to see me, of course, but that's only natural. And she wanted to shut the door because of the cold."

"Why didn't she ask you in?"

Patsy looked at the hearth. "She hardly knew me. Besides, all I had to ask her was whether Claude was there."

"And she said he wasn't."

"Yes."

"And you believed her?"

Patsy's tone hardened. She spoke between clenched teeth. "Of course I did."

"Are you *sure* he wasn't still in the house?"

Ivers leaned forward. "Now wait—"

"Let her answer, Mr. Ivers," Sergeant Hatchley said.

"Caroline said he'd gone. She said he'd just left the record and gone. I hadn't any reason to believe she was lying."

"Was she in a hurry to get rid of you?"

"I've told you, no. Everything was normal as far as I could tell."

"But she didn't invite you inside. Doesn't that seem odd to you, Ms. Janowski? You've already said it was so cold on the doorstep that Caroline Hartley had to hold her robe tight around her. Wouldn't it have made more sense to invite you in, even if just for a few minutes? After all, Mr. Ivers here says he only stayed for five minutes."

"Are you trying to suggest that I *did* go inside?" Patsy exploded. "Just what's going on in that policeman's mind of yours? Are you accusing me of killing her? Because if you are you'd better damn well arrest me right now and let me call my lawyer!"

"There's no reason to be melodramatic, Ms. Janowski,"

Banks said. "I'm not suggesting anything of the kind. I happen to know already that you didn't enter the house."

Patsy's brow furrowed and some of the angry red color drained from her cheeks. "Then I . . . I don't understand."

"Did you hear music playing?"

"No. I can't remember any."

"And you didn't ask to go inside, to look around?"

"No. Why would I? I knew he wouldn't still be there if Veronica wasn't home."

"The point is," Banks said, "that Mr. Ivers *could* have been in the house, couldn't he? You've just confirmed to me that you didn't go in and look."

"I've told you, he wouldn't—"

"Could he have been inside?"

She looked at Ivers, then back to Banks. "That's an unfair question. The goddamn Duke of Edinburg *could* have been inside for all I know, but I don't think he was."

"The thing is," Banks said, "that nobody saw Mr. Ivers leave. Caroline Hartley didn't invite you in, even though it was cold, and you didn't insist on seeing for yourself."

"That doesn't mean anything," Ivers burst out, "and you know it. It was pure bloody luck on your part that anyone noticed me arrive, or Patsy. You can't expect them to be watching for me to leave, too."

"Maybe not, but it would have made everything a lot tidier."

"And if you're suggesting that Caroline didn't let Patsy in because *I* was there, have you considered that she might have been hiding someone else? Have you thought about that?"

"Yes, Mr. Ivers, I've thought about that. The problem is, no one else was seen near the house between your visit and Ms. Janowski's." He turned to Patsy. "When you left, did you notice anyone hanging around the area?"

"I don't think so."

"Concentrate. It could be important. I've asked you before to try to visualize the scene. Did you see anyone behaving strangely, or anyone who looked furtive, suspicious, out of place?"

Patsy closed her eyes. "No, I'm sure I didn't . . . Except—"

"What?"

"I'm not very clear. There was a woman."

"Where?"

"The end of the street. It was very dark there . . . snowing. And she was some distance away from me. But I remember thinking there was something odd about her, I don't know what. I'm damned if I can think what it was."

"Think," Banks encouraged her. The timing was certainly right. Patsy had called at about twenty past seven, and the killer—if indeed the last observed visitor was the killer—only two or three minutes later. There was a good chance that they had passed in the street.

Patsy opened her eyes. "It's no good. It was ages ago now and I hardly paid any attention at the time. It's just one of those odd little things, like a *déjà vu*."

"Did you think you knew this woman, recognized her?"

"No. It wasn't anything like that. I'd remember that. It was when I got to King Street. She was crossing over, as if she was heading for the mews. We were on opposite sides and I didn't get a very close look. It was something else, just a little thing. I'm sorry, Chief Inspector, really I am. Especially," she added sharply, "as any information I might give could get us off the hook. I simply can't remember."

"If you do remember anything at all about the woman," Banks said, "no matter how minor a detail it might seem to you, call me immediately, is that clear?"

Patsy nodded.

"And you're not off the hook yet. Not by a long chalk."

Banks gestured for Hatchley to get up, a lengthy task that involved quite a bit of heaving and puffing, then they left. Banks almost slipped on the icy pathway, but Hatchley caught his arm and steadied him just in time.

"Well," said the sergeant, stamping and rubbing his hands outside the Lobster Inn, "that's that then. I don't mind doing a bit of extra work, you know," he said, glancing longingly at the pub, "even when I'm supposed to be on my honeymoon. I know it's not my case, but I wish you'd fill me in on a few more details."

Banks caught his glance and interpreted the signals. "Fine," he said. "Over a pint?"

Hatchley beamed. "Well, if you insist . . ."

II

"Susan, love, could I have a word?"

"Of course."

Susan and Marcia were sitting in the Crooked Billet with the entire cast of *Twelfth Night* after rehearsal. It had gone badly, and those who weren't busy arguing were drowning their depression in drink. James didn't seem too concerned, Susan thought, watching him listen patiently to Malvolio's complaints about the final scene. But he was used to it; he'd directed plays before. She shifted along the bench to let Marcia Cunningham sit beside her. "What is it?"

Marcia looked puzzled. "I'm not sure. It's nothing really. At least I don't think it is. But it's very odd."

"Police business?"

"Well, it might have something to do with the break-in. You did say to mention anything that came up."

"Go on."

"But that's just it, you see, love. It doesn't make sense."

"Marcia," Susan said, "why don't you just tell me? Get it off your chest."

Marcia frowned. "It's hard to explain. You'd probably think I was just being silly if I told you. Can't you pop around and have a look for yourself? I don't live far away."

"What, now?"

"Whenever you can spare the time, love." Marcia looked at her watch. "I'll have to be off in a few minutes, anyway."

Susan recognized a deadline when she heard one. Now she was with CID she was never really off duty. She wouldn't get anywhere if she put personal pleasure before the job, however fruitless the trek to Marcia's might seem. And the vandalism was *her* case. A success so early in her CID career would look good. What could she do but agree? As Marcia couldn't be induced to say any more, Susan would have to put James off and go with her. It wouldn't take long, Marcia had assured her, so she wouldn't have to cancel their dinner date, just postpone it for half an hour or so. James would understand. He certainly had plenty to occupy himself with in her absence.

"All right," Susan said. "I'll come with you."

"Thanks, love. It might be a waste of time but . . . well, wait till you see."

Susan told James she had to nip out for a while and would be back in half an hour or so, then she buttoned up her winter coat and left with Marcia. They walked north-east along York Road, past the excavated pre-Roman site, where the little burial mounds and hut foundations looked eerie under their carapace of moonlit ice.

"It's just down here." Marcia led Susan down a sloping street of pre-war semis opposite the site. Though the house itself was small, it had gardens at both front and back and a fine view of the river and The Green from the kitchen window. The furniture looked dated and worn, and swaths of material lay scattered here and there, along with stacks of patterns and magazines, in the untidy living room. Marcia didn't apologize for the mess. Her sense of disorder, Susan realized, didn't stop at the way she dressed.

On the mantlepiece above the electric fire stood a framed photograph of Marcia's late husband, a handsome man, posing on the seafront at some holiday resort with a pipe in his mouth. Marcia switched on the fire. Susan took off her coat and knelt by the reddening element, rubbing her hands. She could smell dust burning as it heated up.

"Sorry it's so cold," Marcia said. "We wanted central heat-ing, but since my Frank died I just haven't been able to afford it."

"I don't have it either," Susan said. "I always do this when I get home." She stood up and turned. "What is it you've got to show me?"

Marcia dragged a large box into the center of the room. "It's this. Remember I told you yesterday I was patching up some of the damage those hooligans did to the costumes?"

Susan nodded.

"Well, I have. Look." She held up a long pearl gown with shoulder straps and plunging neckline.

Susan looked closely. "But surely . . . ?"

"Cut to shreds, it was," Marcia said. "Look." She pointed out the faint lines of stitching. "Of course, you'd never get away with wearing it for a banquet at the Ritz, but it'll do for a stage performance. Even the nobs in the front row wouldn't be able to see how it had been sewn back together."

"You're a genius, Marcia," Susan exclaimed, touching the fabric. "You should have been a surgeon."

Marcia shrugged. "Can't stand the sight of blood. Anyway, it was just like doing a jigsaw puzzle really." And she showed Susan more dresses and gowns she had resurrected from the box of snipped-up originals. That so untidy a person should be able to bring such order out of chaos astonished Susan.

"You didn't bring me here just to praise you, did you?" she said finally. "I don't mean to be rude, but I told James I'd be back in half an hour."

"Sorry, love," Marcia said. "Just got carried away, that's all. Forget how impatient young love is."

Susan blushed. "Marcia! The point."

"Yes, well." Marcia reached into the box and took out a simple burgundy dress. "This is the point. I worked on this one all afternoon." She held it up, and Susan could see that the sleeves had been cut off up to elbow-level and a large patch of the front, around the breasts, was also missing.

"I don't understand," she said. "Haven't you finished?"

"I've done all I could, love. That's the point. This is it. All there was."

"I still don't understand."

"And you a copper, too. It's simple. I managed to sort out the bits and pieces of the other dresses here and patch them together, as you've seen."

Susan nodded.

"But when it came to this one, I couldn't find all the pieces. Some of them've plain disappeared."

"Disappeared?"

"Wake up, lass. Yes, disappeared. I've looked everywhere. Even back at the center to see if they'd fallen on the floor or something. Not a trace."

"But it doesn't make any sense," Susan said slowly. "Who on earth would want to steal pieces of a ruined dress?"

"My point exactly," Marcia said. "That's why I asked you to come here and see it for yourself. Who would do such a thing? And why?"

"There has to be a simple explanation."

Marcia nodded. "Yes. But what is it? Your lot didn't take any for analysis or whatever, did they?"

Susan shook her head. "No. They must have dropped out somewhere. Maybe when you were bringing the box home."

"I looked everywhere. I'm telling you, love, if there'd been pieces I would've found them."

Susan couldn't help but feel disappointed. It was hardly an important discovery—certainly not one that would lead to the identity of the vandals—but Marcia was right in that it was mystifying. It was slightly disturbing, too. When Susan picked up the dress and held it in front of her, she shivered as if someone had just walked over her grave. It looked as if the arms had been deliberately cut off rather than torn, and two circles of fabric around the breasts had been snipped out in a similar way. Shaking her head, Susan folded the dress and handed it back to Marcia.

III

"Chief Inspector Banks! Have you any news?"

"No news," Banks said. "Maybe a few questions."

"Come in." Veronica Shildon led him into her front room. It looked larger and colder than it had before, as if even all the heat from the fiercely burning fire in the hearth couldn't penetrate every shadowy corner. Two small, threadbare armchairs stood in front of the fire.

"Christine Cooper let me have them until I get around to buying a new suite," Veronica said, noticing Banks looking at them. "She was going to throw them out."

Banks nodded. After Veronica had taken his coat, he sat in one of the armchairs and warmed himself by the flames. "It's certainly more comfortable than a hard-backed chair," he said.

"Can I offer you a drink?" she asked.

"Tea would do nicely."

Veronica brewed the tea and came to sit in the other armchair, placed so they didn't face each other directly but at an angle that required a slight turning of the head to make eye-contact. The fire danced in the hollows of Veronica's cheeks and reflected like tiny orange candle flames in her eyes.

"I don't feel I thanked you enough for letting me come to London with you," she said, crossing her legs and sitting back in the chair. "It can't have been an easy decision for you to make. Anyway, I'm grateful. Somehow, seeing Ruth Dunne gave me more of Caroline than I'd had, if you can understand that."

Banks, who had more than once spent hours with colleagues extolling the virtues and playfully noting the faults of deceased friends, knew exactly what Veronica meant. Somehow, sharing memories of the dead seemed to make them live larger in one's mind and heart, and Veronica had had nobody in Eastvale to talk to about Caroline because nobody here had really known her.

Banks nodded. "I don't really know why I *am* here, to tell the truth," he said finally. "Nothing I learned in London really helped. Now it's early evening on a cold January day and I'm still no closer to the solution than I was last week. Maybe I'm just the cop who came in from the cold."

Veronica raised an eyebrow. "Frustration?"

"Certainly. More than that."

"Tell me," she said slowly, "am I . . . I mean, do you still believe that *I* might have murdered Caroline?"

Banks lit a cigarette and shifted his legs. The fire was burning his shins. "Ms. Shildon," he said, "we've no evidence at all to link you to the crime. We never have had. Everything you told us checks out, and we found no traces of blood-stained clothing in the house. Nor did there appear to be any blood on your person. Unless you're an especially clever and cold-blooded killer, which I don't think you are, then I don't see how you could have murdered Caroline. You also appear to lack a motive. At least I haven't been able to find one I'm comfortable with."

"But surely you don't take things at face value?"

"No, I don't. It's a simple statistic that most murders are committed by people who are close to the victim, often family members or lovers. Given that, you're obviously a prime suspect. There could have been a way, certainly, if you'd been planning the act. There could also be a motive we don't know about. Caroline *could* have been having an affair and you *could* have found out about it."

"So you still think I might have done it?"

Banks shrugged. "It's not so much a matter of what I think. It's maybe not probable, but it certainly is possible. Until I find out exactly who did do it, I can't count anybody from Caroline's circle out."

"Including me?"

"Including you."

"God, what a terrible job it must be, having to see people that way all the time, as potential criminals. How can you ever get close to anyone?"

"You're exaggerating. It's my job, not my life. Do you think doctors go around all the time seeing everyone as potential patients, for example, or lawyers as potential clients?"

"Of the latter I'm quite certain," Veronica said with a quiet laugh, "but as for doctors, the only ones I've known get very irritated when guests ask their advice about aches and pains at cocktail parties."

"Anyway," Banks went on, "people create their own problems."

"What do you mean?"

"Everyone lies, evades or holds back the full truth. Oh, you all have your own perfectly good reasons for doing it—protecting Caroline's memory, covering up a petty crime, unwillingness to reveal an unattractive aspect of your own personality, inability to face up to things or simply not wanting to get involved. But can't you see where that leaves us? If we're faced with several people all closely connected to the victim, and they all lie to us, one of them could conceivably be lying to cover up murder."

"But surely you must have instincts? You must trust some people."

"Yes, I do. My instincts tell me that you didn't kill Caroline, but I'd be a proper fool if I let my heart rule my head and overlooked an important piece of evidence. That's the trouble, trusting your instincts can sometimes blind you to the obvious. Already I've told you too much."

"Does your instinct tell you who did kill her?"

Banks shook his head and flicked a column of ash into the fire. "Unfortunately, no. Gary Hartley confessed, in a way, but . . ." He told her what had happened in Harrogate. Veronica sat forward and clasped her hands on her lap as he spoke.

"The poor boy," she said when he'd finished. "Is there anything I can do?"

"I don't think so. He's undergoing psychiatric tests right now. But the point is, whatever he did do, he didn't kill Caroline. If anything, toward the end, when he knew the full story, he felt pity for her. It was his father he turned on, with years of pent-up hatred. I still can't imagine what torture it must have been for both of them. The old man unable to help himself, unable to get out of bed, starving and lying in his own waste; and Gary downstairs getting drunk and listening to the feeble cries and taps growing fainter, knowing he was slowly killing his own father." Banks shuddered. "There are some things it doesn't do to dwell on, perhaps. But none of this gets us any closer to Caroline's killer."

"It's the 'why' I can't understand," Veronica said. "Who could possibly have had a reason for killing Caroline?"

"That we don't know." Banks sipped some ice tea. "I thought it might have had something to do with her past, but neither Ruth Dunne nor Colm Grey, the father of her child, had anything to do with it. Unless there's a very obscure connection, such as a dissatisfied customer come back to wreak revenge, which hardly seems likely, all we can surmise is that it was someone she knew, and someone who hadn't planned to kill her."

"How do you know that?"

"There was no sign of forced entry, and the weapon, it just came to hand."

"But she didn't know many people," Veronica said. "Surely that would be a help."

"It is and it isn't. If she didn't know many people very well, then how could she offend someone so much they'd want to kill her?"

"Why do you say offend? Maybe you're wrong. Perhaps she found out something that someone didn't want known, or she saw something she shouldn't have."

"But according to what everyone tells me—yourself included—she wasn't acting at all strangely prior to her death. Surely if something along those lines was bothering her she would have been."

Veronica shook her head. "I don't know . . . she could have been holding back, pretending . . . for my sake."

"But you didn't get that impression? Your instinct didn't tell you so?"

"No. Then, I never know whether to trust my instincts or not. I've made mistakes."

"We all have," Banks said. "But you're right to consider other motives. We shouldn't overlook the possibility that someone had a very practical reason for wanting her out of the way. The problem is, it just makes the motive harder to get at, because it's less personal. Let's say, to be absurd, that she saw two spies exchanging documents. In the first place, how would she know they were doing anything illegal, and in the second, how would they know she was a threat?" He shook his head. "That kind of thing only happens in books. Real murders are much simpler, in a way—at least as far as motive is concerned—but not necessarily easier to solve. Gary Hartley might have had a deep-seated reason to kill his sister, but he didn't do it. Your estranged husband had a motive, too. He blamed Caroline for the separation. But he seems happy enough in his new life with Patsy. Why would he do anything to ruin that? On the other hand, who knows what people really feel?"

"What do you mean?"

"He could have done it, if Patsy Janowski is in it with him or is lying to protect him. He delivered the record, we know that for a fact. As to who put it on the turntable . . ."

Veronica shook her head slowly. "Claude couldn't murder anyone. Oh, he has his moods and his rages, but he's not a killer. Anyway, do you really think the music is important?"

"It's a clue of some kind, but it didn't mean what I thought it did. I believe Caroline opened it out of curiosity. She wanted to know what Claude thought was so special to you. Beyond that, your guess is as good as mine. Maybe she would even play a little of it, again to satisfy her curiosity, but I can't believe she'd leave the arm up so it would repeat forever."

Veronica smiled. "That's just like Caroline," she said quietly. "Such curiosity. You know, she always wanted to shake all her Christmas presents. It was well nigh impossible to stop her opening them on Christmas Eve."

Banks laughed. "I know, my daughter's the same."

Veronica shook her head. "Such a child . . . in some ways."

Banks leaned forward. "What did you say?"

"About Caroline. I said she was such a child in so many ways."

"Yes," Banks whispered. "Yes, she was." He remembered something Ruth Dunne had said to him in London. He tossed his cigarette end into the fire and finished his tea.

"Does it mean something?" Veronica asked.

"It might do." He stood up. "If it does, I've been a bit slow on the uptake. Look, I'd better go now. Much as I'd like to stay here and keep warm, I've got more work to do. I'm sorry."

"It's all right. You don't have to apologize. I don't expect you to keep me company. That's not part of your job."

Banks put the empty teacup on the table. "It's not a task I despise," he said. "But there are a few points I have to review back at the station."

"When you find out," Veronica said, twisting the silver ring around her middle finger, "will you let me know?"

"You'd find out soon enough."

"No. I don't want to find it out from the papers. I want *you* to let me know. As soon as you find out. No matter what the time, day or night. Will you do that for me?"

"Is this some sort of desire for revenge? Do you need an object to hate?"

"No. You once told me I was far too civilized for such feelings. I just want to understand. I want to know why Caroline had to die, what the killer was feeling."

"We might never know that."

She put her hand on his sleeve. "But you will tell me, won't you, when you know? Promise?"

"I'll do my best," Banks said.

Veronica sighed. "Good."

"What about the record?" Banks said at the door. "Technically, it's yours, you know."

Veronica leaned against the doorjamb and wrapped her arms around her to keep warm. "I can live in this house," she said, "especially when I get it redecorated and bring new furniture in. But do you know something? I think that if I ever heard that music again I'd go insane."

Banks said goodnight and Veronica closed the door. It was a shame, he thought, that such a glorious and transcendent piece of music should be associated with such a bloody deed, but at least he thought he now knew why the record had been left playing, if not who had put it on.

IV

Susan systematically picked the strips of glittering silver tinsel from her tiny artificial Christmas tree. Carefully, she replaced each flimsy strand on the card from which it came, to put away for next year. She did the same with the single string of lights and the red and green colored balls, the only decorations she had bought.

When she had finished with the tree, she stood on a chair and untaped the intricate concertinas of colored crêpe paper she had draped across the ceiling and folded them together. Apart from the Father Christmas above the mantelpiece, a three-dimensional figure that closed like a book when you folded it in half, that was it.

When she had put all traces of Christmas in the cupboard, Susan stood in the center of her living room and gazed around. Somehow, even without all the festive decorations she had dashed out and bought at the last moment, the place was beginning to feel a little more like a home. There was still a lot to do—framed prints to buy, perhaps a few ornaments—but she was getting there. Already she had found time to buy three records: highlights from *Madama Butterfly, The Four Seasons* and a recording of traditional folk music, the kind she had heard a few times at university many years ago. The opening chords of "Autumn" were playing as she walked into the kitchen to make some cocoa.

James hadn't seen the inside of her flat yet. She would have to invite him soon if he was going to keep on taking her to dinner—not that he paid, Susan always insisted on going Dutch—but something held her back. Perhaps it was the same thing that had held her back so far from stopping in at his place for a nightcap. Damn it all, the man had been her teacher at school, and that was a difficult image to throw out. Still, at least she would make sure she had a few more books and records when she did invite him. She wouldn't want him to think she lived in such a cultural vacuum.

She poured out her cup of cocoa and sat down to listen to the music, curling her feet under her in the small armchair. If she was honest with herself, she decided, her resistance to James had little to do with the fact that he had been her teacher, and was only partly related to his involvement in the case. As far as Susan was concerned, Veronica Shildon was guilty, and it was simply a matter of proving it, of finding evidence that she had returned earlier than she said and murdered her lover—such a distasteful word, Susan thought, when applied to a relationship like theirs—out of jealousy, self-disgust or some other powerful, negative emotion. Either that or the estranged husband had done it because Caroline had corrupted and stolen his wife. So, although James and the theater crowd were officially suspects, Susan couldn't believe that any of them were really guilty. No, it was something else that kept her at arm's length from James.

She had for some reason stayed away from sexual relationships over the past few years. And, again if she was honest, it wasn't only because of her career. That was important to her, yes, but many women could manage both a lover and a career. Some of her colleagues, and, stranger still, a couple of the more charming villains she had nicked, had asked her out, but she had always said no. Somehow they had all been too close to home. She didn't want to be talked about around the station. She had dated occasionally, but had never been able to commit herself to anything. She supposed that, as far as the men were concerned, there always seemed to be a million things she would rather be doing than being with them, and they were right. Because of that, she had spent too many evenings alone in her soulless flat. But also, because of that, she had passed all her examinations and her career was flourishing.

She certainly found James attractive, as well as charming and lively company. He was a great ham, had a fine sense of the dramatic. But there was more to him than that, an intensity and a kind of masculine self-assurance. He would probably make a fine lover. So why was she avoiding the inevitable? Her excuse was the case, but her real reason was fear. Fear of what? she asked herself. He hadn't even tried to touch her yet, though she was sure she had seen the desire in his eyes. Was she afraid of enjoying herself? Of losing control? Of feeling nothing? She didn't know, but if she was to change her life in any way at all, she would have to find out. And that meant confronting it. So, when the case was over . . .

A skin had formed on the top of her cocoa. She had never liked that, ever since childhood. That sweet and sticky skin made her shudder when, inadvertently, she had sipped without looking and it had stuck like a warm spider's web to her lips. Carefully, using her spoon, she pushed it to the edge of the cup, dredged it out and laid it in the saucer.

For some reason, that photo of Marcia Cunningham's handsome husband with his pipe at a rakish angle came into her mind. He reminded her of James just a little. Not his looks, but his expression. She found herself looking at the mantelpiece. Now that the Father Christmas was gone, it seemed so empty. She would like to have a photo or two there, but of whom? Not her family, that was for certain. James? Much too early for that yet. Herself, the graduation picture from police college? It would do, for a start.

Then she remembered the dress Marcia had dragged her all that way to look at. There was a puzzle, to be sure. No doubt the vandals would have an explanation, when and if they were caught. Still, it was a strange thing for someone to do. Maybe they had taken strips of material to fasten around their foreheads as Rambo headbands or something. There was no telling what weird fantasies went on in the adolescent mind these days.

Susan put her cup down. The record had finished, and even though it wasn't late she decided to go to bed and have an early night. There was still that American tome on homicide investigation for bedtime reading. Or should she do a little advance reading of Shakespeare from the cut-price *Complete Works* she had picked up at W. H. Smith's?

In a couple of days it would be twelfth night, the first night of the play. She just hoped that no police business came up to stop her from attending. James seemed so much to want her there, even though her knowledge of Shakespeare left a lot to be desired. And she was looking forward to the evening. She couldn't see how any of the present cases would get in her way. There wasn't much else they could do on the Caroline Hartley murder until they got new evidence, or until Banks took his head out of the sand and gave Veronica Shildon a long, hard, objective interrogation. Besides, Susan was only a helper, a note-taker on that one. And as for the vandals, until they were caught red-handed there wasn't much to be done about them, either. Picking up the heavy *Complete Works* from her bookshelf, she wandered off to bed.

V

"A message for you, sir," Sergeant Rowe called out as Banks walked into the police station after his visit to Veronica Shildon. He handed over a piece of paper. "It was a woman called Patty Jarouchki, I think. Sounded American. Anyway, she left her number. Said for you to call her as soon as you can."

Banks thanked him and hurried upstairs to his office, grabbing a black coffee on the way. The CID offices were quiet, the tapping of a keyboard from Richmond's office the only sign of life. He picked up the phone and dialed the number

Sergeant Rowe had given him. Patsy Janowski answered on the third ring.

"You had a message for me?" Banks said.

"Yes. Remember you asked me to try and recall if I'd noticed anything unusual in the area?"

"Yes."

"Well, it's not really . . . I mean, it's not clear at all, but you know I said there was a woman?"

"The one crossing King Street?"

"Yes. What about her?"

"I didn't get a good look or anything—I'm sure it wasn't anyone I knew—but I do remember she was walking funny."

"In what way?"

"Just . . . funny."

"Did she have a limp, a wooden leg?"

"No, no, it was nothing like that. At least I don't think so."

"A strange kind of walk? Some people have them. Bow-legged? Knock-kneed?"

"Not even that. She was just struggling a bit. There was snow on the ground. Oh, I know I shouldn't have called you. It's still not clear, and it's probably nothing. I feel stupid."

Banks could imagine her eyes ranging about the room, resting on the tongs by the fire, the old snuff-box on the mantelpiece. "You did right," he assured her.

"But I've told you nothing, really."

"It might mean something. If you think of anything else, will you stop accusing yourself of idiocy and call me?"

He could almost hear her smile at the other end of the line. "All right," she said. "But I don't think it'll get any clearer."

Banks said goodnight and broke the connection. For a moment he just sat on the edge of his desk, coffee in hand, staring at the calendar. It showed a wintry scene in Aysgarth, Wensleydale. Finally, he lit a cigarette and went over to the window. Outside, beyond the venetian blinds, the market square was deserted. The Christmas-tree lights still twinkled, but nobody passed to see them. It was that time of year when everyone had spent too much and drunk too much and seen too many people; now most Eastvalers were holed up in their houses keeping warm and watching repeats on television.

The day's depression was still with him, and the mystery of Caroline Hartley's death was still shrouded in fog. There had to be some way of making sense of it all, Banks told himself. He must have overlooked something. The only solution to his bleak mood was mental activity. As he stood at the window looking down on the forlorn Christmas lights, he tried to recreate the sequence of events in his mind.

First of all, he discounted the arrival of yet another visitor after the mysterious woman at seven-twenty. He also accepted that by the time Patsy Janowski had called and talked to Caroline Hartley briefly at her door, Claude Ivers was busy doing his last-minute shopping in the center and getting ready to head back to Redburn, and Veronica Shildon was shopping too.

A woman, perhaps the same one Patsy said walked strangely, knocked at Caroline's door and was admitted to the house. What had happened inside? Had the woman been an ex-lover or a jilted suitor? Had she called to remonstrate and ended up losing her temper and killing Caroline? Presumably there could have been sex involved. After all, Caroline had been naked, and the kind of sex she was interested in wouldn't oblige by leaving semen traces for the forensic boys to track down.

There was just no way of knowing. Caroline's life had been full of mysteries, a breeding ground for motives. As a working hypothesis, Banks accepted that the crime was spur-of-the-moment rather than a planned murder. The use of the handy knife and the lack of precaution about being seen, or caught by Veronica, who had been likely to arrive home at any moment, seemed to point that way. And unless Caroline had been involved in some unknown criminal activity, the odds were that passion of one kind or another lay at the root of her death.

After the murder came the clearing up. The killer had washed the knife, removed any possible fingerprints she might have left, and either put the Vivaldi record on the turn-table or lifted up the arm. Given the savage nature of the wounds, the killer must also have got blood on her own cloth-ing. If she had removed her coat before the deed, she could easily have covered her blood-spattered clothing with it and destroyed all evidence as soon as she got home.

Banks went to refill his coffee mug and returned to his office.

Something in Patsy Janowski's sketchy description of the woman bothered him, but he couldn't think what it was. He walked to the filing cabinet and dug out the reports on inter-views with Caroline Hartley's neighbors. Nothing much there helped, either. The details were vague, as the evening had been dark and snowy. Again, he read through the descriptions of the mystery woman: Mr. Farlowe had said she was wearing a mid-length, light trenchcoat with the belt fastened. He had seen her legs beneath it, and perhaps the bottom of a dress. She had been wearing a head-scarf, so he had been able to say nothing about her hair. Mrs. Eldridge had little to add, but what she remembered agreed with Farlowe's account.

Despite the coffee, Banks was getting tired. It really was time to go home. There was nothing to be gained by pacing the office. He slipped on his camel-hair overcoat and put the Walkman in his pocket. After he'd walked down the stairs and said goodnight to Sergeant Rowe at the front desk, he hesitated outside the station under the blue lamp and looked at the Queen's Arms. A rosy glow shone warmly from its smoky windows. But no, he decided, best go home and spend some time with Sandra. It was a clear, quiet night. He would leave the car in the station car-park and walk the mile or so home.

He put the headphones on, pressed the button and the open-ing of Poulenc's "Gloria" came on. As he walked on the crisp snow down Market Street, he looked at the patterns frost had made on the shop windows and wished that the odd bits and pieces of knowledge he had about the Hartley case could make similar symmetrical shapes. They didn't. He began to walk faster. Christ, his feet were cold. He should have worn sheepskin-lined boots, or at least galoshes. But he had never really thought about walking home until the impulse struck him. Then something leaped into his mind as he turned into his cul-de-sac and saw the welcome lights of home ahead, something that made him forget his cold feet for the last hundred yards.

Patsy Janowski had said the woman walked strangely. She couldn't explain it any better than that. But Mr. Farlowe said he was sure the visitor was a woman because he had seen her legs below her long coat. If that was the case, then her legs were bare; she either wasn't wearing boots at all, or she was wearing very short ones. It had been snowing quite heavily that evening since about five o'clock, and the snow had been forecast as early as the previous evening, so even a woman going to work that morning would have known to take her boots. Even before the snow, the weather had been gray and cold. Most of December had been lined-boots and overcoat weather.

Now why would a woman be trudging around in the snow without boots at seven-twenty that night? Banks wondered. She could have been in a hurry and simply slipped on the first pair of shoes that caught her eye. She could have come from somewhere she hadn't needed boots. But that didn't make sense. In such weather, most people wear boots to work, then change into more comfortable shoes when they get there. When it's time to leave, they slip back into their boots for the journey home.

The woman might have arrived by car and parked close by. The nearest space, where Patsy said she and Ivers parked, was a fair distance to walk in the snow without boots. The woman might have driven to Caroline's, found she couldn't park any closer and ended up having to walk farther than she'd bargained for. Which meant it could have been someone who didn't know the area well.

Given what Patsy had said about the walk, it sounded as if the woman had probably been wearing pumps or high heels—most likely the latter. That would explain her odd walk; trying to make one's way through four or five inches of snow in high heels would be difficult indeed. And wet.

Was it, then, someone who had nipped out of a local function, committed the murder and dashed back before she was missed? There had probably been a lot of parties going on that night, Hatchley's wedding reception among them. It couldn't have been anyone from there, of course, as Banks knew most of the guests. But it was an interesting avenue to explore. If he could find someone who had been at such a function that night, someone who had a connection with Caroline Hartley, then maybe he'd get somewhere. Feeling a little more positive about things, he turned off the tape and went into the house.

THIRTEEN

I

Teresa Pedmore rented a two-bedroom terrace house on Nelson Grove, in a pleasant enough area of town south of the castle, close to the river. The houses were old but in good repair, and their inhabitants, though only renting, took pride in adding individual touches to the outside trim. A low blue gate led to Teresa's house, where her matching door was edged in white. Lace curtains hung in the windows.

Teresa professed to be surprised to see Banks, though he was never sure what to believe when dealing with actors. Faith could have told Teresa about the visit Banks had paid her earlier, though he thought it unlikely. That would have meant confessing what she had said about Teresa.

The front door led straight into the living room. Cream-and-red-striped wallpaper covered the walls, where a number of framed prints hung. Banks, who had learned what little he knew about art from Sandra, recognized a Constable landscape, a Stubbs horse and a Lowry. Perhaps the most striking thing about the room, though, was that it was furnished with antiques: a Welsh dresser, Queen Anne writing-desk, Regency table and chairs. The only contemporary items were the tan three-piece suite arranged in a semicircle around the hearth and a small television set. Remembering the importance of the music, Banks looked around for evidence of a stereo but could find none.

Teresa gestured toward one of the armchairs and Banks sat down. He was surprised by her taste and impressed with her farm-girl looks, the blushes of red in her creamy cheeks. Her wavy chestnut hair framed a rather chubby, heart-shaped face with a wide, full mouth, an oddly delicate nose that didn't quite seem to belong and thick brows over large almond eyes. She certainly wasn't good-looking in the overtly sexual way Faith Green was, but the fierce confidence and determination in her simplest movements and gestures more than compensated. She was as tall and well-shaped as Faith, and wore a white silky blouse and knee-length navy skirt.

She picked up an engraved silver box from the low table and offered him a cigarette, lighting it with an old lighter as big as a paperweight. It was years since Banks had been offered a cigarette from a box, and he would certainly never have expected it in a small rented terrace house in Eastvale.

The cigarette was too strong, but he persevered. His lungs soon remembered the old days of Capstan Full Strength and rallied to the task. Almost before he had a chance to say yes or no, Teresa was pouring amber liquid from a cut-glass decanter into a crystal snifter. As she handed Banks the glass, the edges of her wide mouth twitched up in a smile.

"I suppose you're wondering where I get my money from," she said. "Policemen are always suspicious about people living above their means, aren't they?" She sat down and crossed her long legs.

Banks swirled the glass in his hand and breathed in the fumes: cognac. "*Are* you living above your means?" he asked.

She laughed, a low, murmuring sound. "How clever of you. Not at all. It only looks that way. The furniture isn't original, of course. I just like the designs, the look and feel of it. And one day, believe me, I'll have real antiques. I think the only valuable objects in the room are the decanter and the cigarette box, and they belonged to my grandfather. Family heirlooms. The Lowry is genuine, too, a present from a distant, wealthy relative. As for the rest, cognac and what have you . . . What can I say? I like to live well. I don't drink a lot, but I drink

the best. I make decent money, I don't run a car, I have no
children and my rent is reasonable."

Banks, who wondered why she was telling him all this,
nodded as if he were suitably impressed. Perhaps she was
trying to paint a picture of herself as someone who had far
too much class and refined sensibility to commit so tasteless
an act as murder. He sipped the cognac. Courvoisier VSOP,
he guessed. Maybe she was right.

"I suppose you think I should have stayed on the farm,"
she went on. "Married a local farmer and started having ba-
bies." She made a dismissive gesture with her cigarette.

For Christ's sake, Banks thought, do I look so old that
people immediately assume I'm a fuddy-duddy? Still, Teresa
couldn't have been more than twenty-two, twenty-three; there
were sixteen or seventeen years between them, which made
it technically possible for him to be her father. He just didn't
feel that old, and he could certainly understand young people
wanting to escape what they felt to be claustrophobic social
backgrounds.

"What do you want to do?" he asked.

"Act, of course."

She reminded Banks of Sally Lumb, another, albeit
younger, Dales hopeful he had met during the Steadman case
eighteen months ago. The memory made him feel sad. Such
dreams often turn to pain. But what are we if we don't dream?
Banks asked himself. And at least try to make them come
true.

"James is trying to fix things so I get a part in *Weymouth
Sands*. He's doing the script for the BBC, you know. He
knows all the casting people. It's terribly exciting." The Dales
accent was still there, despite the evidence of elocution lessons, and it made the upper class phrase "terribly exciting"
sound very funny indeed. "More cognac?"

Banks noticed his snifter was empty. He shook his head.
"No, no thanks. It's very good, but I'd better not."

Teresa shrugged. She didn't press him. Fine cognac is, after
all, very expensive.

"You're still on good terms with James Conran, then?" Banks asked.

Her eyebrows rose. "Why shouldn't I be?"

"I heard rumors you'd had a falling out."

"Who told you that?"

"Are they true?"

"It's that common little tramp, Faith, isn't it?"

"Was James Conran paying too much attention to Caroline Hartley?"

The name stopped Teresa in her tracks. She reached for another cigarette from the box but didn't offer Banks one this time. "It's easy to exaggerate things," she continued quietly. "Everyone argues now and then. I'll bet even you argue with your wife, don't you? But it doesn't mean anything."

"Did you argue with James Conran over Caroline?"

Her eyes flashed briefly, then she drew on her cigarette, tilted her head back and blew out a long stream of smoke through narrow nostrils. "What has Faith been saying about me?" she asked. "I've got a right to know."

"Look," Banks said. "I haven't told you who passed on the information. Nor am I going to. It's not important. What counts is that you answer my questions. And if you won't do it here, you can come down to the police station and answer them."

"You can't make me do that." Teresa leaned forward and flicked off a column of ash. "Surely?"

"What did you do after the rehearsal on December twenty-second?"

"What? I . . . I came home."

"Straight home?"

"No. I did some Christmas shopping first. Look—"

"What time did you get home?"

"—what is this? Are you trying to imply I might have had something to do with Caroline Hartley's death?"

"I'm not implying anything, I'm asking questions." Banks pulled out one of his own Silk Cuts and lit up. "What time did you get home?"

"I don't know. How can I remember? It was ages ago."

"Did you go out again?"

"No. I stayed home and worked on my role."

"You didn't have a date with Mr. Conran?"

"No. We . . . I . . ."

"Were you still seeing him at that time?"

"Of course I was."

"As a lover?"

"That's none of your damn business." She mashed her cigarette out and clasped her hands in her lap.

"When did you and Mr. Conran stop being lovers?"

"I'm not answering that."

"But you did stop."

There was a pause, then she hissed, "Yes."

"Before Caroline Hartley's murder?"

"Yes."

"And did Caroline have anything to do with this parting?"

"No. It was completely amicable on both sides. Things just didn't work out that way. We'd never been very deeply involved, anyway, if you know what I mean."

"A casual affair?"

"You could call it that, though neither of us is married."

"And Caroline Hartley came between you?"

Teresa scratched her palm and looked down.

"Am I right?" Banks persisted.

"Look," Teresa answered. "What if I say you are? It doesn't mean anything, does it? It doesn't mean I'd kill her. I'm not a fanatically jealous woman, but every woman has her pride. Anyway, it wasn't Caroline I blamed."

"Was Conran having an affair with Caroline?"

She shook her head. "I don't think so. We didn't know she was gay, but even so there was something about her, something different. Elusive. She could keep the men at bay while seeming to draw them to her. It's difficult to explain. No, I don't think he even saw her outside rehearsals and the pub."

That seemed to square with what Veronica Shildon had said.

"But he was attracted to her?"

"A bit smitten, you might say," said Teresa. "That was what annoyed me, him chatting her up in public like that when everyone could see, the way he looked at her. That kind of thing. But then James is like that. He goes after anything in a skirt."

"Am I to take it you don't much care for him any longer?"

"Not as a man, no. As a professional, I respect him a great deal."

"That's a very neat distinction."

"Surely you sometimes have to work with people you respect but don't like?"

"Did you argue over his attentions to Caroline?"

"I told him to stop drooling over her in public. I found it embarrassing. But that was only a part of it. What I said before was true. It wasn't much of a relationship to begin with. It had run its course."

"Do you think you'll get this part in *Weymouth Sands*?"

"James still appreciates me as an actress," she said, "which is more than he does that gossipy bitch who told you all about my personal life."

"Who's that?"

"Faith bloody Green, obviously. There's no need to be coy. You know damn well it was her who told you. And I can guess why."

"Why?"

"Why do you think? Because she couldn't get him herself."

"Did she try?"

Teresa gave Banks a disdainful look. "You've met Faith, Chief Inspector. What do you think the answer is?"

"But Conran wasn't interested?"

"It appears not."

"Any reason?"

"Not that I know of. Not his type, perhaps. Too much woman, too aggressive . . . I don't know. I'm just guessing."

"What did he think of her? Did they have any arguments?"

"If she's been trying to imply I had a good reason for

killing Caroline Hartley, it's probably because she had an even better one."

Banks sat up. "Why? Over her interest in Conran?"

Teresa sniffed. "No. It wasn't that. I think she soon realized that her tastes run to rougher trade than James. It was just that she had to try, like she does with every man. No, it was something else that happened."

"Tell me."

Teresa leaned forward and lowered her voice dramatically. "It was after rehearsal that night, the night Caroline was killed."

"What happened?"

"Most people left early because it was close to Christmas, but James wanted to spend half an hour or so with Faith and myself, just getting the blocking right. Our parts are large and very important, you see. Anyway, James wanted Faith to stay behind, so I left first. But I forgot my scarf, and it was cold outside, so I came back. I don't think they heard me. I was in the props room, you know, where we leave our coats and bags, and I heard voices out in the auditorium. I'm not a naturally nosy person, but I wondered what was going on. Anyway, to cut a long story short, I walked a little closer and listened. And guess what?"

"What?"

Teresa smiled. "They were arguing. I bet she didn't tell you about *that*, did she?"

"What were they arguing about?"

"Caroline Hartley. As far as I could gather, James was telling Faith that if she didn't do a better job of learning her lines, he'd give her part to Caroline."

"What was Faith's reaction?"

"She walked out in a huff. I had to be quick to hide behind a door without being seen."

"Can you remember their exact words?"

"I can remember what Faith said to James before she left. She said, 'You'd do anything to get into that little slut's pants, wouldn't you?' I wish I'd been there to see his face. Of course, he can't have meant it about giving her part away. James would know quite well there wasn't enough time for Caroline to take over Faith's role. He was just trying to get her to try a bit harder."

"What happened after that?"

"I don't know. As soon as Faith left, I got out of there pretty quickly. I didn't want to be caught snooping."

"Where was Conran?"

"Still in the auditorium, as far as I know."

"Could he have left by the front door?"

Teresa shook her head. "No, we always use the back during rehearsals. The front's kept locked after the gallery closes, unless there's some sort of an event on."

"Who has a key to the back door?"

"Only Marcia and James from the Dramatic Society, as far as I know. Usually one or the other would be last to leave. James, more often than not, as Marcia was always first to arrive, and she tended to disappear to the pub early if she knew she wasn't needed."

"What time did this argument occur?"

"Six. Maybe a little after."

"What were you wearing?"

Teresa frowned and sat back in her chair. "What do you mean?"

"What clothes were you wearing?"

"Me? Jeans, a leather coat, my wool scarf. Same as usual for rehearsals."

"What about footwear?"

"I had my boots on. It *is* winter, after all. I don't see what—"

"And Faith?"

"I can't remember. I doubt I paid much attention."

"What did she usually wear? Jeans? Skirt and blouse? Dress?"

"She usually wore a skirt and blouse. She is a teacher, believe it or not. She came straight from school. But I don't know for sure what she was wearing that day."

"What about her overcoat?"

"What she always wore, I suppose."

"Which is?"

"A long coat, like a light raincoat with epaulettes, but lined."

"Belted?"

"Yes."

"And her footwear?"

"How should I know?"

"Was she wearing boots or shoes?"

"Boots, I should think. Because of the weather."

"But you can't be sure?"

"No. I can't say I pay Faith's feet much attention."

"Why didn't you tell me all this earlier?" Banks asked.

Teresa sighed and shifted in her chair. "I don't know. It didn't seem all that important. And I didn't want any trouble, anything spoiling the play. It was bad enough with Caroline getting murdered. When I heard about her being gay, I was sure her death must have had something to do with her private life, that it didn't involve any of us. I know I sound hard, but this play is important to me, believe it or not. If I do well, the TV people will hear about me . . ."

Banks stood up. "I see."

"And as for Faith," Teresa went on. "I know I sounded bitchy right now, but it was only because I was annoyed at what she'd said to you. She'd no right to go talking about my personal life. But she's not a killer. Not Faith. And certainly not over a petty incident like that."

Banks buttoned his overcoat and headed for the door. "Thanks very much," he said. "You've been a great help." And he left her reaching for another cigarette from the engraved silver box.

Damn them all! he cursed as he walked out into the cold night. Of course Faith could have killed Caroline. Perhaps not over a petty matter, such as the argument Teresa had described, but there could have been another reason. A woman like Caroline Hartley, whether intentionally or not, causes violent emotion in all who come into contact with her. Even Veronica Shildon had admitted to Banks that she'd never understood lust until she met Caroline.

Faith could have simmered for a while after the row—it would certainly have been a blow to her pride—and then, if she had something else against Caroline, too, she could have gone to visit her and remonstrate. Faith certainly worked hard at her Mae West role, but what if it was just an act? What if her true inclination lay elsewhere, or she leaned both ways?

It didn't seem likely that James Conran would kill the goose he hoped would lay a golden egg. He had high hopes for Caroline as an actress and he was sexually attracted to her as a woman. He didn't know she was gay. Given his masculine pride and confidence, he probably assumed that she would come around eventually; it was just a matter of time and persistence. Still, there might have been something else in the relationship that Banks didn't know about.

Caroline had seemed to bring out the worst in both Faith and Teresa. How could he be sure either of them was telling him the truth? Instead of feeling that he had cleverly played one off against the other, he was beginning to feel that he might be the one who had been played. Cursing actors, he pulled up in front of his house feeling nothing but frustration.

II

The bell was ringing in the distance. All around lay dark jungle: snakes slithered along branches, phosphorescent insects hummed in the air and squat, furry creatures lurked in the lush foliage. But the bell was ringing in the dark and she had to find her way through the jungle to discover why. There were probably booby traps, too—holes lightly covered with grass matting that would give way under her weight to a thirty-foot drop onto sharpened bamboo shoots. And . . .

She was at least half-awake now. The jungle was gone, a

figment of the night. The ringing was coming from her telephone, in the living room. Hardly a dangerous journey, after all, though one she was loath to make, being so comfortably snuggled up under the warm blankets.

She looked at the bedside clock. Two twenty-three in the morning. Bloody hell. And she hadn't got to bed until midnight. Slowly, without turning on the light, she made her way through to the living room by touch. She fumbled the receiver and put it to her ear.

"Susan?"

"Mmm."

"Sergeant Rowe here. Sorry to disturb you, lass, but it's important. At least it might be."

"What's happened?"

"We've caught the vandals."

"How? No, wait. I'm coming in. Give me fifteen minutes."

"Right you are, lass. They'll still be here."

Susan replaced the receiver and shook her head to clear the cobwebs. Luckily, she hadn't drunk too much at dinner. She put on the living room light, squinting in the brightness, then went into the bathroom and splashed cold water on her face. There was no time for make-up and grooming, just a quick wash, a brush through the hair and out into the cold quiet night. With luck, there would be fresh coffee at the station.

Holding her coat around her she shivered as she got into the car. It started on the third try. Driving slowly because of the ice, she took nearly ten minutes to get to the car-park behind the station. She nipped in through the back door and walked to the front desk.

"They're upstairs," Sergeant Rowe said.

"Any background information?"

"Aye. Tolliver and Wilson caught them trying to jimmy their way into the Darby and Joan Club on Heughton Drive. Our lads had enough sense to let them jimmy open the lock and step over the threshold before pouncing. A slight altercation ensued"—Sergeant Rowe stopped and smiled at his use of jargon—"in which said officers managed to apprehend the suspects. In other words, they put up a bit of a fight but came off worst."

"Do we know who they are?"

"Rob Chalmers and Billy Morley. Both spent time in remand homes."

"How old are they?"

"We're in luck. One's eighteen, the other seventeen."

Susan smiled. "Not a case for the juvenile court, then. Have they been cautioned?"

"Charged and cautioned. We've got the jimmy and the gloves they were wearing bagged and ready for testing."

"And?"

"They're not saying owt. Been watching American cop shows like the rest. Refuse to talk till they've seen their lawyers. Lawyers! I ask you."

"And I assume said lawyers are on their way?"

Rowe scratched his bulbous nose. "Bit of trouble tracking them down. I think we might manage it by morning."

"Good. Where are they?"

"Interview rooms upstairs. Tolliver's with one, Wilson's with the other."

"Right."

Susan poured herself a mug of coffee and went upstairs, still feeling the same thrill as she had on her first day in CID. She took a few sips of the strong black liquid, hung her coat up in the office, then took a quick glance in her compact mirror and applied a little make-up. At least now she didn't look as if she had got straight out of bed. Satisfied, she smoothed her skirt, ran her hand through her curls, took a deep breath and walked into the first interview room.

PC Tolliver stood by the door, a bruise by the side of his left eye and a crust of blood under his right nostril. Sitting, or rather slouching, behind the table, legs stretched out, arms behind his head, was a youth with dark, oily, slicked-back hair, as if he had used half a jar of Brylcreem. He was wearing a green parka, open over a torn T-shirt, and faded, grubby, jeans. Susan could smell beer on his breath even at the door.

When he saw her walk in, he didn't move. She ignored him and looked over at Tolliver.

"All right, Mike?"

"I'll mend."

"Who've we got?"

"Robert S. Chalmers, age eighteen. Unemployed. Previous form for assault, damage to property, theft—all as a juvenile. A real charmer." Susan winced in acknowledgment of his joke. Bad puns were a thing with PC Tolliver.

Susan sat down. Tolliver went to the chair by the small window in the corner and took out his notebook.

"Hello, Robert," she said, forcing a smile.

"Fuck off."

The animosity that came from him was almost over-whelming. Susan tensed up inside, determined not to react. On the outside she remained calm and cool. He had acted in this hostile way partly because she was a woman, she was sure. A thug like Chalmers would take it as an insult that they sent a small woman rather than a burly man to interrogate him. He would also expect to be able to deal with her easily. To him, women were probably creatures to be used and discarded. There wouldn't be any shortage of them in his life. He was good-looking in a surly, James Dean, early Elvis Presley way, his upper lip permanently curved in a sneer.

"I hear you've been attempting to gain unlawful entry to the Darby and Joan Club," she said. "What's the problem, can't you wait till you're sixty-five?"

"Very funny."

"It's not funny, Robert. It's aggravated burglary. Do you know how much time you can get for that?"

Chalmers glared at her. "I'm not saying anything till my lawyer gets here."

"It might help you if you did. Co-operation. We'd mention that in court."

"I told you, I ain't saying nothing. I know you bastards. You'd fit me up with a verbal." He moved in his chair and Susan saw him wince slightly with pain.

"What's wrong. Robert?"

"Bastard over there beat me up." He grinned. "Don't worry, love, he only bruised a rib or two—he didn't damage my tackle."

Susan bit her tongue. "Be sensible, Robert, like your friend William."

Susan saw a flicker of apprehension in the boy's eyes, but they quickly regained their hard-bitten look and he laughed. "I'm not stupid, you know, love," he said. "Pull the other one."

Susan stared at him, long and hard, and made her assessment. Was it worth pushing at him? She decided not. He'd been through this kind of thing too many times before to fall for the usual tricks or to scare easily. Maybe his accomplice would be softer.

She stood up. "Right, I'll just go and have another word with your mate, then. He'll be able to fill in all the details. That should give us enough."

Though hardly anything perceptible changed in Chalmers's expression, Susan somehow knew that what she had said worried him. Not that the other had talked already; he wouldn't fall for that. But that Billy Morley was less tough, more nervous, more likely to crack. Chalmers just shrugged and resumed his slouch, gritting his teeth for a second as he shifted. He put his hands in his pockets and pretended to whistle at the ceiling.

Susan went to the next room, stopping to lean against the wall on the way to take a few deep breaths. No matter how often she came across them, people like Chalmers frightened her. They frightened her more than the people who committed crimes out of passion or greed. She could hear her father's voice going on about the younger generation. In his day, the story went, people were frightened of coppers, they respected the law. Now, though, they didn't give a damn; they'd as soon thump a policeman and run. She had to admit there was a lot of truth in what he said. There had always been gangs, youngsters had always been full of mischief and sometimes gone too far, but they certainly used to run when the police arrived. Now they didn't seem to care. Why had it happened? Was television to blame? Partly, perhaps. But it was more than that. Maybe they had become cynical about those in authority after reading about too many corrupt politicians, perverted judges and bent coppers. Everyone was on the fiddle; nothing really mattered anymore. But it wasn't Susan's job to analyze society, just to get the truth out of the bastards. Taking a final deep breath, she walked into the next office to confront Billy Morley.

This lad, guarded by PC Wilson, who sported a small cut over his left eye, seemed a little more nervous than his friend. Skinny to the point of emaciation, he had a spotty, weaselly face and dark, beady eyes that darted all over the place. He was sitting straight up in his chair rubbing his upper arm and licking his thin lips.

"You the lawyer?" he asked hopefully. "This bastard here nearly broke my arm. Hit me with his stick."

"You were resisting arrest." PC Wilson said.

"I wasn't doing nothing of the kind. I was minding my own business."

"Aye," said Wilson, "you and your jimmy."

"It's not mine. It's—"

"Well?" asked Wilson.

He folded his arms. "I'm not saying anything."

By this time Susan had sat down and arranged herself as comfortably as she could in the stiff, bolted-down chair. First she gave PC Wilson the signal to fade into the background and take notes, then she took a good look at Morley. He didn't frighten her nearly as much as Chalmers. Basically, she thought, he was weak—especially alone. He was also the younger of the two. Chalmers, she suspected, was a true hard case, but Morley was just a follower and probably a coward at heart. Chalmers had known that, and the knowledge had flitted across his face for a moment. Being a woman would put Susan at an advantage with someone like Morley, who probably jumped each time his mother yelled.

"I'm not your solicitor, William," Susan said. "I'm a detective constable. I've come to ask you a few questions. It's a serious charge you're facing. Do you understand that?"

"What do you mean?"

"Aggravated burglary. Under section ten of the Theft Act, you could do life. Add to that resisting arrest, assaulting a police officer, and I'm pretty sure any judge would come down hard on you."

"Bollocks! That's crap! You can't get life." He shook his head. "Not just for . . . I don't believe you."

"It's true, William. You're not a juvenile now, you're an adult. No more fun and games."

"But—"

"But nothing. I'm telling you, William, it doesn't look good. Do you know what *aggravated* burglary means?"

Morley shook his head.

Susan clasped her hands on the table in front of her. "It means committing a burglary while carrying an offensive weapon."

"What offensive weapon?"

"The jimmy."

Susan was interpreting the law with a certain amount of license. "Aggravated burglary" usually involved firearms or explosives.

She shook her head. "The best we could do for you is drop the charge to going equipped for stealing. That's thirteen years. Then there's malicious damage to property. . . . Whichever way it cuts, William, you're in a lot of trouble. You can only help yourself by talking to me."

Morley pinched his long, sharp nose and sniffed. "I want my lawyer."

"What were you after?" Susan asked. "Did someone tell you there was money there?"

"We weren't after no money. We—I'm not saying anything till my law—"

"Your solicitor may be some time, William. Solicitors like a good night's sleep. They don't enjoy getting up at two-thirty in the morning just to help a pathetic little creep like you. It'll be better if you cooperate."

Morley gaped at her, as if her insulting words, delivered in such a matter-of-fact, even tone, had pricked him like darts. "I told you," he stammered. "I want—"

Susan rested her hands on the table, palms down, and spoke softly. "William, be sensible for once in your life. Look at the facts. We already know the two of you broke into the Darby and Joan Club. You used a jimmy. It'll have your fingerprints on it. You must have handled it at some time. It's being tested right now. And there'll be fibers we can match with the gloves you were wearing, too. We also have two very reliable witnesses. PC Wilson here and his colleague caught you redhanded. There's no getting around that, solicitor or no solicitor. We've followed correct procedure so far. You've been warned and charged. Right now we're reviewing your options, so to speak."

"He hit me," Morley whined. "He's broke my arm. I need a doctor."

For a moment Susan thought that might be true. Morley was pale and his sharp, narrow brow looked clammy. Then she realized it was fear.

"Look at his eye, William," she said. "Nobody's going to believe he attacked you for no reason."

Morley fell silent for a while. Susan could almost hear him thinking, trying to decide what to do.

"It'll go easier for you if you tell us what you were up to," she said gently. "Perhaps you were only trespassing." That would never wash, she knew. Trespassing, in itself, wasn't an offense except in certain special circumstances, such as poaching and espionage, and breaking the lock of a club with a jimmy was a long way from simple trespass. Still, it wouldn't do Morley any harm to let him look on the bright side.

He remained silent, chewing at the edge of his thumb.

"What's wrong, William? Are you frightened of Robert? Is that what it is?" She was about to tell him Chalmers had already talked, tried to put the blame on him, but realized just in time that such a ploy could ruin any advantage she had. He might suspect a trick then, no doubt having seen such tactics used on television, and her carefully constructed house of cards would fall down.

"There's nothing to be afraid of. You'll be helping him too."

Ten tense seconds later, Morley took his thumb from his mouth and said, "We weren't burgling anything. That wasn't it at all."

"What were you doing there, then?" Susan asked.

"Just having fun."

"What do you mean, fun?"

"You know, it was something to do. Smashing things and stuff. It wasn't no aggravated burglary, or whatever you call it. You can't charge us with that."

"It looks like burglary to us, William. Are you trying to tell me you were going to vandalize the place?"

"We weren't going to take anything or hurt anyone. Nothing like that."

"Were you going to cause damage?"

"Just a bit of fun."

"Why?"

"What do you mean, why?"

"Why would you want to do such a thing?"

"I dunno." Morley squirmed in his chair and grasped his arm again. "Fucking hurts, that."

"Will you please not use language like that in front of me, William," Susan said. "I find it offensive. Answer my question. Why did you do it?"

"No reason. Do you have to have a fucking reason for everything? I told you, it was just fun, that's all."

"I've told you once," Susan said, mustering as much quiet authority as she could, "I don't like that kind of language. Learn some manners."

Morley tried hard to glare at her, but he looked more ashamed and defeated than defiant.

"Was it the same kind of fun you had in those other places?" Susan asked.

"What other places?"

"Come on, William. You know what I mean. This isn't the first time, is it?"

Morley remained silent for a while, then said quietly, still rubbing his arm, "I suppose not."

"Suppose?"

"All right. No, it's not. But we never hurt anyone or anything."

Susan could taste success. Her first real case. She was only assisting on the Hartley murder, but this one was all hers. If she could wrap up a four-month problem of vandalism with a neat confession, it would look very good on her record. As she listed the dates and places vandalized over the past few months—mostly youth clubs and recreation centers—Morley nodded glumly at each one, until she mentioned the Community Center.

"Come again?" he said.

"Eastvale Community Center, night of December twenty-second."

Morley shook his head. "You can't do us for that one."

"What are you saying?"

"I'm saying we didn't do it, that's what."

"Come on, William. What's the point in denying it? It'll all be taken into account. You're doing yourself no good."

He leaned forward. Spittle collected at the corners of his mouth. "Because we didn't f—. . . . Because we didn't do it, that's why. I wasn't even in Eastvale that night. I spent Christmas with my mother down in Coventry. I can prove it. Call her. Go on."

Susan took the number. "What about Robert."

"How should I know. But *I* didn't do it. He wouldn't do it by himself, would he? Stands to reason. Rob—now, wait a minute, wait a minute! He was out of town, too. He was down in Bristol with his brother over Christmas. We didn't do it. I'm telling you."

Susan tapped her pen on the desk and sighed. True, it didn't make sense for the lad to lie at this point, when he had confessed to everything else. Damn! Just when she thought she had got it all wrapped up. That meant there must be two sets of vandals. One down, one to go. She stood up. "Take his statement, will you, John? I'll go and make out a report for the chief inspector. We'll check the alibis for the Community Center job tomorrow morning." As she passed the room where Robert Chalmers was being held, she almost went in for another try. But there was nothing more to learn. Instead, she carried on down the corridor to her office.

III

"Of all the times to come pestering me! It's opening night tonight. Don't you know that? How did you even know I'd be here? Normally I'd be at school at this time."

"I know," Banks said. "I phoned. They told me you'd taken the day off."

"You did what?" Faith Green was really pacing now, arms folded under her breasts. She wore purple tights and a baggy, hip-length sweater with red and blue hoops around it. Her silver hair and matching hoop earrings flashed in the morning sunlight that shone through her large picture window.

"How dare you?" she went on. "Do you realize what damage that could do my career? It doesn't matter that I'm guilty of nothing. Just a hint of police around that place and the smell sticks."

"Why don't you sit down?" Banks perched at the edge of his armchair, faintly amused by Faith's performance. It certainly differed from his last visit. His amusement, however, was overshadowed by irritation.

She stopped and glared at him. "Am I making you nervous? Good."

Banks leaned back in the chair and crossed his legs. "Remember last time I called, I asked if you'd noticed anything odd about the rehearsal on December twenty-second?"

Faith resumed pacing again, stopped in front of the Greta Garbo poster, as if seeking inspiration, and said, with her back to Banks, "So?"

"Were you telling me the truth?"

"I'm not in the habit of lying."

"It'd be easier if you sat down," Banks said.

"Oh, all right, damn you!" Faith flounced toward the sofa and flung herself onto it. "There," she said with a pout. "Does that suit you?"

"Fine. I must say you're not quite as welcoming as you were last time."

Faith looked at him for a moment, trying to gauge his meaning. "That was different," she said finally. "I didn't see why we had to have such a boring time just because you were asking silly questions."

"And this time?"

"I should be rehearsing, going through my lines. I'm tense enough as it is. You're upsetting me."

"How?"

"Asking questions again."

Banks sighed. "All right. How about if I stop asking and start telling?" And he relayed what Teresa had told him about the argument between Faith and James Conran. The further he got, the paler Faith's face turned and the more angry her eyes became.

"Who told you this?" she demanded when he'd finished.

"That doesn't matter."

"It does to me. It couldn't have been James, surely. The last thing *he'd* do is make himself look bad." She paused; then slapped the arm of the sofa. "Of course! How stupid of me. It was Teresa, wasn't it? She must have stayed behind and eavesdropped. I thought she'd been behaving oddly toward me lately. Did you tell her what I told you?"

"Look, it really doesn't—"

"The snooping bitch! She's no right, no right at all. And neither had—"

"Is it true?" Banks asked.

"It's none of her—"

"But is it true?"

"—business to listen to my private—"

"So it *is* true?"

Faith hesitated, looked over to Garbo again and sighed deeply. "All right, so we had a row. I've got nothing to hide. It's nothing new. Happens all the time in the theater."

"It's the timing that interests me most," Banks said. "You could conceivably have been angry enough at Caroline Hartley to stew over it for a couple of drinks, then go pay her a visit. You didn't know she lived with anyone."

Faith's jaw dropped. When she finally spoke, it was in a squeaky, uncontrolled voice, far different from her stage speech.

"Are you suggesting that I killed the damn woman over some stupid argument with the director of a small-town play?"

"You did call her a 'little slut.' I think that suggests a bit more than a tiff over a part in an amateur production, don't you?"

"It's just a figure of speech, a . . ."

"Why did you call her a slut, Faith? Was it because Conran fancied her but he didn't fancy you? Is that why you told me about him and Teresa, too? Out of jealous spite?"

For the first time, Faith seemed speechless. But it didn't last long. Finally, red-faced, she stretched out her arm dramatically and pointed at the door.

"Out!" she yelled. "Out, you wretched, insulting little man! Out!"

"Calm down, Faith," Banks said. "I need answers. Is that why?"

Faith let her arm fall slowly and sat in silence for a few moments contemplating the upholstery of the sofa. "What if I did call her a slut?" she said finally. "Heat of the moment, that's all. And I'll tell you something, the way I felt at the time, if I'd killed anybody it would have been our bloody philandering director. It's unprofessional, letting your prick rule your judgment like that. It happened with Teresa, it was happening with Caroline . . ."

"But it didn't happen with you?"

"Huh! Do you think I really cared about that? I've no trouble finding a man when I want one. A *real* man, too, not some artsy-fartsy wimp like James Conran."

"But maybe he hurt your pride? Some people don't handle rejection well. Or perhaps it wasn't Conran that really bothered you. Was it Caroline herself?"

Faith stared at him, then spoke slowly. "Look, you asked me about that the last time you were here. I told you I'm not a lesbian. I told you I could prove it to you. Do you want me to prove it now?"

She sat up, crossed her arms and reached for the bottom of her sweater.

Banks held his hand up. "No," he said, "I'm not asking you to prove it. And quite honestly, it's not really the kind of thing you *can* prove, is it?"

Faith let her hands drop but remained sitting cross-legged on the sofa. "You mean you think I'm bi?"

Banks shrugged.

"Well, you can't prove that either, can you?"

"We might be able to, if we talk to the right people."

Faith laughed. "My ex-lovers? Well, good luck to you, darling. You'll need it."

"What did you do after the argument?" Banks asked.

"Came home, like I said." She put her hand to her brow. "Quite honestly, I was shagged out, dear."

Faith seemed to have regained her composure since her outburst, or at least her poise. She pushed her fringe back from her eyes and managed a brief smile as she went on. "Look, Chief Inspector, I know you have to catch your criminal and all that, but it's not me. And I've got a lot of work to do before curtain tonight. Besides, I need to be calm, relaxed. You're making me all flustered. I'll blow my lines. Be a darling and bugger off. You can come back some other time, if you want."

Banks smiled. "I shouldn't worry about being nervous. I've heard a bit of anxiety adds an edge to a performance."

Faith narrowed her eyes at him for a moment, as if wondering whether she was being had. "Well . . ." she went on. "If that's all . . . ?"

"Far from it. You argued with James Conran in the auditorium, am I right?"

"Yes."

"What happened next?"

"I left, of course. I don't put up with that kind of treatment—not from anyone."

"And you went straight home?"

"I did."

"Was anyone else in the center at the time?"

"Well, obviously Teresa bloody Pedmore was, but I didn't see her."

"Anyone else?"

Faith shook her head.

"Are you sure?"

"I told you, I didn't see anyone. But then I didn't see them all leave, either. There are plenty of cubby-holes behind the stage there, as you know quite well. The whole bloody cast could have been hiding there and listening, for all I know."

"But as far as you know, the only person there was James Conran, and you left him in the auditorium."

Faith nodded, a puzzled expression on her face. "And Teresa, I suppose, if she saw me leave."

"Yes," Banks said. "And Teresa. What were you wearing that evening?"

"To rehearsal?"

"Yes."

Faith shrugged. "Same as I usually wear, I suppose, when I come from school."

"Which is?"

"They're very conservative, you know. Blouse, skirt and cardigan is required uniform."

"How long was the skirt?"

She arched her eyebrows. "Why, Chief Inspector, I didn't know you cared." She stood up with exaggerated slowness and put the edge of her hand just below her knee. "About that long," she said, then she shifted her weight to her left leg, dropping her right hip in a half-comic, half-seductive pose. "As I said, they're very conservative."

"What about your overcoat?"

"What is this?"

"Can you tell me?"

"I can do better if it'll get you out of here quicker." She walked to the hall cupboard and pulled out a long, heavily-lined gabardine. "It's not quite warm enough for the weather we've been having lately," she said, "but it'll do until some-one buys me a mink."

"What about footwear?"

She raised one eyebrow. "You *are* getting intimate, aren't you? Whatever will it be next, I wonder?"

"Footwear?"

"Boots, of course. What do you think I'd be wearing in that weather? Bloody high heels?" She laughed. "Tell me, have you a shoe fetish or something?"

Banks smiled and got to his feet. "No. Sorry to disappoint you. Thank you very much for your time. I'll see myself out."

But Faith followed him to the door and leaned against the frame, arms loosely folded. "You know, Chief Inspector," she said, "I *am* very disappointed in you. I might be persuaded to change my mind, but it would take a lot of doing. I've never been so insulted and abused by a man as I've been by you. But the funny thing is, I still like you." She took him by the elbow and steered him out the open door. "And now you really must go."

Banks headed down the corridor and turned when he heard Faith calling after him.

"Chief Inspector! Will you be there tonight? Will you be watching the play?"

"I'll be there," Banks said. "I wouldn't miss it for anything." And he went on his way.

FOURTEEN

I

The community hall was surprisingly full for the first night of an amateur production, Banks thought. There they all sat, chattering and coughing nervously before the play started: a party of fourth-formers from Eastvale Comprehensive, present under sufferance; friends and relatives of the cast; a group of pensioners; members of the local Literary Institute. The old boiler groaned away in the cellar, but it didn't seem to be doing much good. There was a chill in the hall and most people kept their scarves on and their coats draped over their shoulders.

Banks sat beside Sandra. Their seats, compliments of James Conran, were front and center, about ten rows back. Further ahead, Banks could make out Susan's blond curls. The director himself sat beside her, occasionally leaning over to whisper in her ear. He could also see Marcia talking animatedly to a gray-haired man beside her.

It was almost seven-thirty. Banks eyed the moth-eaten curtains for signs of movement. Much as he enjoyed Shakespeare, he hoped the performance would not last too long. He remembered an actor telling him once in London that he didn't like doing *Hamlet* because the pubs had always closed by the time it was over. Banks didn't think *Twelfth Night* was that long, but a bad performance could make it seem so.

Finally, the lights went off abruptly, there being no

dimmer-switch in the Eastvale Community Center, and the curtains began to jerk open. Rusted rings creaked on the rail. The audience clapped, then made themselves as comfortable as they could in the molded-plastic chairs.

> If music be the food of love, play on,
> Give me excess of it, that, surfeiting,
> The appetite may sicken, and so die. . . .

So spoke the Duke, and the play was underway. The set was simple, Banks noticed. A few well-placed columns, drapes and portraits gave the impression of a palace. Banks recognized the music, played on a lute, as a Dowland melody, fitting enough for the period.

Though he was no Shakespeare expert, Banks had seen two other performances of *Twelfth Night*, one at school and one in Stratford. He remembered the general plot but not the fine details. This time, he noticed, too many cast members shouted or rushed their lines and mauled the poetry of Shakespeare's language in the process. On the other hand, the groupings and movements on stage constantly held the attention. The way people faced one another or paced about as they talked kept everything in motion. From what little he knew of directing, Banks assumed that Conran himself was responsible for this. Occasionally, a member of the audience would shift in his or her seat, and there were quite a few present suffering from coughs and colds, but on the whole most people were attentive. When an actor or actress hesitated over lines, waiting for a prompt, nobody laughed or walked out.

Faith and Teresa were good. They had the poise and the skill to bring off their roles, even if it was difficult to believe in Faith's masquerade as a man. In their scenes together, though, there was an obvious tension, perhaps because Faith knew who had told Banks about her row with Conran, and Teresa knew who had told him about her jealousy over Caroline Hartley. Ironically, this seemed to give an edge to the performances, especially to Viola's initial rudeness on their first meeting. The ambiguity of their relationship—Viola, dressed as a man, courting Olivia on her brother's behalf—soon absorbed Banks. To hear Faith complimenting Teresa's beauty was an odd thing indeed, but to watch their love blossom was even stranger.

For Banks, this had a dark side, too. He couldn't help but think of Caroline and Veronica, knowing, as the characters themselves did not, that both Viola and Olivia were female. Maria, the role that Caroline would have played, was an added reminder of the recent tragedy.

During the intermission, Banks felt distracted. He left Sandra chatting with some acquaintances and nipped out onto North Market Street for a cigarette in the icy cold. The dim gaslights glinted on the snow and ice, and even as he stood, a gentle snowfall began, flakes drifting down like feathers. He shuddered, flicked his half-smoked cigarette end into a grate and went back inside.

The vague connection between the play and reality was beginning to make Banks feel very uneasy. By the fourth act, his attention began to wander—to thoughts of his recent interviews with Faith and Teresa and the pile of unread paperwork in his in-tray, including a report on the arrest of the vandals that Susan had stayed up half the night to prepare. Then his attention would return to the play in time to hear the Clown and Malvolio chatting about Pythagoras's opinion of wild fowl, or Sebastian in raptures about the pearl Olivia had given him. He couldn't maintain lasting concentration. There was something in his mind, a glimmer of an idea, disparate facts coming together, but he couldn't grasp it, couldn't see the complete picture yet. There was an element still missing.

By the final act, Banks's back and buttocks hurt, and he found it difficult to keep still in the hard chair. Surreptitiously, he glanced at his watch. Almost ten. Surely not long to go. Even before he expected it, true identities were revealed, everybody was married off, except for Malvolio, and the Clown began to sing:

When that I was and a little tiny boy,
With hey, ho, the wind and the rain,
A foolish thing was but a toy,
For the rain it raineth every day.

Then the music ended and the curtains closed. The audience applauded; the cast appeared to take bows. Soon the formalities were all over and everyone shuffled out of the hall, relieved to be leaving the hard seats.

"Time for a drink?" Banks said to Sandra as they fastened their coats on the front steps.

Sandra took his arm. "Of course. Champagne. It's the only civilized thing to do after an evening at the theater. Except go for dinner."

"There aren't any restaurants open this late. Maybe Gibson's Fish and—"

Sandra pulled a face and tugged his arm. "I'll settle for a lager and lime and a packet of cheese-and-onion crisps."

"A cheap date," Banks said. "Now I know why I married you."

They set off down North Market Street to the Queen's Arms, which was much closer to the front exit of the Community Center than was the usual cast watering-hole out back, the Crooked Billet.

It was only twenty past ten when they got there, enough time for a couple of pints at least. The pub was quiet at first, but many of the theater-goers following Banks and Sandra seemed to have the same idea about a drink, and it soon got crowded. By then, Banks and Sandra had a small, dimpled, copper-topped table near the fireplace, where they warmed their hands before drinking.

They discussed the play against a background buzz of conversation, but Banks still felt uneasy and found it hard to concentrate. Instead, he couldn't help but put together what he knew about the Caroline Hartley murder, trying different patterns to see if he could at least discover the shape of the missing piece.

"Alan?"

"What? Oh, sorry."

"What the hell's up with you? I asked you twice what you thought about Malvolio."

Banks sipped some beer and shook his head. "Sorry, love. I feel a bit distracted."

"There's something bothering you, isn't there?"

"Yes."

She put her hand on his arm. "About the case? It's only natural, after seeing the play, isn't it? After all, Caroline Hartley was supposed to be in it."

"It's not just that." Banks couldn't put his thoughts into words. All he could think of was the woman who walked strangely in the snow and Vivaldi's burial music for a small child. And there was something about the play that snagged on his mind. Not the production details or any particular line, but something else, something obvious that he just couldn't bring into focus. Faith and Teresa? He didn't know. All he knew was that he felt not only puzzled but tense, too, the kind of edginess one has before a storm breaks. Often, he knew, that feeling signaled that he was close to solving the case, but there was even more this time, a sense of danger, of evil he had overlooked.

Suddenly he became aware of someone tapping him on the shoulder. It was Marcia Cunningham.

"Hello, Mr. Banks," she said. "Wondered if I'd find you here."

"I'd have thought you'd be at the Crooked Billet with the rest," Banks said.

Marcia shook her head. "It was all right during rehearsals, but I don't know if I can handle the first-night post-mortems. Besides, I'm with a friend."

She introduced Banks to the trim, middle-aged man standing behind her. Albert. There was one more chair at the table, and Banks offered his as well to the two newcomers. They demurred at first, then sat. Banks leaned against the stone fireplace.

"Last orders!" called Cyril, the landlord. "Last orders, please!"

In the scramble for the bar, Banks managed to get in another round. When he got back to the table Marcia Cunningham was chatting to Sandra.

"I was just saying to Sandra," she repeated, "that I was wondering if you'd solved the little mystery of the dress?"

"Pardon?"

"The dress, the one with the pieces missing."

"I'm sorry, Marcia." Banks said, "I've no idea what you're talking about."

Marcia frowned. "But surely young Susan must have told you?"

"Whatever it is, I can assure you she didn't. It was her case, anyway. I've been far too preoccupied with the Caroline Hartley murder."

Marcia shrugged and smiled at Albert. "Well, I don't suppose it's very important, really."

"Why don't you tell me anyway?" Banks asked, realizing he might have been a little abrupt. He remembered what Veronica Shildon had said about people asking doctors for medical advice at cocktail parties. Sometimes being a policeman was much the same; you were never off duty. "We've caught the vandals, you know," he added.

Marcia raised her eyebrows. "You have? Have they told you why they did it?"

"I haven't had time to read Susan's report yet. But don't expect too much. People like that don't have reasons you and I can fathom."

"Oh, I know that, Mr. Banks. I was just wondering what they did with the pieces, that's all."

Banks frowned. "I'm sorry. I don't follow."

Marcia took a sip of mild and launched into her story. Albert sat beside her, still and silent as a faithful retainer. His thin face showed an intricate pattern of pinkish blood vessels just below the skin. He nodded from time to time, as if in support of what Marcia was saying.

"What do you make of it, then?" Marcia asked when she'd finished.

Banks looked at Sandra, who shook her head.

"It's odd behavior for vandals, I'll give you that," he said. "I can't think of any reason—" Then he suddenly fell silent, and the other images that had been haunting him formed into some kind of order—vague and shadowy as yet, without real substance, but still something resembling a pattern. "That's if . . ." he went on after a pause. "Look, Marcia, do you still have it, the dress?"

"Of course. It's at home."

"Could I see it?"

"Any time you want. There's nothing more I can do with it."

"How about now?"

"Now? Well, I don't know . . . I . . ." she looked at Albert, who smiled.

"Is it really so important, Alan?" Sandra asked, putting a hand on his arm.

"It might be," he said. "I can't explain yet, but it might be."

"All right." Marcia said. "We were going home in a minute anyway. It's not far."

"My car's parked behind the station. I'll give you a lift," Banks said. He turned to Sandra. "I'll see you—"

"No you won't. I'm coming with you. I'm damned if I'm walking home alone."

"All right."

They grabbed their coats and made for the door.

II

"What did you think of it?" James asked Susan after they had carried their drinks to a table for two in the Crooked Billet. His eyes were shining and he seemed to exude a special kind of energy. Susan thought that if she touched him now, she would feel an electric shock like the ones she sometimes got from static.

"I enjoyed it," she said. "I thought the cast did a terrific job." As soon as she'd spoken she knew she had said the wrong thing, even before James's eyes lost a little of their sparkle. It wasn't that she hadn't mentioned his direction, but that her comment had been hopelessly pedestrian. The trouble was, she knew nothing about Shakespeare beyond what James himself had tried to teach her at school. What a confession! And she had forgotten all that. She hadn't got far reading *Twelfth Night* at home, either; the language was too difficult for her to grasp much of what was going on. Next to James, with all his knowledge and enthusiasm, she felt inadequate.

James patted her arm. "It could have been better," he said. "Especially the pacing of the third act, that scene . . ."

And Susan sat back with relief to listen. He hadn't wanted intelligent comments after all, just someone to sound out his theories on. That she could do, and for the next twenty minutes she listened and gave her opinion whenever he asked for it. It wasn't so difficult when he got technical. She found she could easily remember scenes that had seemed dull, awkward or over-long, and James confirmed that there were good reasons for this, things he hoped to put right before the next performance tomorrow night.

Occasionally, she drifted off into thoughts of work: her interviews with Chalmers and Morley, the torn dress she hadn't yet told Banks about, the damn nuisance of having even more vandals to chase. But she put her lack of concentration down to tiredness. After all, she had been up most of the night before, and all day.

At eleven-twenty, glasses empty and no prospect of another drink, James asked if Susan fancied a nightcap back at his house. A drink and a talk with a friend, perhaps some music . . . what could be wrong with that? She couldn't put him off forever. Besides, she needed to relax. She still felt nervous about being alone with him, but she reached for her coat and followed him out into the night anyway. It was just for a drink, after all; she wasn't going to let him seduce her.

They pulled up in the alley at the back of the house, where James parked his car, and entered through the back door. Susan made herself comfortable in the armchair by the fire, while James busied himself with drinks in the kitchen. Before he settled, he put a compact disc of Beethoven's "Pastorale" Symphony on.

"Makes me think of spring," he said, sitting down. "Somehow, if I close my curtains and relax, I can almost believe winter's over."

"It soon will be," Susan said. She felt herself relaxing, becoming warm and heavy-limbed.

"Perhaps when the good weather comes we could take a ride out into the dale now and then?" James suggested. "Or even venture a little farther afield? A short hike and a pub lunch?"

"Sounds marvelous," Susan murmured. "Believe it or not, I've hardly ever made time to take advantage of the countryside."

"You know what they say, 'All work and no play . . . ' "

Susan laughed. James sat on the floor by her knees, his shoulder resting against the armchair so he could look at her when they talked. It was closer than she would have liked just yet, but not uncomfortably so.

"How's business, anyway?" he asked. "Caught any big criminals lately?"

Susan shook her head. Then she told him about the previous evening. "So we're still hot on the trail of your vandals," she said, cupping the large glass of brandy in both hands. "They're a strange lot. Can you imagine why any young yob would snip up a dress and then run away with some of the pieces?"

"What?"

Susan explained what Marcia had told her and what she had seen.

"So Marcia still has the dress, then?" he said.

"What's left of it."

"What's she going to do with it?"

"I don't know," Susan answered. She was feeling drowsy and vulnerable from the heat and the brandy. "I suppose I should take it in for analysis. You never know . . ."

"Never know what?"

"What you might find." She looked down at the top of his head. "Why are you so interested, anyway, James?"

"Just curiosity, that's all. I suppose they must have had some reason for doing it. Maybe one of them cut himself and used it as a bandage. Another drink?"

Susan looked at her glass. "No thanks, I'd better not." Already she felt that warmth, tiredness and alcohol were making her let her guard down more than she cared to, and she certainly didn't want to lose control.

"Busy day at the nick tomorrow?"

Susan laughed. "Who knows?"

"Excuse me while I get one."

"Of course."

While he was gone, Susan listened to the music. She could have sworn she heard a cuckoo in one section, but doubted that anyone as serious as Beethoven would use such a frivolous gimmick.

"Perhaps one of them was a fetishist," James suggested, after he had sat down at her feet again.

"And liked to wear only little bits of women's clothes? Don't be silly, James. I don't see why you have to keep harping on about it. It's nothing."

"You'd be surprised the things people like to dress up in."

"Like you in that policeman's uniform that day?"

"That's different. That was just a joke."

"I didn't mean to suggest you were kinky or anything," Susan said. "But didn't you tell me you were just a little bit shy of making a direct approach to a woman?"

"Yes, well. . . . Acting's in my blood, I suppose. Hamming it up. Maybe there are deep-rooted psychological reasons. I don't really know." He shrugged.

Susan laughed. "You're always doing melodramatic things like that. Dressing up, arranging for that singer in Mario's. A real practical joker, aren't you?"

"I told you," James said, a little irritably. "I'm just a bit insecure. It helps."

"Especially with women?"

"Yes."

As soon as Susan realized what she had said, a tiny shiver went up her spine. She could feel the chill, as palpable as the winter night outside, fall between them. James fell silent and Susan sipped at her brandy, thinking, and not liking what she thought: James's penchant for play-acting and dressing up, the vandals' denial of breaking into the Community Center, James's attraction to Caroline, the burgundy dress. No, it couldn't be. Not possibly. It was too absurd. But her thoughts suddenly spanned two cases. It was like hot-wiring a car; the engine jumped to life. Now she could think of at least one good reason why the dress had been cut up the way it had.

Before long, she became aware of a slight tickle up the side of her leg. She looked down and saw that James was touching her, very gently. She shifted in her seat—not too abruptly, she hoped—and he stopped.

The music ended and Susan finished what little she had left in her glass. "I'd better be going," she said, sitting forward in her chair.

"Don't go just yet," James said. "It's been such a wonderful evening. I don't want it to end."

Susan laughed. Didn't he feel the same unease she did? Maybe not. Better for her that he didn't. She must act naturally, then investigate her vague fears later from a more secure position. Surely, she would then discover how absurd they were. No doubt the beer and brandy had caused her imagination to run wild. It was most important now, though, that she make an early exit without letting James see that she entertained any suspicions at all.

"Don't be such a romantic," she laughed. "There'll be plenty of other evenings."

She tried to sit up, but he was on his knees, blocking her way.

"James!"

"What's the harm in it?" he said, leaning forward toward her.

He put his hands on her shoulders and she pushed them off. "If this is what first night does to you . . ." she said, trying for a light tone. But she couldn't think of a way to end her sentence.

Finally, he moved aside and she managed to get to her feet. She felt as if she were treading on thin ice. Did he know what she was beginning to suspect? How could he? Was it obvious that she was humoring him and trying to get out fast? All she knew was that she had to stay cool and get out of there. Maybe then she would be able to dismiss her fears. But she couldn't stay, not after the frightening images had started in her mind. Crazy or not, she had to talk seriously to Banks about James, no matter how difficult it might be to swallow her pride and her feelings.

"Don't sulk," she said, tousling his hair. "It doesn't suit you."

"Damn you!" he said, jerking away from her touch. Anger flashed in his eyes. "What's wrong with you? Don't you think I'm man enough for you? You're just like her, aren't you?"

Susan felt as if she had been thrust under a cold shower. Every nerve-end tingled. She edged closer to the door. "Like who, James?" she asked quietly.

He turned to face her, and she could see that he knew. It was too late. "You know damn well who I'm talking about, don't you?"

"I don't even know what you're talking about," Susan lied. Somehow, she thought, if she didn't say the name, there was still a chance.

"Don't lie. You can't fool me. I can tell. I can tell what you're thinking. You've been toying with me, leading me on all this time, trying to get me to confess. It's all been a game hasn't it?" He moved quickly so that he was standing between Susan and the door.

"Don't be stupid," she said. "I don't know what you mean. And move out of the way, please. I want to leave."

Conran shook his head slowly. "You're thinking about me and Caroline, aren't you?"

There was no point pretending any longer. Susan looked at him and said. "You went to her, didn't you? That night."

"It was an accident," Conran pleaded. "It was a ghastly accident."

"James, you've got to—"

"No! That's where you're wrong. No, I don't. It was all an accident. All that stupid bitch's fault." And suddenly, he didn't look like the James she knew any longer. Not at all like the James she knew and thought she trusted.

III

The four of them stood in Marcia Cunningham's front room and looked at the remains of the dress.

"Who would do something like that?" Sandra asked.

"That's the point," Banks said. "No casual vandal would go to such trouble, at least not for any reason we can think of."

"But it must have happened then," Marcia said. "I'd have noticed if it had been done before. And certainly no one from the cast would have done it."

"I'm not saying it was done before," Banks said. "What I'm saying is that it's possible vandals didn't do this."

"Then who?"

"Look at this." Banks passed the dress to Sandra, who studied the remains of its front. "Look at those spots."

"What are they? Paint?"

"Could be. But I don't think so. They're hard to see because the dress is so dark. And we can't be sure, not without forensic examination, but if I'm right . . ."

"What are you getting at, Alan?" Sandra asked. "You're not making much sense, you know."

"The last person seen entering Caroline Hartley's house was a woman, according to all our witnesses. And Patsy Janowski said she saw a woman who walked funny at the end of the street. I thought it was because she might have been wearing high heels."

"But that's stupid," Sandra said. "In that weather?"

"Exactly."

"Are you suggesting that the killer wore this dress?" Marcia asked. "I can't believe it." She pointed at the dress. "And that's . . . that's blood!"

"The way Caroline Hartley was stabbed." Banks said, "there was no way the murderer could have avoided blood stains. If she was wearing this dress, it would have been easy enough to put her raincoat on again and get away from the scene, get time to think. I don't think the murder was planned, not right from the start. But then there was still a bloodstained dress to explain. Why not simply cut off the sleeves and the stained front, then stage a break-in and cut up the other dresses? That would raise much less suspicion than just doing away with the dress altogether. If our killer had done that, Marcia would have missed it and started to wonder what might have happened. But how could the killer know that Marcia would be so diligent as to try and sew them back together again?"

"But that means," Marcia said slowly, "that the killer was someone who knew about our costumes, someone who had access to them. It means—"

"Yes," said Banks. "And if she was wearing shoes, not boots, what does that suggest?"

"We don't have any boots," Marcia said. "Not that I know of. Shoes, yes, but not boots."

"The killer couldn't find any suitable boots to complete the disguise, so had to make do with women's shoes."

"I still don't understand," Marcia said.

"It was the play gave me the idea, that and what Patsy said. All that stuff about a woman walking funny, and a play about confused identity. Couldn't it have been a man dressed as a woman? Would any of the shoes have been big enough?"

"Well . . . yes, of course," Marcia said. "We have all kinds of sizes. But why? Why would anybody dress up and do that?"

"We don't know," Banks said. "A sick joke? Maybe someone knew Caroline was a lesbian, someone who wanted her badly. Do you have a plastic bag?"

"I think so . . . somewhere." Marcia gestured vaguely, her brows knit together.

"There's one in the larder, by the newspapers, love," said Albert, who had remained silent until now. "I'll go and get it."

Albert brought the bag and Banks put the dress in it.

"What about the break-in?" Marcia asked.

"It could have been staged later, when the killer discovered what he'd done." Banks looked at his watch. "It's after eleven thirty," he said. "Let's try the Crooked Billet and see if they're still there."

"Who?" asked Marcia.

"Susan and Conran," Banks said. "I assume they *are* together." He turned to Marcia. "When did you tell Susan about this dress?"

"The other day. She couldn't make anything of it."

"That's hardly surprising. Does James Conran know?"

"I haven't told him," Marcia said.

"Has Susan?"

"I don't know. I mean, she's seeing him. She might have mentioned it. Why?"

Banks looked at Sandra. "I don't want to alarm anyone," he said, "but if I'm right, we'd better try to find Susan right away. Excuse us, Marcia, Albert." And he took Sandra by the arm and led her to the door.

"But why?" Sandra asked.

"Because I think James Conran's the killer," Banks said on their way down the path. "I think he wanted Caroline Hartley so badly he went over to the house to see her. I don't know why he dressed up, or what happened in there, but he's the only one in the society apart from Marcia who had access to the prop room."

They got in the car and Banks cursed the ignition until it started on his fourth attempt. "Don't you see?" he said as he skidded off. "According to Faith and Teresa, Conran was the last one to leave the center. And even if he did go to the pub, he had a key. He could have easily gone back there and changed. Why do you think he was paying so much attention to Susan? He wanted to know how the investigation was going, how close we were."

"My God," said Sandra. "Poor Susan."

IV

James blocked Susan's way. "She asked for it, you know," he said. "She was nothing but a prick-teaser, then she . . ."

"Then she what?" Susan felt real fear now, like ice in her spine. Her mind was racing in search of a way out. If only she had told Banks about the dress, then maybe he would have been able to put two and two together before she had. If only she could keep Conran talking. If only . . .

"You know what," he said. "It turned out she didn't like men, she was just playing, leading me on, just like you were, playing me for a fool."

"That's not true."

"Stop lying. It's too late now. What are you going to do?" James asked.

"What do you think?"

"Turn me in? Can't you let it go?"

"Don't be an idiot."

"What is it with you, Susan? Just what makes you tick? Professional all the way?"

"Something like that," Susan muttered, "but it doesn't really matter anymore, does it?"

"You could forget this ever happened," James said, moving forward and reaching for her hand. She noticed a sheen of sweat on his forehead and upper lip.

She snatched her hand away. "No, I couldn't. Don't be a bloody fool, James. Let me go. Don't make things worse." He was still rational, she thought; James was no madman, just troubled. She could talk sense to him, and he might listen. The main problem was that he was highly-strung and, at the moment, in a state of near panic. She would have to be very careful how she handled him.

"Where do you want to go?" he asked.

"To the phone," she said calmly.

Conran stood aside and let her pass. But no sooner had she picked up the receiver than he grabbed it from her and pulled her back into the front room.

"No!" he said. "I can't let you. I'm not going to jail. Not just because of that perverted slut. Don't you see? It wasn't my fault."

"Don't be a fool, James. What's the alternative?"

Conran licked his lips and looked around the room like a caged animal. "I could get out of here. Go away. You'd never have to see me again. Just don't try to stop me."

"I have to. You know that."

"I mean it. I don't want to hurt you. Look, we could go together. I've got some money saved up. Wherever you want. We could go somewhere warm."

"James," Susan said softly, "you've got a problem. You don't necessarily have to go to jail. Maybe you can get help. A doctor—"

"What do you mean, problems? I don't have any problems." Conran pointed at his chest. "Me? You tell me I've got problems? She was the one with the problem. Not me. I'm not queer. I'm not a homosexual. I'm normal."

His face was flushed and sweaty now and he was breathing fast. Susan wasn't sure if she could talk him down and persuade him to give himself up. Not if he didn't want to.

"Nobody says you're not normal," she said cautiously. "But you're obviously upset. You need help. Let me help you, James."

"I'm not going with you," he said. "And if you phone, I won't be here when your friends arrive."

"You're making it worse," Susan said. "At least if you come in with me, it'll look good. It's no use running. We'll get you in the end. You know we will."

"I don't care. I'm not going to jail. You don't understand. I couldn't live in jail. The things they do in there . . . I've heard about them." He shuddered.

"I told you, James. It might not mean prison. Perhaps you can get help in a hospital."

"No! There's nothing wrong with me. I'm perfectly normal. I'll not have doctors poking about in my head."

Susan got up and walked toward the front door. She held her breath as she turned her back on him. Before she even got to the hallway, she felt his hands around her neck. They were strong and she couldn't pry them apart. Because he was standing behind her, all she could do was wriggle, and it didn't help. She flailed back with her hands but met only empty air. She tried to swing her hips back into his groin, but she couldn't reach him. Her throat hurt and she couldn't breathe. She lashed back with one foot, felt it connect and heard him gasp. But his grip never slackened. She felt all the life and sensation going out of her body, like water down the drain. Her knee buckled and he let her sink forward to the floor, his hands still locked tight around her throat. The blackness had seeped in everywhere now. She thought she could hear someone hammering on the door, then she heard nothing at all.

V

"I'll call an ambulance and stay with her," Sandra said, kneeling over Susan.

Banks nodded and dashed back to the Cortina. He had heard Conran's car start up as they broke in. There was only one way his back lane led, and that was to the main Swainsdale road. Once there, he could turn back toward Eastvale or head out into the dale. As Banks negotiated the turns, he radioed for help from Eastvale and from Helmthorpe, which had one patrol car. If Conran didn't turn off on one of the sideroads, at least they could make sure the main road was blocked and he could get no further than the dale's largest village. At the junction, Conran turned left into Swainsdale.

The Cortina skidded on a patch of ice. Banks steadied it. He knew the road like the back of his hand. Narrow for the most part, with drystone walls on either side, it dipped and meandered, treacherous in the icy darkness. He kept Conran's taillights in view, about a couple of hundred yards ahead.

When he got closer, he put his foot down. Conran did the same. It was almost like racing through a dark tunnel, or doing a slalom run. Snow was piled almost as high as the walls at the roadsides. Beyond, the fields stretched up the daleside, an endless swath of dull pearl in the moonlight.

Conran screeched through Fortford, almost losing control as he took the bend by the pub. The car's side scraped against the jutting stones in the wall and sent a shower of sparks out into the night. Banks slowed and the Cortina took the turn easily. He knew there was a long stretch of straight road before the next bend.

Conran had gained a hundred yards or so, but once around the corner, Banks put his foot down and set about catching up. The red taillights drew closer. Banks glanced ahead for landmarks and saw the drumlin with the six leaning trees silhouetted by the moon about a mile in front of them. Just before that, there would be another kink in the road.

He was right behind Conran's car now, but there was no

easy way to stop him. He couldn't pull in front in such conditions on a narrow road. If he tried, Conran would easily be able to nudge him into the wall. All he could do was ride his tail and push, hoping Conran would panic and make a mistake.

A few moments later, it happened. Either through ignorance, or just plain panic, Conran missed the bend. Banks had already slowed enough to take it, but instead he eased on the brake as he watched Conran's car slide up the heaped snow in slow motion, take off the top of the drystone wall, spraying sparks again as it went, and land with a loud thud in the field.

Banks turned off his engine. The silence after the accident was so deep he could hear the blood ring in his ears. On a distant hillside, a sheep bleated—an eerie sound on a winter's night.

Banks got out of the car and climbed the wall to see what had happened. There was very little damage as far as he could tell by the moonlight. Conran's car lay on its side, the two free wheels still spinning. Conran himself had managed to get the passenger door open and was now struggling up the hillside, thigh-deep in snow. The farther he went, the deeper the snow became, until he could move no more. Banks walked in his wake and found him curled up and shivering in a cot of snow. He looked up as Banks came toward him.

"Please let me go," he said. "Please! I don't want to go to jail. I couldn't stand being in jail."

Banks thought of Caroline Hartley's body, and of Susan Gay laid out on the floor, her face purple. "Think yourself bloody lucky we don't still have hanging," he said, and dragged Conran up out of the snow.

FIFTEEN

I

Only the sound of thin ice splintering underfoot accompanied Banks on his way to Oakwood Mews later that night. Eastvale was asleep, tucked up warm and safe in bed, and not even the faint sound of a distant car disturbed its tranquillity. But the town didn't know what had gone on between Caroline Hartley and James Conran in that cozy, firelit room with the stately music playing. It didn't know what folly, irony and pride had finally erupted in blood. Banks did. Sometimes, as he walked, he thought that his next step would break the crust over a great darkness and he would fall. He told himself not to be ridiculous, to keep going.

Apart from the dim, amber light shed by its widely-spaced, black-leaded gas-lamps, Oakwood Mews was as dark as the rest of the side-streets at that time of night. Not one light showed in a window. Easy, Banks thought, for a murderer to creep in and out unseen now.

For a moment, he stood by the iron gate and looked at number eleven. Should he? It was two-thirty in the morning. He was tired, and Veronica Shildon was no doubt fast asleep. She wouldn't be able to get back to sleep after what he had to tell her. Sighing, he opened the gate. He had a promise to keep.

He pressed the bell and heard the chimes ring faintly in the hall. Nothing happened, so he rang again and stood back. A few seconds later a light came on in the front upstairs window. Banks heard the soft footsteps and the turning of the key in the lock. The door opened an inch or two, on its chain. When Veronica saw who it was, she immediately took off the chain and let him in.

"I had an idea it was you," Veronica said. "Will you give me a few moments?" She pointed him toward the living room and went back upstairs.

Banks turned on a shaded wall-light and sat down. Embers glowed in the grate. It was cool in the room, but the memory of heat, at least, remained. Banks unfastened his heavy carcoat but didn't take it off.

In a few minutes, Veronica returned in a blue-and-white track-suit. She had combed her hair and washed the sleep out of her eyes.

"Sorry," she said, "but I can't stand sitting around in a dressing-gown. It always makes me think I'm ill. Let me put this on." And she switched on a small electric heater. Its bar shone bright red in no time. "Can I offer you a cup of tea or something?"

"Given the night I've had," Banks said, "a drop of whiskey would be more welcome. That is, if you have any?"

"Of course. Please forgive me if I don't join you. I'd prefer cocoa."

While Veronica made her cocoa, Banks sipped the Scotch and stared into the embers. It had all been so easy once they had got back to the station: wet clothes drying over the heater in the cramped office; steam rising; Conran spilling his guts in the hope of some consideration at sentencing. Now came the hard part.

Veronica sat in the armchair near the electric fire and folded her legs under her. She cradled the cocoa mug in both hands and blew on the surface. Banks noticed that her hands were shaking.

"I always used to have cocoa before bed when I was young," she said. "It's funny, they say it helps you sleep when it's got caffeine in it. Do you understand that?" Suddenly she looked directly at Banks. He could see the pain and fear in her eyes. "I'm prattling on, aren't I?" she said. "I assume you've got something important to tell me, or you wouldn't be here at this time." She looked away.

Banks lit a cigarette and sucked the smoke in deeply. "Are you sure you want to know?" he asked.

"No, I'm not sure. I'm frightened. I'd rather forget everything that happened. But I never got anywhere by denying things, refusing to face the truth."

"All right." Now he was here, he didn't know where to start. The name, just the bald name, seemed inadequate, but the *why* was even more meaningless.

Veronica helped him out. "Will you tell me who first?" she asked. "Who killed Caroline?"

Banks flicked some ash into the grate. "It was James Conran."

Veronica said nothing at first. Only the nerve twitching at the side of her jaw showed that she reacted in any way. "How did you find out?" she asked finally.

"I was slow," Banks replied. "Almost too slow. Given Caroline's life, her past, I was sure there was a complex reason for her death. There were too many puzzles—Gary Hartley, Ruth Dunne, Colm Grey . . ."

"Me."

Banks shrugged. "I didn't look close enough to home."

"Was there a complicated motive?"

Banks shook his head. "No, I was wrong. Some crimes are just plain . . . I was going to say accidents, but that's not really the case. Stupid, perhaps, certainly pointless and often just sheer bad luck."

"Go on."

"As far as the evidence was concerned, we knew that Conran was attracted to Caroline, but there's nothing unusual about that. She was a very beautiful woman. We also found out he tended to prefer her over other actresses in the cast, which gave rise to a certain amount of jealousy. Caroline dealt with normal male attention by doing what she knew best, what she'd learned on the game—teasing, flirting, stringing them along. It was an ideal way for her because it deflected suspicion away from her true sexual inclinations," he looked at Veronica, who was staring down into the murky cocoa, "and it kept them at a distance. Many flirts are afraid of real contact. It's just a game.

"But as I said, I was looking for deep, complex motives—something to do with her family, her time in London, her way of life. As it turns out, her death was to do with all those things, but not directly concerned with any of them."

"Another drink?" Veronica had noticed his glass was empty and went to refill it. Banks didn't object. Embers shifted with a sigh in the fireplace. It was much warmer now the electric fire had heated the room. Banks took his coat off.

"What happened?" Veronica asked, handing him the tumbler.

"On December twenty-second, after rehearsal, everyone went their separate ways. Caroline came straight home, took a shower and made herself comfortable in the living room with a cup of tea and some chocolate cake. Your husband called with the present, which Caroline opened because he had said it was something special and she wanted to know what could be so special to you. I'm sure she intended to rewrap it before you found out. I'm speculating, of course. No one but Caroline was in the house at this time, so we'll never know all the details. But I think I'm right. It couldn't have happened any other way. Anyway, shortly after Claude Ivers left, Patsy Janowski arrived, checking up on him. She thought he was still involved with you." Veronica sniffed and shifted position. Banks went on. "She spoke to Caroline briefly at the door—very briefly, because it was cold and Caroline was only wearing her bathrobe—then she left. On her way down the street, she saw a woman who appeared to be walking oddly, heading across King Street, but thought nothing of it. By then it was dark and the air was filled with snow. It was difficult to look up and keep your eyes open without getting them full of cold snow."

"What about James Conran?" Veronica asked. "How does he fit in?"

"I was getting to that. It had been a particularly difficult rehearsal. He had insulted Faith Green by telling her that Caroline could play her part better, and Teresa Pedmore was probably still angry at him for being so obvious about his lust for Caroline in public. By this time, he was pretty well besotted with her, and he's one of those types who's like a little boy who breaks things when he doesn't get his own way. Because of the bad atmosphere, everyone went their separate ways, including Caroline. After he locked up, Conran went to the Crooked Billet and drank several double Scotches very quickly. His row with Faith made him want Caroline all the more. After all he thought he was doing for her, he was getting very impatient that she didn't seem to be keeping up her end of what he thought was the bargain.

"Then he had an idea. He was always a bit of a theatrical type, the kind who got dressed up and recited 'The Boy Stood on the Burning Deck' at parties when he was a kid, so he thought that, as a joke, he'd dress up as a woman and go see Caroline. *Twelfth Night*, as you know, is about a woman who passes herself off as a man, you see, and that's where he got the idea. It would make her laugh, he thought, if he passed himself off as a woman, and when you make women laugh you soften them and break down their reserve. Also, he'd had enough drinks to make it seem a good idea and to make him feel brave enough. He knew where she lived, but he didn't know that she lived with anyone.

"He went back to the Community Center—only he and Marcia Cunningham from the Dramatic Society had keys to the back door—chose a dress, a wig, and found some women's shoes that fit him. But it must have been an uncomfortable walk for him. The shoes were a little too tight and pinched his toes, and it's very hard to walk in high-heels in the snow, I should imagine. Especially if you're a man. That's what Patsy Janowski noticed, but she didn't realize what it meant.

"He said Caroline seemed to recognize him, laughed and let him in. She had no reason not to. Apparently he'd done things like that in rehearsal—dressed up, played practical jokes, clowned around—so as far as she was concerned it wasn't out of character for him. She may have been puzzled by his visit, even worried that you would come back and wonder what was going on, but as far as she knew, she had no reason to fear him."

Veronica grimaced and massaged her right calf. Banks took a sip of fiery Scotch. "Are you sure you want me to go on?" he asked. "It isn't very pleasant."

"I didn't expect it to be," Veronica said. "I've got a touch of cramp, that's all. It's not what you're saying that's making me grit my teeth. I want to know everything. But I think I've changed my mind about that drink." She limped to the cocktail cabinet, poured herself a glass of sherry and sat down again carefully. "Please go on. I'll be fine."

"Conran was a little drunk and feeling his oats. Caroline must have seemed especially inviting dressed in only her bathrobe. Eventually, it happened. Conran made a pass and Caroline ducked it. According to him, she made some reference to the way he was dressed and told him she preferred real women. She accused him of playing some kind of sick joke. He was stunned. He had no idea. When he started to protest, she laughed at him and told him the clothes suited him, maybe he ought to consider going after some of the men in the cast. Then he hit her. She fell back on the sofa, stunned by the blow, and her robe fell open. He said he couldn't help himself. He wanted her. And if rape was the only way he could get what he wanted, then so be it. He had to have her right there."

Veronica was gripping the sherry glass tightly, her face pale. Banks paused and asked if she was all right.

"Yes," she whispered. "Go on." She closed her eyes.

"He couldn't do it," Banks said. "There she was, a beautiful, naked woman, just what he'd dreamed about ever since he'd met her, and he couldn't function. He says he doesn't remember the next part very well. He just remembers blind rage, the color red. Everything was red inside his eyes, he said. And then it was done. He saw what had happened. He'd picked up the knife from the table and stabbed Caroline. When the rage passed and the realization dawned, he didn't panic, he started thinking clearly again. He knew he had to find some way of covering his tracks. First he washed the knife and rinsed the blood off his hands. When he went back into the room he was horrified by what he'd done. He said he sat down and just stared at Caroline, crying like a baby. That's when he saw the record she'd opened. He knew the piece because he'd had a lot to do with church choral music ever since he was young. He knew that the *Laudate pueri* was played at the burial services of small children. That's another reason I should have thought of him sooner, but then almost anyone could have known the significance of the music, or someone might simply have thought it sounded right."

"But I don't understand," Veronica said. "Why did he play it?"

"He said he put it on as a genuine gesture, that Caroline had always seemed childlike in her ways and in her enthusiasms, and she seemed to him especially like a child now as she lay there."

"So the music was for Caroline?" Veronica asked.

"Yes. A kind of requiem. It was right there in front of him. He was hardly going to search through the whole collection for something else, especially as it seemed so fitting."

Veronica looked down into her sherry glass and said quietly. "Then maybe I *can* listen to it again. Go on."

"You have to remember, too, Veronica, that Conran's a theater director. He has a sense of the dramatic, a feel for arrangement. He told me that when he had stopped crying for what he'd done, he began to see the whole thing as a scene or a tableau of some kind, and the music seemed right. What he'd done wasn't real to him anymore, it was a part of a drama, and it needed the appropriate soundtrack.

"Next he made sure he'd tidied everything up, then he left.

He noticed the stains on the dress but could do nothing about them. At least his coat would cover him up until he got home and formed a clear plan. He was just about to burn the dress when he had a better idea. He knew it would be missed if he simply destroyed it. Marcia was in charge of costumes and he knew she was careful and diligent. That was when he came up with the idea of a break-in. There'd been a lot of vandalism in the area lately, and he saw it would make a perfect cover for getting rid of the evidence. Remember, he had no idea he would end up killing anyone and ruining the dress when he first put it on and went out, but now he had a serious problem. He went back later that night, careful not to be seen this time, broke in, scrawled a little of the usual graffiti and snipped up the dresses. He also replaced the wig and the shoes, which he'd cleaned carefully. When he got home, he snipped his coat into small pieces and burned them in a metal wastebin, a bit at a time; after that, he cut the sleeves and part of the front off the dress he'd worn and burned them too. He missed a few tiny spots, but the dress was a dark burgundy color so they were very difficult to see. And that was it. All he had to do was try to stay cool when the questions started. That was easy enough for someone with actor's training, especially as he seemed so able most of the time to divorce himself from the reality of what he'd done. It had been an act, a role, like any other. And there was no reason why we should connect the break-in with the murder."

"How did you catch him?" Veronica asked.

"It was partly the play. At least that started me thinking about the possibility of someone dressing up. And there were a few other clues. That report about the woman visitor wearing high-heels on such a snowy night. The vandals denying that they had wrecked the Community Center. Marcia being unable to find the missing pieces of that particular dress. Not to mention that I was running out of other suspects." But he didn't tell Veronica that Susan Gay had known about the cut-up dress for two days and hadn't thought it important enough to mention, nor that he hadn't read her report on the

vandals until Conran had already been caught. He had been
too concerned about Susan to stop in at the station and check,
and as it turned out, his instinct had been right.

"How is she?" Veronica asked, when Banks had told her
about the scene at Conran's house.

"She'll be all right. Sandra acted quickly and got her
breathing. She won't be talking or eating real food for a
while."

"How does she feel?"

"I don't know. Sandra's still with her at the hospital, along
with Superintendent Gristhorpe. She's sedated right now, but
when she comes around she'll probably be very hard on herself." He shrugged. "I don't know how she'll deal with it."

And he didn't. Susan had made mistakes, yes, but mistakes
that could be easily understood. Everyone new to the job
made them. After all, why on earth should she link a partially
destroyed dress to a murder? And no matter what anyone said,
she would go on believing that she should have linked them,
should have known. But she should at least have passed on
the information, and verbally, too, not only in a routine report
that might get stuck at the bottom of the chief inspector's
in-tray for days, especially when he was busy on a murder
investigation. And Banks should have read the report. In a
perfect world, he would have done. But police, perhaps more
than anyone else, get notoriously behind in their paperwork.
And so mistakes are made. Susan's career hung in the balance, and Banks couldn't guess which way it would go. Certainly he would support her as far as he could, but it would
be her own decisions and actions that counted in the long run,
her own strength.

"It all seems so . . . pointless," Veronica said, "so abso-
lutely bloody senseless."

"It was," Bank agreed. "Murder often is." He put down his
glass and reached for his coat.

"I'm glad you told me," she said. "I mean, I'm glad you
came right away like you said you would."

"What are you going to do now?"

"I'll go back to bed. Don't worry about me. I probably won't be able to sleep but . . . your job's over, you don't have to take care of me."

"I mean in the future. Have you any plans?"

Veronica uncurled her legs and got to her feet, rubbing her calves to restore the circulation. "I don't know," she said. "Maybe a holiday. Or maybe I'll just struggle on with work and life. I'll manage," she said, attempting a smile. "I'm a survivor."

Banks fastened his coat and headed for the door. Veronica held it open for him. "Once again," she said, "thank you for coming."

On impulse, Banks leaned forward and kissed her cool forehead. She gave him, a puzzled look, then smiled. He hesitated on the path and looked back at her. He could think of nothing else to say. If Conran were mad, his actions might have been easier to explain, or to dismiss. Madmen did strange and evil things, and nobody knew why; it just happened that way. But he wasn't mad. He was highly-strung, egotistical, with a deep-rooted fear of his own latent homosexuality, but he wasn't mad. He had sat at that desk in Banks's office and spilled his heart out for over an hour before Banks, disgusted with the man's whining self-pity, had left the task for Phil Richmond to finish.

Veronica's face, shadowed by the hall's soft light, looked drawn but determined. She held herself stiffly, arms crossed, yet there seemed a supple strength in her limbs to match the strength in her spirit. Perhaps that was why he liked her: she tried; she wasn't afraid to face things; she made an effort at life.

At the end of Oakwood Mews, Banks remembered the Walkman in his pocket. He needed music, not so much as the food of love but as something to soothe the savage breast. The tape he had in was at the last movement of Messiah "Quarter for the End of Time." That eerie, fractured and haunting music would do just fine for the walk home. In the other pocket he felt the catapult he had confiscated from the kid on the riverbank and forgotten about.

He walked up to the market square listening to the music. Piano chords sounded like icicles falling and the violin notes stretched so tight they felt as if they would snap any second. As he walked, he thought about Veronica Shildon, who had now to face some difficult truths and start a new life. He thought about how that life had been shattered, just like the ice under his feet, by a stupid, drunken, pointless act—lust beyond reason—and about how she would go about putting it together again. Veronica was right, she was a survivor. And Shakespeare was right, too; lust often *is* "murderous, bloody, full of blame,/Savage, extreme, rude, cruel, not to trust."

Banks passed the police station with hardly a glance. Sometimes, the formality of the job and its cold, calculated procedures just didn't reflect what really happened, the pain people felt, the pain Banks felt. Perhaps the rites and rituals of the job—the forms to be filled in, the legal procedures to be followed—were intended to keep the pain at a distance. If so, they didn't always succeed.

About twenty yards beyond the station, on Market Street, he stopped and turned. That damn blue light was still shining above the door like a beacon proclaiming benign, paternal innocence and simplicity. Almost without thinking, he took the catapult from his pocket, scraped up a couple of fair-sized stones from the icy gutter, put one in the sling and took aim. The stone clattered on the pavement somewhere along North Market Street. He took a deep breath, sighed out a plume of air, then aimed again carefully, trying to recreate his childhood accuracy. This time the lamp disintegrated in a burst of powder-blue glass and Banks took off down a side-street, the back way home, feeling afraid and guilty and oddly elated, like a naughty schoolboy.

*Here is a chilling excerpt from
Peter Robinson's Inspector Banks novel*

COLD IS THE GRAVE

*Available now
in bookstores everywhere*

The Charlie Courage murder occurred in early December, about a month after Banks had delivered Emily Riddle to her father's house, a little battered and shop-soiled, but not too much the worse for wear. Judging by her silence on the train journey back to Yorkshire, he imagined she might lie low for a while before taking on the world again. In the meantime, Banks had been preoccupied with major changes at Eastvale Divisional Headquarters.

The county force had been reorganized from seven divisions into just three, and Eastvale was the new headquarters of the large Western Division, which took in just about the entire county west of the A1 to the Lancashire border, and from the Durham border in the north to the border with West Yorkshire in the south. There were vast areas of wilderness and moorland, including most of the Yorkshire Dales National Park, and the main occupations were the service industry, tourism, agriculture and a smattering of light industry. There were no major urban areas, but a number of big towns such as Harrogate, Ripon, Richmond, Skipton and Eastvale itself.

There was, of course, plenty of crime, and in keeping with its new status, the Eastvale station had been extended into the adjoining building, where Vic Manson's fingerprints unit, scenes-of-crime, computers and photography departments had all set up shop. Renovations were still going on, and the place was filled with noise and dust.

While the section stations would continue to police their areas as before—indeed, they were to be given even more autonomy—Eastvale was now to be responsible for most of the criminal investigation within the new Western Division. Nobody was sure yet how many CID officers—or Crime Management Personnel, as some now liked to call them—they would end up with, or where they would all be put, but staffing increases had already begun.

One of the first moves that the Director of Human Resources, Millicent Cummings, had made was to transfer Detective Sergeant Annie Cabbot to the new team. Millie told Banks that she thought Annie had worked well with him on their previous case, no matter what Chief Constable Riddle thought of its messy outcome, and that as Annie was going for her inspector's boards as soon as she could, the experience would be good for her.

Millie, of course, along with Riddle and everyone else, didn't know about Banks's affair with Annie, and Banks could hardly say anything now. This was a good opportunity for her to get back in the swing of things, and he certainly wasn't going to stand in her way. Annie *was* a good detective, and if she could handle working with Banks, he could at least try to accommodate her.

The county also had a new Assistant Chief Constable (Crime) in the shape of Ron McLaughlin, known jokingly as "Red Ron" because he leaned more to New Labour than most senior policemen. ACC McLaughlin was known to be a hard but fair man, one who believed in using his officers' abilities to the best, and he was also rumored to enjoy a wee dram of malt every now and then.

It was a misty, drizzling day—what the locals called "mizzling"—when Riddle got the chance to make good on his promise to Banks. Over the last year or so, all serious crimes in the division that couldn't be handled by Detective Superintendent Gristhorpe, Detective Sergeant Hatchley and whichever DCs happened to be assigned to Eastvale Divisional Headquarters at the time, had been passed on to other divisions, or to the Regional Crime Squad, leaving Banks free to devote all his duty hours to paperwork and administration.

Since he had done Riddle the big favor of bringing Emily back home, since the big changes around the station, and since things had finally come to an end with Sandra, the thought of moving from his Gratly cottage and starting a new job with the NCS had begun to lose its appeal, and Banks had withdrawn his application. Eastvale was starting to seem like a good bet again, and it was where he wanted to be.

Despite the drizzle and the filthy gray sky, Banks felt in a buoyant, optimistic mood. He was reading a report on the sudden increase of car theft in rural areas, and in need of a break, he went to stand by the window to smoke a proscribed cigarette and look down on the market square in the late afternoon.

The renovators were mercifully silent, no doubt planning their next major assault, and Banks's radio played quietly in the background: Prokofiev's Piano Concerto No. 3. The Eastvale Christmas lights, turned on in the middle of November by some third-rate television personality Banks had never heard of, made a pretty sight outside his window, hanging across Market Street and over the square like a bright lattice of jewels. Soon they'd be putting up the huge Christmas tree by the market cross, and the church choir would be out singing carols at lunchtime and early evening, collecting for charity.

Brian thought he would be busy with the band over the holidays, but Tracy had phoned the previous day and promised to spend Christmas with her father before heading down to London to see her mother on Boxing Day. Banks had never been much of a fan of Christmas—far too many holiday seasons spent working and witnessing the gaudy excess of suicides and domestic murders that peaked around that time of year had taken care of that—but this called for celebration; this year he would make an effort, buy a small tree, presents, put up some decorations, cook Christmas dinner.

Last year had been a complete washout. He had turned down all offers of meals, drinks and parties from friends and colleagues and spent the entire holiday alone in the Eastvale semi he had once shared with Sandra, wallowing in his own misery and keeping up his maintenance buzz with liberal tots of whiskey. Brian and Tracy had both phoned, of course, and he had managed to bluff his way past any worries they might have had about him, but there was no denying it had been a grim time. This year would be different. Delia Smith had a book about cooking for Christmas, he remembered; perhaps he would go to Waterstone's and buy it before going home.

The telephone brought him back to his desk. "Banks here."

"Chief Inspector Banks? My name's Collaton, Detective Inspector Mike Collaton. I'm calling from Market Harborough, Leicestershire Constabulary. I just called your county headquarters and they put me onto you."

"What can I do for you?"

"Earlier today a motorist stopped by the roadside near here and nipped down a lane into the woods for a piss. He found a body."

"Go on," said Banks, tapping his pen on the desk, still wondering what the connection was.

"It's one of yours. Thought you might be interested."

"One of my what?"

"Local villains. Bloke by the name of Charles Courage. Same as the brewery. Lived at number seventeen Cutpurse Lane, Eastvale." He laughed. "Sounds like it could hardly be a more appropriate address, going by his record."

Jesus Christ, Charlie Courage! *Dutch,* as his cronies jokingly called him on account of that was about the only courage he ever exhibited. Charlie Courage had been a thorn in the side of Eastvale Division for years. In truth, he was a petty villain, a minor player, but around Eastvale he was still a big fish in a small pond. Charlie Courage had done a little bit of everything—except anything that involved violence or sex—from handling stolen goods to sheep-stealing, when it was worth stealing them. You had to give Charlie his due; he was a character. Two or three years ago, he used to have a stall in Eastvale market, Banks remembered, right in front of the police station, where he blithely sold videos and CDs that in all likelihood had "fallen off the back of a lorry." While questioning him about a local break-in once, Banks had even bought the Academy of Ancient Music's CD of Mozart's C Minor Mass for £3.99. A bargain at twice the price. He didn't ask where it had come from. To his credit, Charlie had also acted as police informer on a number of occasions. Rumor had it that he had been going straight lately.

"You've heard of him?" DI Collaton went on.

"I've heard of him. What happened?"

"Shot. Looks like the weapon used was a shotgun. Made a real mess, anyway."

"Any chance it was accidental, or self-inflicted?"

"Not unless he shot himself in the chest, then got up after he was dead and hid the weapon. We can't find any sign of it."

"Are you sure it's Charlie? What on earth was he doing all the way down there? It's not like Charlie to leave his parish."

"I'm afraid we can't shine any light on that just yet, either. But it's definitely him. I got the ID from fingerprints. Seems he did two years once for something involving sheep. I've heard about you lot up there and your sheep. Some sort of unspeakable deed, was it?"

Banks laughed. "Stealing them, actually. They used to be worth a bit. You might remember. As for the other, I can't say I've any idea what Charlie got up to in his spare time. Far as I know, he was single, so he could please himself. Anything more you can tell me?"

"Not much. I've checked around, and it seems he doesn't have any living relatives."

"Sounds like Charlie. I don't think he ever did."

"Anyway, I thought I'd ask you to have a look around his house, if you would, see if there's anything there. Save my lads some legwork. We're a bit short-staffed down here."

"Aren't we all? Sure. I'll have a look. What about his car?"

"No sign of any car. Maybe you'd like to come down here tomorrow morning, see the scene, toss a few ideas around, that sort of thing? I've a feeling that if there are any answers to be found, they're probably at your end. The postmortem's tomorrow afternoon, by the way."

"Okay," said Banks. "In the meantime I'll go have a quick poke around Charlie's place right now and see about organizing a thorough search later. If he's dead, I won't have to worry about a warrant. I'll drive down tomorrow morning."

Banks took Collaton's directions to the Fairfield Road police station in Market Harborough, then hung up and went into the main CID office. Since the reorganization began, they had been assigned three new DCs and were promised three more. DC Gavin Rickerd was a spotty, nondescript sort of lad given to anoraks and parkas. Banks couldn't help feeling he must have been a train-spotter in a previous lifetime, if not in this one. Kevin Templeton was more flash, a bit of a jack-the-lad, but he got things done, and he was surprisingly good with people, especially kids.

The third addition was DC Winsome Jackman, who hailed from a village in the Cockpit Mountains, high above Montego Bay, Jamaica. Why she had wanted to leave there for the unpredictable summers and miserable winters of North Yorkshire was beyond Banks's ken. At least superficially. When it came right down to it, though, he imagined that a village in the Jamaican mountains was probably no place for a bright and beautiful woman like Winsome to forge ahead in a career.

Why she hadn't become a model instead of joining the police was also beyond Banks. She had the figure for it, and her face showed traces of her Maroon heritage in the high cheekbones and dark ebony coloring. She could certainly give Naomi Campbell a run for her money, and from what Banks had read about the supermodel in the papers, Winsome was a far nicer person. Some of the lads called her "Lose-Some" because of the time, back in uniform, when she had chased and caught a mugger in a shopping center, only to have him then slip out of her grasp and escape. She took it good-naturedly and gave as good as she got. You had to when you were the only black woman in the division.

As it turned out, everyone was out of the office except Kevin Templeton and Annie, who looked up from her computer monitor as Banks entered.

"Afternoon," she said, flashing him a quick smile. Annie had a hell of a smile. Though not much more than a twitch of the right corner of her mouth, near the small mole, accompanied by a quick blaze of light from her almond eyes, it was dazzling. Banks felt his heart lurch just a little. God, he hoped this working together wasn't going to be too difficult.

"See what you can dig up on a local villain called Charlie Courage," he said. Then, more or less on impulse, he added, "Fancy a ride down to Market Harborough tomorrow?" He found himself holding his breath after the words were out, almost wishing he could take them back.

"Why not?" she said, after a short pause. "It'll make a nice break."

"Much on?"

"Nothing the lads can't handle on their own."

Kevin Templeton grunted from his corner.

"Okay. I'll pick you up here around nine."

Back in his office, Banks found himself hoping that things worked out with Annie on the job. He liked working with female detectives, and he still missed his old DC, Susan Gay, with all her uncertainties and sharp edges. When he had worked with Annie before, he had come to value her near-telepathic communication skills and the way she could mix logic and intuition in her unique style of thinking. He had also cherished her touch and her laughter, but that was another matter, one he couldn't let himself dwell on anymore. Or could he?

He left the office in a good mood. For the moment, Riddle had proved true to his word, and Banks finally had a case he might be able to get his teeth into. It was DI Collaton's call, of course, but Collaton had asked for help right off the bat, which led Banks to think that he probably didn't want to spend too long away from hearth and home tracking the roots of the crime up in dreary Yorkshire, especially with Christmas being so close. Well, good for him, Banks thought. Co-operation between the forces and all that. His loss was Banks's gain.

It was after five when Banks pulled up behind a blue Metro in front of Charlie Courage's one-up-one-down. Cutpurse Lane was a cramped ragbag of terraced cottages behind the community center. Dating from the eighteenth century for the most part, the mean little hovels had privies out back and no front gardens. During the yuppie craze for "bijou" a few years ago, a number of young couples had bought cottages on Cutpurse Lane and installed bathrooms and dormer windows.

As far as Banks knew, Charlie Courage had lived there for years. Whatever Charlie had done with his ill-gotten gains, he certainly hadn't invested it in improving his living conditions. It was a syndrome Banks had seen before in even more successful petty crooks than Charlie. He had even known one big-time criminal who must have brought in seven figures a year easily, yet still lived hardly a notch above squalor in the East End. He wondered what on earth they used the money they stole for, except in some cases to support mammoth drug habits. Did they give it to charity? Use it to buy their parents that dream home they had always yearned for? People had odd priorities. Charlie Courage, though, had not been a drug addict, was not known for his charity, and he didn't have any living relatives. A mystery, then.

First, Banks knocked on the neighbor's door, which was opened by a short, stocky man in a wrinkled faun V-necked pullover, who looked unnervingly like Hitler, even down to the little mustache and the mad gleam in his eyes. He stood in the doorway, the sound of the television coming from the room behind him.

Banks showed his identification. "Knightley," the man said. "Kenneth Knightley. Please come in out of the rain." Banks accepted his invitation. The drizzle was the kind that immediately seemed to get right through your raincoat and your skin, all the way to your bones.

Banks followed him into a small, neat living room with rose-patterned wallpaper and a couple of framed local landscapes hanging above the tile mantelpiece. Banks recognized Gratly Falls, just outside his own cottage, and a romantic watercolor of the ruins of Devraulx Abbey, up Lyndgarth way. A fire blazed in the hearth, making the room a bit too hot and stuffy for Banks's liking. He could already smell the steam rising from his raincoat.

"It's about your neighbor, Charles Courage," he said. "When did you last see him?"

"I don't have much to do with him," said Knightley. "Except to say hello to, like. He always keeps to himself, and I've not been the most sociable of fellows since Edie died, if truth be told." He smiled. "Edie didn't like him, though. Thought he was a wrong 'un. Why? What's happened?"

"I'm afraid Mr. Courage is dead. It looks as if he's been murdered."

Knightley paled. "Murdered. Where? I mean, not . . ."

"No. Not next door. Some distance away, actually. Down Leicester way."

"Leicester? But he never went *anywhere*. One time I did talk to him, I remember him telling me you'd never catch him going to Torremolinos or Alicante for his holidays. Yorkshire was good enough for him. Charlie didn't like foreign places or foreigners, and they began at Ripon as far as he was concerned."

Banks smiled. "I've met a few people like that, myself. But one way or another, he did end up in Leicestershire. Dead."

"That's probably what killed him then. Finding himself in Leicestershire." Knightly paused and ran his hand across his brow. "Sorry, I shouldn't be so flippant. A man's dead, after all. I don't see how I can help you, though."

"You said you saw him last a couple of days ago. Can you be more precise?"

"Let me think. It was early Sunday afternoon. It must have been then because I was just coming back from The Oak. I always go there on a Sunday lunchtime for a game of dominoes."

"About what time would this be?"

"Just after two. I can't be doing with all these new hours, all-day opening and whatnot. I stick to the old times."

"How did he seem?"

"Same as usual: a bit shifty. Said hello and that was that."

"Shifty?"

"He always looked shifty. As if he'd just that minute done something illegal and wasn't quite sure he'd got away with it yet."

"I know what you mean," said Banks. Charlie Courage usually *had* just done something illegal. "So there was nothing odd or different about his behavior at all?"

"Nothing."

"Was he alone?"

"Far as I could tell."

"Coming or going?"

"Come again?"

"Was he just arriving home or leaving?"

"Oh, I see. He was going out."

"Car?"

"Aye. He's got a blue Metro. It's usually . . . just a minute . . ." Knightley stood up and went to the curtain, which he pulled back a few inches. "Aye, there it is," he said, pointing. "Parked right outside." Banks saw the car in front of his and made a mental note to have it searched.

"Did you see or hear anyone with him in the house over the last few days?"

"No. I'm sorry I can't be much help. Like I said, there was nothing unusual at all. He went off to work, then he came home. Quiet as a mouse."

"*Work?* Charlie?"

"Oh, aye. Didn't you know? He'd got a job as a night

watchman at that new business park down Ripon Road. Dale-view, I think it's called."

"I know the one."

Business park. Another to add to Bank's long list of oxy-morons, along with military intelligence. That was an inter-esting piece of news, anyway: Charlie Courage with a job. A night watchman, no less. Banks wondered if his employers knew of his past. It was worth looking into.

"Is there anything else you can help me with, Mr. Knight-ley?"

"I don't think there is. And it's no use asking Mrs. Ford on the other side. She's deaf as a post."

"I don't suppose you have a key to Mr. Courage's house, do you?" he asked.

"Key? No. Like I said, we didn't do much more than pass the time of day together out of politeness's sake."

Banks stood up. "I'm going to have to have a good look around the place. If there's no key, I'll have to break in some-how, so don't be alarmed if you hear a few strange noises next door."

Knightley nodded. "Right. Right, you are. Charlie Courage. Murdered. Bloody hell, who'd credit it?"

Banks walked around the back of the terrace block to see if he could find an easy way into Charlie's place. A narrow cobbled alley ran past Charlie's backyard. Each house had a high wall and a tall wooden gate. Some of the walls were topped with broken glass, and some of the gates swung loose on their hinges. Banks lifted the catch and pushed at Charlie's gate. It had scratched and faded green paint and one of the rusty hinges had broken, making it grate against the flagstone path as he opened it. It wasn't much of a backyard, and most of it was taken up by a murky puddle that immediately found its way through his shoes. First, out of habit, Banks tried the doorknob.

The door opened.

Perhaps Charlie hadn't had time to lock up properly before being abducted, Banks thought, as he made his way inside the dark house. He found a light switch on the wall to his right and clicked it on. He was in the kitchen. Nothing much there except for a pile of dirty dishes waiting to be washed. They never would be now.

He walked through to the living room, which was tidy and showed no signs of a struggle. Noting the new-looking television and DVD setup, not what you could afford on a night watchman's salary, Banks got some idea of what Charlie had done with his money. He went upstairs.

There were two small bedrooms, a bathroom with a stained tub and a tiny WC with a ten-year-old *Playboy* magazine on the floor and a copy of Harold Robbin's *The Carpetbaggers* resting on the roll of toilet paper. One bedroom was empty except for a few cardboard boxes filled with magazines— mostly soft porn—and secondhand paperbacks, and the other, Charlie's, revealed only an unmade bed and a few clothes.

Downstairs, in one of the sideboard drawers, Banks found the only items of interest: the title deed to the house, Charlie's driving license, a checkbook, and a bankbook that indicated Charlie had made five cash deposits of £200 each over the past month, in addition to what seemed to be his regular pay-check. A thousand quid. Interesting, Banks thought. That would at least account for the new TV and DVD setup. What had the crooked little devil been up to? And had it got him killed?

Wednesday morning dawned every bit as dismal as Tuesday. It was still dark when Banks drove into Eastvale, sipping hot black coffee from a specially designed carrying mug on the way. The other CID officers were already in the office when he got there, and DS Hatchley, in particular, looked down-hearted that he had missed the opportunity of a day trip to Leicestershire. Or perhaps he was jealous that Banks had An-nie's company. He gave Banks the kind of bitter, defeated look that said rank pulled the birds every time, and what was a poor sergeant to do? If only he knew.

"You'll be driving, I suppose?" Annie said when they got out back to the car park.

That was another thing Banks appreciated about Annie: she was a quick learner with a good memory. It *was* unusual for a DCI to drive his own car. Having a driver was one of the perks of his position, but Banks *liked* to drive, even in this weather. He liked to be in control. Every time he let someone else drive him, no matter how good they were, he felt restless and irritated by any minor mistakes they made, constantly wanting to get his own foot on the clutch or the brake. It seemed much simpler to do the driving himself, so that was what he did. Annie understood that and didn't question his idiosyncrasy.

Banks slipped a tape of Mozart wind quintets in the Cavalier's sound system as he turned out of the car park. "Mmm, that's nice," said Annie. "I like a bit of Mozart." Then she settled back into the seat and lapsed into silence. It was another thing Banks liked about her, he remembered, the way she seemed so centered and self-contained, the way she could appear comfortable and relaxed in the most awkward positions, at ease with silence. It had also taken him a while to get used to her complete lack of deference to senior ranks, especially *his,* as well as to her rather free and easy style of dress, learned from growing up in an artists' commune surrounded by bearded artistic types such as her painter father, Ray Cabbot. Today she was wearing red winkle-picker boots that came up just above her ankles, black jeans and a Fair Isle sweater under her loose suede jacket. Rather conservative for Annie.

"How are you liking it at Eastvale?" Banks asked as they joined the stream of traffic on the A1.

"Hard to say yet. I've hardly got my feet under the desk."

"What about the traveling?"

"Takes me about three-quarters of an hour each way. That's not bad." She glanced sideways at him. "It's about the same for you, as I remember."

"True. Have you thought of selling the Harkside house?"

"I've thought of it, but I don't think I will. Not just yet. Wait and see what happens."

Banks remembered Annie's tiny cramped cottage at the center of a labyrinth of narrow, winding streets in the village of Harkside. He remembered his first visit there, when she had asked him on impulse for dinner and cooked a vegetarian pasta dish as they drank wine and listened to Emmylou Harris, remembered standing in the backyard for an after-dinner smoke, putting his arm around her shoulders and feeling the thin bra strap. Despite all the warning signs . . . he also remembered kissing the little rose tattoo just above her breast, their bodies, sweaty and tired, the unfamiliar street sounds the following morning.

He negotiated his way from the A1 to the M1. Lorries churned up oily rain that coated his windscreen before the wipers could get through it; there were more long delays at roadwork signs where nobody was working; a maniac in a red BMW flashed his lights about a foot from his rear end and then, when Banks changed lanes to accommodate him, zoomed off at well over a ton.

"What did you find out about Charlie?" he asked Annie when he had got into the rhythm of motorway driving.

Annie's eyes were closed. She didn't open them. "Not much. Probably not more than you know already."

"Tell me anyway."

"He was born Charles Douglas Courage in February 1946—"

"You don't have to go that far back."

"I find it helps. It makes him one of the generation born immediately after the war, when the men came home randy and ready to get on with their lives. He'd have been ten in 1956, too young for Elvis, perhaps, but twenty in 1966, and probably just raring for all the sex, drugs and rock and roll you lot enjoyed in your youth. Maybe that was where he got his start in crime."

Banks risked a glance away from the road at her. She still had her eyes closed, but there was a little smile on her face. "Charlie wasn't into dealing drugs," he said.

"Maybe it was the rock and roll, then. He was first arrested for distribution of stolen goods in August 1968—to wit, long-playing records. *Sergeant Pepper's Lonely Hearts Club Band*, to be exact, stolen directly from a factory just outside Manchester."

"A music lover, our Charlie," he said. "Carry on."

"After that comes a string of minor offenses—shoplifting, theft of a car stereo—then, in 1988, he was arrested for theft of livestock. To be exact, seventeen sheep from a farm out Relton way. Did eighteen months."

"Conclusion?"

"He's a thief. He'll steal anything, even if it walks on four legs."

"And since then?"

"He appears to have gone straight. Helped Eastvale police out on a number of occasions, mostly minor stuff he found out about through his old contacts."

"Got a list?"

"DC Templeton's working on it."

"Okay," said Banks. "What next?"

"A number of odd jobs, most recently working as a night watchman at the Daleview Business Park. Been there since September."

"Hmm. They must be a trusting lot at Daleview," said Banks. "I think one of us might pay them a visit tomorrow. Anything else?"

"That's about it. Single. Never married. Mother and father deceased. No brothers or sisters. Funny, isn't it?"

"What is?"

Annie stirred in the car seat to face him. "A small-time villain like Charlie Courage getting murdered so far from home."

"We don't know where he was murdered yet."

"An inspired guess. You don't shoot someone in the chest with a shotgun and then drive him around bleeding in a car for three hours, do you?"

"Not without making a mess, you don't. You know, it strikes me that Charlie might have been taken on the long ride."

"The long ride?"

Banks glanced at her. She looked puzzled. "Never heard of the long ride?"

Annie shook her head. "Can't say as I have."

"Just a minute . . ." A slow-moving local delivery van in front of them was sending up so much spray that the windscreen wipers couldn't keep up with it. Carefully, Banks changed lanes and overtook it. "The long ride," he said, once he could see again. "Let's say you've upset someone nasty—you've had your fingers in the till, or you've been telling tales out of school—and he's decided he has to do away with you, right?"

"Okay."

"He's got a number of options, all with their own pros and cons, and this is one of them. What he does—or rather, what his hired hands do—is they pick you up and take you for a ride. A long ride. It's got two main functions. The first is that it confuses the local police by taking the crime away from the patch that gave rise to it. Follow?"

"And the second? Let me guess."

"Go on."

"To scare the shit out of him."

"Right. Let's say you're driven from Eastvale to Market Harborough. You know exactly what's going to happen at the end of the journey. They make sure you have no doubt about that whatsoever, that there's going to be no reprieve, no commuting of the death sentence, so you've got three hours or thereabouts to contemplate your life and its imminent and inevitable end. An end you can also expect to be painful and brutal."

"Cruel bastards."

"It's a cruel world," said Banks. "Anyway, from their perspective, it acts as a deterrent to other would-be thieves or snitches. And, remember, it's not as if we're dealing with lily-whites here. The victim is usually a small-time villain who's done something to upset a more powerful villain."

"Charlie Courage, small-time villain. Fits him to a tee."

"Exactly."

"Except that he was supposed to be going straight, and there aren't any major crime bosses in Eastvale."

"Maybe he wasn't going as straight as we thought. Maybe he was just avoiding drawing our attention. And they don't have to be that big. I'm not talking about the Mafia or the Triads here. There are plenty of minor villains who think life is pretty cheap. Maybe Charlie fell afoul of one of them. Think about it. Charlie worked as a night watchman. He put a thousand quid in the bank—above and beyond his wages— over the past month. What does that tell you, Annie?"

"That he was either selling information, blackmailing someone or he was being paid off to look the other way."

"Right. And he must have been playing way out of his league. Maybe we'll get a better idea when we talk to the manager up there tomorrow. Nearly there now."

Banks negotiated his way around Leicester toward Market Harborough, about thirteen miles south. When they got to the High Street there, it was almost noon, and it took Banks another ten minutes to find the police station.

Before they got out of the car, Banks turned to Annie. "Are we going to be okay?" he asked.

"What do you mean?"

"You know what I mean. This. Working together."

She flashed him a smile. "Well, we seem to be doing all right so far, don't we?" she said, and slipped out of the car.

DI Collaton turned out to be a big bear of a man with thinning gray hair, a red face and a slow, country manner. A year or so away from retirement, Banks guessed. No wonder he didn't want to get involved in a murder inquiry. He looked at his watch and said, "Have you two eaten at all?"

They shook their heads.

He grabbed his raincoat from the stand in the corner of his office. "I know a place."

They followed him to a small pub about two streets away. Judging by the smiles and hellos exchanged, Collaton was well-known there. He led them to a corner table, which gave a little privacy, then offered the first round of drinks. Annie asked for a tomato juice, though Banks knew she enjoyed beer. He ordered a pint of the local best bitter. A fire burned in the hearth and Christmas decorations festooned the walls and ceiling. Apart from the buzz of conversation around the bar, the place was quiet, which was the way Banks liked his pubs, and all too rare these days. As was Annie's habit in pubs, she seemed to mold herself to the hard chair and stretch her legs out, crossing them at the ankles. DI Collaton raised his eyebrows at her red winkle-pickers, but said nothing.

After Banks had ordered game pie, on Collaton's recommendation, and Annie, being a vegetarian, went for the Ploughman's Lunch, he lit what he realized with some surprise was his first cigarette of the day.

"We don't get a lot of murders down here," said Collaton after his first sip.

That didn't surprise Banks. From what he had seen, he supposed Market Harborough to be a bit smaller than Eastvale—maybe seventeen or eighteen thousand people—and Charlie Courage was Eastvale's first murder victim of the entire year so far. In December, no less. "Any idea why they might have chosen your patch?" he asked.

Collaton shook his head. "Not really. It's handy for the M1," he said, "but a bit off the beaten track. If they were taking him somewhere, and he got troublesome . . ."

"Any witnesses?"

"Nobody saw or heard a thing. It's out Husbands Bosworth way, toward the motorway, and at this time of year there's nobody around. More in summer, tourist season, like."

Banks nodded. Same as Eastvale. "Any physical evidence?"

"Tire tracks. That's about all."

"Anything interesting or unusual on his person?"

"Just the usual. Except his wallet was missing."

"I doubt robbery was the motive," Banks mused. "Maybe a London mugger might blow away someone with a shotgun, but not in some leafy Midlands lane."

"My thoughts exactly," said Collaton. "I thought maybe they'd taken it to help keep his identity unknown a bit longer. Maybe they didn't know he'd got form and we'd find out that way."

"Possibly."

"Had he been up to anything lately?"

"We don't know yet," said Banks. "Rumor has it he's been going straight. Had a job as a night watchman. We know he made five cash deposits of two hundred quid each over the past month, though, and I doubt that he came by the money honestly."

Their food arrived. Collaton was right about the game pie. Annie nibbled at her cheese and pickled onion. Collaton kept looking at her out of the corner of his eye, when he thought no one noticed. At first Banks thought he was simply puzzled by her, as people often were, then he realized the dirty old bugger fancied her. And him old enough to be her father.

Suddenly, Banks felt himself struck almost as physically as a blow with the memory of Emily Riddle in his hotel room. Not so much by her white and slender nakedness, the spider tattoo or the feel of her body pressing against his as by her torn dress, her fear, the little question mark of blood, and Barry Clough. Why on earth hadn't he followed up on that? The next morning he had simply gone out to Oxford Street as soon as the shops opened and, not being skilled at shopping for women's clothing, bought her a tracksuit because it seemed easiest. Though he had questioned her about the previous night, she had given away nothing, maintaining a surly silence all the way home. Did she even remember how she got to his hotel room and her awkward attempt at seducing him?

When he had driven her home from the station and left her with her parents, she had given him a look he found hard to interpret. Sad, yes, partly, and perhaps also a little let-down; defeated, a little hurt, but not completely without affection, a sort of complicit recognition that they had shared something together, been through an adventure. Banks had decided on the way that he had no reason to tell Riddle what happened down there. If Emily wanted to do so, that was fine, but his part of the bargain was over; she was Riddle's problem now.

Still, it had gnawed at him over the past few weeks—Clough especially. Perhaps, if he had time over the next couple of days, he could make a few discreet inquiries of old friends on the Met, see if Clough had form, find out what his particular line of work was. Dirty Dick Burgess ought to know; he had been working with one of the top-level criminal intelligence departments for a while now. But Riddle had asked Banks to be discreet, and sometimes, when you set things in motion, you couldn't always stop them as easily as you wanted to, and you didn't know in which direction they would spin. That was Banks's problem, as Riddle had told him more than once: he had never learned when to leave well enough alone.

"Sir?"

Banks snapped back from a long distance when he felt Annie's elbow in his ribs. "Sorry. Miles away."

"DI Collaton asked if we wanted to have a look at the scene after lunch."

Banks looked at Collaton, who showed concern in his eyes, whether for Banks's health or the lapse in attention wasn't clear. "Yes," he said, pushing his empty plate aside. "Yes, by all means let's go have a look at poor old Charlie's final resting place."

After viewing the spot where Charlie Courage's body had been discovered, just off a muddy track in some woods near Husbands Bosworth, they attended the postmortem in Market Harborough Hospital.

Courage's body had already been photographed, finger-printed, weighed, measured and X-rayed the previous day. Now, the Home Office pathologist, Dr. Lindsey, and his assistants, worked methodically and patiently through a routine they must have carried out many times. Lindsey began with a close external examination, paying special attention to the gunshot pattern.

"Definitely a shotgun wound," he said. "Twelve-bore, by the looks of it. Range about two or three yards." He pointed out the central entrance opening over the heart and the numerous single small holes around it from the scattered shot. "any closer and it would have been practically circular. Much farther away and the shot would have spread out more into smaller groups. There's still some wadding embedded in the wounds, too. Look." He held up a piece. "Depends whether they used a sawn-off, of course, as the shot patterns don't hold as far. Even so, it was pretty close range. And judging by the angle of the main wounds, it looks as if either his killer was very tall or the victim was on his knees at the time."

Banks guessed that if he was right in assuming Charlie had been taken for the long ride, then his killer would have used a sawn-off shotgun. The legal length for shotgun barrels was twenty-four inches, not including the stock, and no villain is going to walk or drive around with something that big.

"Then there's this bruising," Dr. Lindsey went on, pointing out the discoloration around Courage's stomach and kidneys. "It looks as if he was beaten either with fists or some hard object before he was killed. Enough to make him piss blood for a week at least."

"Perhaps somebody wanted him to tell them something?" Collaton said.

"From what I knew of Charlie, he'd give up his grandmother if you so much as waved your fist in his face. They might have wanted him to tell them something, but my bet is that he did, and then they carried on beating him up just for the fun of it."

Next, Dr. Lindsey began his dissection with the Y-incision.

He took blood samples, then removed and inspected the inner organs, working from the trachea, esophagus and what was left of the heart, down to the bladder and spleen.

As all this was going on, Banks kept a close eye on Annie. He didn't know how good she was at postmortems on fairly fresh corpses, as the last one they had been to was of a skeleton disinterred after fifty years. Though she paled a little when Dr. Lindsey opened up the body cavity and swallowed rather loudly as he squished out the various organs as if he were shucking oysters, she stood her ground.

Until, that is, the power saw started ripping into the front quadrant of the skull. At that, Annie swayed, put her hand to her mouth and, making a gurgling sound, dashed out of the room. Dr. Lindsey rolled his eyes and Collaton glanced at Banks, who just shrugged.

Dr. Lindsey pulled out the brain, looked it over, tossed it from hand to hand as if it were a grapefruit, then put it aside for weighing and sectioning.

"Well," he said, "until we get the tests back on the blood and tissue samples, we won't know whether he was poisoned before he was shot. I doubt it, myself, Judging by the blood, I'd say the gunshot wound was the cause of death. It blew his heart open. And going by the lividity, I'd also say he was killed at the same spot he was found."

"Did you determine time of death?" Banks asked, though he knew it was the question all pathologists hated the most.

Dr. Lindsey frowned and searched through a pile of notes on the lab bench. "I made some rough calculations at the scene. Only rough, of course. I've got them somewhere. Now, where . . . ah here it is. Rigor, temperature . . . allowing for the chilly weather and the rain . . . he was found on Tuesday, that's yesterday, at about four P.M. and I surmised he'd been dead at least twenty-four hours, perhaps longer."

Charlie had been seen by his neighbor on Sunday afternoon at around two o'clock, and if he had been killed sometime Monday afternoon, that left over twenty-four hours, the last twenty-four hours of his life, unaccounted for. When they got back to Eastvale, Banks would have to initiate some house-to-house inquiries in the neighborhood, find out if anyone had seen Charlie later than Sunday lunchtime, and if anyone had seen him *with* anyone. He hadn't got to the lane near Husbands Bosworth in his own car, and he certainly hadn't walked there. The fresh tire tracks that Collaton's men had found most likely belonged to the car that had taken him there, as the lane was an out-of-the-way place. Depending on how good the impressions were, it might be possible to match them up with a particular car—if, of course, they found the car, and if the tires hadn't been changed.

They had learned just about all they could from Dr. Lindsey for the moment, and Banks thanked him for his prompt postmortem and left with Collaton, looking out for Annie as he walked along the corridors.

They found her standing out in the misty, gray afternoon taking deep breaths. When she saw them, she looked away and ran her hand over her chestnut hair. "Christ, I'm sorry. I feel such an idiot."

"It's all right," said Banks. "Don't worry about it."

"It's not that I haven't been to one before." She pulled a face. "I was okay, honest I was, until . . . It was the smell, the saw burning the bone, and the noise it made. I couldn't . . . I'm sorry. I feel like such a fool."

It was the first time Banks had seen any real break in Annie's on-the-job composure. "I told you," he said. "Don't worry about it. Are you up to going home?"

She nodded. He imagined it would be a quiet journey. Annie was clearly pissed off at herself for showing signs of weakness.

Banks looked at Collaton. The indulgent expression on his face indicated he would probably have forgiven Annie *anything*.

It was late when Banks finally got home, after calling in at the station to issue some actions for the following morning. The traffic on the M1 was murder, especially around Sheffield, and patches of dense fog on the A1 meant they had to move at a crawl, keeping in view the rear lights of the lorry in front of them. Banks was reminded of the time when he was lost in the fog, heading for a friend's house, and had blindly followed the car in front right into a private drive. He had been damned embarrassed when the irate driver came to ask him what the hell he thought he was doing.

Annie recovered from her little spell of embarrassment a lot quicker than Banks expected. He had to remind himself that this wasn't Susan Gay, and that Annie didn't worry so much about appearing weak or incompetent; she simply got on with her work and her life.

The fog in the dale slowed him down most on the last leg of his journey. Wraiths of gray mist muzzled up the daleside and swirled on the road before him. The road ran several feet up the hillside from the valley bottom, where the River Swain meandered through The Leas, and most of the fog had settled low. Banks knew the road well enough not to take too many foolish risks.

Back at the cottage, he found two messages waiting. The first was from Tracy, asking him for ideas about what she should buy her mother for Christmas. A wedding dress, perhaps? Banks thought. But he wouldn't say that to Tracy.

The next caller didn't identify herself, but he knew immediately who she was: "Hello, it's me. Look, I'm sorry I haven't been in touch . . . it was probably very rude of me . . . I mean, I never really thanked you and all, did I, you know, for what you did for me? I suppose I was pretty fucked up." There, she broke off and Banks could hear her suck on a cigarette and blow out the smoke. He thought he could hear background noise, too. "Anyway, you must let me buy you lunch at least. Hey, look, I'll be over in Eastvale tomorrow, so why don't you meet me at the Black Bull on York Road over from Castle Hill, say about one o'clock? Is that all right?" There was a silence on the line, as if she were actually expecting an answer. Then she sighed. "Okay, then, hope to see you tomorrow. And I'm sorry. Really, I am. Ciao."

•

Banks remembered the last time he had seen Emily at the door of the old mill house, in the pink tracksuit he had bought for her on Oxford Street, an outfit she obviously loathed, giving him that enigmatic look as he delivered her to her parents. He remembered Jimmy Riddle's clipped thanks and Rosalind's cool silence. It was all unspoken, but he had sensed Riddle's awkward, hidden love for his daughter and Rosalind's distance.

So Emily Riddle wanted to thank him. Should he go? Yes, he thought, reaching for the bottle of Laphroaig; hell, yes, he would go.